Praise for Bartholomew Gill
and the Peter McGarr Mysteries

"Cunning . . . witty . . . fun . . . Another clever puzzle
mystery for the brainy detective Peter McGarr."
The *New York Times Book Review*
on *The Death of an Ardent Bibliophile*

"Prepare to be swept away."
The New York Times Book Review on *Death on a Cold, Wild River*

"A joy to read, and a pleasure to be in the
company of as lively a set of characters as ever
sparked a yearning for Dublin. . . .
The chase is headlong and fun to follow."
Philadelphia Inquirer on *The Death of a Joyce Scholar*

"Wonderful . . . fascinating . . . marvelously intricate . . .
I haven't had this much fun since—
well, since Sherlock Holmes."
Los Angeles Times on *The Death of Love*

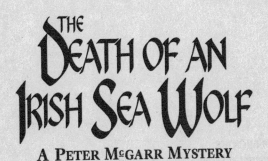

THE DEATH OF AN IRISH SEA WOLF

A PETER McGARR MYSTERY

BARTHOLOMEW GILL

AVON BOOKS
An Imprint of HarperCollinsPublishers

AVON BOOKS
An Imprint of HarperCollins*Publishers*
10 East 53rd Street
New York, New York 10022-5299

First Avon Books Printing: October 1997

Avon Trademark Reg. U.S. Pat. Off. and in Other Countries, Marca
Registrada, Hecho en U.S.A.
HarperCollins® is a trademark of HarperCollins Publishers Inc.

Printed in the U.S.A.

WCD 10 9 8 7 6 5 4

For Bert:
Great, good-hearted companion
and loving friend.
We miss you.

═══════════

WILLIAM MAKEPEACE THACKERAY, writing of Clew Bay, County Mayo, in 1842:

The most beautiful view I ever saw in the world . . . . The mountains were tumbled about in a thousand fantastic ways and . . . the bay . . . which sweeps down to the sea, and a hundred islands in it, were dressed up in gold and purple, and crimson with the whole cloudy west in a flame. Wonderful, wonderful!

PART I

Island Man

CHAPTER 1

CLEMENT FORD HEARD the phone ring in the hall of the Clare Island cottage that he had occupied now for over fifty years. He glanced at the clock on the mantel—4:15.

"Strange hour of the afternoon to be ringing up," said his wife, Breege, who was sitting in the other wing chair across the hearth from him.

Like a cracked red eye, a mound of peat was glowing in the fireplace, the white smoke tracking quickly up the flue. Outside a chill wind that had brought drenching rains was whining through the eaves. It was the last gasp of a wild and wet spring, Ford hoped. Apart from the clock, the clicking of Breege's knitting needles was the only other sound.

"Shall I answer it?"

"No, of course not," said Ford, clenching his pipe between his teeth and grasping the arms of the chair. "I've always answered the phone round here, and I've no intention of stopping now."

"Mind your poor knees. Or are they feeling better today?"

Ford glanced at her. Although her hands were moving at a furious pace, her star-burst blue eyes, which he had always considered the most beautiful he had ever seen, were staring up into the shadows on the other side of the room. Breege had been blind since birth.

A dark woman with long, finely formed features, she was thin with good shoulders that had remained square even as she had aged. In fact, with only a touch of gray in her jet black hair, Breege scarcely looked a day over fifty, though she was nearly as old as Ford himself.

A *proper* woman in everything, she kept herself, her house, and all she touched shipshape. And he loved her still, as he had from the moment she and her aunt had pulled him half-dead from the sea all those years ago.

"If you must know, my knees are beyond hope, says the specialist in Dublin. So there's no sense discussing the subject further. If I don't use them, they'll seize up, and then we'll be in the soup right enough." One blind and the other a cripple who was now pushing eighty, Ford thought.

In spite of his age, Ford's shoulders and arms were still well muscled and strong, and he easily pushed himself up from the chair. He had to wait a tottering moment, however, before knowing if his legs would bear his weight, which was twenty stone. A massive man by any measure, he had "shrunk"—Breege was wont to tell people who asked—to six feet six inches tall. "I can see him diminishing by the day," she'd say with a slight smile.

"Well, whoever it is, they know enough to keep ringing," she now observed.

The phone was maintaining its manic, two-ring jingle in the hall.

"Maybe it's one of the children calling." The Fords had no offspring of their own, nor had they raised any. Yet their mantel was filled with framed photos of several dozen young people in various stages of growth. "We should really get one of those radio telephones that Mirna rang up on the other day," Breege continued. "She bought it in Westport, and she can even carry it up to her pasture and down to the harbor. It's rigged to one of the American satellites. I'm afraid I'll never understand how it happens, but she sounded like she was sitting where you are, Clem."

It was the last thing they needed, Ford thought—as he moved stiffly—another modern device that would put him on his duff and keep him there, until the both of them were ready for some "home." Ford planned to live at least as long as

Breege, who needed him more than she knew.

How? By staying active. "Chinese exercise," Breege's own maiden aunt had called it, and Peig O'Malley had died at an even hundred years. "I've had to hack, scratch, and claw for everything I've ever needed," it was her wont to say, "and 'tis *work* that's kept me fit." And would Ford too, if he could just persevere and fight through the pain. Clare Island practices had saved him once before and would keep him alive now, if he let them.

"Hah-loo. How may I help you?" Ford said, forcing a bit of affability into his voice. His accent was decidedly British.

"Clem—Paul here. I've got another one for you." A distant relation of Breege, like so many others on Clare Island, Paul O'Malley meant another boat. His was the highest dwelling on the harbor side of the island and commanded nearly a complete view of the surrounding sea. As a shut-in, he was known as the "eyes of Clare Island," and he phoned Ford whenever any vessel of size put into the harbor.

For the favor, Ford bought O'Malley the odd pint when the quadriplegic's parents took him out for an airing. Also, it was believed that Ford had performed several extraordinary services for the large clan, who had inhabited the island at least since the notorious Grace O'Malley of Elizabethan times.

There was the matter of Padraic "Packy" O'Malley's surgery in Dublin, where he was taken after having caught his hand in the winch of his lobster boat. A specialist had to be flown in from London, but miraculously the bill had arrived at Packy's tiny cottage marked "Paid in Full." When Packy had inquired by whom, he was told a "giant Englishman" with a great white beard, though Ford had denied everything. He made mention of his modest lifestyle in the cottage that Breege had inherited, the three meager fields that he farmed assiduously, and the fact that he did not own even an automobile. Or a boat.

Also a number of O'Malley children had been sent to universities in Ireland and abroad, courtesy of the anonymously endowed Clare Island Trust. Businesses on the island and in County Mayo, of which Clare Island was a part, had been started, churches repaired, and libraries supported through the Trust.

And it seemed that whenever Clement Ford was informed of a native Clare Islander or a good cause that was in need, the matter was set to rights, later rather than sooner. There was always an appreciable lag between Ford's learning of a problem, and its happy resolution. Clare Islanders, who believed they knew the source of the bounty, called it "the Ford gap."

Ford now thanked Paul O'Malley and inquired after his health and that of his parents. "Will I see you at the hotel?"

"Saturday, as usual." It was the night Paul was taken to the island's only hotel for a bit of a gargle. "Nine sharp."

"I'll stop round, and we'll have a jar."

"I'd like that. Bring Breege." Perhaps because they were both disabled, the two cousins got along famously and seemed to buck each other up.

"Sure, I couldn't get out of the house without her." Ford rang off and reached for his storm anorak and hat. To Breege he called, "I'm stepping out for a moment, dear heart. Don't hold tea—I might be late."

"Who was that—Paul?"

From the cabinet beneath the hatrack, Ford added the pair of Zeiss night-seeing binoculars that he had treated himself to when last in Dublin. They were heavy, bulky, and had cost the better part of two thousand quid. As always, he had trouble fitting them under the rain gear.

"Don't you think you could stop this foolishness after all these years?"

It was a question that Ford had often asked himself when having to go out into weather like this. But he always came up with the same answer: He had been placed in trust, as he thought of it, over the cargo that he had brought with him to the island in 1945. It wasn't his. In fact, after the passage of time and all the changes that had taken place in the world, it probably wasn't anybody's.

But the uses it could be put to were important to Ford. Granted, the impulse to acquire the cargo had not been selfless. But during his long recovery from the pummeling that the ocean had given him, Ford had realized that there was something operating in the world that was bigger than he or his personal needs. That something had saved him. And it had given him Breege and Clare Island, which was like a kind of paradise. It was right to use the resources at his disposal to serve that something. And so he had.

The others that Ford had, well, "stolen" the cargo from? They were predators and would never forget. As long as even one of them was still alive, there was a chance that he might be out there in the harbor someday, and Ford had to guard against that possibility, if not for himself then for Breege and for the Trust.

"I'll try to make it fast." But all depended on how quickly the crew of the vessel would show themselves on deck.

Ford lowered his head and glanced at himself in the hatrack mirror. With his full beard and long hair, which was now going white, he looked rather like Father Time. His nose was long and beaked, his cheeks now hollow with age. Snugging the woolen fisherman's hat over his brow, he clamped his pipe between his teeth. "Good-bye!" he called, opening the front door.

But before he could amend his words, Breege snapped, "Don't *ever* say that! You know how I don't like it."

"Cheerio, then."

"Well, I hope it isn't cheery, and the storm drives you home. I'll hold your tea."

"I said don't. Don't!"

"And who are you, out on a fool's errand, to tell me anything at all." Breege stood to take herself into the kitchen at the back of the cottage.

As Ford closed the door, he saw her reach toward the table beside the chair, her fingers feeling for the diamond ring he had given her all those years ago. The surround of brilliant sapphire stones was just the color of her eyes, and too large to wear when knitting. "Foolish man," she muttered, as she slipped it on her finger.

The blast of the storm staggered Clem Ford the moment he stepped out of the small vestibule that was necessary protection on an island that fronted the Atlantic Ocean. Between his home on Clare Island and New York lay nothing but ocean, over three thousand miles of it.

Still, Ford paused out of habit, while the wind buffeted him, to push the small Judas stone against the edge of the door. Glancing up, he scanned the ragged edge of the storm front that was sweeping in off the ocean from the northwest.

Like a black curtain—dark and impenetrable—it was closing down over the brilliant tones of the setting sun. More tellingly, the barometer had begun to plummet. Reaching toward the panel of instruments that he had fixed above the frame of the door, Ford tapped the glass face. They had lost a full inch of mercury in the last hour; the storm would strike soon and hard.

Ford pulled the hood of the anorak over his woolen hat and knotted the scarf about his neck. It might be high time for early summer on the calendar, but Nature heeded her own schedule. Bitch-goddess that she was, she would do as she list.

Turning, Ford launched his large body into the gale.

CHAPTER 2

FORD KNEW THE boat—or at least the type—since he had sailed one in his youth between the wars.

Then his father had operated a legitimate import/export business by day, but by night he had made his real money. From Harwich in England he had smuggled alcohol, tobacco, gasoline—any commodity that was in short supply or heavily taxed—into the Weimar Republic.

An eighty-foot North Sea pilot schooner made little more noise than the water cut by her sharp bow. Drawing a mere eight feet, she could sneak into the sleepy, shallow ports off the Friesland coast that the authorities never thought of patrolling. Yet her beam was great enough for substantial cargoes of contraband. "Why risk confiscation for a pittance," his father had instructed him. "If you're going to steal, steal big." Words that had later come to haunt Ford.

Now he wondered at the fluke of an exact replica of such a boat sailing back into his life at the end of his seventh decade. Clement Ford was not given to superstition, but his life on Clare Island had made him attentive to the vagaries of chance. According to more than a few of the island's inhabitants, there was no such thing as coincidence.

God—they had it—spoke to us through other persons,

9

places, and even things. Could the boat now be a warning?
Ford thought it might.

A sliver of waning sunlight was still striking the graceful,
white hull, where she was anchored in the harbor not far from
the granite breakwater and short quay. From the crosstrees of
her two tall masts, working lights had been hung. Once the
sun faded, the deck would be awash in achromatic light.

Raising the binoculars to his eyes, Ford discovered he did
not need their night-seeing capability. He had positioned himself, as he always did on such an occasion, in the topmost
open window of the small O'Malley castle. Now a national
monument, it had guarded the harbor in ancient times and did
so again for Ford.

From there the quay with its short jetty and tall protective
wall were about a hundred yards away and the schooner perhaps two hundred where she was riding easily on her anchor
in a stiff chop. Bracing his elbows against the castle wall,
Ford focused the vessel in.

There were two men working the rigging, furling and securing the sails, while a third hand, who moved like a woman,
was belaying line and stowing running gear. All were dressed
in bright orange foul-weather gear that displayed the name of
the vessel—*Mah Jong*—on the back in Chinese-like letters.

When the schooner swung on her anchor, Ford noted that
her home port was "New Orleans, La." and he wondered if
the boat had embarked from there. If so, the crew had time
and good weather to work on the boat. The topsides bore none
of the encrusted salt or dull bronze that an ocean crossing
inevitably produced. Everything from her paint through her
brightwork to her sheets and canvas seemed fresh or recent-
lyitted out.

Or could the boat itself be new—a reproduction of a North
Sea pilot schooner? If so, Ford wondered where the plans had
been got, who had built her, and at what cost. She was something he would like for himself, or would have, were he
younger and less beset by his history. Apart from Breege's
ring, Ford had assiduously avoided any display of wealth that
would raise questions.

Now another figure appeared on deck, who was not garbed
in storm gear. Instead, he wore a simple Norwegian fisher-

man's cap and pea jacket, both navy blue. Below were denim trousers and storm boots. A small but broad, older man, he looked jaunty and nautical with his gloved hands clasped behind his back and a lidded pipe in his mouth. On the blast off Clew Bay, puffs of blue tobacco smoke bolted past the antennae on the cabin top.

It was only then that Ford realized how well provided the vessel was with modern communications equipment. In addition to the standard Loran, radar, and VHF arrays in the masts, he counted four other aerials and dishes that he did not recognize, not having kept himself up on every advance in marine electronics.

Now the female deckhand began loading duffel bags into the large jolly boat at the stern of the schooner. As the old man approached her, Ford realized that there was something vaguely familiar about his bearing and the way he moved. Stiffly, proudly, as though unable to conceal a swagger.

More so, when the right hand came up, and he spoke some order. The hand chopped down to make his point, stiffly, all in one piece. The woman immediately stopped what she had been doing and followed his commands. Turning, the man then peered up into mast lights and said something to the two men above him, who were now climbing down and had nearly reached the deck. Ford froze.

What? Was his imagination playing a trick on him? Was all the superstitious claptrap of the last fifty-years causing him to make too much of this boat that was like the one from his past? No, he thought not. Even allowing for the passage of time, it could be nobody but Angus Rehm, the man he had bested all those years ago. Granted Rehm's face was creased with age and the hair that was visible along the sides of his temples white, not blond. But there was no mistaking the face, the eyes, the gestures. And the hand.

Ford tightened the binoculars to his eyes and reached for the automatic-focusing button.

Which was when the mast lights were extinguished.

Ford flicked on the night-seeing capability, but he had not even accustomed his eyes to the greenish-yellow, infrared image, when a hooter aboard the schooner began blaring. At first Ford supposed it was some warning system, telling the crew that the bottom was too shallow or the anchor had lost its grip. Or that fuel or gasoline was leaking.

Until he saw the man in the cap and pea jacket reach inside the companionway and retrieve what looked like a scanning device. With it, he began sweeping the beach, the hills, the hamlet of cottages and houses that bordered the harbor, the pub, and finally the quay, the jetty, and the castle. He stopped there with the device virtually pointed at Ford.

Ford heard a command shouted from the boat, and then a klieg light—as bright as burning magnesium—swept him standing there in the open window of the castle, and then returned.

Like a large, old, slow animal caught in headlamps, Ford stood there, blinking. Only then did he realize that one of the electronics systems aboard the schooner must have detected the infrared illuminator in his binoculars, and Rehm had then used the scanner to locate him.

Ford switched off the infrared, and stepped into the shadow of the castle wall. But too late. Or was he imagining all of it. Or getting soft, as the Irish spoke of senility. No, damnit—the arc light was still emblazening the open window. What to do?

Flee—back to Breege and see if he could get her out of the house and to some safe haven at least for the night, and then off the island altogether in the morning. Rehm would see him, of course, the moment he got beyond the wall that surrounded the castle. Clare Island was treeless, and Ford could only hobble on his gimpy knees. And realizing how truly helpless he was, they would swoop down on him like the predators they were.

Instead, Ford chose a different course. Demonstrating the daring that had marked his naval career, he stepped back into the light and trained the binoculars on the boat. There he found Rehm—he was sure of it!—staring back at him with another pair of glasses.

Rehm then lowered his binoculars, and Ford watched and read his lips as he said, "It's him. The Sea Wolf," before the klieg light was switched off.

Ford had to wait until his eyesight returned before making his way down from his precarious perch in the dark castle.

Once outside, he paused to look back at the schooner in the harbor, still scarcely able to credit what he had seen. Even with all his years of strict vigilance, Ford had been caught out nearly from the moment the bastard had dropped anchor. If he couldn't now hear the chop rushing past the boat's long white hull, he might again think it a cruel dream. Or a hallucination.

Breege, who was guiltless, was his first concern. Not that Ford himself felt any guilt. If anybody, it was Rehm who had been the criminal and a special class of being—a kind of devil. Witness the fact that he had hardly aged. Ford should have stamped him out when he had the chance, those many years ago.

The black curtain of the storm had descended, and Ford only managed to keep to the muddy path that was lined with bogs because he knew it so well. He tried to think of his options. Years ago, when he fully believed in the possibility that Rehm would one day arrive, he had developed a complicated escape plan. Now he could scarcely remember the details. And how to get himself and a blind, frail woman off the island at night in the midst of a storm?

The wind was howling about his ears, and a cold rain stippled his face whenever he turned to the west. In the far distance, he could see the yellow lights of his snug cottage. How he longed to sit himself down by the fire and smoke his pipe. Had he not earned that much in his old age?

No, he had *earned* nothing. But much less so Angus Rehm.

CHAPTER 3

AT THE DOOR of his cottage, Clement Ford did not bother to remove his hat or coat. He merely stepped inside, threw the bolts on the cubby and main doors, then divested himself of the heavy pair of high-tech binoculars. Making his way quickly to the kitchen, he found Breege busy about their tea.

"Back so soon? Was it a party boat, or did the storm prove too much for you? I haven't heard the wind howl like this all the year long." She was working at the cooker, holding out a hand to feel the heat from a burner before setting down a pot.

The kitchen was warm, the air redolent of the cooking meal. Again Ford thought he would give almost anything just to be able to collapse into his chair and forget what he had just seen. But there was no time for comfort. And how to tell her so she would listen and heed his words. Breege could be stubborn in her own pleasant way, and she had as much as ruled him, lo these many years.

"You haven't taken off your coat," she said, being able to smell the dampness on him. "Or your boots. There's muck on them." Suddenly she stopped what she was doing and turned to him, her beautiful, blind eyes finding his own, as though she could actually see him.

"Ah, Breege"—Ford began in lament, which he knew was

14

a blunder—"it's wrong that it should arrive at a time, like
this, when we're so old. But remember how I said years ago
there would come a day when I would ask you to leave this
place—no questions asked?"

She nodded the perfect arrangement of dark hair that only
recently had begun to turn silver. She had always set it herself—by feel!—and the process had never ceased to entrance
Ford. At that moment he believed he had never loved her
more. "Well—that day has come."

The slight smile that pouted her definite cheeks did not
fade. "Clem—is this a joke?"

"I *wish* it were. I don't know how to tell you, Breege, so
you'll believe me—but after all these years he's here. Rehm."

She paused for a moment before continuing her labors over
the cooker. "Really? What did you say his name was again?"

"Rehm. Angus Rehm."

"*Rehm.* What a curious name! And Scots! How it fits what
you told me about him at Oxford and during the war. I mean,
like the word, the one in Latin. Ar ee em. Oh"—she raised
a finger—"and there's a rock group by that name now. I
heard them over the wireless the other day." Breege moved
toward the fridge. "Tell me now—how do you know it's
Rehm?" She removed a plate of butter from its depths. "Or
are you after nipping into the pub."

Ford sighed in exasperation. "Breege—listen to me. It *is*
Rehm, the man I told you about. I'd know him anywhere. It's
like"—Ford glanced behind him down the hall toward the
door—"he's hardly changed. And he's got three others with
him that I could count."

"But, sure, even if it is, couldn't we just ring up Kevin
O'Grady, who'll have them off the island by noon?" She
reached for a pot handle and gave it a shake.

O'Grady was a retired guard. Otherwise Clare Island did
not have—or want—a resident police officer. Nor did Ford
wish to bring the police into the matter, since they might ask
questions that he would rather not answer. And Breege was
innocent of everything in every way; she deserved to live out
her days as she would have, had he never entered her life.
Ford turned back to the front door.

There at the pegs he removed her storm coat, a woolen hat,

and a muffler. In their bedroom he found her warmest stockings. From a drawer in his own dresser, he removed the Webley automatic that had still been strapped to his side that morning in the spring of 1945 when Breege and her aunt had found him on their beach half-dead, washed in with the tide.

While recuperating, Ford had stripped down the weapon to its component parts, then desalinized, lubricated, and reassembled the pieces. Through a connection in Dublin, where Ford went from time to time, he had obtained a stock of ammunition. Over Breege's objections, he had also taught her to shoot as straight as she could at what she could hear. Now Ford slid a clip of seven bullets into the Webley and dropped it into his anorak.

Back in the kitchen, he found Breege standing on her side of the table. She was pouring tea from the kettle. On platters there were lamb chops, green vegetables, and potatoes along with a tureen of fish chowder that was one of Ford's favorite dishes. Suddenly he was hungry. And angry.

"Now sit down and eat," she said. "You'll soon find yourself feeling much better. Did I tell you what's coming over the telly this evening? You'll like it—all about the Russian Navy. They're selling it piecemeal to anybody who can pay the price. And what they can't sell is just being left to rust."

When Breege sat, Ford merely swung her chair round so he could take the slippers from her feet and slip on the stockings and Wellies.

"What are you doing, Clem?" she asked in her usual pleasant tone of voice, although he was handling her.

"Breege, my love," he began, hoping she might credit his concern, "I don't think you fully understood what I said. That . . . *bastard* is on the island. And he's equipped and not alone. No. When I flicked on the infrared, some device on his vessel detected me."

"You? How? Detected what?"

"The infrared illuminator in my new binoculars, I assume."

"Well, how did it do that? What's infrared?"

Ford only shook his head, knowing any explanation would be pointless and probably fatal at this juncture. "They caught me in their floodlights," he went on. "He—Rehm—saw me.

He won't wait until morning. One question in the pub, and he'll be onto where we are, and a quick strike is best for him. A storm? Better still." Ford pulled off her slippers and began fitting on the stockings.

The wind was now keening around the house.

"After fifty years you still know what this Rehm looks like?"

"Yes. The size, the shape of him. The way he walks. He even had gloves on his hands."

"But it's cold. That's a storm you're hearing outside. Everybody *should* have gloves on his hands. Even yourself."

"Breege—I looked into his face! In the glasses. It's him."

She put a hand on his arm to stop him. "Luveen—look at me and listen."

Ford glanced up into her pretty face.

"Has it never occurred to you that we're getting old? And you have been ... *consumed* by this matter and this man many a long year. Could it be that he has now come alive *in your imagination*? Sometimes things I think about over much assume a reality of their own. Sure, I say this because I love you, and for no other reason."

"Keep your foot still," Ford replied. "I'm going to dress you for outside so you'll be warm. You are my life, and if you won't walk yourself, I'll carry you."

"You, with your bad knees? Clem—where would we go?"

It certainly was *the* question. Years ago Ford had maintained a boat that he kept on the other side of the island in an isolated cove. But it had been destroyed in a rogue storm, and Ford had not replaced it, *because* of the time that had passed. "Out of here. We'll find some place to stay for the night. It'll give us time."

"And him time too, if he's real. Clem—what'll people say, our just leaving in the dead of night? They'll be worried sick about us. Think of the talk! They'll call the guards."

"Let them say what they will, as long as it's not over our dead bodies. I'll figure something out." It came to him then that he'd seen Packy O'Malley's boat docked at the jetty. It was small but fast and able, even in a storm sea, and the man would be glad to do him a favor. "And if not of yourself, think of the Trust—the good it can do. And will, if we can keep it out of Rehm's hands.''

''But isn't it *his*?''

''*No,* damnit!'' Ford had on Breege's Wellies now, and he tried to stand so he could help her to her feet. But his knees would simply not support him, and he staggered against the door to the press. ''As I told you, what he had was stolen itself, from whom I don't know.''

''But you have an idea.''

''Yes, but that's not *knowing*!'' he said far too strongly. ''And if he gets it now, after how we watched over it all these years and made it grow, it would be a double shame.'' Having regained his balance, Ford reached down for her elbows.

''Wait,'' she objected, trying to pull his large hands away. ''Clem, luveen. Let me go, please. Please!''

He released her, and she reached for and found his hands.

Again she looked up at him. ''If that's what's so important to you—why don't you tell somebody else where it is and how to keep it safe. That way, if this Rehm does come for us, and the worst happens, the Trust will continue.

''Now, please—sit down with me and eat your tea, which is what I have every intention of doing myself. Come Armageddon or Angus Rehm.'' Obviously she still did not believe him.

Ford released her and straightened up. She had a point. Confiding in somebody else was something that Ford had been considering now over the last several years, since it would be necessary eventually. He would not live forever. But who? He could never decide. Who could he possibly trust with such a secret? Well, now he had to.

Breege herself had *never* wanted to know the details of the Trust with its Dublin connection or even the location of the cache here on the island. ''Why,'' she had asked, ''when I could never see the blessed hidey-hole anyhow? And even you think it's dangerous going up there.''

Also, Breege was a woman who lived in the present. ''As long as I have you, Clem, and we're happy here—I don't care how much we have or haven't. Before you, my aunt and

I lived on the little we could get for ourselves—her even then an old woman and me blind.''

Ford now sat in his chair beside her. "Like who?" to confide in, he meant. "We should have decided this long ago."

Breege rearranged her chair and picked up her knife and fork. "Now, try a chop, Clem. They come from Achill, and you know how nice the spring lamb tastes from there. They say the sheep feed on clover the year round."

"Breege—*who*?"

"Oh, I don't know. You know more people than I." She began carving the meat on her plate. "What about Mirna? She's a quiet, careful person and educated. And *she* would probably sympathize with our intentions for the Trust. No— she *would* sympathize, being the artist that she is. Are you eating, Clem?"

Pondering what he knew about Mirna Gottschalk, Ford did not answer.

"Well, since you aren't, why don't you go tell Mirna, and I'll finish my tea. If you're still . . . disturbed about this when you get back, why, I'll leave here with you. For the hotel. I can register as . . . I don't know. Mary Robinson"—who, of course, was the president of Ireland—"and you can hide in the cellar, since you're so conspicuous." Breege had a sense of humor, though Ford did not appreciate it at the moment.

He sighed again; it was hell getting old. Certainly he wouldn't be able to carry her very far under any condition, and she was right about one thing—it was time to confide in somebody. Maybe Mirna *was* the one. She had a fine young son in Dublin, who had already benefited substantially from the Trust and could deal with the details on that end. And Mirna's house was but a long, if arduous, mile away, over the hill in back of the house and then along the cliff.

He stood. "Right—we'll compromise. Here are my terms. After your tea, you take this and sit with it in your chair in the sitting room with your face to the door. If anybody comes into the house apart from Kevin O'Grady, you're to use it, as I taught you."

Breege turned her head to him. "Use what?"

"This." He placed the Webley on the table beside her plate.

She put down her fork and felt it. "The pistol?" she asked incredulously. With a click she dropped the knife on the plate. "Clem—have you quit your senses? *Me* use that? Why I—" but she thought better of it.

"All right," she relented. "Anything you say. I'll take myself into the chair and sit in it. If anybody but Kevin comes in, I'll . . . well, I'll do what I must. When you return, we'll leave. Perhaps the air will do me good. But you must speak to Mirna first."

She retrieved her knife and fork. "I don't mean to be difficult about this, but I would like to know what excuse you'll give when asking Kevin to come *'sit'* me? And don't think to tell him I'm the frightened one."

Ford moved toward the phone in the hallway. "I'll just ask him to come." And bring a gun, he thought. He had never requested anything scurrilous of O'Grady, and the man would do his bidding.

How long did he have? Ford tried to think of how Rehm would proceed.

He would make no direct inquiry of, say, the barman there at the island's only pub in the harbor. Instead, he would engage some local in conversation. Dressed in their storm gear with the name of their vessel, *Mah Jong,* on their backs, they would order drinks, and the topic of their voyage or the boat would soon come up, given the interest of island folk in boats and visitors. Rehm had been a charming, engaging man back when Ford had known him, and he was undoubtedly more practiced now. But he had also been a careful man.

He'd say something like "We were wurried aboot this place," in his heavy Scot's burr that even in their Oxford days was devised. "While we were anchoring, we glammed a hoary great giant, peeking out at us from the castle walls. Are there Druids on the island?"

The locals would laugh. "Oh, that's just Clem Ford, our *resident* Druid," as Ford had once overheard himself described. "He's harmless, really. Just likes to get a look at any new boat that puts in."

"Strange—we didn't see him again. It was as though he melted off into the hills."

"Not to worry. Clem lives up on the flanks of Croaghmore,

the mountain you can see looking west. A pretty, rambling cottage that was left to his wife. She's an O'Malley, like so many of us on the island.''

And Rehm would have him. Another, say, ten or so minutes to change the topic of conversation, finish their drinks, and amble off. ''We'll go up to the hotel now, have ourselves a night ashore. Cheerio. See you tomorrow.'' Then maybe a half hour to pretend registering in the hotel, and an hour to get their bearings and travel by the road in the dark here to Ford's cottage. They'd not risk an overland route with the chance of walking into a bog or waking a dog.

By then, O'Grady would be firmly in place. Seeing him armed, they would make up some story and take themselves off on such a night, returning either to the hotel or their boat. The storm, which Ford could now hear moaning through the thatch, was simply too foul.

Three hours, Ford decided. He had three hours to trace the difficult overland path to Mirna's, tell her the tale that would seem incredible to her after all the years she had known him, then get himself back and Breege into O'Grady's car.

He'd also ring up Packy and have the fast boat ready to put off the moment they reached the harbor. They'd head due north toward Achill Island but continue on to Belmullet, which was a fishing port. There he might be able to hire a car.

He picked up the receiver and dialed.

O'Grady was just finishing his tea. Ford could hear kitchen sounds and O'Grady's children in the background. But he agreed to come. ''If you think you need me, Clem, I'll be right up. But—why the gun?''

''Just bring one, please. And be prepared to use it.''

There was a pause before O'Grady asked, ''How's Breege keeping?''

''*She*'s fine. It's me who wants you. I'll explain everything when I get back. And don't forget the gun.'' Explain what, Ford wondered? He didn't know, but some credible story would come to him when needed. He told O'Grady where he would leave the key, then rang off.

Breege, who scarcely ate enough to keep a bird alive, had

finished her meal. Ford made her sit beside the hearth in the chair that faced the door.

He then stuffed the Webley down between the cushion and the padded arm of the chair and pulled the chair shawl over it. "Kevin knows where the latchkey is, so you won't have to get up to let him in. When you hear him at the door, call out. Make sure he answers, and you recognize his voice. If not, use this." Taking her left hand, he made her feel the butt of the weapon. "Remember how I taught you to shoot?"

Breege wagged her still lovely, dark head. "But that was years ago, Clem. And this is all so cloak-and-dagger. Are you sure you're *right*?"

In *every* way, Ford suspected she meant.

"I could not be wrong. It's Rehm. He's come for the cargo and to kill me. And anybody who gets in his way, make no mistake."

"Did you tell Kevin that?"

"No, of course not. How could I?" Reading her expression, Ford thought for a moment that she finally believed him. "There's still time to change your mind. Come with me to Mirna's. She's got the big new Land Rover. She can take us to the harbor. Packy is probably in the pub, and we'll be gone by midnight."

Breege turned her head and listened to the wind, her eyes seeming to track its passage from the distant Western ocean, over the cliffs and pinnacle of Croaghmore, and past the house. "No, Clem—I'm just not up to it. And as long as you say Kevin is on his way, I'll rest easy. And, sure, I've got this." She patted the side of the chair where he had lodged the Webley.

Bending to the fire, Ford picked up the special tong-like device that he kept among the fire irons there. He knocked aside the few remaining lumps of peat that were still smoldering, and he pried up a deep stone from the inner hearth. A strongbox came next. From it he extracted the manila packet that was all the box contained.

Years before they had discussed it—Breege noting that, after they were gone, older Clare Islanders might think to look under the bricks of the hearth. "It's there in times past a family's valuables were hidden from the tax collectors, revenuers, and Lawlife's bailiffs." Lawlife being the London insurance company that had owned Clare Island before the turn of the century.

With the packet now in hand, he replaced the box and the stone, and with a briquette of solid parafin he built a new fire for Breege.

Reaching for a notepad of his stationery Ford sat in his wing chair and scribbled the two addresses in Dublin that Mirna would need. He also added the name "Angus Rehm."

Ford was left-handed and his script had a curious backward slant that was even less legible because of the mild arthritis that afflicted his large hands. He had to concentrate to form the letters, and it took more time. Seven minutes by the clock on the mantel.

Placing the slip of paper into the packet and then stuffing the packet into the liner of his hat, Ford stood up.

"Do you have everything you need?" Breege asked.

"If you mean the Trust envelope. I do."

"Now, hurry back."

"I will, and you be ready to leave, when I am."

It took Ford another ten minutes to batten all the window shutters and to lock the front and cubby doors. Leaving by the rear, he locked that door as well, then walked round through the soggy soil to the front and left the key under a rock for O'Grady, as they had discussed. With a toe he eased the Judas stone against the door and checked his wristwatch by the light from the transom.

Forty-seven minutes had elapsed since Rehm had seen him on the hillside. He deducted that plus the hour it would take him to go and come back from Mirna's. He would then have something less than an hour to tell her—no, to *convince* her of what he wished her to know, which was nothing less than fifty or so years of history. And, then what he wished her to do, which would change her life irrevocably.

CHAPTER 4

MIRNA GOTTSCHALK HAD been born on Clare Island in 1941, four years before Ford arrived. Her father, Rudolph—then a young painter from Vienna—had once summered on the island, and in 1940 he came to stay. He told people he was attracted by the quality of light, the vistas of Clew Bay, and the island's tranquility. Also, being a Jew did not seem to matter as much here as it did in Austria after the German occupation in 1938.

From Austria, Gottschalk had gone to Spain to fight for the Republic. But he had no sooner recovered from the wounds that he had suffered in the siege of Barcelona, than the Insurgents, led by Franco, took Madrid, and the bloody civil war was over. Fleeing across the border into France, he met a beautiful, young Basque woman who was also a political refugee. Together and with little more than their talents, they arrived in Ireland.

The house that they squatted in on Clare Island had been abandoned during the famine of the last century and was nothing but crumbling walls and dung, since sheep and cattle had sought shelter there over the years. It took the Gottschalks nearly a decade and plenty of hard work, but they created the most handsome and unusual dwelling on the island, Ford judged. With bits of the considerable flotsam that had washed

up on Irish shores during the war, they fitted out and furnished their building. They used everything they could get
their hands on—packing crates, ships' timbers, the entire
cabin of an old freighter that had been finished in Philippine
mahogany.

They added a studio in 1951 and, with the help of the Clare
Island Trust, several long white outbuildings that served as a
kind of factory. There they made "Clare Island sculpture"—
also fabricated from driftwood, which they sold throughout
Ireland and England. It was the enterprise that had provided
the elder Gottschalks a living, and (now that they had passed
away) allowed Mirna the freedom to paint what she would.

Topping the crest of the hill, Ford was relieved to look
down at a light in the studio windows. It meant that Mirna
was in there painting and would be alone.

But descending the steep trail seemed almost harder on his
ruined knees than the climb up had been. Ford staggered several times, then slipped on the muddy slope, and fell in a
long, bruising tumble that nearly brought him up against the
door of the studio. His hat blew off, and he tried to scramble
after it and the all-important envelope that it contained.
"Christ!" he shouted. Finally in one, last, desperate effort
before the hat swept over the cliff Ford's hand grabbed the
envelope. The hat, however, sailed off into the darkness and
tumbled toward the sea, some four hundred feet below on the
western side of the island.

Feeling hopeless, as though he could never respond to the
challenge that Rehm represented, Ford cursed himself and his
old age and with difficulty pulled himself to his feet. In a bit
of moonlight that now appeared briefly as if to illuminate the
event, he caught sight of his hat, still airborne and spiraling
out into Clew Bay. The clouds closed again. Ford reached for
the handle of the door—which, like most on Clare Island—
was never locked.

Mirna Gottschalk turned from the canvas, then said, "Oh,
Clem—I thought I heard a voice." She began walking toward
him. "But, I'm sorry, you can't come in."

Ford stopped. "What? Why not? Are ye' not alone?"

Stepping in front of him as though to keep him from seeing
into the room, she smiled. "Certainly I'm alone. Or are you

here with a proposition?'' To show him she was fooling, she touched a hand to her hair which had turned gray early and was now closer to white. She kept it in braids.

In her mid-fifties now, Mirna Gottschalk-Byrne was still an attractive woman with a lithe body and the dark Spanish, good looks of her mother. The only bit of her father that Ford had ever been able to discern in her was her long, straight nose and hazel eyes.

Divorced now, she lived mostly alone, although she was visited from time to time by her son, Karl, and ''suitors,'' she called them, who never stayed more than a few weeks. During weekdays, of course, she was surrounded by other island women, who came to work on the driftwood ornaments that she designed and produced in the shop.

Ford tried to move around her, but she again stepped in front of him. ''Really, Clem—can we go into the house? I'll make you a cup of tea. You look''—her eyes ran down his muddy anorak and soiled trousers—''like you could use one. Did you fall? Where's your hat.''

''No,'' said Ford, easily pushing past the thin woman. ''There isn't time.''

''But''—she reached for his sleeve—''you'll only ruin the surprise.''

''What?''

''The surprise that I'm making for your birthday. It's not done, and I only have the week.''

She tried to prevent him, but Ford's eyes swept the studio and fixed on the canvas and easel that was illuminated in the center of the room.

It was a large oil portrait of Breege, painted after Ford's favorite photograph of her that had been taken in 1948. A print was clipped to the easel. He moved toward it.

''Well, so much for the surprise,'' said Mirna.

It was Breege as Ford always saw her in his mind's eye— as the dark, fey, young angel who had nursed him back to health and made him believe in life again. There was her slight smile and her full red lips, and the definite youthful sparkle in her bright, blind but very blue eyes. It was the same smile she had when Ford had declared his love for her, the one that said I love you too, and I'm yours. She had a rose in her hair, and her long graceful neck was the color of ivory. She was wearing the ring that Ford had only then recently given her, the one with the large diamond and sapphire surround.

Tears filled his eyes, and he had to wipe them away. "It's beautiful, but—" He pulled out his handkerchief.

"But what?" Mirna now moved beside him, obviously wishing to hear his reservation.

Ford blew his nose. "But nothing. It's beautiful, *better* than the photograph, but"—he turned to Mirna—"I only hope to God that we'll live to savor it. It's why I'm here like this." He swept his hand down his clothes. "I've only got"—he checked his wristwatch; it had taken him twenty-three minutes, longer than he thought, to get there—"a short time before Rehm gets to the cottage, and I must tell you something. For the good of—" of whom? Of Breege and him, certainly, but perhaps not for the good of Mirna herself, who would most assuredly be burdened with the knowledge. "For the good of the island." He reached for her hands and shook them. "Will you listen to me, Mirna? As a favor to me and Breege?"

Mirna Gottschalk's eyes were wide and round. "Why—what's happened? Is it Breege?"

"No, I don't think so. Not yet, anyway."

"Who's Rehm?"

"Angus Rehm—he's the worst, the very worst!" Ford glanced at his wristwatch. "But you must listen to me." Ford's eyes flickered up at the black, rain-spattered wash of the studio windows. Where to start? There was so little time.

He straightened up. "I am not Clement Ford, I never was. Who I am doesn't matter anymore. What does matter is this." He waved the packet. "It's the Trust, the Clare Island Trust. And it's meant everything to Breege and me. It's given our lives purpose and done much good for people who otherwise would have had little.

"Anyhow, it's all in here. And you and your son, Karl—of all the people that we know in the world—deserve to control it. The first name and address on the top sheet is the firm you should contact to take control. They're solicitors in Merrion Square. You need only to present yourself to them and say exactly, 'Dorfmann sent me.' When she says back, 'But I don't know a Mr. Dorfmann,' you're to say, 'Klimt says you do.' Do you have that?''

Mirna cocked her head quizzically, her smile brittle, her eyes glassy. "I think so."

"Repeat it."

She complied, adding, "Don't you want to sit down. I can get you—"

But he cut her off. "The second name and address is another firm that will help you dispose of what's left in the cave, which is now the lesser part of the cargo I brought to the island. I haven't had to trade with them in years, but the old man there is fair. It's him you should see.''

"Cave?'' Mirna asked, shaking her head, her brow furrowed. From her expression it was plain that she thought him daft and babbling, and she was concerned for him.

"Yes, cave. The map to it is also in here."

"I know of no actual cave on Clare Island."

"Well, damnit, there is one. Peig showed it to me when I first got here. Back in forty-five.''

She cocked her head quizzically. "And *what's* in it?''

"Just something I put together at the end of the war. You'll see. Now—the final name is of this man, Rehm, whom you should avoid at all cost. He's my age or thereabouts, small, square, blond. Well . . .'' Ford glanced at the windows, realizing that he no longer knew what Angus Rehm actually looked like. "He could be white or bald or . . . but, if he thinks he knows who you are, he'll probably approach you as somebody else. Or he'll have confederates, so you must be on your guard. Or''—Ford straightened up, the thought only now striking him—"he *is* somebody else by now.''

"Oh, Clem—can't I make you some tea?'' Her voice was filled with concern.

"No, you must promise me. You must avoid this man and take yourself away, ever should you know of his presence.''

Mirna shrugged and nodded. "Whatever you say.''

"I'll come back, if I can, and answer your questions. And help you, because you'll need help. But I must get back to Breege. This packet is now yours to do with as you see fit. I should have given it to you a long time ago. I know you and

Karl will handle it well, but promise me you won't open the sealed pouch until you've taken a look at the cave and visited the solicitors in Dublin.''

Mirna nodded, but she was plainly dismayed.

''Promise?''

''I promise.''

Ford thrust the manila packet into her hands and turned for the door.

''But—I don't understand. Why are you telling me this? What's in here? What's happened?''

The blast swept into the room, as Ford pulled open the door. ''Whatever you do, keep it to yourself. Tell *nobody* but Karl, and only after you swear him to secrecy!'' Ford launched himself into the darkness.

CHAPTER 5

FORD STAGGERED AND fell again. He had imagined the descent down the muddy and slick slope to Mirna's compound on the cliffs would be hardest on his old bones, but the climb back up proved far worse. He could barely get his knees to lock and unlock with each step. How could he ever hope to defend himself or even flee with Breege, when he could barely walk himself?

Fighting through the pain, he forced himself to think of how Rehm had got onto him, after all these years. He had scuttled the boat in a trench off the continental shelf. Could it have broken up and some of its pieces been caught, say, by one of the modern draggers that now fished Irish waters? It was unlikely, since the boat had been designed never to break up, even under the most harrowing fire.

No—Ford stopped to brace himself after blundering off the trail into a slough of mud—it was probably the release of all the war records now that the fifty-year most-secret limit had passed. Before scuttling the boat, Ford had sent a final radio communiqué to his confederates on land, in case he perished. Granted it had been mere coordinates, naming the final position of the boat, but the signal might also have been picked up by some other source and recorded.

After the war a few "tourists" did visit Clare Island,

snooping around, asking questions. But for the first four or five years, Clem Ford had remained almost exclusively with his new wife at their isolated home on the far side of the island. Scarcely a cart track led to them then. And Breege's aunt Peig had put it about that Ford—in spite of or perhaps because of his British accent—was an I.R.A. man on the run. A "strong woman" with known "Republican connections," her word was heeded.

Below him now, Ford could see the lights of his own house glowing dimly in the distance. As he got closer, he also caught sight of Kevin O'Grady's old car parked in front. The sitting room lights were on too, and, of course, the Judas stone had been moved, when O'Grady let himself in.

The wind was now wailing about Ford's bare head, and he felt a sudden chill. More acutely, when, stepping cautiously toward the front cubby, he noticed that the front door, the one that opened into the hall, was slightly ajar.

No Clare Islander—not Kevin O'Grady, not Breege— would ever allow any door, especially one facing the blast, to stand open even a crack. He reached for his belt where he sometimes tucked his Webley, but, of course, he had given it to Breege.

What to do? Go back round to the kitchen cubby and try the door there? If it were open, then he'd know something had definitely happened and Rehm was there.

But it was locked. The little Ford could see through the salt-spattered windows and between the curtains was the cooker with his tea on it, warming. Suddenly he felt cold, old, ravenous, and weak.

Because then he noticed something else beyond the kitchen on the floor, something he could not make out distinctly with his old eyes. When he reached into his breast pocket for his spectacles, he discovered that he had smashed them, falling.

Turning his head suddenly to the outbuildings in the haggard behind him, he thought he sensed somebody there, among the tools and farm implements. But all was dark and quiet. In horizontal sheets, the rain pelted him, as he stepped around the windward side of the cottage to approach the front door again.

All he could think of was Breege—if Rehm was in there,

he had to get her out one way or another. After all, their secret and the Trust were now in good hands, and all they had to do was get away and live out whatever days they had left.

At the cubby door, Ford took a deep breath and scanned O'Grady's banger—a large, old Ford Granada—but there was nobody in it, or behind it, that he could tell. With a trembling hand, he turned the handle on the cubby door and pushed it open. But the front door did not crash back with the force of the storm that now swept into the cubby.

The reason was soon apparent. There was something behind the door stopping it. Something heavy. Ford had to put his large shoulder into the door and shove to squeeze himself inside. Looking down, he was horrified by what he saw.

Kevin O'Grady was spread out in the hall, his eyes open, his hands clutched to his chest. There was a spot on his forehead, dark, like something from Ash Wednesday. Most of the back of his head was gone, having been blown away. A spray of blood and brain and bone coated the wall, the mirror, and the framed photographs Ford had taken of Breege and Peig over the years.

With two fingers Ford reached out and touched the spattered glass surface over the very same photo Mirna was using to paint Breege's portrait. And the enormity of Kevin O'Grady's death and what it would mean to his wife and children descended upon Ford. O'Grady had been the very best sort of neighbor and friend—a *guard* in every sense— and now he was dead, because of Ford himself. Nobody else.

Then, heedless of his own person or who might have murdered O'Grady, Ford shouted, ''Breege!'' and bolted into the sitting room.

There she sat, her blind blue eyes staring up at him as though he had never left. Her knitting was in her lap. One hand was stuffed down beside the shawl over her legs, the other was resting upon the doily on the arm of the wing chair. Her ring finger had been chopped off cleanly at the last knuckle but had bled only a trickle.

Ford fell to one knee beside her, only to realize from the slackness of her jaw that she too was dead.

''It was the on'y way I could get the bloody thing off her finger,'' said a Scot's voice behind him. ''Trust me—I tried everr'athing else. And the coincidence is really quite remarkable. D'ye' know the woman it was taken from, the lass who owned it first? Why, it had to be chopped from her mitt in the verra' same manner, or so I was told.''

Slowly, Ford turned to behold Angus Rehm sitting in the far corner of the room, the Norwegian fisherman's cap that Ford had seen him wearing earlier in his lap. Again Ford noted that apart from the snowy white hair and his creased and weathered face, Rehm looked unchanged from 1945.

Rehm opened one hand to reveal a bloodstained handkerchief. In it was Breege's finger with the ring still round it. In the palm of the other hand lay a pistol that Ford had never seen before with three gathered barrels and a long curving banana clip.

Standing behind him were two young men with short-barreled automatic weapons hanging from long slings. A woman now appeared in the doorway to the hall, carrying another gun. Those three were still dressed in the bright orange oilskins Ford had seen them wearing on the boat. The *Mah Jong*.

It was only then that Ford realized how changed the room was. The contents of every drawer and cabinet had been tossed into a heap in the center of the room. Years of correspondence was everywhere. Even the stuffed chairs had been flayed, including the one Breege was sitting in. The stuffing from it was scattered all over.

Was there any hope that the Webley was where Ford had concealed it? Breege looked as though she hadn't stirred an inch from how he had left her. Maybe out of respect for the dead they had let her be.

Ford's eyes shied to the hearth. He was shocked to see that the fresh fire he had started had been pushed aside and the deep stone prized up.

''Clem—is that yehr handle these days, laddie?—ye' underestimate us. Don't ye' think we would have done our homework?'' Rehm's manner was colloquial and jovial almost. ''Heather here''—he gestured to the young woman—''is a student of your adopted culture.

''Knowing you could only be here or in Scotland, given yehr dearth of crew and fuel, we made it our business to study

this country, its habit of mind, its culture and traditions, its
. . . texture. But then back in the old days, ye' always favored
Irish waters, di' y'not?

"Pity about the old girl—yehr wife, I take it from the pictures." Rehm waved his stiff, gloved hand at the photographs
on the floor. "I don't believe her heart could take the shock
of what happened in the hall. If it's any consolation, she was
a'ready dead before I took the ring."

Which meant the handgun might still be where Ford had
placed it, between the cushion and the chair. If it was time
for him to die, he would take Rehm and maybe one of the
others with him. Maybe all, if he could manage it. That would
leave Mirna Gottschalk with a free hand with the Trust. One
thing—he would not allow himself to be tortured. He could
see from the way everything in the room had been pulled
apart, and even floorboards ripped up, that they had already
conducted a thorough search. The kind Rehm had been good
at, all those years ago.

Ford glanced back down at poor, generous, innocent, and
wonderful Breege, and tears popped from his eyes. She had
been so gentle and so undeserving of this sort of violent death.

"Come, come now, Clem—or is it Clement?—that's no
way for a thief of yehr caliber to behave. Ye' knew I was
coming one day. Yehr excellent Zeiss binoculars tell me as
much. How did ye' ever allow yehrself to buy German? But
why not with yehr money!"

Ford said nothing, as he tried to gather himself.

"May I introduce ye' to my family? For years I've been
distressing them with my apocryphal—they thought—story
about some great, lost fortune and the legendary 'Sea Wolf'
who stole it from me. Now at least they no longer think me
a dotty old fool who was dreaming of the good old days, the
halcyon days of the war. How's that poem go, Clem? The
one ye' used to spout at university when ye' were in yehr
cups?

> "Two things greater
> than all things are,
> The first is Love
> and the second War.

"Kipling, wasn't it? Another bloody bellicose Brit, like you. Could you stand and show my children how tall ye' are?"

Ford managed to find his voice. "I'd . . . I'd prefer to remain here beside my wife."

"Granted. Ye're allowed. But please first stand for a moment so we can be sure ye're not armed. I'd like to keep this reunion as pleasant as possible, our being old comrades and so forth. Ye' canna' know how yeh've given my life point, Clem. All the success that I've had in my second life—or was it my third?—I owe to ye'. 'Twas the thought of ye' and nobody else that kept me young and vital, and my sons and daughter should thank ye' for it. Year after year I kept tellin' meself, I need the money, the health, the time to right the wrong of forty-five, and by gum, I'll do it. Clem and I will meet again, and here we are at last."

Sighing contentedly, Rehm motioned to his sons to move forward. "So tell us now, what's left? From yehr modest lifestyle, one might hope much. For yehr sake."

As the young men approached him, Ford considered reaching for the Webley and perhaps taking them both out. But he could not remember if he had slid off the safety (or know if Breege had thumbed it back on), and another, better plan now occurred to him. He had not been called Sea Wolf for nothing.

Slowly Ford got to his feet, his knees now not paining him in any way. It was as if all of him—body, mind, and soul— had decided that he would accomplish this last act, and this would be his final day on earth. Knowing he could not and *would not* go on without Breege, Ford only hoped that her spirit was still somewhere close by, so he could now join her.

"Please, Clem—ye' have not answered any of my questions. Ye' have not really even acknowledged our presence, which is impolite."

The two young men, while considerably smaller in stature than Ford, were well muscled and strong. Spinning him round, they threw him against the mantel. Like police, one spread out his legs, while the other patted him down. Satisfied that he was unarmed, they slowly moved away, the assault rifle of the third one—the girl—having been trained on him all the while.

"Which question do I answer first?" Ford straightened up. "May I remain here beside my wife?"

Rehm nodded. "*If* we can keep the discussion on this level, certainly. If it degenerates, we'll take you out into the kitchen."

Ford lifted Breege's legs from the footstool and eased himself down onto it. Like that, he was but a reach away from the Webley, and the chair between him and the woman in the doorway.

"The primary question, of course—is there much left?"

Ford shrugged and reached for his pipe.

"It's even better than that. There's more, *much* more, than in forty-five. I invested the lion's portion, and it's grown, as you can imagine."

Rehm smiled, and his eyes swept his three children. "See? I kept telling ye' my Sea Wolf was no fool. If he lived, the treasure would still be intact. How much would yeh say there is, Clem?"

Ford struck a match into his pipe and puffed up a cloud of Yachtsman, a strong blend that produced dark blue, aromatic smoke. In times past he had thoroughly clouded the sitting room. He shrugged. "Millions." It was no lie.

"How many millions?" one of the sons asked.

Ford cocked his head. "Many. The sum fluctuates, as markets change and currencies vary. But, fear not—it's safe." He was hoping Rehm's avarice would make him unwary. But then, it could as easily have the opposite effect.

"Take a guess. How many?"

"It's hard to say, but many."

"Ten?"

"No—more than that."

"Twenty?"

Ford shook his head. "I couldn't be sure without tallying what's invested and what's still on the island. Much of the cargo, of course, couldn't be brokered—you know that yourself—and so it remains where I concealed it. But twenty easily. Och"—Ford allowed himself a Celticism—"what am I saying? It's many times that."

"In pounds or dollars."

"Oh, pounds of course."

"Irish or British."

"British, mainly. This is such a small country, it would have been foolhardy to have made a show of it."

There was a pause in which the four others in the small room considered that.

Finally Rehm spoke. "By on the island yeh mean in this form?" Rehm waved the handkerchief that still held Breege's finger and the ring.

Ford nodded. "As I said, you know yourself, many of the better pieces were far too well known to sell. And why get rid of them when—"

"The price of well-cut diamonds keeps going up. Still, ye' can always find somebody to take such things, regardless of their origin. Greed supersedes all."

As demonstrated by your presence, thought Ford, and by my wife's and Kevin O'Grady's deaths. For which you will pay the highest price. "My first concern was security, always. I did nothing that would alert the authorities."

"Or would alert me!" Rehm positively crowed. "Yeh see, I was right! Each of us has kept the other alive. Without my anger and yehr—is 'fear' the right word, Clem? Why, we would both now probably be dead."

Ford glanced at Breege, then reached for her damaged hand and placed it in her lap. "Would you put that handkerchief down, please. It's—"

"Ghastly. I know. And ye' *are* cooperating, it seems. Now—how do we receive our share?" Rehm placed the handkerchief on the table beside him.

Ford pulled on his pipe and blew a long stream of blue smoke into the room. "It depends on how much of a share you require." He waited a long moment before turning his eyes to Rehm. "I hope you understand, only I can touch the invested funds. I've had the time—decades—to set all that up. If you kill me, you'll have only what remains on the island, which I'm willing to turn over to you now as the price of my release. Later we can arrive at an additional, equitable settlement. I wish only to live out the few days I have left in peace. As you can see, I require little. Personally."

The elder of the two sons now bent to his father and whispered something in a language that Ford did not recognize.

Said Rehm, "Well—if yeh say there's millions and, of all who were involved in this, only ye' and I are left, shouldn't we split it too? For good faith, yeh'll surrender what's left here on the island. And when ye' also surrender half of the invested funds, why then, we'll let ye' go, and yeh'll be free to do as ye' list."

"What about him?" Ford gestured toward the hallway with his pipe, meaning Kevin O'Grady. "Unfortunately, he's a former policeman and a father of seven. Breege—like us—was ready to die. But killing O'Grady is a complication. His wife knows I phoned and asked him to come here. Armed."

"So we discovered." Rehm raised the fisherman's cap from his lap to reveal a shiny nickel-plated revolver. "But the problem is easily solved. We'll simply take him, your wife, and you with us. No corpses, no murder. Maybe even no police."

"In your conspicuous North Sea schooner? You won't make it to Westport, once the authorities know we're missing."

"No—actually, we have another boat. The schooner was just a way of smoking you out, and now that its usefulness is over, we'll scuttle it with the bodies."

"Frankly, I believe none of what he's just told us," said the young woman. Her English was curious. It was flat, nasal, and American-sounding, but it was not American. "How could anybody with the money he claims he has possibly *live* like this? Like a *peón*."

Ford removed the pipe from his mouth and considered the stem for a moment. "Well, whatever we do, we should do it quickly. O'Grady's wife will be phoning here any minute, wishing to speak to him."

"And where was he?" asked one of the sons.

Said Rehm, "Yes—where were yeh, Clem, between the time that we first saw yeh in the window of the castle and yehr arrival here at the house?"

Ford had already phrased an answer. "I went straight to the hotel and rang up O'Grady, asking him to come up here and watch over Breege. Then I tried to make it back on my own. It's dark, there's a storm out there, and my knees have been bad ever since the war. I fell. I lost my hat and my way for a bit." He pointed to his muddy trousers, his soiled anorak. His hair and his beard were still matted with dampness.

Again Rehm and the older of the two young men conferred. Said Rehm, "We've decided you're right, Clem. We should leave here immediately. It's also obvious—if you accompany us, you can never come back. My son wishes to know if you can live with that?"

"Tell him I can live with anything, as long as I *live*."

"Tell me"—Rehm pointed at Breege and then toward the hall "—what will happen here by way of an investigation?"

"They'll send a team out from Dublin."

"Specialists?"

Ford nodded. "With the death of a former guard, they'll spare nothing."

"But, as we agreed—I hope we've agreed?—there's the remainder of the cargo."

"It can be done, and tonight. But we must act quickly."

Yet again the son conferred with Rehm, this time joined by the youngest man.

Ford was tempted to reach for the Webley, but he had his plan.

After a few moments, Rehm tugged the ring off Breege's severed finger and slipped it in the pocket of his pea jacket. Standing, he said, "As long as Commodore Dorfmann is going to cooperate with us—I see no illogic in cleaning this place up. You two"—he pointed to his sons—"put the bodies in the trunk of the car."

Ford raised a hand. "No—please. Grant me this one thing. My wife will stay with me. I will hold her. I will put her in the car and take her aboard the boat. And I will commit her to the deep. Completely." He pointed at the finger that was now on the side table. "It is the sailor's way, and I will ask you for nothing else."

Rehm cocked his head. "Who is in charge here, Commodore? Ye' or I? Could it be that we had this discussion before, much to my chagrin?"

"You are very definitely in charge, Colonel, but she stays with me. Completely." Again he pointed to the table.

With deliberation, Rehm folded the handkerchief over the finger and handed it to Ford. "Remember now—any misstep

and we will begin with ye'.'' He held up his own gloved
hand that concealed a prosthetic device. He had lost all the
fingers on his right hand, joint by joint, while being interrogated during the war. Or so he had told Ford in 1945.

"And *you* remember, Angus—without me there is nothing." Ford waited until the two sons had returned from placing O'Grady's body in the boot of the car. He wanted all of
them to be present before he made his move.

When they returned he stood towering over the smaller
men. Ford reached down for Breege's body, his right hand
pushing into the gap between the cushion and the side of the
chair. And there he felt it—the butt of the Webley.

Pretending to have to struggle with her mere seven stone,
Ford eased the handgun under her body. As he lifted Breege,
he made certain her pleated, woolen skirt draped his hand.
With his thumb, he eased off the safety and swung her toward
the door; he wanted to get as close as he could to the car,
which he now heard start up, before opening up on them.

Passing the young woman, he looked into her dark eyes
and wondered if she were actually Rehm's daughter, and he
suddenly felt sorry for her. Here, over fifty years later, the
killing of the Second World War was continuing, and it
should stop. Was Rhem's old life or even his own and
Breege's worth her death, no matter how she had been raised
by her obsessed father? No matter from whom and by what
means Rehm and his true cohorts of a bygone generation had
obtained their treasure?

But Ford suspected she and the others of Rehm's family
were no better than their father; otherwise they would not be
with him and wouldn't have killed Kevin O'Grady and
Breege. In so doing, they had sealed their fates.

The smart thing, if possible, would be to shoot the young
men first, then the daughter, and finally Rehm, who posed the
least threat. But if he got the chance, Rehm would die. Without him, none of this would have happened.

Both right doors of the right-hand-drive car were open; the
car was running, and the bonnet pointed down the hill. Standing by the doors, the two young men had their weapons at
the ready.

Rehm now walked between the car and Ford, who was still

carrying Breege and the Webley beneath her, saying, "Malcolm will get in the back first, Clem. Then you and your wife will be next. Dugald will sit on the other side of you. That way your wife can remain in your lap, and you won't have to worry about the doors. I'll drive. Heather will sit in front with me." And you will be covered from three directions, went unsaid.

With the strange machine pistol still in his good hand, Rehm waited until the elder son had followed his orders and slipped into the back on the other side, before he stepped toward the driver's door. That put the open rear door, as a shield, between Ford and Rehm. Heather, the daughter, was now moving around the bonnet, which left only Dugald behind Ford with a clean shot. It was time to act.

Ford began lowering himself and Breege through the open rear door, the Webley still fully concealed under her skirt yet free to fire at the eldest son, who was now seated on the other side of the car. "Could you give me a hand with her?" Ford asked. "The position is awkward."

When the son reached forward, his light blue eyes flashing up at him, Ford said, "Angus?"

"Yes, Clem?" Rehm was now positioned behind the wheel.

"This is for Breege." Ford pumped a 9 mm round into Rehm's son's head.

As a ruse, Ford staggered back into the drive with Breege, saying, "*Why*? I don't understand—he *shot* me!" Spinning round, he turned Breege's back toward the nearer young man and fired at his chest, knocking him flat on his back.

Rehm had begun to get out of the car, his one good hand reaching for the top of the open door to pull himself up. But Ford, pivoting on his heels, squeezed off two quick shots that shattered the door window and thwacked through the sheet metal of the roof. He then raised the gun slightly and fired the three remaining bullets at the young woman, who had dived toward the cover of the doorway of the house.

Tossing Breege's body into the back beside the elder son, Ford slammed the door shut and lunged for Rehm's one good hand that was reaching for the machine pistol. He caught it just as Rehm's finger wrapped the trigger, and the burst of automatic fire from the three joined barrels was frightful. In a wild arc it blew out the windscreen, peppered the night sky, and—with Ford now directing the barrage—raked the cubby of the house where he had last seen the girl. With the clip spent, he braced a foot against the side of the car, stiffened his arms and swirled his shoulders. Rehm tumbled out into the gravel of the drive.

But Ford's legs were too long for the position of the seat, and he could only manage to release the hand brake before a spray of fire from the woman's assault rifle pocked the car. A jagged fragment slammed into Ford's upper right arm, breaking it, he was sure.

But the car was moving down the steep, switchback drive to the dirt road below. Driving now with his left hand, he could just see the bright orange oilskins of the girl plunging down through the cabbage field that bordered the steep drive. She was firing as she ran.

Bullets pinged off the bonnet. The windows on the left side suddenly exploded and rained slivers of glass over Ford. But leaning away, he took only a shard of bullet low in the left leg.

It was then that the car made the road. Flooring the accelerator, Ford bolted toward the harbor that was four long miles away. And where he also knew what he would do. If he could.

CHAPTER 6

THERE WAS NO light in Packy O'Malley's tiny cottage by the harbor, but his fishing boat was still tied to the jetty wall, as it had been earlier. It meant that he was either at the pub or up in the hotel. Ford could use Packy's help, but at the same time, he did not want to involve anybody else or have to do any explaining. Stopping the car beside the boat, he doused the lights and dragged himself out.

Ford was now bleeding profusely from the arm wound. Tugging the belt from his trousers, he bound his upper arm and pulled the cinch tight above the puncture. He had thought the leg wound only a scratch, until he attempted to move toward the back door and discovered his left leg numb from the knee down. He had to pretend he could feel it to walk.

Peering out into the harbor at the large, white-hulled North Sea schooner rocking on her anchor, he also caught sight of the vessel's launch. It was plunging wildly on a line that was sprung from the quay wall. Would Rehm and his daughter now flee with their dead or wounded? Or would they try to track him down, get what they could from him, and finish him off? In a way he hoped they would try. To make a clean sweep of them or him would be best for everybody. And now—tugging open the back door and seeing poor Breege—Ford's anger surfaced with an intensity that made him dizzy.

But he had dropped the Webley when he had lunged for
Rehm, so he would have to take them by surprise. Which was
not likely, given his condition. Also, he was now weak, and
without the use of his right arm, it took him whole minutes—
five at the very least—to pull Breege's tiny body out of the
backseat, where it was tangled with Rehm's elder son, almost
in the position of lovers.

Loading her onto his good shoulder took more time. Any
moment Rehm and the daughter might arrive. They were sure
to have seen the donkey in the haggard and the cart nearby.
Or even the daughter alone. She had seemed athletic, and with
the storm at her back and rage pushing her on, she might
sprint the four miles—much of it downhill—in no time at all.

Once here in the harbor, they would spot the car easily.
Ford had dared not park farther than a few feet from Packy's
boat. Now his weak knees were nearly buckling, as he tried
to keep hold of Breege. And down they went when he tried
to step into the boat.

It took forever, it seemed, for Ford to pick himself up and
drag Breege into the small cuddy cabin that provided some
shelter from the storm. Propping her against the fiberglass
wall, he tried to close her eyes and firm up her mouth, which
was drooping open pitifully.

It took more time to find a pencil and for Ford to gain use
of his arthritic good hand. Across the chart of Mayo waters
that was fixed to a shelf near the wheel, he wrote in labored
letters:

*Packy—bury her beside Peig. Yourself, so nobody will
know. No stone. I'll take care of that later, if I can. If
I can't, I thank you for every good turn you've ever
done us in our lives. I'm leaving you a little something
by way of a pension. And let the O'Gradys know they'll
be seen after as well. My apologies to the Island.*

Clem

Burying Breege was something that the rough but loyal
man would do for a friend.

When Ford straightened up, he thought he saw—yes!—a

flash of orange down by the long boat on the quay, fifty or
so yards away. And another figure dressed in dark clothing
and dark hat. Reaching for Packy's cabin binoculars, he focused them in.

It was Rehm riding in the back of Ford's ass rail with the
assault rifle strapped over a shoulder. The daughter was running beside the donkey, driving it on.

Rehm now leaned down and the second son, the one Ford
had shot in the chest, appeared behind the cart. Ford couldn't
believe his eyes. He had shot him point-blank; he could not
have missed.

Reaching the quay, they stopped the cart, the girl pulling
the assault rifle off her shoulder, and screwing something
down on the muzzle of the gun. She then broke into a jog,
passed by the cart, and made straight for Ford, the boat, the
car, and Packy's cottage.

If she caught him in the tiny cubby cabin, she would kill
him like a mouse in a box. Or, worse, she would take him
aboard the schooner to get from him what they had come for,
one way or another. And doubtless it would be the other.
They wouldn't spare him now.

Ford panicked, his eyes darting about the small space. He
would not allow himself to be tortured.

The engine. Perhaps if he were to open the hatch and crawl
in, she might not think to open it. But there was Breege. Once
she discovered Breege's body, she would search the boat; yet
it was his only chance.

Wrenching open the hatch with his one good arm, Ford
hooked the binoculars back up on their peg, then tried to
lower himself—all six feet six inches—past the top of the
engine and into the darkness on the port side of the hull. But
with the use of only one arm and one leg he fell on top of
the hard spikes of the injectors. Summoning what little
strength he had left, Ford worked his body through the me-
chanics, wires, and pipes of the boat. Until—miraculously, it
seemed to him—his left hand, reaching out, slid into something smooth and soothing.

Fish? Yes, of course. In fact, herring, he could tell by the
feel of the scales. Packy's new boat, which had been financed
in part by the Clare Island Trust, was cold-molded. Con-

structed of thin strips of wood bonded with epoxy, it was light but strong and required only minimal bulkheads. Packy must have run into a school of herring and taken so many that they had nearly spilled into the engine compartment.

Slowly, silently—in a way almost like swimming—Ford now wriggled his large body in among the cool, soothing herring to a place where, he judged, he would not be visible from either deck hatch.

All the while he listened to the sounds of the woman at work—kicking open Packy's cottage door and (what was that sound?) spraying the interior with silenced bullets. It was the phut! phut! phut! that Ford remembered from the war. A few moments went by before he heard a thump on deck, and the boat listed slightly under her weight.

At the cuddy cabin, she cursed, then squeezed off another half clip, the bullets punching through the fiberglass and epoxy and—Ford imagined—Breege's corpse. For which she would pay, Ford vowed, if he survived the night.

Finally there was the engine compartment hatch, which she raised and fired off a volley to left and right. And the fish hatch, where she did the same. But Ford had positioned himself between them, and the angle was impossible.

"You old bastard!" she shouted into the blast. "You son of a bitch! I know you're fucking here someplace, and we'll be fucking back! Sooner than you think."

With any luck at all, thought Ford; he only hoped he'd be present to meet them.

She then stepped toward the cabin, where he heard her rip the chart that he had written on from its brace. In a leap she was off the boat. A whole minute went by, before Ford heard a loud pop from the direction of the launch.

Gripped suddenly with cold, he coaxed his hands into the pockets of his anorak where he felt something. It was Breege's severed finger. Grasping it tight, he believed he could still feel her warmth, and, he imagined, they were together again as one, if only in spirit. Which was as much as he could hope for, as he felt himself fading.

PART II

Seoinini

CHAPTER 7

CLARE ISLAND WAS just as Peter McGarr remembered it—a bright green and treeless eminence rising from the sea, the last and largest of the three hundred and sixty-five islands in Clew Bay, so said a sign in the Roonagh Point ferry terminus. It was as if the land had raised a three-by-five-mile, fifteen-hundred-meter shoulder against the fury of the ocean. Today it was mounting a thundering offensive against the Mayo coast.

Under a brilliant early-summer sun that had been swept clean of every cloud, mist, or color but a blistering robin's egg blue, Clew Bay was a boil of turquoise wave. Approaching the breakwater and harbor, the boat that had been sent to fetch McGarr bobbed like a cork in a cauldron. Only the skill of the captain—playing one engine off against the other—kept it from dashing its side into the jetty.

But there it waited, two yards maybe three from the wall, until the captain waved an arm. "Are yeh comin' aboard?"

McGarr nodded.

"The feck are yeh waitin' for?"

Hesitating, half hoping conditions would change, McGarr launched himself off the jetty and over the rail. Only the mate, catching him, prevented an ugly fall. The boat then lurched away from the wall, and again McGarr nearly went down.

49

"Pig of a blow last night," the mate confided. "As you can see."

McGarr had been seeing nothing but for the past two hours. His Dublin office had paged him while he was fishing Lough Eske in nearby Donegal. It had been early morning—around 7:00—and McGarr had only just returned to the lodge for breakfast, having fished the dawn for the salmon that were entering the lake. Two and a half hours later, he arrived at Roonagh point, only to be made to wait two more by the owner of the "water taxi."

"The price is forty-five bloody quid for guards, God, or gombeen men," the owner of the concession had said when McGarr had rung him up. The alternative was the twice-daily ferry, which would have meant a six-hour wait.

McGarr now had a feeling that it was the captain he had spoken to on the phone. For a forty-five-pound skiting, he should get more than a sea-sickening, eight-mile crossing. Already his stomach was feeling queasy.

In his early fifties, McGarr was a short, well-knit man with an aquiline nose and pale gray eyes. What little hair he had left was a lustrous red and curled at the nape of his neck. Having been on holiday fishing in Donegal when the call came through, he was wearing a short-brimmed khaki cap, windbreaker and trousers to match. On his feet was a pair of stout but supple walking shoes which, he knew, would be well suited to the rough terrain of Clare Island. He had spent a summer holiday there several years before. Apart from the blousyness of the jacket that concealed a 9 mm automatic, there was nothing to suggest his occupation.

"Rough day," he said by way of making conversation.

But the curly-headed captain with the ginger beard and weathered face did not so much as glance his way.

"Was it you I spoke to on the phone?"

Still the man did not reply. He was wearing a bright yellow rain slicker and bib overalls.

Could he be deaf? No, he had shouted to McGarr on the jetty.

"So—what gives on Clare Island?"

That got him. Shoving forward the throttle levers, the man cut the speed of the boat that pitched and heaved yet more violently as it lost momentum. The captain's eyes were hazel and angry. "Hear me—I couldn't care less who you are or why you've come, you'll bring *me* no bother. Now, I'll have me forty-five pound or it's back to the mainland with you." He tapped the flat top of the control console.

McGarr did not move. He could imagine the flap if this "captain" returned to the island without him. McGarr had been summoned by the superintendent of the Louisburgh barracks because of "a homicide and maybe some others. Whatever happened, we got one dead, three people missin', and there's blood and . . . mayhem everywhere." To McGarr's knowledge there had not been a capital crime on Clare Island in recent times, and its forty or so families would need the reassurance of an official presence.

"The only time we see *seoinini*, like you, is when there's trouble!" the man now went on. "All you ever give us is grief!"

And the odd forty-five pounds, thought McGarr, though he imagined life could be hard here on the rocky edge of the continent. In Irish *Maigh Eo* meant "the Place of the Yew Trees." It had been sacred to the ancient Celts, and certainly the terrain with its many mountains and formidable cliffs was dramatically beautiful.

But Mayo had long been thought of as the most remote of the counties of Connacht, and its people had fiercely resisted every foreign incursion from Christianity, through Cromwell, to the English language. For some, Dublin was now the enemy. *Seoinin* meant aper of foreign ways or jackeen or city slicker, which in many ways McGarr most definitely was. And he'd now give up the forty-five quid when good and ready. If then.

Finally the man wrenched his eyes away and jerked back the sticks, "Ye're hoors and gobshites, all of yiz. Louts, bowsies, and gurriers."

The boat surged into an oncoming wave that burst over the foredeck and thundered against the windscreen. "All piss and cess like a tinker's mule," he went on, having tried and failed to put a bit of wind up the chief superintendent of the Serious Crimes Unit of the Garda Siochana, the national police.

But with no witnesses save the mate, at worst he was out
the price of the ride.

By the time the boat reached the island, the blinding sunlight
had become another medium altogether, and McGarr wished
he had brought a hat with a wider brim. Roiling sparkles now
appeared in the periphery of his vision, as he glanced from
the well-preserved O'Malley Castle that dominated the harbor
entrance to the crowd on the jetty. There perhaps a hundred
people had gathered in two groups—by a cottage and car and
by a two-wheeled cart a few feet off. Which had to be most
of the island's population, McGarr judged.

He did not wait for the boat to tie up. What was good
enough for Roonagh Point, he decided, was even better for
here, and he jumped off when they were three feet from the
jetty wall. The captain howled to the mate, then called out.
But McGarr did not look back.

" 'Tis the only two corpses we can find," said Superintendent Rice from the Louisburgh barracks, pointing to the
young donkey that had been shot point-blank in the side of
the head and was now heaped in its traces.

His finger then moved to the boot of the battered car, the
lid of which was open but covered by a blanket. Standing
there was a middle-aged woman with her head bent and ro-
sary beads in her hands. Grouped tightly around her were
seven children of various ages. Other adults were keeping
themselves at a respectful remove.

McGarr glanced down at the donkey. The muzzle blast had
burned a black aureole around the entrance wound, and the
outer lens of the visible eye was milky blue.

"It's Clement Ford's beast, I'm told," Rice said in an un-
dertone. "He's one of them that's missing."

The animal's mouth was open, and the stiff breeze, bucking
over the edge of the jetty, riffled its upper lip. Now and then
square yellow teeth appeared, and a length of dry-cracked
tongue. It was as though the mute corpse was saying, We
dumb beasts are better than this, but *you*! McGarr turned toward the car and what he suspected was human carnage.

"Apart from the one body in the boot, like I mentioned on
the phone, the rest is just bullets and blood, and plenty o'

both.'' Rice went on, following him. His hand swept over the shiny brass bullet casings that littered the ground in front of a small white cottage, more a kind of converted outbuilding than a house by design. The door had been broken open and was hanging at an odd angle.

McGarr now glanced down at his feet. There were dark stains from the car to the edge of the jetty. The vehicle itself, while old and rusty, looked like it had been caught in a cross fire. The faded blue sheet metal was riddled and pierced by large-caliber bullets, the glass blown out of all windows but one. There were some other holes that appeared to have been caused by smaller-caliber fire, perhaps by a handgun. Or handguns.

''The other crime scene I told you about—the house—is about four miles by road from here at the base of Croagh-more. It's the same. Blood in the hall, in the sitting room, on the gravel drive. Casings all over, one from a handgun in the house.'' Croaghmore was the large mountain behind them, McGarr now remembered.

The crowd broke before him, silent, their eyes on his face, regarding him closely. He was the cop, the government man, the *seoinín* who might make sense of it all, when, in fact, it was they who had the answers. Unlike in Dublin or Cork or Limerick where anonymous crime was common, there was little possibility that the pivotal details of whatever had occurred were unknown to them. The challenge would be in convincing them to give up that truth.

''So, what we have is—three people is missing and one boat,'' Rice went on. A beefy older man in a blue uniform, he toddled and huffed a half step behind McGarr.

''*Two* boats, if you count the one that put into the harbor at nightfall. It was a big white yoke with sails, somethin' like a schooner I'm told. There was at least three people aboard, foreigners from the sound of them. But only one of them called in at the bar over there.'' He jerked a thumb at the largest of the buildings in the harbor front. ''He was a young man, middling height, sandy hair cut short and wearing''— Rice consulted his notepad—''an orange deck suit with 'Mah Jong' on the back.''

''Like the game.''

"And the boat evidently. It was called that too. The bloke spoke good English sort of like an American and was quick to ask after Ford—where he lived. How he could get there? Was it far? That class of thing. When the barman volunteered to ring Ford up, he said no, he wanted his visit to be a surprise. Left most of his fresh pint on the bar."

"Ford's one of the missing?"

Rice nodded. "An Englishman who's lived here for fifty years. Big fella, huge, and a kind man. Great, white beard."

The woman standing by the boot of the car now turned her face to McGarr; it was haggard with woe. McGarr touched the brim of his cap. "Peter McGarr. I'm—"

But she nodded, and Rice interposed. "Jacinta O'Grady. Sergeant O'Grady's wife. *Former* Sergeant O'—" but he had explained about O'Grady on the phone, along with how the man had come to be at the Fords' house armed on the evening before—as a favor to the old couple. "He left his tea on the table, fetched his revolver from the closet, and that was the last seen of him," Rice had reported.

The youngest child now began to cry, and the widow lifted him into her arms.

Because O'Grady had been a guard, a funeral detail would be sent out from Dublin. Radio and television would cover the event. It would do nothing for the family, but maybe somebody would recall having seen a large white schooner leaving the island. Or O'Malley's fishing boat. Already every maritime policing agency had been notified, not only in the Republic but also in the North, in Britain, and in Norway. Planes and helicopters had been dispatched, but so far nothing.

"Would you tell me something?" Jacinta O'Grady took a step closer to the boot of the car, then turned her head to her other children. "The lot of yeh stay where you are." She then tried to raise an edge of the gray blanket, but the wind, sweeping over the jetty, tore the wool from her hand. Only Rice, reaching out, kept the blanket from being swept out into the harbor. "Whatever happened to the back of his poor head?"

McGarr could see at a glance. The bullet had entered the forehead, then exploded, blowing away the skull from the ears back. It made his face look unreal and one-dimensional, like a pasteboard cutout tacked to his shoulders.

But McGarr only shook his head. It was a scene he knew all too well, and no words, no matter how well chosen, could help.

"Don't you know? Can't you tell me?"

Rice signaled to some of the other women who moved forward.

"Who was it? Who could have done such a thing? Taken a life, a husband. Taken a father from his children."

Stepping round the car, McGarr peered into the backseat at a mass of fat green flies that had gathered on the pooled blood. There was plenty of it. Too much for one person to have survived. In the matter of lethal bloodletting, McGarr was rather expert.

"Now—what I mentioned, Chief, is here on the floor under the wheel."

It was a woman's ring that was sparkling even in the shadows. A single shaft of sunlight, angling through a bullet hole in the side window, had caught its large central stone and was spewing rainbows of prismatic light over the pedals. The smaller surrounding stones had the deep blue color of sapphires.

"Could it be real?" McGarr asked.

"Not likely. That big job is the size of a peach pit, and them other ones is too alike to be real. And whyever would it have been left behind." If it were real, Rice meant.

McGarr was tempted to reach for it, but the Tech Squad would be arriving soon by helicopter. Instead, he turned toward the cottage.

It was bachelor digs, he could see as he entered; men's clothes were hung on pegs, and the furnishings were Spartan and few. Dirty dishes were heaped in the sink, most shattered by bullets. Somebody had swept the room with an automatic weapon.

Turning to step back outside, McGarr walked into the chest of a larger man; it was the captain of the boat that had ferried him to the island. He was standing in the doorway with a hand out. "Now, bucko—my forty-five pounds."

McGarr tried to step to one side, but the man moved in front of him. And to the other. Again.

"Did ye not hear me?"

McGarr knew the tone; more, he had seen that squint-eyed smile before. The man in the yellow rain slicker was twenty years younger, twenty pounds heavier, and a good six inches taller. Already his hands had formed fists. He was about to give McGarr a thumping, or at least try. Which posed a dilemma.

McGarr could not appear to be intimidated, especially not here in front of the gathered population of the island whose respect he would need. But neither could he be seen in a brawl that would be reported to the press.

As though wary or frightened, he moved back into the room, drawing the man away from the door. Rice stepped forward to intervene, but McGarr raised a hand. "Sure, if that's all the gentleman wants, I'll give him his twenty-two pounds fifty. He'll get the other half when he takes me back."

The hazel eyes widened and the ears pulled back. Here it comes, thought McGarr—telegraphed, no, carrier-pigeoned maybe a whole second—before the hands leapt for McGarr's throat. Sidestepping, McGarr threw a double jab with his left hand. The first blow caught the small ribs—the soft, cartilaginous, easily broken and sensitive ribs just up from the belt. The second landed smartly on an ear, with a twist to make it sting all the more.

When the right hand jumped up in pain, McGarr loaded his weight into a shot thrown straight from his knees that sank so deep into the stomach he thought he felt backbone from the inside. Buckling up, the man sank toward McGarr, who grabbed a fistful of curly hair and spun him toward the door.

"There's a lesson in this, bucko. *Seoinini* like me? We do this for sport. Or at least it would have been sport, had you been more of a challenge. Like this, it's just plain old police brutality." Raising a foot to the rump, McGarr shot him out the door where he stumbled and fell roughly onto the concrete for all to see.

Stepping out of the house, McGarr pulled some money out of his billfold and showed it to Rice. "How much is this, Superintendent?"

"I count forty-five pounds."

Bending to the man, McGarr said in a low voice, "I'd stick this in your gob, if you didn't need it to suck all that wind. In the future, put into the dock for your passengers. I might've broken my leg. And show some respect for your elders. You never know when they might teach you a lesson." He shoved the money into a pocket of the oilskin, then straightened up.

"Now, Superintendent—I'll see the house."

CHAPTER 8

THE FORD COTTAGE lay some two miles from the harbor overland. But it was a good four by road, much of it along a rough mountain track scarcely wide enough for the ancient Bedford van that Rice had borrowed from the owner of the island's only pub.

The floor of the vehicle was largely gone, a few sheets of steel having been welded onto the frame for their feet. Looking down, McGarr watched the gravel, rocks, and grass flow past them, like an endless, gray-green watercourse. It reminded him of what he would rather be doing.

Rice, who was driving, explained, "The islanders pick up these junks cheap wherever they can, so long as the engine has a bit of life left. Diesel's the thing, since it's cheap and they get the government subsidy." On fuel used while farming or fishing, he meant. "Road tax? Insurance? Even number plates? Why bother, since the car's never going off the island.

"You hear these people complain, and some of them have 'attitudes,' like yehr mahn with the forty-five pounds. But with eight miles of water between them and the government, they have it made."

Unless, of course, they were visited in the dead of the night by a raiding party with murder in mind.

The cottage was set off on a high cliff on the western side

of the island with no near neighbors in any direction. The views were spectacular, especially on a clear day such as this.

To the north across Clew Bay were the mountains of Achill Island and North Mayo, layer upon towering layer, with the ocean defining all in a fringe of silver surf.

To the south the steep shoulder of Croaghmore continued to rise. Two narrow paths wound across it, one leading up to its peak and the pristine sky, the other tracing down through a defile to a beach that was probably exposed only at low tide.

To the east lay a long stretch of green commonage and walled fields. And beyond, the harbor with its collection of white houses, the pub, a shop or two, and the castle. But without so much as a tree for perspective, they seemed leagues away.

Finally, to the west and maybe three hundred feet down lay the blue depths of the Atlantic clear to New York. And wind, McGarr discovered, stepping out at the bottom of the drive so as not to destroy any evidence. Gathering at the base of the cliff after thousands of miles of unimpeded sweep, it surged over the edge and pinned him against the side of the van.

McGarr imagined that the place was virtually uninhabitable most days of the year; the storm of the night before, while severe, was not unusual. Now climbing the steep switchback drive, the wind was so strong that both men had to lean back into it and brace their legs to keep from being hurled forward.

How had Ford and his wife—near octogenarians both, Rice had said—ever managed to leave the house? And why had they remained in such an inhospitable place for "How many years did you say they lived here?" McGarr tried to ask, but the gale swept away his words. What was their support? How had they kept themselves from being prisoners of the wind?

It was then, as they turned through the first switchback and began to mount the next incline, that the wind ceased abruptly, nearly tumbling McGarr. Rice staggered, then righted himself. "It's magic, what? This morning I thought me ears would burst."

The house had been sited with care in a kind dingle or combe that a stream had cut into the side of Croaghmore.

And although still windy there, the swirling breezes lacked the force of the gusts that were wailing overhead.

"Many's the time I wondered how man or beast could live in a place like this, seeing it from down there." Rice pointed toward the ocean. "I fish a bit with the brother-in-law. Now I know."

McGarr stopped and looked behind him down the declivity to the beachlike area and the ocean. "Go through the chronology again for me."

"Like I mentioned on the phone, Chief—the call came to the barracks in Louisburgh around four in the morning. The two men who fish with Packy O'Malley went to roust him out, since he's a bit of a character and usually closes the pub. And they found the boat gone and his kip all shot up. That's when they noticed O'Grady's car with the doors open and blood everywhere. One of them thought to look in the boot.

"I got to the harbor around seven, the brother-in-law bringing me out. Word, of course, had spread, and even at that hour the jetty was packed.

"Says the publican to me, says he, 'You should speak to Paul O'Malley, he's got something to tell you.' 'Who's Paul O'Malley,' says I? 'A crippled fella who lives on Capnagower.' That's another of the hills to the east of the island. 'Paul can do little else each day but monitor local waters with binoculars and sideband.' It's him that told me about the schooner and how Clem Ford would always want to be informed the moment any new boat put in.

"But, sure, by that time I'd already heard from Jacinta O'Grady, saying that Ford had rung up her husband, asking him to come and sit with the wife while he stepped out for a moment. And to come armed. O'Grady thought it a bit daft, but he left his tea nevertheless, worried, like, about the two old-timers."

"And he took along a gun?"

Rice nodded. "So the wife said. A handgun."

"Did Ford mention why he wanted O'Grady to come here?"

"No—he said he'd explain it all later."

"Or where he was stepping out to?"

Rice shook his head.

"Do we have any idea of any later times?"

"Jacinta said she began to get worried when, by midnight, O'Grady hadn't come home or phoned her. It was then she began ringing him here, but the line was busy or off the hook. Also, the publican said Packy O'Malley stayed as usual 'til closing, which was half ten last night, no later. He also says he saw Packy's boat in the harbor when he put out the bottles and locked the back door of the pub fifteen minutes later."

So, if they could assume that O'Malley's boat was gone because he was on it, then he left sometime after 10:45. "What's the connection—O'Malley to the Fords?"

"She—the wife, Breege—is an O'Malley too, and they're probably related somehow. But the publican says Ford and Packy got on famously and often had jars together. But other than that—" Again Rice shook his head, then pointed to the drive that was speckled with the same brass 7.62 mm bullet jackets that had littered the jetty at the harbor. " 'Tis here that the shell casings begin."

And also what McGarr thought of as the "mess" that marked the scene of almost every murder, victims seldom being taken completely unawares. The soft clay-and-gravel drive was pocked with footprints, as was the even softer earth of a small cabbage garden that had been planted between the two legs of the switchback drive. Somebody—evidently whoever had been wielding the automatic weapon—had sprinted across the drive near the cubby entrance to the house and then plunged down through the garden, firing all the while.

"Hard to figure it though—them's small prints for a man or even a boy. Could it have been a woman?"

There was no way of knowing, and at the moment McGarr was merely observing, taking in everything he could. But whoever it had been, he or she had not been afraid of the steep slope through the garden and had leapt four or five feet at a bound, firing all the while. The shell cases looked like bright brass seeds that had been strewn over the earth, which was dark from the rain of the night before.

But there were other prints too, most notably those of a size as large as McGarr had ever seen.

"Ford himself," Rice opined, pointing. "There, there, and

there. Huge man. As tall and broad as we've got in these parts, and Mayo has some big men.''

And *there* carrying something heavy from the house to the car, most of the weight on the heels. The impressions were filled with clayey rainwater the color of milky tea. But they did not lead to where the boot of the car must have been, given the tire tracks, but rather to the backseat that had contained so much blood.

There were also prints of a smaller man leading to the back door on the passenger side, and the prints of yet another even smaller man to the driver's door. Two of those had been partially stepped on by Ford, who appeared to have been in a great hurry getting behind the wheel. One of his immense shoes had slid a half yard before digging deep into the drive as he pushed off.

Stooping, McGarr picked up one of the several, smaller shell casings. Nine mm. Probably fired from the Webley automatic that the car had run over and was partially buried in the drive. It had to be an antique, since to McGarr's knowledge Webleys of that type had not been produced since the Second World War.

And what was that on its grip? McGarr stepped closer. It was an anchor that had been cast in intaglio along with the words "PROPERTY OF THE ROYAL NAVY." Patent and registration numbers were on the barrel.

"These here are the palm prints I told you about."

There were several. It looked like somebody had fallen and scrambled through the wet gravel and clay with one rather small hand fully opened and the other cupped.

From his jacket McGarr pulled out a box of cigarettes and turned toward the house where, maybe, he could find a windless corner and light up. At his wife's insistence, he'd been trying to quit now for . . . oh, ten years off and on. But mainly off. The overconsidered cigarette wasn't worth smoking, and he decided he liked the guilt.

He displayed the packet to Rice, who shook his head and tapped the uniform pocket over his heart. While lighting up, McGarr noticed a pair of high-tech binoculars hanging from a peg. Zeiss, which were high-quality and—could they be?— of the night-seeing variety. They were bulky with a large dome between the lenses. He wondered what something like that cost; doubtless a pretty penny. Whatever the raiding party had come for, it had not been for a simple theft. Turning, he stepped into the house.

Blood. Rice had said there would be blood, and he had not lied. Somebody had died in the narrow hallway, probably O'Grady from the pieces of sandy-colored scalp and whitish gore that McGarr caught sight of. A gush of vital matter covered the array of framed photographs and paintings on the wall; in fact, Ford with his huge footprints had trod through the coagulating blood and then stopped six or so feet from where the corpse had lain. There was an outline of shoulders where the blood had pooled.

Said Rice, "These here are my tracks, Chief, when I came in this morning."

But McGarr was distracted. Something had caught his eye. Turning his head, he again scanned the wall. A picture, one of the black-and-white photographs near where Ford had stopped. In it was a beautiful young woman with raven hair and light eyes.

Smiling into the camera, she had a rose in her hair, and her gracefully formed hands were grouped near her neck. On one finger was the ring that he had seen in the Granada at the harbor, the one with the "diamond" of unlikely size and the surround of "sapphire" stones. Blood had spattered the picture, and somebody with two large fingers had touched the bloodied glass covering it. The fingerprints were definite and now dry.

But the footprints in the hall were worthless, McGarr judged. After O'Grady had died in the hall, his murderers had tossed the place completely, walking back and forth, searching every nook and cranny. Not one drawer or cabinet had been spared, the contents dumped in piles in the center of the rooms.

Correspondence was everywhere. Letters had been ripped open, scanned, and the sheets tossed down. Only one stack of paper was still in some order on a table by a lamp that was lit. Each page had "Clem and Breege Ford, Clare Island, Co. Mayo" printed in fancy script at the top. But the handwriting was so eccentric as to be nearly illegible, with backward-slanting characters that looked almost Gothic. McGarr could make out only a word or two.

Framed photographs—mostly of children and young adults—were also scattered on the hearth, the glass broken. McGarr counted them—eighteen. "Did Ford have that many children or grandchildren?"

"Far as I know he had none. But, like I said, he was a friendly sort."

In other rooms chairs had been overturned and gutted, floorboards ripped up. The hatch to the low attic was still open and a heap of old trunks and cases lay smashed beneath it. The phone was off the hook. Yet the small light on the answering machine was lit, saying there were 0 recorded messages.

With the butt of his pen, McGarr depressed the button to hear the outgoing message. A deep and sonorous male voice said, "You have reached the home of Breege and Clement Ford. We are unable to come to the phone at the moment, but if you would kindly leave a message, we will ring you back at the earliest possible opportunity. Please wait for the tone." The English was precise but neutral, the consonants suspirated crisply but without affectation. In all Ford sounded like somebody from a privileged background.

The kitchen table was still laid with dinner for two, although only one had been eaten; some sort of chowder, lamb chops, brussels sprouts, and boiled potatoes. The other plate had been filled, but the serving remained untouched.

There was no other sign of life or death. The house had been sacked and its occupants were now missing. Pushing open the back door, McGarr stepped out into another but much larger glassed-in cubby that was filled with rows of potted plants. It was hot in there, and the door to the yard was bolted. McGarr opened it and stepped out.

A large, well-tended garden ran up most of the length of the dingle. Because the house blocked the blast, it was nearly windless there. A haggard with a row of outbuildings occupied one side of the cleft, and the mountain stream that had formed the dingle ran down the other, passing well beyond the house. Today it was a sparkling torrent, in full spate with the storm water pouring off the mountain.

Opening one of the sheds McGarr was surprised by geese that bolted past him in a flutter of white feathers and raucous complaint. He found a cow, which he also let out into a grazing yard, and some chickens, but nothing else.

Crossing the garden again, he moved toward the stream and a well-worn path along its higher bank. So—he mused, reaching for another cigarette—a large white sailing vessel arrived in the harbor at sundown, and Paul O'Malley, a shut-in who monitored such events, phoned Clement Ford.

It was suppertime, a storm was raging, yet Ford—a large man nearly eighty who would have to walk two miles each way—pushed himself away from the table and set out immediately. Why? Because he feared (and had been fearing for years) what came to pass?

Ford then hurried back here to the cottage and rang up Kevin O'Grady, a former guard, asking him to come with a weapon and stay with his wife while he . . . ?

McGarr stopped by the stream and looked down into the amber water that had been colored by some tannin-rich mountain bog and was gushing golden down the rocky sluice.

. . . while Ford hid whatever the raiders had tried to find when they tossed the house? Why else would he leave his blind wife at such a moment?

But what and hid where? Certainly *not* in the house or anywhere near it. And whatever it was, it had to be something that an old man, like Ford, could carry during a raging storm.

McGarr looked round him—at the cottage and ocean beyond, at the garden and haggard, and farther up the ravine to the top where the stream seemed to be spewing from the azure sky. Turning, he began to climb toward that point; maybe from there he could see what the rest of the area looked like.

So—Ford left the house, O'Grady arrived and the wife let him in. The *blind* wife, McGarr reminded himself. But before Ford could return, the raiders arrived, murdered O'Grady, and tossed the house. Then Ford, entering by the front door, was shocked to find O'Grady on the floor with the back of his head blown off. It was then that he touched the bloodied picture of his wife. And whatever happened after that was less definite. McGarr thought of all the bloody footprints that had been tracked through the house.

Now he kept his eyes focused on the path where there were
other prints, mostly those of sheep and a donkey—probably
the dead donkey, since there was no other—and here and
there an immense boot print, obviously Ford's. But, then, it
was equally obvious that Ford farmed the property actively.
His prints were probably all over the area.

At any rate, there was the Webley. No, the *antique* British
Navy–issue Webley. McGarr tried to think of when he had
last come across a Webley handgun of that sort. Over a score
of years earlier, and even then it had been unusual.

Somebody in or near the car had fired the Webley at the
house, then dropped it in the drive and jumped into the car
that ran over it. Ford himself, McGarr was willing to bet;
there was the large, skidding footprint just where the driver's
door would have been.

The car then moved off, and the person wearing the small,
narrow boots charged down from the top of the drive, through
the cabbage garden, and out onto the switchback drive again,
firing clip after clip of 7.62-caliber ammunition.

At what? At the car, O'Grady's car, the Granada that had
been left on the jetty wall with O'Grady dead in the boot. It
was pocked and riven mainly with large-caliber bullet holes.
The raiders had then hitched the donkey to the cart and taken
it the four miles by road to the harbor, rather than the two
overland. Why?

Because they did not know the overland route and feared
blundering into a bog? Or because they had found what they
were after here and had to transport it back to their boat? Or
because one of them had been hit by the fire from the Webley,
and the donkey cart was the easiest means of getting their
wounded back?

Then who had lost so much blood in the backseat of the
Granada? Ford's wife. Because she was blind, she could not
have been driving the car. But yet her ring was lying on the
floor by the driver's seat.

Plainly McGarr did not know enough, and he tried to keep
his mind from rushing on. But if the raiders had found what
they were after here at the Ford cottage, why had they then
broken down the door of the fisherman's living quarters on
the quay and sprayed the interior with gunfire? Pique at not

having discovered what they had come for? Or anger that one or more of their number had been killed or wounded by Ford? They must have thought Ford was in there. Or O'Malley.

No, not O'Malley. It all had to have happened before half ten, while O'Malley was still in the pub. Why had nobody heard the gunfire? An assault rifle produced a deafening report, especially when fired in basin of concrete and stone like the Clare Island harbor. Unless, of course, the gun had been silenced, which the Tech Squad would be able to determine by examining the recovered slug.

The raiders had then left on their boat, the large white schooner. How far could it have got in the twelve plus hours between leaving Clare Island and McGarr asking the Coast Guard and Naval Service to search for it? Far. Say, it could motor as well as sail, and it made ... fifteen knots under power. That would be over two hundred miles.

Say then, that it took another four or five hours at the inside for Scottish or Norwegian authorities to be made aware of the alert and to deploy their ships and planes. Or, say, that the boat had simply sailed straight out to sea, or that the raiders had in place some contingency plan for scuttling the vessel. Or abandoning it in some port on the mainland that was only eight miles distant.

McGarr shook his head, before tossing down the cigarette and crushing it under foot. Raiders with silenced assault rifles, who had come to the island for a purpose and were willing to kill, had probably also devised some way of making off. As well, there was the additional problem that there had been few government vessels in Mayo waters on the night before, and that onboard radar could sweep a radius of only twenty miles at the outside.

Now nearing the top of the dingle, McGarr again felt the wind off the ocean pushing him forward, more strongly the higher he climbed. At the top he had to plant his legs to look around.

Three hundred or so yards below him directly to the west, and tucked neatly into the dingle, lay the Ford cottage, looking like a photo for some "Hidden Ireland" promotional campaign. Were there not a road, it would be impossible to tell that there was a house anywhere nearby. Both to north and south the land was nothing but a reach of towering, tree-less mountain and an equally open expanse of rolling fields—bounded by the cliff—all the way to what appeared to be a lighthouse some two long miles away.

McGarr could see only one other group of buildings. An-other cottage with some large buildings nearby had been grouped virtually on the cliff edge maybe half the distance to the lighthouse. It was also the direction in which the path now led, over hill, dale, stile and stream. McGarr set out.

Overhead a young gannet, its dun wings speckled, swooped in a circle, gathering itself before diving toward the edge of the cliff and the deep blue waves below. Farther on, McGarr came upon a patch of alpine sawwort, its yellow leaves thriv-ing at the edge of a bog. Formerly he had thought the exotic plant restricted to special growth areas in Cork and Kerry in Ireland, and he plucked a leaf to make sure. Later—perhaps back in Dublin—he'd look it up. Other than fishing, McGarr's hobby was gardening and plants.

Farther still along the path, he discovered a wallow where Ford—it could have been nobody but—had blundered through the mud. Perhaps walking at night in a storm without a torch because he feared being seen?

The water was deep but the prints still crisp.

McGarr moved on.

CHAPTER 9

MIRNA GOTTSCHALK SAW the man approaching from at least a mile away. She had been scanning the hills with the binoculars she used for birding, ever since she received the first phone call about Breege and Clem and poor Kevin O'Grady. And now Packy O'Malley seemed to be missing as well. His house had been shot up, and his boat was gone.

Her first thought had been to go to the Fords' cottage, her dear friends and nearest neighbors who meant so much to her and her parents in their time. Why? Because she felt guilty, and she wished there was some way she could help, now that it was probably too late.

Why had she thought Clem had been exaggerating or acting a bit dotty when he had come to her studio the night before? To her knowledge Clem Ford had never uttered so much as a fib, and he had been upright and genuine in all his dealings. Maybe she could have prevented whatever it was that had happened to them and the tragedy of O'Grady's death.

How? Well, by having notified the guards in Louisburgh on the mainland. Would they have come on the report of an elderly man acting a bit strange? No, probably not. And even if they said they would, could they have got to the harbor and then all the way out to the Fords' on time? No again.

Worried by what Clem had said and how he had acted, she

69

had rung up Breege shortly after he left but had been unable
to get through to the cottage, even though she let the phone
ring and ring. And Breege could not possibly have been anywhere else on such a night. That alone should have alerted
her to the extraordinary nature of the situation—for the half
century that she had known the Fords, they had been the most
predictable and dependable people on the island.

Instead of taking action, Mirna had told herself she would
stop round in the morning and return the packet. She had
thought it an embarrassment for Clem, a sign that he was
getting old and beginning to lose his grip on reality. But after
the phone calls, she had changed her mind.

With fear and trembling, she had summoned the courage
to look inside. It contained only what Clem had said—two
single sheets of paper. The first listed the names of the two
firms that Clem had told her about and also the name of the
man that she should avoid at all costs: Angus Rehm. Also
there was a paperboard pouch that was sealed with red wax
and felt like it contained papers.

Could the rumors be true? Could Clem and Breege, who
had lived the simplest of lives, have controlled the Clare Island Trust? Is that why they were missing or . . . whatever?
Mirna reflected on how the Trust had helped her, granting her
incipient business venture an immense loan of one hundred
thousand pounds. And it had not foreclosed during the ten
months that she had been unable to meet the repayment
schedule.

As Mirna remembered, Clem and Breege had even offered
to loan her money from ''Clem's pension scheme'' Breege
had put it, to help her through. They had been strange and
wonderful people. No, *were* wonderful people. Mirna would
not give up hope.

The second loose page was a hand-drawn map that showed
how to enter a cave at the steepest face of the Croaghmore
cliffs. Mirna was sure there was none. She had been by the
place perhaps a half-dozen times during slack spring tide,
which was the only time the area was even approachable, as
far as she knew.

Now the possible reality of the cave, which would more
than prove Clem's statements of the night before, terrified her.

In every way, from the bottom of her soul, she wished the packet gone and the night before had never happened. But yet she copied the map onto the back of the other sheet of paper. It was spring, and the tides were low. Maybe in a day or two she would take herself out there, if the police weren't still about.

The police. They had been at the harbor, and one of her employees, phoning Mirna, had said that they had gone out to the Fords'.

Raising the binoculars again, she found that the man was much closer now, no more than a quarter mile away. Short but square and fit, he was moving with a quick, rolling gait, ready and alert. He was dressed casually in khaki, like a golfer or a sportsman. She had seen the face before with its nose that was bent slightly to one side, those pale gray eyes, and red, curly hair. And more than once. But where? Certainly he looked too much of a piece for a country man.

Lowering the binoculars, Mirna looked around the studio. On the television, of course, and in the newspaper. He *was* the police, the detective, the one from Dublin who was sent out on major investigations. She panicked and looked down at the muddied packet and the still-unopened paperboard pouch with the red sealing wax. Why did she feel like she had done something wrong, when, in fact, she should welcome the security that his presence represented? He would protect her, perhaps even set everything right.

But she also remembered Clem's entreaty about the Trust, and how it had given Breege's and his life point and purpose. And certainly it had done great good. Finally, it could be that the Fords were not dead and would come back and take the entire thing off her hands.

Mirna looked down at the sealed pouch that Clem had asked her not to open yet, not until she had gone to the cave and to the solicitors in Dublin. But she just had to understand more completely what she was getting into, before pressing forward as he had asked.

Slipping a fingernail under the flap she slit the wax seal. It contained a sheaf of handwritten pages that were yellowed and timeworn. The top page was dated 1948. It began:

11 November 1947
Clare Island, Mayo
Eire

*I write this while the details are still fresh in mind and
so you who succeed us will know the source of the
cargo that I brought to this island. I write also for posterity and my God, who shall judge me; it was war, but
it was also a struggle between forces. I knew that back
in the mid-1930s. The pity is, not well enough.*

*First, a word about who I am, since beginning in
1945 I had to abandon my true identity, again because
of the cargo. I arrived here under circumstances that
were, at the very least, covert and perhaps even criminal, when viewed in the light of history.*

I was born in . . .

Mirna glanced up. If the memoir or whatever it was now
told her that Clem Ford was some sort of thief or worse, she
could not read on. It was all too much for her. And what was
she seeing out of the corner of her eye, movement close to
the house on the far side of the yard. The man had arrived.

Snatching up the sheaf, she folded the pages hurriedly and
slipped them into the pouch and the pouch into the packet.
Then the map. But where was the top sheet, the piece of
stationery with the names and addresses on it? Glancing
wildly round the table and then under it, Mirna could not
locate the thing, so she emptied the packet again and shuffled
through the documents. Perhaps it had got caught between
some of the pages. No, it was not there, and she had only
just fitted the documents back inside, closed the flap, and
stuffed the packet under the cushion of her reading chair when
a knock came on the door.

Flushing with shame or guilt or . . . she didn't know what—
mortification, maybe—Mirna Gottschalk rushed to the door
and pulled it open. "Yes?" she demanded in a strange,
choked voice that was not her own. Suddenly she felt faint.

The clear gray eyes regarded her calmly. It was as though
he could read her thoughts, and the pause seemed to continue
for an eternity. Finally without taking his gaze from her, he

pointed to the ground by the door. "Clement Ford was here early last evening, wasn't he? He slipped and fell right here."

Even through her tears, which without warning had filled her eyes, Mirna could see a long scrape. It could only have been Clem. There were other impressions from his large boots where he had picked himself up and staggered. Even his muddied tracks were still on the stairs, the print of his large hand on the rail.

"What did he bring you?"

It was the moment of decision. But too soon. Mirna had wanted to think about it some more, to wait for some word about Clem and Breege. She had also wanted to lay the entire matter before Karl, her son. Again, as Clem had requested.

She could lie. She could say that Clem had visited her earlier yesterday, sometime late in the afternoon. Why? Why to view the portrait she was painting of his wife. There it was in the center of the room, a bright blur of color through her tears.

But when she tried to speak, her throat wouldn't let the lie out, and she only sobbed. And the sound of her voice cracking brought on further sobs for Breege and Clem and Kevin O'Grady and Packy, but also for herself and her predicament.

She believed she felt worse—both low and worthless— than she had ever in her life. How could she have lived beside Breege and Clem all these years and ignored the great problem that had created this debacle. Why had she not done something last night? And here she was embracing the problem as her own.

"I'm sorry," she managed, turning away from the door toward a small kitchen. "But the Fords were—*are*—my best friends. Could you come back later, when I'm—" She reached for some tissues and began blotting her eyes. But it did little good, and Mirna just stood at the sink with her hands on the edge, her body racked by sobs.

McGarr studied her for a moment. She was a shapely woman in her early fifties whose braided white hair appeared whiter still because of her complexion. It was dark, like her eyes, and maybe because of the braids or her prominent cheekbones or the way she was dressed—blue cotton work shirt, jeans, and even beaded moccasins on her feet—the woman looked rather Amer-indian.

McGarr let his eyes sweep the studio, fixing on the oil portrait in the middle of the room. The portrait was of the very same woman in the very same pose as the blood-spattered framed photograph in the hallway of the Ford cottage. The wife as a young woman. In fact, a print of the photograph was clipped to the easel.

But the larger portrait was a colorful oil painting, artfully rendered, such that the woman's obvious beauty was enhanced not diminished. And just as in the photograph, the diamond-and-sapphire ring was on her finger, the one that was by now in the possession of the Technical Squad.

"What is your opinion of that ring?" he asked.

Mirna turned her head and tried to focus on the canvas. "What? I don't understand."

"Is it real?"

Mirna began to shake her head, but then thought better of it—realizing suddenly that, all along, she had admired the ring that had seemed so real because it *was* real. And, my God! What must it be worth?

"Did the Fords have money?"

"I wouldn't know."

"I thought you said they were your best friends."

"*Are* my best friends. You're speaking of them in the past tense. Do you know something I don't?"

"Only that whoever came to their cottage was looking for something important enough to commit murder. And we still don't know how many."

When McGarr stepped back to get a different perspective on the painting, he noticed something in the shadows beneath the easel—a sheet of writing paper. Even from where he was standing, he could read the "Clem and Breege Ford" printed at the top of the page. It was the same sort of sheet that he had seen in Ford's sitting room.

Walking over, McGarr squatted down and picked it up. "Is this what Ford brought you last night?"

Mirna decided she would say nothing. If he now ransacked the studio and discovered the packet, well then, it would be all over, and she would be relieved of the burden Clem had placed upon her. If he didn't, she would proceed as she had intended, and either Clem would return and there would be no need for her to act, or she would tell Karl and he would know what to do.

McGarr looked down on the sheet, which was undated. In his peculiar script, Ford had written the names "Monck & Neary, 2 Merrion Square, Dublin" and "Sigal & Sons, the Coombe," which was the name of a street also in Dublin.

The first was a firm of solicitors renowned in Dublin legal circles for handling the legal affairs of the country's "quiet money"—the very few remaining Ascendancy families who had managed to retain their wealth, as well as a select group of newly rich who had the sense not to flaunt theirs. Monck & Neary had the reputation of being most discreet.

The second was the name of a family of jewelers and gold merchants who had been plying a similarly select trade in their own specialty, which was antique jewelry, old gold and silver. McGarr's wife, who was a picture dealer, had dealt with the Sigals often and well, and she recommended them to her own clientele.

Farther down the page was a single name, Angus Rehm, but no address.

Turning the sheet of paper over, McGarr found what looked like a map but drawn with a soft lead pencil of the sort that artists used. He could make sense of nothing but the label, "cave," which—it appeared—was near some wiggly lines that looked like water.

"Is this what he brought you?" he asked again, thinking: over a treacherous mile of boreen and bog, in the teeth of a storm, with a more deadly threat looming? All to deliver a note, the contents of which would as easily be said over the telephone in a minute or two? Also, where was the mud? If Ford had touched it after his fall, there would be mud on the sheet, but there was none.

But neither did she deny it. Only the wind replied, soughing past the eaves of the studio that was perched on the very edge of the cliff.

"You know, I could make one phone call and get permission to search this place. But I'd prefer your help."

As in, "helping" the police. It was the euphemism em-

ployed to describe suspects. "Don't tell me you think that
I'm involved in this?" Mirna asked in a small, incredulous
voice.

McGarr cocked his head. "I hope not. For your sake.
Now"—he raised the sheet of paper—"I'll ask you once
more. Is this what Clement Ford brought you last night? Just
nod." And then I can toss the place legally, he did not add.
Looking for something that had to be mud-covered.

But she only continued to regard him.

Walking over to the wastepaper bin, McGarr peered inside.
But there was nothing muddy visible. Straightening up, he
again surveyed the room. "Of course by now you know what
happened last night to your best friends, the Fords. And to
Kevin O'Grady and probably to Padraic O'Malley?" McGarr
moved slowly about the large room, making sure his eyes
surveyed every surface. "But do you know the sequence of
events? You should.

"Paul O'Malley, the quadriplegic with the binos and sideband—he saw a large white schooner anchor in the harbor.
He rang up your friend. Sometime after that, Ford phoned
O'Grady and asked him to come out here and sit with his
wife. *Armed,* he was so worried.

"Why? Because he knew what the people aboard the boat
had come for, and he had to get it out of the house. So he
came here and gave it to you. Now O'Grady's dead, and the
Fords and Padraic O'Malley are missing, along with
O'Malley's boat. Is this what he gave you? Or is this only
part what he gave you?"

Yet again McGarr waited for a reply before continuing.

"I can understand loyalty to friends. It's important, and
probably all the more so on an island, like this, where you
are so few. But if Clem Ford gave you what those killers
came for, you're now taking a hell of a risk. All they need is
a map. Where else could Ford have come on short notice and
during a storm in the dead of night? And him an old man.
This place is the only possibility. And has it occurred to you
that your friends might not be dead, that your helping me
now might allow us to find them?"

Yet again McGarr waited, but she did not move from the

sink. She was looking out the window there, at the brilliant ocean to the northwest.

"What do these names mean? Who are these people? Why did Ford bring them to you? It was last night, wasn't it?"

McGarr waited at least a whole minute, listening to the wind wail past the eaves of the studio. "I can appreciate that you're distraught. And that you have not actually lied to me."

That brought the woman round. Her face was streaming with tears, her fists clenched by her sides. "Get out." She moved to the door and opened it. "Get out now."

"I'll leave you my card." Slowly, deliberately, McGarr removed one from his pocket secretary and placed it on the sheet from Ford on the drawing table. "I have a feeling you'll need it. For the moment, I'll be at the hotel. Or you can ring any barracks. They'll put you through. Please understand that you're in danger, and I can help."

Tom Rice was waiting at the bottom of the stairs. "The old van we drove to the Fords in? Wouldn't start. I thought I'd hoof it over here to save you time."

"Do you know where Paul O'Malley lives?"

The large older man shrugged. "The place is called Capnagower, but we'll have to ask at the harbor." Rice gazed resignedly at the collection of white buildings that had to be about four miles away. "Maybe we can get the loan of another car when we get there."

McGarr turned to Mirna Gottschalk, who was closing the door. "Is it possible to walk to Capnagower?"

With her palms she pushed the tears from her eyes. "If you know the way. But I wouldn't recommend it. You can take my van and leave it at the hotel when you're through. The key's in the switch."

It was a generous gesture to be sure, and McGarr wondered how much it was by way of apology. A Land Rover with only 492 miles on the odometer, it still bore the rich fragrance of new leather. The powerful engine ticked over on first crank.

As soon as the van disappeared over the crest of the drive, Mirna went straight to the reading chair and pulled the muddied manila packet from under the cushion. She had never felt so compromised in her life, so sullied. Like some criminal

in a docket evading a charge, she had kept silent when she
should have spoken; she had failed to acknowledge the truth.
She had even challenged the man.

Well, she had enough of that and it. Stuffing the note from
Clem in among the other papers, she carried the thing to the
house where she would hide it beneath the hearth where it
belonged. And it would remain there, at least until she heard
more about Clem and Breege or Karl arrived to tell her what
the thing meant.

She would ring him up right now, so he would come out
for Kevin's funeral. And they would decide then what to do.
Together.

CHAPTER 10

AS THE ROVER wheeled slowly along the rutted boreen, McGarr regretted not having taken a more definite tack with Mirna Gottschalk.

He could have simply begun a search of the premises, later saying that he had been "in hot pursuit," since Ford's footsteps led to the studio. If she filed a complaint. But would she? Probably not, given the fact—and he was convinced of it—that Ford had brought her whatever the raiding party had come for.

But it now occurred to McGarr—as they topped a ridge that presented a panoramic view of the verdant island—that her keeping it might be helpful in another way, so long as she was willing to take the risk. And she obviously was.

Said Tom Rice, looking out the windows that were photo-sensitive and had darkened in the strong sunlight, " 'Tis a wonder how tidy the greenskeepers maintain this place. They could use them yokes at Ballybunion," which was one of Ireland's premier golf courses. He meant the sheep that could now be seen in every direction.

"It's rumored there's not an inch of grass on even the most remote ledge of Croaghmore. Time was the south slope of that mountain was three feet thick in heath. Now I don't think you could find a patch. It's the EC or EU—they now call themselves—playing Puck. Anyhow, the bloody Common Market t'ugs from Brussels telling us how to live.''

McGarr nodded, knowing about the policy. Having designated much of the West of Ireland "severely disadvantaged," Brussels had decided that it could keep people on the land by encouraging "traditional farming practices," one of which was raising sheep. But the subsidy did not reward farmers for animals brought to market, which would depress sheep prices. Instead it paid them according to the number of sheep on the land—aged, infirm, or ill; it did not matter—which had led to overgrazing and the destruction of native plant habitats.

On the other hand, an environmentally-conscious farmer was not required to accept Brussels's largess, however hard it might be to pass up. Being "severely disadvantaged."

McGarr stopped the Rover so Rice could get out and open a gate that prevented animals from straying down the road.

"Are those the remains of lazy beds?" he asked when Rice climbed back in. He pointed to the tightly spaced pattern of ridges in the fields that followed the contour of the land right down to the edge of Clew Bay in one direction, and all the way up the flanks of Croaghmore in the other.

"Famine furrows, some call them. Sure, people hereabouts never do nothin' halfway. Now it's the sheep, then it was potatoes. Before the blight in the last century, you had sixteen hundred people on this island with every last patch of ground they could find in potatoes. Compared to other places, like Inishturk"—Rice jerked a thumb at the looming shape of another large island to the southwest—"the land here is good, which was their undoing. When the potatoes thrived, the population grew. When they rotted, people died. I'm a bit of a history buff, don't yeh know.

"Ten years after the blight, there was only six hundred people on Clare Island. Today"—Rice paused dramatically—"a hundred and forty in a good year with them forty kids who leave the island for school at age twelve, some of them never to return for more than a few weeks on holiday or to get in the hay. Here's a fact for you—seventy-five percent of the children born into this parish will emigrate sooner or later.''

Which made the people here indeed severely disadvantaged, McGarr concluded, no matter who had devised the phrase—*seoinini* from Brussels, Dublin, or Mars.

The Paul O'Malley house stood on the top of Capnagower, a word meaning "Hill of the Goats" in Irish. It was a tall but flat bluff on the southeast side of Clare Island, surveying Clew Bay, the Mayo coast from Inishturk to Croagh Patrick, and the shoreline as far as Dooega Head.

Much of Clare Island itself was also visible from there, all the closer—McGarr assumed—when viewed through the lenses of a spotting scope. The instrument sat on a tripod in the middle of the floor and could be rotated to any of the four large windows of the highest room in the building.

"You've heard of houses with widow's walks," the young man said from his curious-looking wheelchair. "Well, this is a quad's quad." Paul O'Malley was disabled from the neck down because of an accident while scuba diving. Clare Island was noted for the sport, there even being a dive school here, McGarr seemed to remember.

"Aran Energy sank a new pipeline in Galway Bay, and nobody thought to mark it. I was a commercial diver, and when I went over the side to check out why a boat was hung up . . . well, here I am." With a gross compression of vertebrae C4 and C5, the mother had told them while leading McGarr and Rice up the stairs to the top of the house. "It's a miracle he can even breathe on his own."

And yet O'Malley could move about the room in a high-tech wheelchair that he controlled by moving his neck, which was fastened to an electronic collar.

His light blue eyes met McGarr's. "After I rang up Clem about the boat, I ate supper, which is a chore that took—" He glanced at his mother, who had remained in the room.

"An hour at least." She was a thin, older woman with sunken cheeks and carefully permed hair that looked like baked meringue.

"Normally, I listen to the sideband"—he pointed to the radio—"and last night was no exception, since there was another odd craft—something like a sportfishing boat—anchored about a mile off Lecknacurra, which is over there." O'Malley spun the chair so that his feet were pointing a few degrees west of due north. "It was lighted, but fishermen passing her couldn't see anybody aboard, nor raise them on the blower. Stranger still, she had neither name nor numbers."

"Was the Naval Service notified?" McGarr asked. "Or the Coast Guard?"

O'Malley's eyes flashed up at him. "Ah, I'm afraid we're not quick to call the authorities round here. Especially not the fishermen, who've got the water bailiffs on their backs, come day go day." He meant the officials of the Board of Fishery Conservators who enforced the Maritime Law against drift-netting and other fishing abuses. The fishermen complained that the three frigates operating off the Irish coasts usually let foreign boats off with a warning, while confiscating the catch, nets, and sometimes even the boats of Irish captains.

The water *seoinini*, McGarr thought.

"What about yourself?" Rice asked.

O'Malley rolled his eyes. "I wouldn't want anybody to think I'm up here watching them day after day, just waiting for the chance to grass. Anyhow, it was nigh on dark by the time I looked again, but the twilight factor on this Swarovski is excellent." Spinning the wheelchair, O'Malley rolled toward the spotting scope in the center of the room. With an elaborate extended eyepiece, it was positioned low on the tripod which, like the chair, bristled with motors and drives. "The focusing is automatic.

"The mast lights of the schooner were on, and the crew was furling sails and what not."

"A crew of how many?" McGarr asked.

"Four, counting the captain. He was an older man, but the three others were young, say, late twenties, early thirties."

It was a different report from the publican, who said only one young man had stopped in there. The three others must have waited outside, careful to keep any possible identifications to a minimum.

"At one point they switched on a strong searchlight—halogen, I think—and played it over the castle."

"That's the Granuaile castle down at the harbor," the mother explained; it was the Irish way of saying Grace O'Malley's name.

"They kept the light on it for a while, and I think I saw a figure in one of the windows."

"Clem," the mother concluded. "Many's the younger man could not have got himself to the harbor by then. But he had great old go in him all the same. Never mattered the time of day or night. Paul would ring him up, and there Clem'd be, fierce soon altogether."

"But I'm not certain it was him, mind, the angle from here being a bit tricky."

"And them walls is thick."

"And, sure, he never once let on why he wanted me to keep him informed about the boats that arrived," the young man lamented, a definite note of sorrow in his voice. "Maybe if I hadn't rung him up, Breege and him and Kevin might still be with us."

Guilt. It ruled all in the Ireland that McGarr knew. "What about the boat, the schooner?" he prompted.

"Well—the four of them come off it in a tender they tied to the jetty wall. Then they moved up toward the pub, where I lost them among the buildings."

McGarr stepped to the window that looked south toward the castle, the breakwater and jetty, and the small group of structures gathered about the harbor. Even under a brilliant afternoon sun, they looked tiny and unimposing from such a distance—the gray cube of the castle, the white pub, some stucco walls and slate roofs. Croaghmore lay to the west, rising in a steady gentle slope that went up and up and up and thoroughly dominated the landscape of the island. He let his eyes trace the four miles of road out to the Ford's; he then tried but failed to find the direct, overland path. "What about later?"

"That's the troubling part. I must've dozed off, because the radio woke me. Whoever they were, they were using a scrambler. But wouldn't you know I've got a little box here that can decode everything from one-twenty-eight to four-oh-nine-six codes automatically. It's computerized and darts through the field of possible codes until it comes up with a match."

"Paulie's gadget-mad, don't you know," said the mother.

"But it didn't help. They were speaking some language I

never heard before. And the schooner itself was gone from the harbor, and the only activity I could see on my three directions of the compass was at the boat, the one that bore no name or numbers and was anchored off Lecknacurra. Its running lights were on. To me the exchange sounded like a ship-to-ship transmission, but I could see only the one set of lights.''

As if the schooner were running without any, thought McGarr.

"Anyhow, it was dark and stormy, and along about then didn't another boat charge out of the harbor, passing the light on the jetty, the one that's on the night long. But no lights on her either, so the moment she hit the dark ocean she was gone from sight.''

"But in the glimpse you'd say it was Packy's,'' the mother prompted.

"I would now, since she was all of forty feet with a small cabin, and wasn't Packy's boat missing in the morn'?''

McGarr thought for a moment. "I know you didn't see the schooner leave, and we don't know if it was she that linked up with the anchored boat off Lecknacurra, but if it was—how long would it have taken her to get out there?''

"Her speed under power can't be much, and it would have taken some time to get the launch back up on the davits and the anchor weighed—forty-five minutes at the very least. Closer to an hour.''

"Which would have made it?''

"Nine forty-five. Or ten. Packy's boat was closer to eleven.''

"In what direction was the boat with the running lights headed?''

"The one off Lecknacurra?''

McGarr nodded.

"West. Round the island.''

"Out to sea?''

"Well, it might have changed course to follow the coast north. You have to go west to round Achill Head.''

Which meant there was no way to tell where the boat was headed.

"A foreign language?''

"Aye, but one I never heard, and I hear quite a few on the sideband, now that the world is raidin' our fishing grounds. At first I thought it Danish or Dutch, but I'm sure it was none of them. But, something like that."

"Would you know it if you heard it again?"

"Whenever I do, I haven't a clue."

McGarr's brow furrowed. "Sorry—I don't think I understand."

"Didn't I tell you? I taped it digitally, like I do whenever there's a storm, so that there's an exact record of the time of any transmission. That way, if a boat gets lost, we at least have some idea of its position the last time a signal was sent. The recorder's over there." O'Malley pivoted the chair so that his feet pointed at a bank of electronic equipment that had been placed against a wall.

"Might I have a copy."

"Of course," said the mother. "I'll make you one now."

"It's only a few words, back and forth, and then a gap and a few more. And a final, like, sign-off. Then not a peep from anybody until four or so, when the other fishermen, going to their boats, found the cart, the car, and Packy's cottage shot up. Then all hell broke loose."

McGarr moved toward the view scope. "May I?"

The mother answered, "Work away. But you'll have to squat. I can't tell you how long it took us to get the thing to the proper height."

McGarr hunkered down and stared into the peculiar eyepiece.

"Clem was always after me to get binos. He said they'd be easier on the eyes, but, as you can see, a scope like this is much more powerful."

McGarr peered into the instrument and was suddenly transported to the jetty at the harbor where the Tech Squad was now conducting their part of the investigation. The optics were so crisp and bright that it was almost as though he were standing there conversing with them.

"Didn't I see you roust Colm Canning from Packy's house this morning," O'Malley went on. "Stormed in there, he did, fists clenched and jaw set. Come out headfirst and legs flying after him."

McGarr imagined that between the Swarovski, the side-band, and the telephone, there was little that escaped the shut-in. He straightened up. "What's something, like this, cost?"

"I've no idea. Clem bought it—" O'Malley managed to say before his mother cut him off.

"Isn't it time for your nap, Paulie."

"A thousand pounds?" McGarr pressed.

"For what—the scope or all of it?"

McGarr nodded encouragingly. "All of it."

O'Malley let out a short laugh. "Try *tens* of thousands. A man came all the way from Indiana just to measure me."

"Oh Jesus Christ," muttered the mother.

"Clem Ford has money then?"

There was a pause, and McGarr could almost hear Paul O'Malley realize he had said too much.

The mother shifted her feet. "Not more than others, but no less. He has his pension. Then, he's a canny English-style farmer who works every last inch of ground in some way or t'other. And with the two of them stuck out there in their mountain airie, what can they spend?" She paused for thought and breath, before continuing. "It's just that, at the time before Paulie's insurance settlement, we didn't have the bobs for any of this." Her hand swept the room.

"And, of course, you paid him back."

She nodded vigorously, but her eyes moved off. "Oh aye, we did. We saw him right. Wouldn't have it any other way."

McGarr looked down at her son in the wheelchair. "What about you, Paul? What is your recollection? Did Clem Ford give you all of this, or did you pay him back?"

O'Malley only blinked. When climbing the stairs, the mother had told McGarr and Rice that the new house with its observation room had been built and ready for Paul when he came home from the rehabilitation clinic.

"A generous sort, our Mr. Ford." McGarr's and Rice's eyes met.

Again at the windows, McGarr gazed northwest toward Mirna Gottschalk's compound of neat white buildings. It could be seen in its entirety. Not so the Ford cottage. None of it—not even the edge of the dingle—was in view. "Is it possible to see the Ford place from anywhere on the island, apart from the top of the dingle?''

"Croaghmore," O'Malley answered without hesitation, as though glad they were no longer speaking of the Fords' finances. "If you look straight down the north cliff face, you can see the roofs and the haggard. I used to climb some, when I could.''

"There's the lighthouse as well," the mother put in. "Well, it's not a working lighthouse anymore, but a guest-house owned by some Belgians. It's brilliant how they put a room right up in the turret. From there you have a clear view of Mirna's with Clem and Breege's cottage beyond. Course, you'd be well served to have one o' them." She pointed to the Swarovski.

Or, say, Ford's high-power, night-seeing Zeiss binoculars, thought McGarr. "But is it open, this lighthouse—for custom?''

"Just, Monday last their season began. It's the finest place on Clare Island. You should stay there yourself, if you're long here.''

There was a question in that, which McGarr ignored.

"So—what happened at the cottage and on the jetty?"

Paul O'Malley only shook his head; the mother looked away.

"The Fords have any enemies?"

"Not that anyone knows of," said the mother. " 'Tis a mystery what happened, coming right out of the blue, like that.''

"Why did Ford ask you to keep an eye on the boats?" he asked the son. "How long ago was that?"

"Just ten years come August, right after I got back here. 'Twas a sailor himself, said he, and he liked the look of a boat's lines.''

"Years ago Clem had others watching the harbor for him, but he always said Paulie's the best.''

"So, Ford's interest in boats dates from when?"

The mother hunched her shoulder. "From whenever he came here, as far as I know. Since I was a little girl. Since" —her eyes flashed at McGarr, who was just about her age— "just after the war. He'd buy you a box of Smarties, like, if you could tell him the type of boat. You know, ketch or lobster boat or trawler or dragger. We used to get one of the lads that knew to tell us the type, then he'd buy the lot of us sweets.''

''An Englishman.''

She nodded. ''Spoke just like a king, he did. You know, precise. Educated.''

''He came here when?''

She only shook her head.

''What brought him here?''

Again. ''Breege?''

''The wife. She have money?''

The mother's head went back in patent disdain. ''Not a dickey bird. She was sent here as a wee blind thing, and Peig took her in. A by-blow—some say—of one of Peig's sisters in England, though others had it she was Peig's own.

''But Peig was a big, strong, heavy woman who did not need and never pined after men. Nor for anybody, living most of the year out there in that gulch where only wild asses had grazed even during famine times. It's Clem what made it bloom.''

''Clem the Englishman,'' McGarr prompted.

''He'd tell English tourists, who inquired, that he was from Harwich.''

''Norwich,'' the son corrected.

''Say what you will, I know for fact it's Harwich. One time when Clem was gone Breege told me he was in Harwich to settle his mother's estate. Sell the house and all.'' She brightened. ''Maybe that's where he got the readies.''

Out at the Rover, she went on, ''Look at that now—Mirna's after giving you the use of her fine new van. Wouldn't you say that's rare generous of the woman? She has an islander's heart all the same.''

McGarr inclined his head, as though for an explanation.

''Gottschalk—the name says it all.''

''Says what?'' Tom Rice asked in a quiet voice.

''Says she's one o' them. You know, a Jew.''

McGarr only stared.

The mother raised her chin and her eyes narrowed. ''There's some who predicted this, who said she'd bring trouble down on us sooner or later. And him too—Clem himself. Wasn't he a bloody Brit all along?''

The same Clem Ford who had equipped her son with the Swarovski scope, the high-tech robotics tripod, and perhaps even financed the house in some way. ''Who, for instance?''

Her eyes held McGarr's gaze; she had something to tell him. ''Fergal O'Grady, for one. Kevin's father and a *senachie*. Time out of mind now, he predicted that no good would come from blow-ins like them. And here now hasn't Fergal's words fallen on Fergal himself? You might speak to him, if you have the chance.''

Why? thought McGarr. He twisted the ignition key, and the engine cranked over.

''I think you'll find the people of Clare Island very helpful, sir.''

Some more than others, McGarr suspected, pulling away.

In silence the two men drove back toward the harbor, one in a contemplative mood, the latter plainly embarrassed.

After a while, McGarr asked, ''Is there any other harbor but the one?''

Rice shook his head. ''There's a second that serves the salmon farm not far south of the lighthouse, and the remains of a third in Portnakilly, which is close to the abbey and the Grace O'Malley tomb. I'll show you on a map when we get back to the harbor.

''But if your question is can somebody slip onto the island without anybody knowing? The answer is yes. In quiet water at low tide there're probably a dozen sandy spots where you could run in a small boat. And isolated enough nobody would see. Getting off would be the problem, if the tide turned or conditions changed. Like I said, the brother-in-law fishes these parts.''

''What about tourist season? When's that?'' He remembered Rice saying there were only one hundred and forty people on Clare Island, and maybe a third of them now in school. With the treeless vistas, the rough coast, and the small and now alerted population, the raiders would find it difficult to return unseen for whatever they had searched for but not found at the Fords.

"It begins right round now, since the weather's broken."

McGarr again scanned what he could see of the island, now as the day wore down. Yes, there was sun. But it was still cool, and the wind was intense even by Irish standards.

"Day-trippers mostly," Rice went on. "People over from Louisburgh for a day on the beach. Accommodations for overnight is scare. There's the hotel, the new lighthouse we just heard about, the pub has a few rooms, and maybe four B and Bs. Oh, and there's a hostel hard by the hotel. Maybe a hundred beds in all.

"There's little to do here, unless nature's your game. I mentioned the beach, but there's also the dive center and some prize shark-fishing when the water warms. And natural history." Rice then explained that Clare Island had been the subject of a Royal Dublin Society study early in the century with a follow-up only a few years past. The reassessment began in 1989.

"A hoard of scientists and scholars descended on the place and found birds and flowers and rocks the islanders themselves didn't know were here. As well as passage graves from antiquity and such truck. It made all the papers, and the odd professor still comes and goes.

"Other than that, the only big event is the 'O'Malley Rally.' That's the roundup and reunion of all the O'Malleys from all over the world. A prolific people, I'd say. They come to find their roots, you know, and hoolie for the better part of a week. It keeps getting bigger and bigger every year. Sometimes upwards of three thousand of them, all here on this little island." Rice let his eyes stray over the barren landscape. "It's bedlam."

"When's that?"

"The coming week, I think. But I can give you the date exact. They moved it up early this year so the footballers among them won't miss the World Cup. I always make sure we're prepared."

From a pocket of his tunic, Rice pulled out a calendar and thumbed to the appropriate page. "Here we have it. This year they'll begin arriving in two days' time. The Chieftain's Dinner in the Bayview Hotel, which wraps everything up, is three days later. It's all the celebrating a human body—even one by the name of O'Malley—can tolerate. To say nothing of us. After that, we tell all the revelers to go back home to O'Malley-ville, wherever that might be. If they haven't had enough of us, we have of them.

"I try to keep the 'police presence' to a minimum, but with that many celebrants on hand *and* mouth, there's always some gobshite to try our patience."

CHAPTER 11

A TRIED PATIENCE was Detective Superintendent Bernard McKeon's condition exactly. For nearly an hour now he had been compelled to listen to a tall young fisherman with a red and swollen left ear and skinned palms hold forth at the bar of the Bayview, Clare Island's only hotel.

The man had been saying how all guards, government men, EU officials, naval service personnel, water bailiffs, Spics, Port-u-gees, Japs, Ruskies, Brits, and others too numerous for McKeon to remember were variously thundering gobshites, blatherskites, bloody scuts, shite-hawkers, bad cess, and pooling hoors' melts along with a host of other overused and less colorful expressions. All the while drinking pints and shorts that improved his spirits not one whit.

At first McKeon was entranced. A confirmed Dubliner who usually manned the Serious Crimes Unit command desk, he was used to the "chat," as it were, of the common run of psychopaths and murderers, and he had not been treated to such quaint and rustic speech in many a year. But the man's *shagraun* soon grew old.

Twice the barman pleaded with him to mend his ways, saying, "Well, my wild rapparee, you fairly destroyed that pint. Go easy, or you'll have 'Her Grace' in here." He meant the older woman, obviously the owner, who could be seen at the desk in the lobby. She was too close not to have heard some of the tirade.

The second warning was more pointed. "Steady up or settle down, Colm. I tell you again, you'll clear off out of here." Which brought a brief surcease, while Colm took himself to "the jacks!" as the three or four other drinkers studiously ignored him. It was then that the barman told McKeon what had happened to Colm Canning's ear and hands, which brought a smile to McKeon's cherubic face.

But Canning was not back for a roar and a swallow before the mistress of the premises appeared. Reaching over the taps, she removed the fresh pint and set it in back of the bar, saying, "There now, Colm—you were warned, and you've done it. You can come back for that on the morrow. But if I hear any more out of you, you won't come back at all," which was a potent threat indeed, McKeon judged, on an island having only two licensed premises that he knew of. It was a category of information that McKeon was quick to learn, wherever he went.

And Colm Canning respected as well. Plainly miffed but feigning proud unconcern, he snapped a dismissive hand at the woman, who waited to be sure of his response. She checked the other drinkers' glasses, smiled at McKeon, and had a quiet word with the barman. In silence, Canning dug out a smoke which he lit. Turning away from the bar, his hazel eyes lit on the only foreign, and therefore less potentially punishing, target in the premises. Obviously, he had not learned his lesson.

For an unsteady moment, he regarded McKeon. "Whatever are you looking at?"

Which was the question in a question, thought McKeon. *Whatever.* But he said nothing, knowing there could be no conciliatory reply, a drunk being a drunk being a drunk.

At fifty-three, Bernie McKeon was a short, wide man with close-set dark eyes and a thick shock of blond hair that was now turning gray. In recent years, he had put on weight, which belied the fact that he had once been a drill instructor in the Irish Army and for a time in charge of the physical training of Garda recruits. McKeon still visited the gym at least once a week, even if, most times, it was just to amble around the track, pump enough iron to work up a thirst, and grab some steam.

"You there. You're starin' at me."

McKeon couldn't keep himself from glancing at the man.

"You're tryin' to turn me to stone."

"You mean, like Gorgon? The Greek bloke with the stony gaze and the snakes in his hair?"

Canning closed his eyes and shook his head. "That bloke was not a bloke. That bloke was a hoor, actually three hoors—Stheno, Euryale, and Medusa."

Ah, a literary fisherman—thought McKeon—with an ego as immense as classical reference. "You mean to tell me, my staring at you has put you in the condition you now find yourself?"

Canning only grunted, his pupils dilating, his ears pulling back as his sodden brain struggled to think of some way of lunging at McKeon while still retaining the right to drink at the hotel bar. But there could be none. 'Her Grace' had returned to the door of the bar and was now watching him.

"I must remember to avoid mirrors," said McKeon.

Which brought quick nervous laughter from the others at the bar.

"I asked you a question—where yeh from?"

But the woman stepped forward, saying, "That's it, Colm. I warned you. Now you're—"

Raising a hand, McKeon stopped the blade of her figurative guillotine; some other man might thank him in the morning. "Me? I thought you'd never ask. Why, I'm from Bawling ass Crieth, and I'll make you a citizen if I have to." The phrase was a corruption of the Irish name for Dublin, *Baile atha Cliath*.

It took a few seconds for the phrase to sink in, but when Canning's eyes cleared, McKeon could tell that the message had hit home. "You mean, you're just another Dublin arse ban—"

"Say that word, Colm Canning, and you'll not only never set foot in this premises again, I'll ring up the civic guards, though I'm not sure I'll have to." She glanced at McKeon, who tried to appear confused. He was supposed to be under-cover.

"Now then, we'll be seeing the back of you. This instant!"

Lurching out the front door, who should Colm Canning run into but Peter McGarr. Drunk though he was, Canning only flushed scarlet and thrashed off into the windy evening.

"But the hotel is in perfectly good nick," McKeon complained a few minutes later when McGarr said he wanted him to take a room at the lighthouse. "And look"—his hand darted to the window—"it's got a clear view of the harbor. With these yokes—why, nothing will escape me."

He hefted the Zeiss night-seeing binoculars that McGarr had brought him; they had yielded only one set of fingerprints, believed to be Ford's. "You can go out and about the island, interviewing and what not, and I'll man the post right here in this window. I won't leave it for . . . well, for anything but a call of nature. Don't we want to monitor arrivals at the harbor?"

They did, but McGarr was not certain how effective it would be with two other docking sites and a number of other potential small-boat landing points around the island. Also, when the raiders returned, they would need a new plan, now that police were on the island and the resident population was alerted.

In the meantime, McGarr's staff could run down the leads in Dublin: the solicitors, Monck & Neary in Merrion Square; the gold merchants named Sigal; and the immense diamond and sapphire ring that he now had in his pocket. That too had yielded nothing but a smeared print and a few flecks of dried blood. Also, there was the final name on Clement Ford's notepaper. Angus Rehm. And Paul O'Malley's tape of the radio conversation, boat to boat.

So far, Ford himself had proved an enigma. He had paid taxes in the Republic of Ireland regularly and completely on a small income beginning in 1947 until the last tax year. But he was not a citizen. Nor was he a citizen of the U.K., as far as could be ascertained at the moment. England listed nine people by that name, but none was as elderly as Ford or resident outside of that country. And none six feet six inches and twenty stone in weight.

Still standing at the window, McKeon now drew in a deep

breath and let it out slowly, as though resigned. "So—where is this lighthouse?"

"About two miles from here. Perhaps a bit more. North."

"All uphill, I assume."

"Well, most lighthouses are situated on promontories. Think of it this way. When you come back, it'll be all down hill."

"Is there anything else up there?"

Wind, McGarr explained, wishing there was an audience to witness McKeon's discomfort. He described the clouds and birds. "There might even be a ganetry. I caught a glimpse of one. And Tom Rice tells me there's an ASI."

"A what?"

"An ASI. Area of Special Interest—it's an EU designation."

McKeon made a face. "What class of interest?"

"Environmental interest. What other class do you think exists here? This one contains Alpine flora found only in some isolated parts of Cork and Kerry and, of course, Switzerland."

McKeon's dark baleful eyes raked the hotel window with the now brooding sky and riotous waters below. "Which could do with some civilizing."

McGarr also explained that he had wanted an old hand to watch the Ford cottage and Mirna Gottschalk, somebody who would quickly determine what activity was normal and usual. And what was not. Also, he had chosen McKeon because, as his chief of staff, he seldom got out of the office on assignment, and such junkets were a perquisite of rank.

"I suppose we could change places—me up there, you down here nosing about."

"No, no—we couldn't have that." It would be unseemly, at least from a police point of view. The ranking fellow on stakeout, the subordinate handling the investigation.

Also, form dictated that McGarr attend Kevin O'Grady's funeral. Finally, McGarr thought he would ring up his wife, Noreen. She and their young child, Maddie, were still at the fishing resort he had left that morning. Noreen had passed an entire summer on Clare Island; apart from weekends, McGarr had been forced to come and go. She would know the island better and might even be remembered by the locals.

"The brochure of the place bills the lighthouse as 'the Last Temptation.'" McGarr stood and moved to the door.

"As in—'of Christ'? If that's the recommendation, I'm poxed. Haven't I seen the film." Like a man condemned, McKeon followed McGarr down the deeply carpeted staircase to the lobby.

His head turned, as they passed through the bar, then the lounge where the national news was just coming over the telly now at 6:00, and finally the sun porch where a number of people had gathered at tables to look out on Clew Bay over tea or drinks.

"What about me bag?"

"I had it put in the car."

McKeon's head went back. "Am I that easy to suss?"

"No, but you're a rare dutiful guardian of civic order." McGarr was having fun. Outside now, McGarr had to shout. "And would you look at that seascape. Where else could you find a view like that?"

Clew Bay was a rip of windblown water, bright green in toward shore but a deep blue beyond. And while a brilliant sun still bathed the myriad of islands to the east, dark clouds with high white thunderheads were now racing in off the Atlantic. In all, the scene was unusual and dramatic but threatening. Another blow was sweeping in off the ocean, and it would storm before morning.

"I've seen better," McKeon said sourly. "In a Guinness advert."

But his mood improved by the time they neared the lighthouse. "'Tis a bigger place than I thought." The Rover rocked and staggered in the stiff breeze that became stronger the higher they climbed. "Belgians, you say the people are?"

"So I'm told. Do you know that Belgium has more breweries per capita than any other country in the world?"

"You're pullin' me leg."

"No, but I imagine some of that goes on too." Beer being beer.

McKeon had to struggle to open the door, and a bitter draught bolted into the car. "I hope they like heat."

Stepping out, the two men were literally driven by the wind

toward a stout iron gate. But just as in the dingle by the Ford cottage, its force diminished considerably a dozen feet into the cobbled courtyard.

In front of them was a large white stucco residence that was ringed by the walls of stables and other service buildings. In fact, in the growing darkness they could see funnels of yellow light from other mewslike areas within the construct, that had been built—like boxes within boxes, McGarr supposed—to wall out the wind. Overhead it was now wailing past the turret of the lighthouse and its cast-iron catwalk that were silhouetted against the gloaming to the west.

There were lights in every window. Approaching the main door, they peered in to see a fire roaring in a large open hearth. Heaped with driftwood, it was displaying a nimbus of rainbow colors as the halogens in the sea salts combusted. But there was nobody in that room, nor in the two other tastefully furnished quarters that were also visible beyond.

"Would you look at that," McKeon said. "A light show, and all for me. Now, if we can just scare up the pooka who runs this place—"

With that, the door swung open, and there appeared a tall wide man with a thick shoe-brush mustache and steel-rimmed glasses. "You must be the gentlemen who rang up," he said in a deep voice that matched his size. "Let me take your bag. Monica is in the kitchen, and I'm afraid that's it. We've just opened for the season, and you've got the place to yourself, Mr.—"

"McKeon," said McKeon.

"And you are staying with us too, Mr.—"

McGarr introduced himself, and was sorry to say he wasn't. Whatever Monica was making in the kitchen smelled appetizing in the extreme, and McGarr suddenly realized that he had not had a bite all day.

"Just a humble *carbonnade*," which, Robert Timmermans explained, was a chunky beef stew cooked in beer.

"Really?" said McKeon. "Beer?"

"Sticks to the ribs. It'll be cold tonight. Speaking of which, may I offer you an aperitif?"

McKeon liked that even better, and Timmermans led the

two men into another room where, miraculously, there was a well-stocked bar.

McGarr let himself be talked into dinner, which exceeded the promise of the aroma. And while sipping an excellent and piquant Calvados that was served with coffee by the fire, he mused that accommodations like this lighthouse were one of the many ways that Ireland—but most particularly the West of Ireland—had changed for the better, largely because of *seoinini* or their cultures.

There had been a time, before the country's entry into the EU, that a stay in a place as remote as Clare Island inevitably included plain, poor fare and a cold, damp room even in the better hotels of the day. Now McGarr could not think of a county that did not offer at least one acceptable accommodation, if not on the level of this lighthouse.

And before sinking too deeply into the comfortable leather chair by the fire, he revealed to the Timmermans who McKeon and he were and why they had come to Clare Island, as if the couple hadn't guessed.

The Timmermans swapped glances, Robert saying, "Poor Kevin O'Grady. He was very helpful to us when we bought this place as a ruin. There was nothing he wouldn't do. And Clem Ford—whenever he came to see us, he came with tools to work."

"Whoever could have done such a thing?" asked Monica, who was a pretty blond woman. It was the question that McGarr had wanted to put. But when he glanced up at her, he saw that her eyes were filled with tears.

Later that night before turning in, McGarr used the private telephone box in the lobby of the Bayview Hotel to ring up his wife. After they had spoken of what she and Maddie had done that day, he said, "Look—I'm going to be here for a while, and—"

"Would we like to join you? On Clare Island? Of course."

Fishing holidays were boring for Noreen, who did not fish. And while his daughter was presently learning the sport, she was only six and her patience flagged.

"Do you know that Clare Island was the subject of an in-depth, multidisciplinary study a few years back?'' Noreen asked.

"To compare to the findings to the Royal Irish Study at the turn of the century.''

There was a pause. ''You know about that?'' Irish antiquities—in fact, anything that pertained to the culture of the country—Noreen considered her exclusive domain, at least within their family.

"Chapter and verse.''

"They discovered a previously unknown megalithic court tomb that's probably five thousand years old and a number of *fulachta fiadh* that we probably walked right by without knowing the summer we were there. You can point them out when we arrive.''

"And just who is Fiadh when he's at home?''

"I thought as much. And speaking of superficial knowledge—the details on the evening news were rather sketchy. They mentioned the name of the former guard who got killed, but said only that three other Clare Islanders were missing. I'll need details, if I'm to be of any help.''

"We'll trade information over breakfast, if you can get here that early.''

"Ah, Peter—we won't be there until lunch or dinner, and you know it. Why don't you fill me in now, so I won't have to waste money on newspapers.'' There was nothing Noreen enjoyed more than having some inside knowledge of one of his murder investigations.

McGarr reached for his glass and took a swallow. ''I didn't see a journalist here the day long. The most they have is what was on the news. My love to you both. I assume she's asleep by now.''

"Of course.''

"Me too.''

CHAPTER 12

JUST BEFORE DAWN, Angus Rehm cut the auxiliary engine and slowed the North Sea schooner over what his depth finder told him was a cleft in the continental shelf off Erris Head. It was some one hundred and seventy nautical miles north northeast of Clare Island.

For the first time in seven hours he switched on an electronic device—the vessel's differential global positioning system that compared the transmissions of a high-altitude satellite system to low-frequency signals sent from shore-based beacons. The computerized result told him exactly where he was, and was accurate to within five meters anywhere on the earth's surface.

Also for the first time in hours, he spoke into the VHF radio that linked him with the smaller sportfishing boat that had been following in his wake. The message—in a language that few in the Northern Hemisphere would understand—informed his daughter, Heather, that they had reached their destination, and she should pull alongside. "Dugald will take your lines."

The surviving son was standing close enough to have heard, and he moved to the rail. Having been wearing a Kevlar vest under his orange deck suit, Dugald had only been knocked unconscious by the force of the 9 mm round Clement

101

Ford had fired into his chest. Malcolm had not been so lucky. His corpse was now lashed to the top of the cabin of the schooner.

Rehm did not wait for Heather to join them. With a stiff prosthetic finger—one of four on his right hand—he began punching the function buttons of the vessel's cockpit computer. Soon he had the area survey map of Clare Island up on the view screen. While he called up an overlay of a tax map, and compared the two, his surviving son and daughter began transferring all the materiel that they would need from the vessel to the boat. Soon they were finished and joined him at the wheel.

Rehm adjusted his half glasses and pointed to the screen with the gloved hand. "Unless he buried the contents of that strongbox under some rock, the only possible place he could have taken it is to this group of buildings. There's nothing else around. What is it, a small village?"

The daughter bent to the screen and studied the cluster of black squares and rectangles that represented Clare Island. Map reading was one of her specialties. "Could be, but the structures are grouped rather close for individual properties. I'd say it's a farm of some sort." She straightened up. "And of course Ford didn't hide the contents under a rock. A man of his age, he would have figured he had little chance of surviving, and if he buried the information about the investments and the hiding place of the rest—I'm assuming it is— and he died, the entire fortune would be lost."

"But what if he did it just out of spite," Dugald put in. "You know—if *he* couldn't have it, nobody else would. Especially us." He glanced at his brother's corpse on the cabin top. "And are we forgetting that he *did* survive?"

"No! Nobody's forgetting that!" Heather barked. "Nobody will *ever* forget that, especially not me."

She tugged her hair free from the nape of her life vest, and the blondish mane lifted in the breeze. She was a tall woman and strongly built with wide shoulders and large breasts; her waist was thin, her stomach flat. She had a deep tan. "And answer me this—if he intended to bury it, why didn't he take the strongbox too? It's wet on that island, you saw so yourself. Anything unprotected would get soaked and ruined in no time. Bank notes, legal documents, maps.''

''If he can be believed—what he told us there in the sitting room.''

She snapped her head to her brother, who, while wide and powerfully built, was an inch or two shorter than she. ''You think he was lying?''

''You thought he was. You said so.''

''At first, after the way we saw how he lived. Meanly, poorly, coveting every shekel like some . . . peasant. But— think about it—that's just how he'd act to keep us from finding him on the one hand, and, on the other, to move the hoard in some anonymous way. Like he said, he had time to do all that—half a bloody century!—and he probably transferred a set amount each year—''

''Enough,'' Rehm cut in. ''I know the man and how he thinks. I lived with him, I studied with him. He told us the truth for one reason and one reason only. Because it *was* the truth and would *sound* like the truth. Anything less would have taken him away from his wife and the pistol he had concealed under her.'' Rehm raised his head to the corpse that was lashed to the cabin top. In a hushed voice he intoned. ''Malcolm—we loved ye', laddie.''

After a while he continued, ''The straight o' it is we failed. There was the darkness and the poor road, and who could have guessed he would live where he did. But—excuses aside—we weren't quick enough. He succeeded in passing off the secret before we arrived, and when he returned to the cottage, he had one purpose in mind and one on'y.''

''To kill as many of us as possible.''

''And nearly did,'' said Dugald. ''Or, at least, another of us.''

Rehm rounded on his second son, the gloved hand smacking his arm. ''What am I hearin', Dugald. Have ye' no stomach for the fray? Does yehr brother's body, lyin' there afore ye' mean nothing? This is war, mahn. The stakes are muckle high. Yeh take losses. Nobody is sorrier for Malcolm, nobody'll grieve him more than I, his father. Nobody. But what would ye' now have us do? Give up the fight altogether? Roll over and surrender? Whimper and take ourselves off into some dark place to pine?

"Nae, boy. Nae, nae—I say 'tis better to die here, like Malcolm, than to die slowly from the memory of defeat. Ye' do na' know what that's like, son, but *I* do."

It took Dugald a few moments to reply. Again his eyes swept the cabin top and his sister, before meeting his father's gaze. It's not my war, he wanted to say, and it's not *people* who died but Malcolm, whose opinion could no longer be sought.

But he also knew that his father was right. Collectively, they understood defeat—specifically, the defeat fifty years ago—having been reminded almost daily, as it had wrankled in Rehm's soul. He viewed his three children more as agents of his ego, there to satisfy his principal needs, than as independent personae. Which had led to this debacle.

On the other hand, Dugald supposed that with Malcolm's death it was now his own defeat too. Older by only a year, Malcolm had been like his twin, and they had been inseparable even in their work. "I couldn't live with myself thinking we came all this way, Malcolm died, and we left empty-handed."

"Good lad, brave lad. We'll acquit ourselves well, I promise ye'."

From the start Dugald had thought the second plan of attack—the anonymous flanking approach—better. It had been their father—backed by Heather—who had insisted upon a direct frontal assault, since both of them had something to prove: Angus to the man who had bested him so many years ago; Heather to herself.

Rehm turned to the daughter. "Ye' think yeh winged him?"

"I don't think, I *know* I did. He took it right here." She indicated her upper right arm.

"Then we should get right back before he has a chance to return or whoever this is"—he tapped the computer screen—"decides to leave the island." Rehm exited the program, switched off the machine, and stepped back so they could take it away.

Only a few minutes later when all three were aboard the smaller boat and a safe distance away, Rehm pointed an electronic remote device at the schooner, saying, "I only wish we could set it alight. The only reason we've gone to this trouble is to give Malcolm a decent burial. But that might attract a passing vessel."

"Like a Viking burial. The warrior sailing to Valhalla," Heather said with almost a thrill in her voice.

Dugald looked away.

"And *yehr* thoughts, son? D'ye have ony last wish for my son and yehr brother?"

Dugald nodded. "Och, aye," he said in a burr as broad as his father's. "I wish that Malcolm *were* alive, make no mistake. And tha' he di'na' die for sweet heady bullshit, Father."

Rehm's head went back. "So, is tha' what ye' think still, even after glammin' the ring on the woman's finger and what the man said?"

Dugald nodded. "Said. There's been too much *said*—by you, by him"—he turned and looked his sister directly in the eye—"by everybody. Now it's time to get what we came for," or join Malcolm, he did not add. For him it had come to that.

"And we will, I assure ye'. It's not like we di'na' prepare." Rehm pressed the button of the remote device, and the image of the schooner blurred for a moment. Next they felt the concussion of subsurface charges; they had been secured in her hold some months earlier for just such a contingency.

The report of the simultaneous explosions, however, was little more than a muffled thump, before the vessel, gutted of its keel, sank swiftly in one clean piece. It was as if a hand had reached up and pulled her down into the deep.

Before leaving the area, Dugald went below into the cabin of the sportfisher and undid the six spring clamps that had kept the entire cabin trunk and flying bridge attached to the hull. With his sister's help, he soon had the lightweight aluminum shell off, revealing a narrow control console protected by a canvas doghouse. Their father was nowhere to be seen, having retired to the cabin in the foredeck to sleep.

Now they removed the black paint or, rather, the opaque Mylar film that covered the white paint below. Once cut into, it came away in broad ribbons that were carried away on the breeze. In less than a half hour, the pair had stripped the exterior down to the waterline. They then added Irish registration numbers on either side of the bow.

Finally, a nameboard was dropped into slots on the transom: *Grainne Uaile*, it said—a variant spelling of the infamous pirate queen's name.

At the wheel, Dugald hit the sticks and directed the powerful craft east, in the direction of the breaking day and the Irish mainland.

PART III

Temptation

CHAPTER 13

WHEN DETECTIVE SUPERINTENDENT Hugh Ward opened his eyes the next morning, he did not know which arms or legs were his and which belonged to Detective Inspector Ruth Bresnahan. They had become tangled during the night. Even now after several years together it was not unusual. Theirs was a torrid relationship.

The trick now was to determine what parts were his and to extricate himself without waking her. While still very much in love with his "colleague" (her term), Ward savored a few moments to himself in the quiet of early morning.

The trouble was, Bresnahan treated Ward just like a Teddy bear, hugging him to her and not wanting to let go. The second problem this morning was that they were rather more completely joined than he had first imagined. Hugh's initial attempt brought an immediate visceral reaction from the somnolent one who locked his head farther between her not insignificant breasts.

Like that, he imagined, he would, albeit pleasurably, soon smother. And so he did the only thing he could, which occupied the next quarter of an hour and left him feeling rather piqued. He had achieved his purpose, however, and was now blissfully free from her collegial embrace.

After he MIC'ed a cup of tea in the kitchen, Ward phoned

Murder Squad headquarters and learned that orders from McGarr had arrived. He was to pay a visit to a certain firm of solicitors and then take a ring, which had also been sent, to a certain jeweler. The stones had proved to be real, and Bresnahan and he were to try to flog it.

There was also an identity search for one Angus Rehm, to say nothing of the countless details of the dozens of other cases that were still being actively investigated. With McGarr away, Ward was in charge. Of what? Given the sheer volume of capital crime and the present paltry staffing levels—of chaos. The most they could do was to give any one murder a couple of intense days' scrutiny, hoping the perpetrator would be found and a book of evidence built, before moving on to the next.

Ringing off, Ward turned round to find his freshly made cup of tea gone; the door to the shower was closed and the water running. Of course, there was nothing preventing the small, dark, well-made man from slipping off his bathrobe and heading into the steamy confines of that quarter.

But if Ward, who was a noted amateur pugilist, had learned anything in the boxing ring, it was never to spar in a tight ring with a younger, taller, perhaps even stronger opponent (after the debilitating exercises of the night before). Also, there was something to be said for maintaining one's emphasis—to say nothing of reputation—with her who mattered most.

But soon Bresnahan was out of the shower and back into her clothes of the night before, so she could drive to her mews apartment in Ballsbridge and change for the day. Some appearance of singularity had to be maintained. "Fraternizing" was strictly prohibited among Garda personnel, and were their "collegiality" made known to the Commissioner, one of them would have to leave the Murder Squad. She—who was less senior—knew who it would be. The "fraternizer."

When Bresnahan reappeared, ready to leave, Ward said, "Today I've got a surprise for you."

"You're going to take me to 'Break for the Border' for lunch." It was a new "theme bistro" that featured a cowboy-and-Indian motif and Tex-Mex chow which Ward had refused to go near.

"No I'm going to give you a ring."

Turning to him in a way that made her angularity conspicuous, she fluffed her damp mane of auburn hair, "How do you mean?"

Ward pointed to the third finger of his left hand.

"No—*really*?" She seemed to have to think for a moment, and Ward panicked. Of course he'd been joking.

"Do we want to do something, like that?"

He was relieved, even though he hated when she told him what *we* wanted, which had been occurring more of late. "Knock your eye out by all reports. The size of a pigeon's egg, says Swords."

She closed her smoky gray eyes and breathed out. "Phew! You mean, the bloody ring from Clare Island." She too had read McGarr's preliminary reports from the day before. "You had me going for a moment." She opened the door and stepped out.

Feeling rejected—even if for all the right reasons—Ward said, "You're to dress accordingly. We'll be visiting those solicitors and the jewelers to see if we can sell it." Making for the shower, he cast a longing eye at the now empty bed.

"Oh, Mother of Mercy—I can't wear that," said Bresnahan, turning the ring this way and that, the many facets of the diamond winking at her. "What if I lost it?"

She was sitting with Ward in her BMW which she had bought a year or so ago after her father had died and left her a substantial bequest along with the largest farm in the South Kerry Mountains.

"It'll be safer on your hand than in me pocket," said Ward, "and it goes with the rig." He meant the car and how she was dressed. Wearing a designer suit of chrome yellow Quantril that fit her like second skin, black pumps, a black pillbox hat and veil, and with her hair in a tight bun, she looked like a caution sign in motion.

And to think—Ward thought proudly, possessively, yea sleazily—no more than two hours earlier, he had had enough of *that*. Or, rather, that glorious creature. He must be off his feed. There had been a time, not so many years ago, that Ward pursued women first, then tried to fit the other activities of life around that regime. The only reason he had joined the Murder Squad or fought in the ring was because their cachet rather enhanced his success in the chase.

Watching the supple flexing of her calf as she climbed the granite steps of the Georgian townhouse where Monck & Neary kept their office, Ward wondered—did the penis rule all men the way it ruled him? Or was he, you know, simply a surd?

Now opening the heavy paneled door, Ward breathed in her fragrance as she brushed by—some heady melange of soap, shampoo, emollient, and scent that had probably cost her more than her weekly pay packet. She spared nothing on her appearance, which was always more than enough to make Ward . . . well, "putty in her hands" was not an apt phrase.

The door to what had once been the sitting room was open. There Ward found an old man seated at a desk in front of a tall arched window that looked out on the street. He was reading a newspaper.

Wearing a swallowtail coat, morning trousers, and dove-gray spats, he turned only his eyes to Ward. They were blue, clear, but agatized with age. In a bank of cages beside his desk, a passel of exotic songbirds in many bright colors was warbling raucously. "I don't get up anymore, unless you have business with us, which you don't. What do you want?"

"To see Monck or Neary." It was hot—no, stifling—in the room. And yet everything was neat and well tended, like the colorful Persian rug in the middle of the floor.

"Monck, which is me, is retired twelve month come July. And Neary will need a reason."

"It's private actually, the matter of an estate."

"You'll have to do better than that. All Monck and Neary matters are private, strictly so. We handle mainly estates."

Bresnahan stepped into the room. "We won't take much of his time. As a matter of fact, we only need a bit of information."

The chair swiveled slowly and the old eyes regarded her, beginning with the pumps and rising to the pillbox hat; no, Ward decided, he was not alone. She handed Monck a card, and his old eyes lingered on the diamond-and-sapphire ring.

"You won't be taking any of *his* time whatsoever, is it, Inspector?"

Bresnahan nodded.

The old man shook his head in wonder. "Information is our stock in trade. We collect it, we save it, we bank it, and I'm afraid we can't pay out as much as a farthing, the capital not being ours to give. But"—placing his hands on the arms of the chair, Monck rose unsteadily to his feet—"Neary has some modern notions about this, and she refuses nobody a see, much less a new-model guard." He turned to Ward. "And who might you be?"

"Her keeper." Ward produced another card.

"And a most fortunate man," Monck muttered, shuffling toward the door. "That hair her own?"

"She's the genuine article in every particular."

"Me—I'm more interested in verbs. Pity mine are all past tense."

They were shown into a drawing room, where a maid served them tea and petits fours. Waiting in virtual silence, they listened to the bells of a nearby church ring in eleven and finally noon before Neary appeared.

She proved to be a slightly older woman in quiet tweeds, with the thin smile and imperturbable manner that Ward had always associated with Ascendancy matrons. It was the bearing of privilege that said, There is nothing you can say or do that will shock or upset me, since I expect the worst of you and know myself to be demonstrably better. Just look at me now—I can even shake your hand with equanimity.

And she knew the tack to take, which was guilt transference. "Please excuse the delay, but I had my schedule to observe. Had you rung up . . ." Astrid Neary widened her eyes, as though she could not imagine simply dropping in.

She then perched on the edge of a chair and folded her hands in her lap, as though to suggest that whatever they had come for would not take long. Her thin legs were grouped gracefully to one side of the seat. "You couldn't possibly be the same person by this name"—she glanced down at Ward's card—"who is the pugilist, could you, Superintendent?" When she looked up, her eyes were dancing; they then took in his double-breasted designer suit, his square shoulders, his dark eyes and dark good looks.

Ward ignored the question, since she would not have asked, did she not know. He had interviewed many like her in his now fourteen years with the Garda Siochana. Instead he explained that the name of her firm had arisen in the course of a murder investigation, and they would like to ask her a few questions.

"Certainly. I will try to cooperate. You can ask me anything you wish." Her pale blue eyes had grown brighter, as though somehow the possibility of helping the police entertained her. "But you should know that any question about a client is off limits, and I simply cannot answer."

"Is Mirna Gottschalk a client of yours?" Bresnahan asked.

"There you go—but she's not. I've never so much as heard the name." Her eyes swung to Ward for approbation; see, she *was* doing what she could.

"What about Clem or Clement Ford."

The hesitation was slight but significant. "Perhaps you don't know this, but we've been brought to court by other government agencies more than a few times, and yet we have never been forced to give up so much as a client's name." She turned her head to Bresnahan, confiding, "It was a bother and a bore, but rather good publicity in the end. However"— her eyes met Ward's—"we do not represent that name either. Not currently, not ever as far as I know, and I am a founding partner."

"What do you do for your clients?" Bresnahan asked. "If you don't mind telling us."

"No, my dear. It's a matter of record. We manage estates, establish funds and trusts, and execute the terms of wills and legal contracts."

"But I don't understand the need for such—is it?—secrecy."

"It is and you would, were you, say, U2 or Liam Neeson, none of whom we represent"—and wouldn't, said her tone— "and you wished to aid some cause anonymously, so you wouldn't then be importuned by other similar efforts or castigated in the press for being . . . invidious or prejudicial."

"Or if you wished to conceal the source of the money of some fund?" Ward asked.

"As in—what is the current term?—money laundering? Heavens, no. We accept no more than a client or two a year, and it takes us a full year at least to decide that we will. No matter—personal, financial, criminal, *social* even—is left unexamined, to say nothing of the many checks we make on any funds that are tendered to our care.

"Because of income taxes, we are most careful in that regard. No scandal has been allowed to darken the luster of our reputation, which is everything in this profession. As in some others that come to mind, I should think."

Did she know about Bresnahan and him, Ward wondered. Or was she just guessing, both of them being young and attractive. They had tried to avoid being seen together socially, but there was only so much "hiding out" they could do, and the Dublin gossip mill was a potent engine indeed. In the two hours that they had been waiting she might well have learned any number of scurrilous things.

"How is it, do you think, that a man named Clement Ford of Clare Island would have written down the name of your firm and this address?"

"Really, now, I have no idea why somebody would do such a thing. We're rather well known in some circles." Astrid Neary glanced at her wristwatch.

"Probably as his last act." Bresnahan put in.

"Last?"

"The last in his life."

"Do you mean this man was murdered?" Neary opened her hand and glanced at Ward's card again.

"He's missing and may well have been. But this is murder as it stands. What about Brigid Honora O'Malley. Do you represent her?"

"I don't know why I'm telling you this. I don't have to, you know. But, no, we don't represent anybody by that name either."

"Do you represent anybody at all on Clare Island?"

Astrid Neary stood. "No. I'm afraid I can't help you there either. None of our clients has a Clare Island mailing address."

Which was a rather fine statement of denial. "Then, you *do* represent somebody on Clare Island, but he has a different mailing address?" Ward asked.

"Really, Superintendent Ward, I haven't been interrogated like this since my student days in mock court. But, again, Monck and Neary represents nobody on Clare Island that we know of."

"Could a client of yours reside on Clare Island without your knowing?" asked Bresnahan.

"Surely—they don't ask our permission nor do they inform us about their places of residence. And, frankly, we don't wish to know more than where to send the quarterly notices of accounts. Or checks. Usually that's a bank or building society."

"And yet you research them thoroughly before deciding to accept them as clients," said Bresnahan.

"The years go by, people move, they die, they leave the country, even. But yet their assets, managed by the proper firm, often carry on without them. In fact, since the inception of the new banking laws, persons of foreign nationality, investing in Irish instruments, might actually nominate a third party to act as a nominal fiduciary agent. The level of privacy they enjoy at least equals that of other tax havens, such as Switzerland or the Cayman Islands."

"Do you represent many foreigners?" Ward asked.

"Some."

"How many?"

"Twelve on last count. Really, I'm afraid I must get back to my office."

"How many clients has Monck and Neary all told?"

Neary began moving toward the door. "Forty-three."

"Then in summary—one last question, please"—Bresnahan rose from her chair and followed the smaller, older woman into the hall. "Monck and Neary might have a client of Irish citizenship or otherwise who asked you to secure and invest assets, the sources of which were not known to you because, at the time, it was not necessary to report them."

Neary stopped on the first step of the stairs to the first floor. She turned to them. "Yes, I suppose so. Years ago. But, as I said, the success of this firm has been based upon its judiciousness in everything, and, as I've said, we represent almost exclusively only the most well-known and respected interests in the country.''

"Or, more recently," Bresnahan pressed, "a foreign national might have been accorded the same treatment, because of the new laws."

"That's it, in a nutshell."

"And you've never heard of Clem or Clement Ford?"

The smile cracked the slightest bit. "We do not represent a person by that name."

"Did you ever?"

Shaking her head in polite exasperation, Neary offered Bresnahan her hand. "You are as clever as you are beautiful, my dear. Did you ever consider the law as a profession?"

Her small hand was dwarfed in Bresnahan's. "I practice it daily.''

"Oh, *touché*. A *bon mot* if I ever heard one. I hope you don't mind if I repeat it to my friends." Doubtless a tale laced with class prejudice, Bresnahan thought. *You should have seen this woman. Big? And wearing a dress the color of a hay field in her native Kerry. Barged right into our office asking the most indiscreet. . . .* "Did you ever represent Clem or Clement Ford?" She had not let go of the hand.

"Not that I remember, my dear. I wonder if you could release my digits? I'm in pain."

Bresnahan complied. "Would you mind if we asked solicitor Monck?"

"Capital idea." Neary turned and began climbing the stairs. "Ask him anything you please. Even to lunch, if you're brave." In the shadows near the landing, the older woman checked her wristwatch again. "He's notorious within at least a long mile of this place. And rightly so."

"No, I don't recall any Clem or Clement Ford," said Monck from his desk where he was now scanning a computer screen; on it ticks from various stock markets were flowing by. "But then, I can scarcely remember my own name most days.''

Bresnahan and Ward exchanged glances; somehow neither believed he was as dotty as he made out. "How many people work here?" asked Ward. "Do you have staff?"

"We don't *work* here, young sir. We *practice* the law and sound, fiduciary, investment banking. Now and again Astrid hires in somebody to type and file and so forth. Low expenses, low fees. Our clients prefer it that way."

"And how many clients do you have?" Bresnahan pressed.

Without taking his eyes from the computer screen, he said, "Last count, forty-three. Eighteen foreign nationals, the balance resident citizens."

"Would you have a list of them?" Bresnahan brought herself within range of his vision.

Like a puppet, his head swung to her. "For you, I would, were there any such thing. But there's not."

"Not even in that computer?"

"*This* computer? Bloody thing's a bloody brute and costly. See this key? I press that to buy, and this one to sell. Used to be you had to think about these things, ring up a broker, get his opinion, chew the fat, with luck perhaps even be taken to lunch. Only then would you plunge." His old eyes again ran over Bresnahan. "Tell you something?"

Bresnahan nodded.

"We'd all be better off the way we were before."

"Which is?"

"Ignorant. It's the best advice I can offer today." Monck's gaze returned to the screen.

CHAPTER 14

COLM CANNING THOUGHT his head was one of the bells when his old Bakelite telephone began ringing shortly before noon. The phone was on the pillow beside his head, and his hand shot out and smacked the receiver from its yoke.

He had placed the telephone there prior to collapsing the night before so he wouldn't miss a "water taxi" summons from any of the well-heeled O'Malleys from Parts Unknown. They would begin arriving some time soon and might think forty-five quid spare change.

"Call-em! Call-em!" the voice on the other end kept saying. Whoever he was, he was local, which would mean no bobs for Canning. But, reaching for the can of Guinness on the nightstand with one hand and the plunger with the other, he also heard, "Call-em, this is *Fisherman's Friend*"—Packy O'Malley's boat. It also sounded like O'Malley's distinctive, gravelly voice, the result of drinking whiskey and smoking unfiltered Woodbines for the better part of fifty-seven years.

Sitting up in bed brought on an instant, piercing headache. But Canning knew enough not to say the man's name. "Where are you?"

"Well, the fish is runnin' great guns, so they are. But them scuts of seals is slashin' through our nets like butter, and we're lucky if we come up with a fish or two unmarred for

sellin' in any one net. A nip gone here, a mouthful there. The
rest is cannery fare, if we can get them there on time. I tell
you it's a dreadful scene altogether."

It was Packy right enough, being cagey because of the
cops.

Cops! Christ! Canning's face went red as beet root, he
could see in the dim dresser mirror, and his heart started
thumping just to think of the public . . . drubbing the old
gouger had given him in Packy's own kip in the harbor. The
fecker had to be, like . . . sixty! Sucker-punched him, so he
did—Canning's ego now decided—there with two hundred
and fifty pounds of blue uniform backing him in the shape of
Tom Rice, the superintendent from the Louisburgh barracks.

"Call-em, are ye' there?"

Canning grunted and remembered his other humiliation—
the one in the hotel. That had been yet more unfair because
he'd been drinking. It nearly got him barred from the place!
By Christ, he hated all the thundering mainland gobshites who
thought they could come out here and play Puck because they
had readies.

The Guinness can was empty. He chucked it at the dusty
shelves of books his wife and he had read in university and
humped out here seven years before, after his mother died
and left him the house. They had thought they could make a
go of the place—him fishing and writing, her painting and
picking up whatever jobs she could get in computers, which
she had studied and were now big.

But with all the high-tech foreign fleets in Irish waters, the
fishing was poor for one man in a small old boat, and the
writing . . . well, just never materialized. The two children
who did, however, took the wife away from the family's only
real income. Shortly after warning Canning that she would
not allow her kids to live in "quaint, West of Ireland pov-
erty," she scraped up plane fare and skipped with them to
her sister in California. A year now, come July.

At first Canning had felt that she had stolen his heart and
soul. But time had passed, and now at moments like this, he
knew the truth—that there was something far wrong with him
altogether. He was a different, but not better, man than when
he first returned to Clare Island.

"Call-em, I want to ask you if you'd bring us out some equipment, like."

"Like what? Out where?" In the scullery, he opened the refrigerator. He had left the radio on, and RTE was playing the "Angelus." Noon already!

"Like equipment with a bit o' metal in it. With some steel."

No Guinness. In fact, no nothing. There wasn't so much as a bite to eat in the fridge; even the cheese looked like a wedge of China plate with blue mold all around. The butter smelled rancid. "I don't bloody know what you mean—steel nets? Don't tell me you intend to drag for salmon?"

"No, not drag. Plink, like—if you know what I mean. Use your imagination. Didn't you always say you wanted to be a writer? We need something so we don't come back to the island empty-handed."

Nothing in the cupboards either. Just all the baking powders and spices from when the wife cooked. Canning pincered his aching temples. Use his bloody imagination? And what was this "always . . . *wanted* to be a writer?" Wasn't he only bloody thirty-one years of age; Joyce didn't publish *Ulysses* until he had gone forty. "Who's we?"

"The big fella and me. My backer and yours."

Clem Ford, Canning thought. So, he had survived; he should have known as much. The fucker was immortal. Steel . . . so they wouldn't come back to the island empty-handed. "Where would I get this steel?"

"You know the place."

Now Canning knew what O'Malley meant. Guns. Even before Packy got his new fast boat with the wide hold and few bulkheads, he had run guns off trawlers into the North for the I.R.A. But with the mangled hand, he had needed help of the sort that Canning could supply. The money had been good and the jars—usually a whole night of them—even better. Canning liked coming home to the wife with all the money still intact but enough of a load on to make him amorous. She could hardly refuse.

It was that, however, that had kept him from the writing, he was now sure of it. He simply did too much, trying to keep up with the cost of four mouths to feed. Christ, wasn't there a beer in the entire kip? He stormed out into the cubby. When the wife had been around, he had always kept a nip there for just this sort of emergency. "What would you need from there?"

"All that's there."

So they could return—two old men—armed to the oxters on his boat? He'd lose it sure, if they shot somebody and it ever got out.

"You'll not find much, you'll see. But we need it at the moment."

Canning prized up a floorboard, and there it was—a jam jar of *potín* that he must have hidden there maybe two years ago, when the wife had put her foot down about the pubs and the money he was spending. No, "Pissing our life's blood over the bar" was her timeless mixed metaphor. But, then, she had done sciences not arts.

Granted, *potín* wasn't something to be guzzling at any time, to say nothing of the noon hour. You could never tell what it was made from or what yeasts had entered the mix. Ketones were created, some molecules of which were poisons, others hallucinogens; a wild batch of *potín* had been the ruination of many a man in Mayo and the West.

But a wee taste would take the edge off his humor and get him on track. He only wished there was something to cut it with. "Need it where?" He twisted open the cap and took a slug, even before he got to the tap at the sink.

"Killala. Nobody'll think much of your coming and going, but take precautions. You're to set off to Roonagh Point, like you're puttin' in there. No, better yet, do it. Then, comin' back, feint a wee bit south toward Inishturk, before cuttin' west of the island where Paulie can't see you. If he thinks anything, he'll think you're out for a few mackerel," which had just begun to run.

The acrid liquor scorched down Canning's throat along with the enormity of the request. Killala was seventy long miles north of Clare Island around Achill, Erris, Benwee, and Downpatrick heads, and then into Killala Bay. With either wind or tide against him or both, a trip like that would take him most of a day and night, all else running smooth.

Twisting on the tap, Canning sucked the cold water straight from the spigot. "Can't." He sucked again.

"What?" O'Malley asked unbelievingly.

Canning straightened up and felt the heat work down through his body, warming his back and ribs which, he now realized, had been galling him only slightly less than his head and *ear*! "I said I can't. Not today, not tomorrow, not for the next week!" Some of the O'Malleys arrive early; others might tarry on the island for a week. Canning's trade would be brisk for at least that long.

"Why ever not?" The old man was aghast. Mate to mate, islander to islander—helping out in a pinch was something that was done, no questions asked. You might need it yourself someday.

"Because it'll burn the arse out of any chance of my making a few quid during the rally, is why. Why can't you get some of your friends up there to provide what you need?" Canning meant the Republicans.

"You scut you, you know why."

Because, after what had happened on the island, the Republicans would want no part of it. And what O'Malley and Ford needed in addition to arms was an anonymous boat. Packy's was probably now under cover in a shed or scuttled.

"Well, I can't, and I won't, and there's the end to it." Canning tugged on the jam jar. Second sip he did not need a chaser. His young, strong body could cope with it, he thought heroically.

"By Jaze, buck—you need a good beatin', so you do," Packy began giving out to him. "Would you remember, now, how ye' got yehr bloody boat? Can ye' tell me who's responsible for that?"

Stepping quickly to the counter, Canning slammed the handset into the cradle. And he had only just got into the toilet to throw some water on his face, when the phone began ringing again.

"Colm—we know you've had trouble of late, but can you not come up here and give us a hand?" Clem Ford asked in his straitlaced English voice but with Irish syntax.

It was all so fecking false Canning could scarcely contain himself. The son of a bitch had bought his way on to the island way back when and had the gall to stay; well, now he could bloody well buy his way back on. But, first, Canning would have his bit of fun with him. He moved back into the kitchen and the jam jar. "Whatever happened to ye' now that ye' need my help?"

"I'm sorry, I can't tell you at the moment. But sometime I will, please God."

The invocation was plain wrong in Ford's mouth, and Canning felt his scalp tighten. "You brought the law down on us, so you did." He raised the jar.

There was a pause, and then, "And, I suppose, you'd like me to pay."

Canning nearly choked on the *potín;* now he was talking, and without Canning having to bring it up. Ford was a blow-in but a smart blow-in at that.

"I'll need to be paid for all the business I'll have missed."

Canning heard Packy grousing in the background, "After all the help, the money, the jars—he's just a cunt, a greedy cunt!" Which was the ultimate term of abuse, man to man, on the island. But Ford said evenly, "By all means. And what do you think that might be?"

Ten trips, thought Canning. No, twenty, the *potín* told him. "A thousand pound!"

"How much?" O'Malley demanded to know.

But Ford said to him, "Please, Packy. Get a grip on yourself." And to Canning, "Just so, Colm. Whatever you say."

There was more roaring in the background.

"When do I get me money?" Canning killed off the jar, thinking that he should soon lay some ballast on his belly or he'd be in no form to take any wheel. But with a thousand quid in the offing—hell, he'd treat himself to a slap-up meal at the hotel.

"Don't worry, you'll get it." Ford said in a voice that sounded tired and—was it?—disappointed, which put a bit of wind up Canning. But another little voice counseled, It's only the *potín,* Colm. Calm yourself. Eat, get on the boat, make your killing. By age or by enemies Ford will soon be gone, and you will have taken your last bite out of him. And a good bite at that.

Still he managed, "When we get back here?"
"If you like. I'll see if I can manage it then."
"And if you can't?"
"I said you'll get your money." Ford rang off.

CHAPTER 15

JUST AFTER NOON, Noreen McGarr stopped the car at the foot of the bald, gray-green mountain that had dominated their view out the windscreen ever since Maddie and she had left Westport. It was time for her six-year-old daughter to learn a thing or two about her country's history and culture.

"This is Croagh Patrick, which means 'Mountain of Patrick.' It's the holiest hill in all of Ireland. Do you remember what happens here?"

Maddie had to crane her head to look up at the top. "It's not a hill, it's a mountain. Do people *climb* it?"

"That's right. Thousands of them all on one day. Can you see the paths winding up the sides? Some of them do it with bare feet. Shall we give it a go?"

"With bare feet?"

"Unless you think you'd prefer your shoes."

A redhead, like both her mother and father, Maddie was quickly out of the car and ahead of Noreen on the rough stony path. But as the grade increased toward the 2,510-foot summit, Maddie's pace slowed markedly. "Wouldn't you say it hurts?"

"Not at the moment, but I'm sure it will in the morning."

"No—wouldn't you say it hurts their feet, climbing this barefoot?"

"It does, sure. Some of them come back all bloody." And sometimes not at all, she did not add; in most years the mountain claimed at least one penitent with a health problem. "But that's why they do it."

"To hurt themselves?"

"Well, to mortify the flesh, I think. That means they hurt themselves to pay for sins they believe they might have committed during the year. Those sins might also be of the flesh."

Maddie waited for a better explanation, and Noreen took her hand. "You see, it's part of a religious observance. Actually *two* religious observances. The first one began many, many years ago—some say as many as two thousand years ago—when this mountain was called *Cruachain Aigle,* which means 'Mountain of the Eagle.' One night in the summer, people from near and far would take food and drink and climb to the top of this mountain so they could watch the sun rise in the morning."

"Like a picnic."

"Exactly. It was their celebration of the first fruits of the harvest that they rightly believed the sun, whom they called Lugh, was responsible for."

"Because without the sun plants can't grow," Maddie chimed in. Her father had a garden, and the two of them had discussed it.

"Right again. They even named the day after Lugh, calling it Lughnassa, which was one of the four great festivals of ancient Ireland."

"But you said there were two ob—"

"—servances. That's right." Noreen had to stop and catch her breath. Although a trim woman still in her thirties, what with the demands of her picture gallery in Dublin and her duties as a wife and mother, she had little time to exercise. "There is now a different observance, because the people of Ireland changed their religion."

"I know about that."

"You do, do you?"

Maddie nodded. "People are either Catholic or Protestant unless, like us, they don't have a religion."

That vexed Noreen. She was from a Protestant background, her husband's was Catholic; they were sending Maddie to a nondenominational school in Dublin, largely so Maddie could avoid thinking in the categories that still scarred Ireland to this day. "You know other children in your school who are neither Catholic nor Protestant."

Maddie nodded. "They're Jews, then. Or, like me, nothing."

Again stung by that, Noreen said too strongly, "That's not true. Just because we have no religious affiliation doesn't mean we don't believe in God." It was the phrase Noreen had used when filling out Maddie's application form. "And some of your other friends are Muslims and Hindus." She could have added Bahaists, Shintoists, Quakers; the school, like much of Dublin itself, was thoroughly catholic. "You can be spiritual without being a member of an organized religion."

Maddie considered that, as they climbed higher. "Is that what we are, then—spiritual?"

"You could say that. It's what all religions aim at."

"Then, we're religious and spiritual."

"Spot on. That's us entirely."

"What about the second festival?"

"Well, that began—as I said—when the people of Ireland were changing their religion to what's called Christianity."

"Is that Catholic or Protestant?"

Noreen was astonished by how thoroughly the schism was invested in the mind of her six-year-old, especially since she seldom heard such distinctions drawn at home. "Actually, it's both. And one early Christian was named Patrick."

"You mean, Saint Patrick."

Jesus, thought Noreen, the Irish fixation with religion must be imbibed in the water or inhaled in the air; to her knowledge nobody in their house or family had ever spoke to Maddie of saints or sinners. "I do, although at the time he was simply Patrick.

"At any rate, it has been recorded that in the year 441, Patrick climbed to the top of this mountain, where he fasted and prayed for forty days that the people of Ireland would embrace his religion."

"The one called Christianity."

Noreen had to pause again. She was winded, but the air—

now that they had gained some height—was fresh, and she
felt more invigorated than she had in many a day. "Yes."

"What's praying?"

"Asking God for guidance and spiritual help."

"What's fasting?"

"Doing without food and only taking wee sips of water
now and again."

"For *forty* days? How many is forty?"

They climbed forty more steps up Croagh Patrick.

"And did he not die?"

Noreen decided to skip the bit about fasting, prayer, med-
itation, and visions. "He was a young man at the time, and
who's to say he didn't nibble the odd wildflower. But I myself
believe that a person of his . . . dedication well might not have
eaten in all that time.

"At any rate, his stay on the mountain was so phenomenal
that it gave rise to a myth."

"What's a myth?"

"A good story that people keep telling over and over, even
if we know it can't be true. Like the stories about Cuchulain
and Finn MacCool," that Noreen had been reading now to
Maddie for years. "This one has to do with the fact that there
are no snakes in Ireland."

"There aren't?"

Noreen shook her head.

"That's good."

"I agree."

"I don't like snakes."

"Why?"

Maddie shrugged. "I don't know, I just don't. How could
you?"

Noreen couldn't herself. "So, this myth says that the reason there are no snakes in Ireland is that Patrick, who had
special powers, collected all the snakes, drove them up this
mountain, forced them to jump off a cliff, and they died."

"How did he do that?"

"It's said he had special powers. It's probably one reason
they call him a saint."

"Saint Patrick."

Noreen sighed, having corroborated the very foolishness

that she wished to avoid. Of course, it was all part of the culture, which Maddie should know.

"Why didn't the snakes bite Patrick?"

"Because, as the myth has it, Patrick stepped on shamrocks all the way up this mountain, and the snakes—being evil and knowing the shamrock is the symbol of good''—to say nothing of its more recent national significance—''couldn't bite him, as long as he remained on the shamrocks.''

For a while they climbed on, Maddie looking to left and right as though for snakes and shamrocks. Noreen loved her concentration; she could virtually hear the wheels of her mind turning. Finally, Maddie asked, "Is it a silly story?"

"That's for you to decide. There are no snakes in Ireland, and in many ways what Patrick brought was good." Noreen was blown; she could not go on. "Have we climbed high enough?"

Maddie looked up. They had not climbed even halfway, and the great mass of the mountain still lay before them. Yet, in turning to look down, they were presented with a glorious view of Clew Bay. In the far distance Clare Island with its own tall, bald mountain looked like a final sentinel in the distant Atlantic.

"Have you had enough information for a day, or can I tell you something else? About the land?" Like her father, Maddie had a definite feel for what Noreen thought of as mise-en-scène or, here, the environment. "See this mountain we're on?"

Maddie nodded.

"And see that mountain on the last island in the bay?"

"The big one?"

"Yes, that's the island we're going to. Don't they look alike? The mountain on the island is a continuation of this mountain, and there are others in the chain to the east. But do you know that not so very long ago in the life of the earth it was possible to walk from this mountain to the mountain on the island?"

"You mean, there was no water?"

"There was, but the ocean was much lower then. All over the world it was far colder than it is today, and when it rained and snowed over the land, the water was frozen to ice and could not flow back into the ocean. At that time, there was a land bridge between Roonagh Point and Clare Island.

"Then around ten thousand years ago the world got suddenly warmer, the ice began to melt, the oceans rose, and Clew Bay filled up with water."

"Whatever happened to the people on the island?"

"There were no people on the island then, as far as anybody knows. People didn't begin to arrive there until around seven or eight thousand years ago, and it had to be by boat, since the bay was filled by then."

"How much is a thousand?"

"How much is ten tens?" Maddie was well into her sums at her school.

"A hundred."

"A thousand is ten hundreds."

Looking out at the island, Maddie thought for a while. "Eight thousands is a great lot altogether."

"Of course, there's another explanation of how Clare Island got where it is."

Maddie's eyes widened, as though to say, There always is, and Noreen wondered at her child's opinion of her. As a girl she could remember being critical of her own mother's serenity in the face of all the bracing details that made sense of the world.

"It's a big boulder that one Druid launched at the head of another Druid."

"Did it hit him?"

Noreen shook her head. "It went wide."

"I like that story better."

CHAPTER 16

"IS SIGAL A Jewish name?" Ruth Bresnahan asked Hugh Ward, as they drove past the shop of the jeweler and gold merchant and tried to find a parking place. The Coombe, however, was a narrow through street and there was not a place to be found.

"It can be, although it's more usually spelled with an *e* after the *i*."

"Odd, but you don't usually think of there being many Jews in Ireland. Remember that passage from Joyce?"

"In *Ulysses*?"

"Was it *Ulysses*?"

Ward nodded. "Deasy saying to Daedalus, the reason there are no Jews in Ireland is because she never let them in. It was dead wrong then, dead wrong now. Jews have been in Ireland for eight centuries that are known about and perhaps even before that. Henry the Third made Peter of Rivall the chancellor of the Irish exchequer and gave him 'custody of the King's Judaism.' That was in 1232."

Bresnahan eyed Ward sidelong. She hated when he knew more about some subject that was—or, at least, should be—common knowledge. Before their liaison they had been rather at each other's throats in Murder Squad meetings. In fact, it had been *Ulysses* and Joyce that had brought their *agon* to a crisis, the resolution of which was their present state of involvement. "How do you know all that? There's a parking place there, if you haven't noticed."

Ward had, but auto theft in that part of Dublin was rife, and a blistering new BMW with every option very much a target. Since they were posing as ordinary citizens, they could not very well pull up in front of the shop and lower the Garda shield on her visor. "You sure?"

"Of course, I'm sure. It's only a motorcar." Her manner was nonchalant even breezy, but Ward could tell she was spoiling for a dustup.

There had been a time—before having become . . . attracted to Bresnahan (it was hardly the right word)—when Ward had proscribed redheaded, left-handed women with light-colored eyes from his scope of amorous activity. He had never met one who was not in some way dangerous or zany.

"Give me more on Ireland's Jews."

With the gauntlet down, Ward could scarcely shrink from the challenge, and humbling her was a definite pleasure. "A quick sketch, or in detail?" Getting out of the car, he tossed her the keys like a hurler a ball on his stick.

"Why the works, of course. Who am I to frustrate your penchant for pedantry? What's that little gem you keep dredging up about genius being the infinite capacity for detail?"

"It's actually 'The transcendent capacity of taking trouble, first of all.' "

"Who said that anyhow?"

Something like it had been uttered by Dickens, Barrie, and Einstein, but Carlyle said it best. But it was safer to stick to Ireland's Jews.

Following her up the narrow footpath with cars and delivery vans passing them only a few feet away, Ward nearly had to shout. "Ireland attempted to naturalize Jews in the early part of the eighteenth century. The act passed the Commons unanimously over the objections of the Peers, only to be struck down by George the Second.

"We tried again later and in 1796, I believe, with the Irish parliament extending full civil liberties to Jews."

"I'll check this with my Jewish friends, don't think I won't."

"Baron de Rothschild? During the height of the famine he sent Ireland ten thousand pounds, a princely sum at the time, to be used by the needy regardless of religious affiliation."

Ahead of him, Bresnahan was walking slowly, careful to keep her chrome yellow suit from brushing against the grimy brick walls of the narrow street. Ward asked himself why—for the love of Yahweh—was he getting into a row with *that*? It wasn't what he wanted and would only complicate his life; but it was as though he could not help himself. "And, of course, you know about 'Little Jerusalem,' " he heard himself say.

There was no reply.

"It was a neighborhood off the South Circular Road around Clanbrassil Street. Around the turn of the century, it was lined with kosher butchers, bakeries, delicatessens, and the like. Bloom himself was born there, according to Joyce. Chaim Herzog, the future president of Israel, grew up on Bloomfield Avenue, which name—it's occurred to me more than once—Joyce might have taken for his 'cultured allaroundman.' "

"Who was a model for his time and ours." They had reached the door of the shop; Bresnahan turned to him. "So tell me—how many Jews are there in Ireland now? Few, I bet."

"Around three thousand, last count."

"There you go. Three thousand out of five million. I was right all along."

"Emigration keeps the number stable. Most of it, like Herzog, is to Israel."

Bresnahan reached a black-gloved finger to the buzzer. "Now I *cop* on—you're about to tell me you're a closet celebrant of said faith. Or is all of this something you learned in your brief *pass* through university." Which Ward had left for the guards, after his father had died and he found himself with a mother and three sisters to support.

"Well, you could say that. But think of the reams of bracing stuff I could regale you with had I stayed."

"Not to worry—I like you fine the way you are."

Dare he ask? "Which is?"

"Oh, cute. Definitely cute. But Monck was not wrong."

A face appeared in the square window—that of an early-middle-aged woman who had done little to enhance her dark good looks. Her hair, which was graying, was cropped short, and no makeup disguised the lines that had begun to appear around the corners of her eyes and mouth. Her long, thinly bridged nose was retroussé in shape, her eyes were blue.

But it was more what she did (or did not do) that caused Bresnahan and Ward to exchange glances. Framed in the door window, she only glanced at Bresnahan before her gaze lingered on Ward for whole seconds. Color came to her cheeks. Turning back into the shop as though for assistance, she looked out at them again with her eyes widened in what looked like panic. Again they fixed on Ward.

"Well, at least it's not me," said Bresnahan. "Did you shave?"

A dark person himself, Ward—while not hirsute—had a beard that looked almost blue when shaved close. He touched his chin. "No less than usual. Or have I egg on me pan?"

Finally her hands darted out and freed the latch. A loud alarm bell sounded in the shop as the door swung wide.

"Oh, hello. Sorry. Please, please come in. It's just that we don't get many people dropping in in this neighborhood. Most of our trade is by appointment."

Again, eyes met; shades of Monck & Neary went unsaid.

The alarm stopped the moment the door was closed, and she led them toward a row of glass cases. With a low tin ceiling, the dark shop at first appeared small and cramped, until their eyes adjusted to the shadows. Beyond—in fact, way beyond—some central display cases, they could see a light source. Aisles appeared, some packed with pianos, musical instruments, clocks, chandeliers and candelabras, others with brass sconces, vases and a vast collection of newel posts, among a host of other items.

She was not a tall woman, Ward noted as she turned to them, but nicely put together for somebody her age, which was what? Late thirties, early forties. All was concealed, however, in a tasteful, if loose-fitting, floral dress. There were plain gold rings in her ears, but none on her hands.

"Our trade is mostly wholesale, broker to broker. Or commissions."

"And you deal in more than jewelry and gold?" Bresnahan's eyes roamed the other items.

"Not really. We call those things my father's 'collection.' When he was alive, there were certain things he couldn't resist. Perhaps one of these days I'll sell them."

Yet again her light eyes flitted over Bresnahan and fixed on Ward. "What can I do for you?"

"I have a ring that was given me." Bresnahan held out her left hand. "I'd like an estimate of its worth, with an eye toward selling it. I was told Sigal and Sons might be able to find me a buyer. Or is it Sigal and Daughter?"

But the woman only directed Bresnahan's hand into the beam of a jeweler's light on the counter. She then fitted on a pair of watchmaker's eyeglasses, with a second lens in front of her right eye. Again she examined the large central stone, and then the eight in the surround. "The valuation, now— would it be for personal or professional use, Inspector?"

Bresnahan's nostrils flared. So much for anonymity. But she supposed that Ward's face had been in the papers and on the telly often enough, and she herself had acted as spokesperson for the squad more than a few times. "Shall I take it off my finger? Perhaps you could see it better then."

"It would help."

Bresnahan had some trouble removing the ring, which was small for her. And after only a moment or so of reexamination, the woman asked, "Do you have the rest of the parure?"

Neither Bresnahan nor Ward knew what she meant.

"Parure. A matched set of jewelry. Don't tell me you never kept up with your French, Superintendent?" she muttered.

Ward's head went back. He opened his mouth to ask the woman what she meant by that, but she continued to speak.

"A ring of this quality and artistry would have been created as part of a matched set. That is, along with a necklace, earrings, and brooch."

"We only have the ring."

"What a shame. I can tell you that Sigal and Sons sees a fair few gemstones in the course of a year—for jewelry, for appraisal, for sale, for insurance valuation. And for the last fourteen years the appraiser has been me." Her blue eyes, magnified through the glasses, flicked up at Ward. "But I've seldom encountered stones of this quality. Shall I tell you why?''

Ward nodded.

"I'll start with the diamond, which is a blue-white. The very best. As far as I can see, there is only one slight inclusion in the entire—I'm guessing here—twenty-eight carats, which is remarkable.''

"What's an inclusion?'' Bresnahan asked.

"Jewelerspeak for flaw. An imperfection. Officially, it's a solid body or a gaseous or liquid substance contained in a crystal mass. Very few diamonds are completely free from flaws. This one comes close.

"Also, it was cut by a master as a 'marquise brilliant' with fifty-eight facets or sides, thirty-three above the girdle.'' She pointed to the widest part of the rectangular-shaped stone. "And twenty-five below. It's spectacular.

"The sapphires are no less so. They're a matched selection of Kashmiris in cornflower blue, which are highly prized both because of the rich light blue color that you see and their rarity. There're very few sapphires of this quality in the world. Like rubies they can be cut so that, in the light''—she held the ring so Ward and Bresnahan could see—"a beautiful, luminous, six-point star appears on the surface of the gem. And finally, star sapphires of this sort are semiopalescent. All that milky iridescence.''

"It's gorgeous.''

"Yes, but imagine it with the other pieces. Now''—she turned the ring over—"as for the shank, setting, and designer. The hallmark says it's twenty-four-karat gold, which is the purest, a karat being a one twenty-fourth measure. But the setting is probably eighteen or fourteen to keep the stones in place. Pure gold is soft and malleable.

"The designer?'' With a jeweler's tool she pointed to a symbol that was concealed on the band in the shadow created by the stone. "Peter Carl Fabergé, Saint Petersburg, which means it was created before Fabergé's removal to Paris. He cut his name only into those creations of which he was proudest.''

"What's it worth?''

She glanced up at Bresnahan. "Depends on the buyer.

Were the other pieces of the set as spectacular and owned by one person, then the ring's value would easily double or triple. A complete matched set of this quality would be of inestimable value, comparable to the parures worn by royalty on state occasions or displayed in national museums. Think of the effect were the queen or princess to possess light-colored blue eyes.'' Hers, which were that color, flickered up at Ward.

"But as it is here in Dublin today," Bresnahan pressed. "What's it worth?"

"The ring alone?" The woman swayed her head from side to side. "A hundred thousand pounds. Maybe a hundred and a quarter were the buyer to possess the wherewithal to use these stones as the basis for creating another matched set. The problem would be *finding* stones of this quality, which would take time and cost . . . millions. May I ask you a question?" Which question was directed at Ward. "Have you researched the ring?"

Ward shook his head. "We only just came by it this morning."

"Something this good might have been written about or, at least, registered in some way or other. With the police, some insurance carrier, a bank or Fabergé. Since it's you, I can take a few photos and fax them to a service we use to locate rare items and document others. They might be able to run it down."

Since it's us, the police? Ward wondered. Or should they know her? "Yes, please. That'd be grand. Any expense—"

"Nary a bit. The service is one price, whether I use it once a month or a hundred times. And I'm rather intrigued now myself." She fitted the shank into a small, chamois-lined vise and trained the light on it. "And if the owner would ever wish to sell it, why then—" Over the top of the glasses her eyes again met Ward's with a glint that he thought for a moment he recognized. But from where?

From beneath the counter she drew out a camera and took several shots of the ring from various angles.

"Would you know a Clem or Clement Ford?" Bresnahan asked, as the woman worked.

"I don't believe so. Who is he?"

Bresnahan turned to Ward; it was up to him to decide how much to divulge.

"He's a man from Mayo who wrote the name and address of your shop on a pad in what may well have been his last act. This ring was his wife's. It was found in a car with the corpse of a murdered former guard."

"You mean, the trouble on Clare Island? It was in this morning's papers."

Ward nodded.

"Ford, you say? I can check our records." She turned into an office area beyond the counter. "Clem or—"

"Clement." Bresnahan lowered her head to examine the stones of the ring again in the bright light.

Ward kept his eyes on the woman; under the billowy dress she was still rather interesting, in spite of her age.

She tapped in the name, waited a moment, then shook her head. "When do you think we might have had dealings with him?"

"Hard to say, but he's described as a man in his late seventies."

"Then maybe my father dealt with him." She turned to a wooden cabinet that looked like it had been a card catalogue in a library at one time.

"What was your father's name?" Ward asked.

"Lou. Short for Aloysius. His mother was a gentile. I have a John Ford, a Reginald Ford, and a Maurice T. J. Forde with an *e* on the end. None from Mayo." Closing the drawer, she yet again stared directly at Ward, a slight smile puckering her dimples. Her eyes were shining.

"Have you ever dealt with anybody from Clare Island? The man is described as tall and broad-shouldered." Ward blocked them off. "Immense. Six feet six, twenty stone."

The woman wrapped her arms around her back, and Ward could see that with even a slight attempt at stylishness she could be fetching. Her brow wrinkled, and she smoothed back her silvery hair. "Do you know—I seem to remember somebody, like that, coming into the shop. But it was years ago, back when I was only a girl. But he was an Englishman, as I recall. With a great beard and a big voice. Always laughing. You know, a 'hearty chap.' "

"That's just the person," said Bresnahan.

"And his name was not Ford. It was—"

They waited, while she tried to recall, but after some time she said, "Sorry. I can't come up with it now, but I will, if I go through the files. We have nothing to hide." She pointed to her father's catalogue. "Would you have a card or something, so I can get back to you?" The request was plainly aimed at Ward.

Said Bresnahan, "Say an ordinary customer walked in here with that." She pointed to the ring. "Wanting to flog it, no questions asked. Would you buy it?"

"Of course. At my price. Or, at least, a fair enough price. Stones like that—" She shook her head.

"How would you go about it?"

"The same way we just did. I'd make inquiries via fax and modem. My service?"

Bresnahan nodded.

"It's updated daily via the Internet with reports from most of the world's major police agencies, including the Garda Siochana and the Interpol master list. For something of this worth I'd do what I just did—take some snaps and fax them out. If nothing came up, we could begin . . . negotiations."

"Does that happen often?"

"Somebody with something like this? Never in my fourteen years. Somebody with something over, say, fifty thousand pounds? Once a year, or twice, depending on referrals. Usually, after the death of some rich individual."

"Are you the sole proprietor here?"

"Since the death of my father."

"Fourteen years ago," said Ward. There was something definitely familiar about the woman, but he did not know what. "I wonder, is there any way you could begin the search now? Perhaps your father noted down Clare Island or Mayo on the cards in his files."

The woman glanced at her wristwatch, then scanned the blotter calender on the desk. "Well, today is out. I have to drive to Cavan to value a number of items in an estate. I'll try to set aside tomorrow or the next day, but it will take some juggling. You're welcome to look yourselves. You might have some trouble reading my father's handwriting, but''—she paused, and her eyes widened—''I could provide you some help. My son can read his grandfather's script, and he's a great fan of yours.''

Of whose? Ward was tempted to look behind him. He waited.

''Hasn't he followed your career in the ring since he was a wee lad? In fact, he's a boxer himself now. Well, let's say he's learning. Do I call him? He'd be crushed, if he didn't meet you.'' She did not give Ward time to reply; turning, she vanished into the dark interior of the shop.

Said Bresnahan, ''Well now—even if the investigation is a bust, at least you'll come away with something.''

Ward waited resignedly, knowing he was about to be slagged.

''Proof positive of the detestable notion that some men have an hypnotic effect over certain women.'' But not over herself went unsaid.

Or some women over certain men, thought Ward, shaking his head; it was as though he had lost his identity, the best of what he had known about himself in what now seemed like the distant past, after only two years with Bresnahan. What would any more permanent arrangement be like? he wondered.

The woman was returning. Behind her was a dark boy, tall and well-made for his age which was his early teens.

''Hugh Ward—this is my son, Lou.''

Ward reached his hand to the boy. ''My pleasure.''

''I'm pleased to meet you, I'm sure,'' the boy blurted out. ''I never thought I—'' He blushed and turned to his mother.

''I told him you might need his help, searching through his grandfather's cards for . . . what was it again?'' She too seemed to have lost her aplomb.

''I'll write it all down,'' said Bresnahan, taking a pen and notepad from her purse.

''And how do we get in touch with you—at Harcourt Street or the Castle or—''

''I'll have that here for you too,'' Bresnahan grumbled.

''I saw you defeat the Dane,'' said the boy, ''in the Utrecht games. For the first two rounds I thought you were a goner.''

''I did too,'' said Ward, studying the boy. He rather reminded Ward of himself at that age, with his slim, strong body and olive-toned complexion.

"How did you come back?"

"Luck. Your man got arm-weary thumping me. My head cleared, and by then he was tired."

Said the mother, "Amn't I after saying he'd tell you the truth?" And to Ward, "How can you take such punishment year after year and still . . . well, look the way you do? It's such a brutal sport, wouldn't you say, Inspector?"

Not brutal enough by half, thought Bresnahan, barely able to keep her temper in check. A breath of fresh air was in order.

"I'm not liable to continue for much longer."

"Ah, don't say that," said Lou. "But I suppose you've your duties with the guards. You're in charge of the Murder Squad now, aren't you?"

Ward glanced at Bresnahan, before saying, "Well no. There's a bit of an impediment in my way. Chief Superintendent McGarr."

"Oh yes," said the mother. "McGarr."

"But, sure, he's an old man."

Ward laughed. "Don't let him hear you say that. He could still give you a few brisk rounds." He turned toward the door. "Where do you work out?"

"At the P.A.C." The Powerscourt Athletic Club was a new sports facility with every amenity. "And you?"

"The Irishtown Gym," which was little more than an old industrial facility with a ring, a few weights, and occasionally running water in the showers. "Come round sometime, and I'll introduce you to the lads. We might even go a few rounds. But you'll want to be quick about it now, before you're out of my weight class."

"Sorry," said Bresnahan to the mother, "I didn't catch your name."

But the woman seemed preoccupied. Her arms were folded at her waist, and her smile was masklike and her eyes overbright, as she watched her son and Ward shaking hands.

"Excuse me. Hello. Your name, please, if you don't mind. I need it for my report on the ring."

"Oh, sorry—Leah. Leah . . . Sigal."

"And this is also your residence?"

"Yes, we live in the back. I'm pleased to have met you."

But enthralled to have met Ward, Bresnahan glowered. Taking his hand in both of her own, Leah Sigal looked searchingly into his eyes. "I'll be in touch."

Obviously the operative word. Stepping out into the sunlight, Bresnahan moved quickly up the narrow footpath of the traffic-busy street.

"You have a problem?" Ward asked, when he caught her up.

"Me? None. I'm not the one with the problem, it's you."

Ward thought he knew what was wrong. "Don't tell me *you,* of all people, are jealous."

Bresnahan stopped. "*Of all people?* What's *that* supposed to mean?"

"Only that you have people—*men*—eating out of your . . . black glove, come day go day. And you obviously enjoy it. Look at the way you've got yourself up."

"And which way is that?"

"Why, to be attractive. To men. If you were out in the desert, you could be seen at sixteen miles in that costume."

"And to women. Women like to see other women—"

"Ah Jesus," Ward cut her off. "Don't give me that"—he decided against shite—"guff."

"And who, may I ask, do you think I've been attractive to today?"

"Monck, of Monck and Neary. That's who."

"Sure, he's old enough to be my grandfather."

"And what about"—Ward waved his hand at the top of the street—"that woman in the shop? Leah Sigal."

"That woman's a well-preserved thirty-eight and not a day older. With a little care and that haughty nose and those eyes, she'd look like a younger, thinner, and"—Bresnahan swirled her hands in front of her chest—"more attractive Liz Taylor than Liz Taylor was at that age. And that's going some."

Maybe that was who Leah Sigal reminded Ward of. Stepping out into the street and around Bresnahan, Ward took note of the two bright patches on her cheeks. A full-blown Murphy was in the offing, he could tell. But he could not keep himself from muttering, "And the care you take of yourself, now—

who does it make *you* look like? Or shouldn't I ask?"

"Like myself, of course, and nobody but. Unless you have some idea of who else. And if you do, I'd like to know who. Now." She virtually chased him to her car, which was gone. Stolen. Garda shield on the visor, Garda radio, cellular telephone, and all.

"Not to worry—it won't be hard to find." Ward pulled a trim cellular phone from a jacket pocket and punched up Auto Theft. "Just think if we'd left the *ring* in the car."

Bresnahan looked down at it. "Shite on the ring. I'd trade it and you in a heartbeat for my bloody chariot."

"Chop shop," said the desk officer. "It's probably being stripped down as we speak."

CHAPTER 17

THE TURRET ROOM of the Clare Island lighthouse was like a revelation to Bernie McKeon. When he awoke in the morning, he thought he'd died and gone to heaven, which was surprising of itself.

First came the voices—or, rather, a whole choir of voices singing, wailing, howling—even before he opened his eyes. When he did, he was treated to a panorama of shimmering clouds lit by a new sun; they were hurtling past the window, enveloping the turret in a quicksilver gauze.

Looking out the south-facing window, McKeon only occasionally caught a glimpse of the corrugated green sward with its countless sheep and the high rugged cliffs that plunged straight into the sea. Mirna Gottschalk's compound of buildings was nowhere to be seen.

Clouds were not something McGarr or he had planned on. How could they have, being two city fellas? McKeon showered and shaved. He even pulled on a fisherman's-knit jumper that he'd been given for Christmas some years past and now had occasion to wear. Alone, that is, where nobody he knew could see him. Plucking up the Zeiss binoculars, he sat himself down in a large stuffed chair by the window. To wait.

As the day wore on, however, the clouds seemed to grow lighter both in color and weight, and—fascinated—McKeon watched them rise up and dissolve into the pale blue ether. Just as the sky cleared, Robert Timmermans, the great Belgian bear of a man who ran the place, arrived with a breakfast tray, again offering to help. "Anything you need, just ask. Did you bring any rain gear?"

"Well, a mac, and I have me hat." McKeon pointed to his felt fedora.

"Useless here. I took the liberty of bringing you an anorak." Timmermans tossed it on a chair. "I hope it'll fit. And boots. Did you bring boots?"

McKeon shook his head.

"Try these. We're about the same size."

In my bravest dream, thought McKeon. The man was two of him.

"Remember, *anything*!" Timmermans closed the door, and as he moved down the lighthouse stairs, McKeon glanced out the east turret window at the rest of the lighthouse; it had been only partially visible on the night before.

What he saw amazed him. The entire complex of—how many?—a dozen buildings, some large, was perched on the very edge of the cliffs that formed the northwest corner of Clare Island. All had been painted a blistering white with doors and shutters bright blue or red or green so that, in the now brilliant sun, the entire place had a Mediterranean look. McKeon felt as though suddenly he had been transported to another land, different from any he had ever even imagined. He was enthralled.

Looking out the north window, he felt as though he were on the bow of a ship that was sailing the sky toward the mountains of Mayo where peak was stacked upon peak until the mountaintops were lost in the mist. There a new cloud system was marching in off the Atlantic, reinforced by phalanx after phalanx of deep blue waves that were attacking the pale green waters of Clew Bay. Farther to the east, the sun was a brilliant disk of hammered brass.

But it was mainly the silence that impressed McKeon the most. True, there was noise, in fact, an utter blather of wind song and occasionally birdsong. But there were no clamorous sounds, no human sounds, no *Dublin* sounds. McKeon never until now realized how much he had needed a rest from that hubbub.

A baker's dozen women now began arriving at the Gottschalk place, only to be sent back by Mirna Gottschalk—it could only be her with her braids, jeans, and moccasins. Through the binoculars he watched her shake her head, then hunch her shoulders, as though to say she did not know when they would work again.

Easing his back into the comfortable chair, McKeon turned the glasses toward the line of clouds that were following what he knew was the Gulf Stream—how many?—fifty, sixty miles offshore since the clouds were so tall and he was perched so high. Watching its slow, steady drift north northeast toward the Shetland Islands and Norway, McKeon asked himself how he could have allowed his life to have progressed this far without such simple and grand pleasure, so simply achieved, as sitting in the window of that turret. Or some other turret, or on some cliff, or some mountaintop or high perch.

It was as though he were participating in one of the major events of nature and was a part of it, rather than continuing to be the pasty dodger who nipped from bus to office to pub to home. And staring out on the silent immensity of the Mayo coast, he began asking himself every eminently relevant question that he had stuffed down for . . . oh, a good thirty years, is all.

But not without guilt, given what Bernie McKeon—father of eleven children and a man so constant in his habits, both good and bad, that you could set your watch by him—allowed himself the liberty of imagining. He imagined what his life might have been like, living out here on this or some other island on the edge of the continent in the clamorous silence, watching the transit of wind and wave from an aerie such as this.

He supposed it was the human condition—locked in one body, the spirit yearning to soar. But he found the entire experience so seductive that he did not once desire a drink. Even through his lunch that was served with a bottle of wine, and his dinner, when Timmermans arrived with a bottle of malt in one hand and two glasses in the other. Why? He did not know. But he could scarcely concentrate on the little work that he had been set, and now night was coming on.

He was shocked, therefore, when he suddenly caught sight of a figure about a hundred yards from the Gottschalk house. Snapping up the binoculars, he had trouble finding the person, but with relief he discovered it was she, the Gottschalk woman. But where could she be going now with the day winding down and the gloaming coming on.

With her braids flying to windward, she was wearing a brushed leather jacket with Buffalo Bill fringes and a rucksack was strapped over her shoulders. And she sure could shift, her thin legs and legging moccasins hurrying her along the rough path.

What to do? He could stay where he was, which was his first choice; from his perch he would only lose sight of her when she dipped down behind one of the ridges that rumpled the topography of the island, there at the edge of the cliff. That way, he could continue his blissful stakeout undisturbed. To the east the first few brilliant stars had appeared, and the westering sun had transformed the clouds over the Gulf Stream into a riot of fiery color.

But thirty-plus years of police work could not be squelched by a day of solitary reflection, and McKeon soon found himself on his feet and slipping his arms into Timmermans's jacket, which fit him like a tent. The boots were only somewhat better. Strapping the binoculars over his neck, he snugged his Heckler & Koch automatic under his belt where he could feel its comforting weight.

The first maxim he had been made to shout in surveillance training with the Irish Army was "Never let a Mark out of your sight! Nor Matthew, Luke, or John!" Mirna Gottschalk, however, was nowhere to be seen.

She had spent the day at sixes and sevens with herself. Her first mistake was to have sent the women, who had come to work, home. She didn't want it ever to be said (and it would) that, Jew that she was, she had made any of them work so soon after the murder of Kevin O'Grady and the disappearance of the Fords, who had been so good to her.

But had the women been there, she might have been able

to forget about the entire debacle and the packet that Clem had thrust upon her. Finally, she had decided—she didn't care how much money was in the Clare Island Trust or what "good" she might do with it. So far, the blasted thing had succeeded only in ruining lives and now her own equanimity. She would see for herself if any of what Clem had told her was true. Her son, Karl, would be arriving in the morning for Kevin's funeral, and she would not burden him with false stories.

An experienced climber—like her father and mother before her—Mirna had thought to pack climbing tools and several long lengths of rope, in case the location of Clem's purported cave was higher on the cliff face than she thought. She had also brought along a bright electric torch and a down sleeping bag, since she would have to wait a full twelve hours to the next low tide before she could leave. And finally, she included her Polaroid camera. That way, if what Clem claimed was real, she would have proof to show Karl.

It was nearly dark when she reached the dingle near the Fords' that led down to the ocean. During low tide, for just twenty or thirty minutes, the water ebbed enough to reveal a narrow fringe of beach along the cliffs. Mirna hoped she had timed it right; climbing in wet boots on wet rock could be dangerous, unless she fitted on crampons and spikes, which would take more time.

Now all that was left of the day was a thin blush of mulberry—her artist's eye told her—tinting the horizon. Yet the phosphorescent wash of the waves, breaking for a good quarter mile past treacherous shallows, rocks, and sudden deep pools, guided Mirna along the cliff bottom. She paused when she believed she had reached the series of upthrust rocks that jutted out of the water, like teeth, and were repeated on the face of the cliffs of Croaghmore.

She even dug out the map from her rucksack to check. Mirna had brought along the entire packet, remembering what the policeman—McGarr—had told her of how Clem and Breege's cottage had been sacked. She would not give up Clem's secret just because she'd been careless and not until she saw for herself what it was.

Satisfied that she had reached the spot, Mirna replaced the

map, then trained the beam of the torch on her feet. Fortunately, her climbing shoes were still dry, but the cliff face was dripping wet both from waves and the dampness that was leaching from the mountain after the storms of the days before.

But she was a careful climber who had all night. She would anchor a rope at the mouth of the cave, wherever it was. It would make the descent quick and easy and leave the cliff face unmarred.

With the rucksack again on her shoulders, Mirna started up slowly, having to feel her way. It would have been so much easier, of course, in the daylight. But she wished to honor what Clem had asked of her, and the cliffs hereabouts often had divers off them, fishing boats, and lobstermen tending their traps.

Bernie McKeon did not know what had happened to the woman and could only assume that she had been lost. The only place she could have gone was the cliff face, and surely the pounding sea would have swept her away.

Bucking the wind, which was as fierce as any he had ever felt, McKeon had followed her to the cut in the cliffs near the Ford place, only to see her in the last bit of light that was left at a bend maybe two hundred yards ahead of him. And rounded it, she did. He saw her.

But when he got there himself, not only was he slogging through a foot of wave wash, utter darkness had also descended, and he could scarcely see his hand in front of his face.

Worried now—about her, about getting back himself—McKeon called out, "Hello! Hello there! Miss Gottschalk! Hello!" But the roar of wind and wave, boiling across a long low tide terrace and through cuts and rocks, made his voice sound pitiful in comparison.

Frightened for himself, he turned and waded through the now knee-deep frigid water. He only just made the cut at the Ford place—the binoculars raised above the chest-high water in one hand, his automatic in the other.

*   *   *

Perhaps three hundred feet up the cliff face, Mirna came upon a curious geological structure where, it appeared, a shard of some dense metamorphic rock had become wedged against the cliff face. Taking out her pocket torch, she discovered it was yet another of the "teeth" that were situated both lower on the cliff and out into the water. Behind it she could see a cavity where a wide band of limestone had been eroded, either by some stream or by waves before that part of Croaghmore had been thrust up.

A cave had been created, she could see, but one that was not visible from below because of the metamorphic shard. In fact, there was only a narrow notch through which a person could fit. But the moment Mirna squeezed through and found herself on the other side, she knew it was the cave that Clem had meant.

First, it was wide, high, and deep. When Mirna pointed the halogen torch with a full sixty thousand candlepower and new batteries at the entrance gallery, her beam was stopped dead by the deep, dustless darkness about forty feet away. The cave was dry and still. The floor was covered by fine washed beach sand that undoubtedly had been trapped there for however long it had taken the cave to be lifted from the surface of the sea. Thousands of years, perhaps even millions.

Yet there were footprints. Because of the protecting veil of rock, it was utterly still within the cave, and the footprints in the sand of the last persons to step there were still as complete as the day they were made. And most could only have been made by Clem Ford. Who else had feet that big? Here and there were some others of either a small man or a large woman.

Breege? No—she was a fine-boned woman with narrow feet. And because of her blindness, she undoubtedly would have never been there.

The answer to who it had been was printed on the wall about twenty feet in. What looked like an animal—an elk or a deer stylized in the manner of the ancient Celts—had been chipped into a flat surface. Near it somebody else had written in Irish, in faded reddish-colored paint, "*Gearoidi Vairnh.*" It meant "Gerard's Cave." Clare Island, however, had not been a stronghold of the Irish language, and even at the turn of the present century there had been few Irish speakers, which rather dated the graffiti.

Finally, large white letters announced,

> "2 SEPT, 1916
> TOUCH NOTHING OR YOU'LL HAVE
> PEIG O'MALLEY TO DEAL WITH
> UP THE REPUBLIC!"

Tucked into the wall were stacks of empty, wooden rifle crates stenciled "Springfield Armory, Springfield, Mass." Guns from America. Peig must have hidden them here after the ill-fated Easter Rising at the Dublin GPO when the British scoured the country for caches of arms.

Mirna thought she should go on, having come this far. But she was exhausted from all her worrying and the long dark climb. Also, the torch seemed to grow dimmer and dimmer, the farther she got away from the mouth of the cave. And finally she came to an aven that plunged sharply to what could only be some other, deeper gallery.

Lining the shaft was a wide and smooth, wooden skid— built from the wood of other gun cases—that was scarred, as though having been used to lower some things that were heavy below. A large winch with a great bale of cable wrapped around its drum and powered by a donkey engine stood before it.

Mirna decided to sleep the night, before carrying on farther. Maybe the twinge of fear that was tracking up her spine would have left her by then. One thing she knew without ever having to see what was down there—what Clem had told her was true, and probably all of it.

CHAPTER 18

PETER McGARR WAS waiting in the wing chair in Mirna Gottschalk's sitting room when she arrived home at 8:11 the next morning.

The sun had come up at 4:22, but McGarr had been in the house since around midnight, after receiving a phone call from McKeon. There was no nook or cranny in any of Gottschalk's four buildings that McGarr had not searched. But he had found nothing related to the Fords, beyond their telephone number written on the inside kitchen cabinet near the phone.

"Well, Chief Superintendent McGarr—aren't you the true *guard* in every sense. A woman steps away for a night, and there you are, securing her portals."

"Which were open."

"As they always are."

"Even now during tourist season?"

"What tourists would I get out here? Only the odd lost soul."

McGarr cocked his head, as though to say, My thought exactly. "I also came to return your Rover. It was in the way, still sitting in front of the hotel with all the O'Malleys arriving."

Pulling her rucksack off her shoulders, Mirna let it down

onto the flagstones beside her in the hall. There was color in her cheeks, and her dark eyes were bright and clear. McGarr could see no sign of what McKeon had reported as her probable fate. Her clothes were dry, and she even looked rested.

"Sure, my parents and I spent most of our lives without owning a motorcar. Even now it sits idle in the shed until some one of my employees needs to get home. But as luck would have it, I have to collect my son at the ferry and take him to the funeral." She pulled off her jacket, and a clump of fine beach sand sprayed over the flagstones.

"Could I catch a lift there myself?"

"*Mais oui*. A lift is in order. I like the sound of that, don't you?"

"Lift?"

"Lift. I feel so rejuvenated after my hike."

McGarr studied her. "May I ask where you've been?"

"Oh, of course, you may. You may ask anything you wish." But she only cocked her head and eyed him; she was a different woman from the one he had met two days earlier. She was insouciant, playful, and even—was it?—cocky.

"May I take a look at what you have in the sack?"

"Better, I'll show you." She pulled open the straps and dumped the contents. "And tick it off—crampons, spikes, chocks, nuts, pitons, carabiners, climbing harness, climbing ropes, swami belt, down bag, halogen light, camera. A large part of Croaghmore is an ISO. I enjoy photographing wildlife." The last phrase was said with a smile. "Dawn is the best time."

But the camera was a Polaroid, meant for portraits and close-ups. McGarr wondered what class of wildlife she would be photographing with that.

"Now then, Chief Superintendent, I must shower and change. If you continue to need me for any reason, just follow the sound of water."

And what was that—a proposition?

Beyond picking up the camera, Mirna Gottschalk did not move. Instead, she stared at him quizzically, as though waiting.

Which left McGarr in no doubt. He only held her gaze. She had made her choices in life, he his.

*   *   *

In the shower, Mirna wondered how much the policeman could know. Surely not the totality of what Clem Ford had left. Had she not snapped some photographs to show Karl, she would scarcely credit it herself. And then there was Dublin.

Mirna was elated. What she could do for Mayo, for Ireland, for the arts! When the ice-cold water in the shower, plumbed from deep in the cliff courtesy of the Clare Island Trust, struck her face, it shocked her, but she felt renewed and suddenly powerful.

She flexed her muscles and wished the policeman had decided to give her a tumble. She needed sex, a man . . . *something*. It was just mind-boggling that Clem and Breege had sat on such worth for so long without ever using it. There was a lesson in that, and Mirna understood why she, of all people, should have been chosen by Clem.

They were the same. Worldly goods, things, possessions meant little to her, witness the fact that only a short while past she had been standing in the midst of incomparable wealth, and it had never dawned on her to take a thing. Like Clem and Breege, she had no personal need for wealth other than what she already possessed. She only hoped Karl would see it that way too. But, of course, he would, being her son.

Karl Gottschalk was a tall, dark, young man who was thin almost to the point of gauntness. With wide shoulders—made larger by the padding of a dark, square-cut suit—he appeared to lope when he walked. His eyes were deep-set and dark, like his mother's.

When he was introduced to McGarr by his mother, his smile was quick, his gaze steady. "This *is* a pleasure," he said in the designedly neutral voice that could be anything—British, Canadian, American, Australian even—that McGarr placed as the lingua franca of preferment. Karl Gottschalk knew how people of privilege spoke.

"I've always wanted to meet the man beneath the bowler. My friends will be envious. I'm sure they'll make me 'play' McGarr. I hope you don't mind if I observe you closely."

"The bowler?" McGarr asked with mild dismay. "Sure I wear that only during photo ops."

Which elicited a vulpine smile and an unhurried look of assessment from Gottschalk. Taking the wheel, he said he was an architect practicing in Dublin now five years.

"With a firm?"

"Someday, maybe. Right now, I'm on me own."

And struggling, McGarr could hear from his tone.

"It's difficult to get started if you don't fancy building shopping centers or housing estates," his mother put in.

"Or bloody Georgian restorations, or neo-Georgian . . . *anythings*. I swear there's not a person in all of Dublin who doesn't have graven on his subconscious mind the ideal of the fanlight, cornices of white stone, and tall arched windows, even if he claims he doesn't.

"I show a client my drawing, and I can tell from his reaction there's something wrong. I take something away here, add something there. Still wrong. Throw in a Georgian window—it doesn't matter where; on the bloody roof even—'Ah there, young sir, you're getting the hang of it now.' "

McGarr and Mirna laughed.

Karl Gottschalk was a pleasant sort—Trinity grad and then on to Italy and London. He had worked in England for a while, but, like so many other émigrés, he had always planned to settle in Ireland, and he had returned at the first opportunity. "But it's been dribs and drabs, so far, I'll admit."

Presently he was living in Herbert Park, a decidedly staid and pricey section of Dublin. "Five of us from Trinity—house sharing," which was the practice for young people who found themselves with mortgages they could not afford.

"Your place?" McGarr asked.

"Oh Lord no. A friend is trying to own it. And he's got the proper license."

"And which would that be?"

"The license to steal, legally. He's a barrister."

Again Mirna Gottschalk laughed; as it turned out, for the last time that morning.

There were two churches, a burial ground, and a holy well at the abbey. Or, rather, a white stucco church that looked to have been built fairly recently and the fifteenth-century abbey where Grania Uiale was said to be interred. Presently the frescoes of the old, graceful stone structure were being restored, and it bristled with rusting iron scaffolding.

"A Board of Works project," Karl said. "Handled right, it could become a career for at least several people."

A Cistercian abbey had been on the site since the twelfth century, Mirna Gottschalk informed McGarr. "Actually, some think the holy well was a Druidic worshipping place before Christianity established itself here. There's a standing stone in the graveyard that might mark a Bronze Age burial site."

"The Bronze Age," McGarr mused, "just when was that? After Copper and before Brass?"

"The Bronze Age around here was about two thousand B.C. But the 1989 study of the island turned up a Stone Age passage grave that's been conservatively estimated to be at least fifty-five hundred years old."

"And to think we're still waiting for the Gold." McGarr opened the door and stepped out.

The laneway in front of the newer church was packed with a motley assortment of "island" vehicles, and the new Rover rather amplified the Gottschalks' difference from other Clare Islanders—Mirna, the entrepreneur who put the others to work; Karl, the professional who had been forced to emigrate only as far as Dublin from which he could return easily, as now, when needed. She was divorced, a blow-in, a Jew.

And she looked all of the part: dark, *tanned*, wearing some simple black summer dress that was at once decorous and fetching. With her white hair brushed out and the knobs of her shoulders exposed, she collected the eyes of many of the people there. A woman sitting near the rail beckoned, and Karl and Mirna took the places that had been saved. Born-and-raised Clare Islanders, they were not without friends, *seo-inini* that they were. McGarr himself took a seat among the police presence. There were guards from Galway where Kevin O'Grady had put in ten years, Wicklow Town where he had also served, and from Phoenix Park which was Garda Siochana headquarters in Dublin.

"Which one is O'Grady's father?" McGarr asked Tom

Rice in a whisper. "What's his first name again?"

"Fergal. He's the one in the *brat* with the *sugan* belt," Rice muttered in patent disdain. "And the mane in need of shearing."

By *brat* he meant the long Celtic-style cloak with a ruffled collar that O'Grady was wearing; the *sugan* belt around his waist resembled a link of braided beige rope but was probably straw or dried heather. Together the costume was a bit much but obviously designedly so; nobody looked like that without wanting to.

"There's them that claims he's a *senachie*," Rice went on. "He's got a regular following here on the island." The word meant wise man or soothsayer.

Like Paul O'Malley's mother, McGarr remembered, with her saying O'Grady had predicted trouble would come because of the presence of "strangers" like the Gottschalks and Clem Ford.

"But there's others that say he's a shite-hawking, poor-mouth hoor with a good word for nobody but himself and his toadies."

"And what do you say?"

Rice cocked his head. "This might sound hard, given the situation, but if he's a *senachie*, then he's a *senachie* with an 'attitude'—as is said. He never deserved a son like Kevin. What you see there is just how he *looks*. Worse is his carry-on and blather. The antics of the man are beyond belief."

In the churchyard, McGarr found himself standing beside the ancient Bronze Age burial stone that Mirna Gottschalk had spoken of earlier. It was at least twice McGarr's height and had a Latin cross engraved on its surface, probably cut by some early Christian attempting to consecrate the Druidic worshipping place.

In that way it was little different from the land where EU sheep now grazed on the corrugations of former potato beds, some of which had been cut through *fulachta fiadh*—ancient cooking sites, McGarr had been told by his wife.

As the priest droned on, McGarr thought of the waves of people who had invaded Ireland with its good harbors and deep rivers, immigrants after a fashion. The first were from Brittany or Spain or perhaps even the Tagus area of Portugal, it was thought. Then came the Celts, the Danes, the Normans, the British, the Spanish, the British, and now individuals from who knew where who had money and could tolerate island life. Or who had discovered a way of providing themselves with an income. Like Mirna Gottschalk and Clem Ford.

Somehow, Ford had a personal source of wealth that was beyond the scope of other Clare Islanders. Witness his wife's magnificent diamond-and-sapphire ring. And whatever it was that the raiders had searched for and not found.

True, McGarr had not known Kevin O'Grady, former guard and father of seven. But it was strange and sad how, after a lengthy career in the guards that had probably exposed him to his share of danger, lethal violence had found him out in his retirement in this remote place.

The general prayer had begun, and McGarr joined the assembled mourners in the communal chant. The priest then said that there was no doubt life was linked through death to an afterlife. McGarr looked away. He supposed something had to be said to give the family hope, but the certitude of the pronouncement rang hollow.

After the ceremony, McGarr found himself chatting with some other guards he did not know. But two of them knew somebody who knew him vaguely and had said to say hello, so they gabbed about him. It was a closer conjunction than McGarr had experienced at some other police burials. Either the country was too large; or there was too much crime, too many police, and too many police burials.

When he looked around, he discovered that O'Grady's father had left. He was not among the family, nor in the church, nor on any of the roads McGarr could see from there. Using another police Land Rover that Rice had succeeded in ferrying over from the mainland, he checked the shop of the Clare Island Co-op—a small grocery store that was nearby—and then the pub in the harbor and the bar at the hotel. No Fergal O'Grady.

Finally, after a quick inquiry for directions, McGarr drove out to O'Grady's house. It was an old-style Irish cottage, built perpendicular to a hill with two small windows to either side of the door. The roof, which was in good thatch, was held down by a netting of rope that looked handmade; the corners

were staked to the ground. There was no car; in fact, there
were no wires leading into the buildings.

McGarr knocked but got no reply. When he tried the door,
it was open. Inside, there was a strong smell of paraffin, and
a ship's lantern hanging over the central table was lit by wick.
McGarr shouted, only the wind replied.

Walking past the house, however, he caught sight of a figure about a half mile off on the heath, footing turf—O'Grady
himself, McGarr could see as he got closer. Standing with his
back to the wind so that his wild mane was shielding his face,
the old man was punching a slane down through the moist
peat, the bright blade coming away with a dark divot with
every thrust.

O'Grady had doffed the *brat,* which now lay carefully
folded across the yoke of the panniers that draped his donkey's back. A black-and-white sheep dog met McGarr halfway and barked at his heels for the better part of a quarter
mile.

Working in a loose tunic that looked handmade, O'Grady
was also wearing woolen trousers of a coarseness that resembled cottage weave. Probably all of eighty, he was nevertheless hale, his thin muscles gnarled and strong.

"I wonder if I might have a word with you," McGarr said
over the dog's continuing harangue.

O'Grady did not look up. *"Ná bí ag cainnt Bearla."*

"I'm afraid we'll have to speak English. My Irish isn't up
to it."

"I don't have to speak nothin' to the likes of you." Raising
the slane, O'Grady shook the sharp right-angled blade at
McGarr.

"And what likes is that?"

"The likes of them that murdered my son, is what likes.
The likes of foreigners and scuts, like you. Yeh've ruined this
country, this island, and now my son who served his time
and then did everything in his power to get clear of you.
Frauds and gobshites, all of yiz. Mots, bowsies, and gurriers."

McGarr had heard that before—from Colm Canning on the
"water taxi." "Ruined this country how?" The point was to
keep him talking; maybe he might have some idea of who
the raiders were, *senachie* that people claimed him.

"By taking the king's shilling is how." It was an old phrase alluding to a traitorous act. "The Europeans paid you hoors twenty billion pounds since 1973, and what did they want in return? Not just our bodies in Brussels. *No*—they knew they could get that. This time they wanted our *souls* too! It was you that sold them." He shook the slane again, his old eyes wide in anger, his mane flaring.

"And you Dublin swine, you were first into the trough—snouts, jowls, trotters, and all—with one GUBU outrage after another." It was an acronym that had been coined in the press to describe ever-unfolding government scandals and stood for *G*rotesque, *U*nbelievable, *B*izarre, *U*nprecedented. "Shoddy housing estates, poor roads, payoffs, kickbacks, nepotism, and plain old theft.

"The slops that splashed out? Why, they fell to us gruntlings. With twenty billion in play, why, even the fools in the West could get some. Grants for houses, lights, toilets, piped poor water, the bloody telephone, farm this way, fish that way, even put your rubbish out their way. And with every sort of backhander along the way for government men like you." O'Grady stuck out a hand behind his back as though to accept bribe money.

McGarr dug a smoke from his pocket. He had heard the twenty-billion figure before; in fact, he knew people—his wife's father, for one—who had made a great deal of money since 1973 because of his associations with politicians and his knowledge of the workings of government. But he had never been accused of any misdeed, nor had any of his friends. Also, since 1973 life had got better for almost everybody in Ireland, at least on a material level. But it was that which seemed to bother the old man most.

"What else did we get?" Now O'Grady was pointing a finger at McGarr. It was shaking noticeably, he was so exercised, and McGarr wondered if the man was entirely right. Maybe his son's death had put him over the top. "Illegitimacy—one in five born in Ireland today is a bastard."

McGarr managed to light the cigarette. Apart from the term, it was nothing new in a country where, formerly, all means of contraception had been illegal. Over the years more than a few Irish women had gone to England for abortions or to give up a child for adoption. The difference was—now unwed Irish women were keeping their children, the stigma having eased in many circles. Thankfully.

"Ireland has the youngest population in all of Europe. More than half are under twenty-five, and no jobs for them. No sir. They're the children of Lir!"

Who were changed into swans by a jealous stepmother and made to wander the earth for centuries, McGarr seemed to remember. He blew out the smoke that bolted past the old man. Again McGarr wished he was out in a boat with his favorite gillie, dropping flies through the clear water to the salmon that were entering Loch Eske.

Now O'Grady climbed out of the bog, slane still in hand. "Now we even have divorce, and why shouldn't we. We're practiced at it. We've been divorcing our children for two bloody centuries as a matter of *policy*! But not *your* child, buck!" O'Grady darted the slane in McGarr's direction. "Not now that you've banked the twenty billion that would have kept ours at home. No, you'll send yours to Trinity on government grants."

Please, God, thought McGarr.

"Then she'll waltz right into the art shop on Dawson Street and have her weekends in Dunlavin reported in the press."

O'Grady took another step toward McGarr, who wondered where he had come up with that. But people talked, and it was all public information.

"See this?" Now the old man had the slane only inches from McGarr's face. "I'm probably the only cottier on this island who still cuts turf for heat or grows potatoes for sustenance or raises sheep for his food and clothing."

You're a piece of work, all right, thought McGarr. I'll give you that.

"Now it's all coal from Poland or spuds from bloody Cyprus! And alcoholism, drug addiction, child battering, divorce, and abortion advocates. Kids on the telly making fun of everything from the Irish language, which they, like you, canna speak, read, or write, to taking off their parents and teachers! Taking off Republicanism! Taking off religion and God!"

McGarr raised a hand and pushed the blade away from his

face. "I came here to ask you if you know who killed your son."

"And *you* just heard it." With the tool O'Grady riffled the air above McGarr's head.

Not knowing how much more he could take or should, McGarr turned and began making his way back toward the house.

But he had only moved a few steps before O'Grady shouted, "The voice that Paul O'Malley taped was speaking Afrikaans. It was just a discussion of course bearing and the gap that should be kept between the two boats, the schooner and the dark sportfisher that was lacking numbers. 'Northwest' it said. 'Bearing three hundred and twenty-two degrees.' The man's voice was elderly, and he advised the other boat not to break radio silence again until they reached their destination, which was not discussed. He—the elder—signed off by using the word 'Helmet.'

"The second voice, who spoke nothing beyond calling for the *Mah Jong* and asking for the bearing, speed, and delay, was that of a pubescent boy or a young woman, I'm thinking."

"How do you know all this?"

"Don't I be known as a *senachie*." It was not a question and was said with perfect surety.

"You speak Afrikaans?"

"Monck of Monck and Neary represented Paul O'Malley in his action against Aran Energy. Paul was put onto them by Clem Ford, who had them on retainer through the Clare Island Trust. Monck settled for three million pounds. Ford thought it too little and paid Monck's fee and all Paul's medical expenses."

"And built the house."

O'Grady nodded.

"And bought him the automated wheelchair, the robotics scope, the transceiver, and scanner."

"The works."

"Why?"

"Why not?"

"Clem Ford is rich."

O'Grady looked away and forked his fingers through his

hair. "I wouldn't say he is, which is the one thing I admire him for. He has great inhuman restraint."

And you inordinate pride, thought McGarr. "So, the Clare Island Trust is well funded and Ford controls it through Monck and Neary?"

"I know nothing about the Clare Island Trust, apart from the fact it's brought grave trouble down upon us, as I said it would from the very beginning. Which is this."

"I've called into most of the houses on the island. Why did nobody else tell me of the Clare Island Trust?"

"Because it's their fiddle too, and they're afraid you'll ruin it for them. Me, I couldn't care less. I wouldn't take a farthing from that scut."

McGarr waited, before asking, "Anything else?"

O'Grady shrugged, as though considering. Finally, he said, "I only hope you're different from the others of your kind and know your job. And you should get some help. Packy O'Malley is a Republican, tried and true. He won't let what happened to Kevin and Breege Ford go unpunished. He's got Clem with him and maybe some others, and he'll be back."

"Back where? Here?"

O'Grady nodded.

"Why here?"

O'Grady turned and moved away toward the bog.

Back at the desk of the hotel, McGarr asked for his messages and confirmed what Fergal O'Grady said about the language on the tape being Afrikaans. A Tech Squad report said the second voice was definitely that of a woman. She had called herself Hester or Ester when signing on. The Naval Service had dispatched a long-range reconnaissance aircraft to search the area along a line of the compass bearing, but McGarr expected little from the effort. Too much time—nearly three days now—had elapsed.

The registration number on the Royal Navy Webley automatic placed it last in the possession of one Lieutenant Owen Hoarsely whose gunboat never returned from patrol off the coast of Scotland at the beginning of the war.

And finally there was a note from Tom Rice to the effect that while chatting in the pub over jars after the funeral, he was told that Clem Ford was said to have controlled a charitable and philanthropic institution called the Clare Island Trust, "that has done wonders for the island and Mayo."

McGarr signaled to the desk clerk. "When a message comes in for me, how is it dealt with?"

"It's put right into the box for your room." She stood and showed him a cabinet of numbered pigeonholes.

"Do you read them?"

"No, sir. I was told when I started—all that is private, strictly so, and none of my affair. Don't so much as look at it. If I did, I'd be sacked."

"And you never leave the desk."

"Oh, of course I do. I fill in for the barman on his break. Or when it's slow I find something else to keep me busy, like."

So much for Fergal O'Grady, *senachie*.

Two hours later, McGarr was standing in the hallway of the Ford cottage with his wife, Noreen, by his side. Over Maddie's complaints they had left her in the Garda Land Rover out in the drive.

The flies that had been attracted by the surfeit of blood had already produced maggots. The hall floor was teeming with them, and the reek was nearly enough to make McGarr retch. Noreen remained in the cubby, a handkerchief covering her nose and mouth.

McGarr punched down the playback button of the voice message on the answering machine, and after a pause Clem Ford's deep voice came on, saying, "You have reached the home of Breege and Clement Ford. We are unable to . . ."

"Hear it again?"

"Don't have to. From the precise way he suspirates his consonants, to say nothing of his lazy nasalized vowels and dropped Rs, it's Ox-bridge. Or something like it. A good public school—Harrow, Eton, one of those. Also, I don't think he's a native speaker. Did you hear that 'message' of his?"

McGarr had not, so they heard it again.

". . . if you would kindly leave a meszage—"

"Notice the gutteralization of that final *S*. And also in the way he says 'please.' "

They heard that too, which sounded slightly like, "Pleasze wait for the. . . ."

"Doesn't it remind you a little of Henry Kissinger or—I don't know—Boris Becker? Finally the giveaway is the way he pronounces his own name. It's like he's saying, 'Khlemt.' In phonetics, that's the non-English velar fricative sound. Native English speakers don't say it and often can't without practice.

"And another thing—on the other tape, the one of the Afrikaans speaking boat to boat?" Although neither Noreen nor McGarr spoke that language, they had listened to it several times over on the drive out from the hotel. "Couldn't the 'Helmet' that the man calls himself be 'Helmut,' to keep everything tribal and within the range of gutteralized languages."

Back out in the Rover, they listened to it yet again, and she was right. It now sounded more like Helmut which seemed to make more sense.

All the advantages of a university degree, McGarr thought. But then, of course, by marriage he had acquired three of them without having to carry around a burden like "velar fricatives" in his head. He had all he could to remember the details from his backlog of open cases.

Before retiring to their room in the hotel, McGarr rang up his Dublin office and asked the desk sergeant to put in a request to Scotland Yard for a search of any and all possible Oxford, Cambridge, and British public school graduates by the names of Clem or Clement Ford.

"And as long as they're about the check, let's add the name of Angus Rehm," since it was the only other name they had. And on a whim, McGarr now said, "And Helmut Rehm." Noreen had mentioned keeping everything "perfectly tribal," and, whereas, Angus was an identifiably Scots name, Rehm was something else entirely—German or Dutch or perhaps even Afrikaner.

Some one of their inquiries was bound to turn up some information at least on Clem Ford. The recording apparatus of modern society was too pervasive and complete for anybody, even an old man in the West of Ireland, to get lost. After all, Ford hadn't just sailed up Clew Bay in a bubble;

there had to be facts on file about him someplace.

"What about Ward and Bresnahan?" He wanted them there by the morning, when Rice said the O'Malleys would begin coming over for their "rally."

"As far as I know, they're on their way here now, Chief."

"Any word on the diamond ring?"

"Other than its authenticity and value, nothing. Yet."

McGarr then spent the better part of an hour going over the progress of the other open murder investigations and the preliminary details of a death in Cork that local guards thought suspicious.

After ringing off, he phoned his contact in the Naval Service about the search for the schooner and sportfishing boat.

"Nothing unusual—the Spanish tuna fleet is beginning to assemble in the Stream, three larger sailing craft, no schooners. There's a Norwegian trawler and two draggers working a bit farther north off Donegal, and a fair few of our own boats plying coastal waters."

CHAPTER 19

MIRNA GOTTSCHALK WAITED until after dinner to tell her son about Clem Ford's visit, the packet, and the cave. For good reason.

With the tide coming in, Karl would not be able to thrash off into the night and find the cave. Though an experienced climber, he would at least have to sleep on it, prudence dictating that he wait at least until morning or the evening of the coming day.

Better still, he might be satisfied with the photos Mirna had taken. She showed them to him in the studio. Breege's portrait was still on the easel.

"It's a complete cave in every sense with four galleries that I know of and what looks like an aven leading up into the mountain."

"In addition to the cave entrance, the one you went in?" Karl was intrigued.

"Yes, I could feel a draft there, but my light only carried thirty or forty feet."

"Meaning there could be a second entrance somewhere up on the mountain?"

"It would seem so, but where? I thought I knew every inch of that mountain."

Karl nodded, being well acquainted with Croaghmore himself.

"Which brings me to what I discovered inside. Do you know that immense ring that Breege always wears?" Mirna pointed to the painting. "I always thought it couldn't possibly be real."

Karl nodded. "Because of its size."

Standing beside the chair he had taken at the long drawing table, Mirna placed a Polaroid snapshot in front of him. "Here are the pieces that go with it—the earrings, the necklace, the brooch. The central stone in the necklace is the single largest diamond I have ever seen."

Mirna waited while Karl studied the photograph and the eleven others that she had taken of the . . . treasure, it could only be. She had shot one Polaroid roll.

"My God, Mother. This stuff is magnificent. How do you know it's real?" His dark eyes flashed up at her, but he knew it was. "Where could Clem have come by it? Was he a pirate with all his bother about the boats that put into the harbor?"

Mirna glanced at Clem's packet on the other side of the table; she had not again opened the pouch with the memoir or explanation or apologia or whatever it was, not wishing to learn anything worse about Clem. His reputation was already being destroyed now by Fergal O'Grady and his toadies on the island. Also, Mirna's head was still filled with the possibilities for doing good. And finally she suspected that Clem, by asking her to wait before reading the memoir, had wanted them to suspend judgment of him until they heard whatever the solicitors at Monck & Neary in Dublin would tell them.

Karl shuffled through the other photos: one British Navy ammunition box after ammunition box filled with heaps of gold jewelry encrusted mostly with diamonds, but with rubies, emeralds, sapphires, topazes, and tourmalines looking like bright ribbons of golden Christmas candy. There was also a variety of metal-working equipment: cylinders of gas, torches, crucibles, ladles, and molds for creating ingots that were still lined with gold droplets and gold dust.

"What are those things heaped in that corner?" Karl asked, pointing to a pile of strange cone-shaped objects with propellers.

"I have no idea. There are ten of them, but I was so over-come by everything else, I didn't pay them much mind."

"And Clem said this was the *lesser* part? What you could *do* with this! I mean, in a positive way."

Mirna squeezed Karl's shoulder, who was surely her son right down to the way he thought.

His eyes darted at the packet on the other side of the table. "Is that Clem's? Is that what he gave you? What's in it?" His hand darted out. Mirna tried to stop him, but the flap of the packet popped open and the contents spilled onto the ta-ble. They both stared down at the two pieces of paper and the pouch with the red wax seal that was broken.

"I think we should respect what Clem asked of us."

Karl glanced at the two sheets with the names and the map, then picked up the pouch. "But, look—it's been opened. Did you open it?"

Mirna nodded. "After I heard what had happened at the Fords', I thought I should know more about it. But I didn't read much."

"Oh please, Mother. I *know* you."

"Well I didn't, I read only a page."

"And you *stopped*? Why?"

"Because I decided it was wrong. As I said, I decided that we should honor what Clem asked of me."

"That wasn't the reason."

Mirna sighed and looked away. She supposed that, in her heart of hearts, she had been thinking that here lay a glorious future for Karl. Without taking so much as a *sou* from the cave or the Trust, he would wield power and influence in matters architectural, social, educational, and moral even.

Life was short; Mirna had blinked, and here she was a middle-aged woman with a small business on a small island in a small country on the edge of Europe. In her youth, she had wanted so much else for herself—fame in the arts, no-toriety, the haut monde of talent and achievement in some place like London or Paris—but now what she had was about as much as she could expect. In that way.

"But since you did open it, where's the harm?" Karl's finger slid under the flap, but he waited for Mirna's permis-sion.

"No—if we can agree that Clem knew what he was doing all these years, then we should follow his instructions to the letter."

"But that's a specious argument. He obviously didn't know everything that he should, since the whole thing came acropper when he was elderly and least able to defend himself. It ended in disaster. A debacle.

"Also, from what you've told me and how Clem acted about the boats and all, I should think it had something to do with the origin of all this stuff."

As did Mirna; it was the reason she had not read on, the reason she had closed the pouch up. She was just not being brave, and suddenly she remembered what the policeman had said to her about whoever it was—Angus Rehm—coming back on her. *He* had obviously killed Kevin and done whatever he had to three other Clare Islanders whom she had known all of her life.

Mirna sighed; she was about to violate a trust. It did not come easy, but at the same time she had Karl and herself to think of. "I think it's wrong, considering what Clem asked of me—"

"But what he asked of you might well have been wrong in itself," Karl quickly interjected. "Think, for a moment, what happened to them. Also, Clem told you they were coming for this, which we can well imagine.

"Shall I?" With his other hand, Karl reached for the flap.

Mirna hated herself, but she nodded. "Perhaps we should."

For about an hour they read. Rapt. Engaged. Shocked. And ultimately dismayed. After Karl folded the yellowed papers and slipped them back into the pouch, he sat back in his chair.

Several long minutes elapsed before Mirna said, "This isn't the Clem Ford I've known all my life. It can't be. It's like he was two different people, and the other one—" she shook her head. There was another pause. "Well, what do we do now?"

Karl sighed. "Certainly we can't go to the authorities, given the state of leadership in Dublin."

"Or even go public," Mirna put in.

"Who knows how much of it would disappear."

"Into the wrong pockets." Mirna did not wish to sound

like Fergal O'Grady, but a good bit would surely be lost to
"the State." And doubtless there would be other "States"
before any individuals were even considered. What with the
courts and lawyers and judges, who would steal their share
legally, Mirna could imagine the entire fortune—the Trust
included—being wrapped up in litigation for years. And dis-
sipated. Ireland's legal system was as notorious as her lawyers
were clever at "making a good thing last."

"Tell you what—tomorrow night on the low tide I'll go
out to the cave and retrieve the other parts of Breege's parure.
In Dublin I'll try to determine its provenance and value. I'll
also visit Monck and Neary, utter Clem's passwords, and see
what they say.

"In the meantime, I'll make a copy of this to take back to
Dublin and see if I can learn anything more about this Angus
Rehm. Then we'll put all of it"—Karl indicated the two
sheets as well as the time-yellowed memoir—"back into the
packet and back under the keystone in the hearth where none
of the *seoinini*," he said with a smile meant to calm her, "will
think to look. And we'll pretend we never opened the blasted
box."

Which scarcely contained hope at the bottom, thought
Mirna. To her way of thinking, what she could now see in
the pictures that were scattered on the table was no longer a
cave of riches. It had become a cave of corruption, a contam-
ination that Clem Ford had tried to bury and purge by estab-
lishing the Trust. But Clem had failed. And all these years
later it had surfaced, more malignant still for the wait in a
defenseless place like Clare Island.

CHAPTER 20

WITH A CRASH and a curse Colm Canning arrived at the public dock in Killala harbor. It was a few minutes past 4:00 in the morning, and the sky to the east was just growing light.

Sixteen hours it had been since the phone call from Packy and Clem. Canning's boat—bought with a generous stipend and a no-interest loan from the Clare Island Trust—made an easy twelve knots cruising. Granted he had had to feint into Roonagh Point, then motor due west round the island before heading north. But still the ninety-mile journey could have been covered in half the time, especially in an emergency, as Canning had known all along it was. And here he was hours late.

Clem Ford—Canning could see from the size of his silhouette—snagged a scupper with a boat hook and pulled him back toward the dock. But Canning, trembling totally now that the boat had made the dock and he no longer had to force himself to stay awake, let his body slump down the companionway. In the fo'c'sle, he collapsed into a berth.

Already he could hear Packy roaring. "Where's that cunt! He skite off, or he below?"

"Easy now, Packy. There's nothing to be done about it now," Ford counseled.

"You don't think so? I'll moor-door the scut! I'll have his

173

guts for garters. He's fecking dog's piss, he is. Dog's piss! What neck! I'll put the bastard on the flat of his back, I will.''

Unless he was already there, the last of the new jar of *potín* that Canning had finished a half hour earlier made him think. Without it he would now be terrified; and without it he wouldn't be in such a spot. But Canning could not imagine himself without it. If only he could get more.

And there Packy was, filling the hatch—short, broad, almost comically square and compact which, of course, only reinforced the sublimity of his name. But enormously powerful, even now as an old man.

''You hoor!'' The boat rocked, as he forced himself down through the narrow companionway. ''D'ye' not know what happened to Kevin and Breege? Did we not make it clear? Where the *fuck* have ye' been?''

Canning had never heard Packy utter an actual—as opposed to a euphemistic—curse, and the emphasis was not lost on him. Along with the thought, why answer? He's going to beat me anyway, like the cop did in Packy's house. But the difference is, this time I want it. *What?* another part of him asked.

Too late.

''Oh, aye—I see what it is.'' By the craw Canning was plucked from the berth and shoved so high into the low cabin top that Packy could barely swing the stump of his mangled hand. But the arc was enough. Slaps, they were, back and forth, snapping Canning's head from side to side.

''Ye' bloody deceivin' bastard. How many times have I told ye'—drink will be your ruination!''

And he didn't know the half of the deception, thought Canning.

''Ye're a drunk, yeh fuck. First, last, and always, it's yehrself ye' think of, and yehr gullet. And not like some—you got your chance. You had university, all expenses paid.''

My first mistake, thought Canning. No, not a bit of it—it was Clem Ford's mistake, just because I could pass the exams. Him and his meddling Trust. Was I ever *asked* did I want to go? No. I did the subjects and passed the tests, the money was there so the parents said go. And I did, only to end up back on the island but unsuited to it because of . . . expectations.

"But you failed that."

Writers don't need degrees; in fact, degrees had hurt the ones Canning knew of—himself included—just going for it!

"Then you dragged the wife out here where you no longer belonged, and you failed her and the kids and the fishin', and now this. If we've missed those bastards because of you"— like a blow from a short flat bat, Packy knocked him clear across the cabin into the other berth—"I'll feed you to the seals, piece by piece."

Which was when Clem Ford intervened. "Packy—check the tanks. We should cast off immediately." Pronounced imeejitly. The British prick.

"As a favor to me, please."

Having bought him too, thought Canning, who was not angry with Packy. He'd only given him what he deserved; and more, if they knew the whole of it. Drunk, staggering, *hallucinating* even while still on Clare Island, he had loosened his gob to Fergal O'Grady. The *senachie* almost seemed to have been waiting for Colm there by the bog where Packy kept the guns. As Canning had told all to O'Grady, wraiths of people he had known or partially known in his life had flitted around them, shaking their heads, condemning Canning while the words spilled out.

Trembling more totally now, Canning tried to wipe away the blood that was tracking through his beard, but his hand flitted past his face. With a handkerchief, Ford reached toward him, but Canning ripped it away. "I'll do it myself *imeejitly*." It was a poor jibe, but that was the *potín* again—you had no thoughts but *potín* thoughts and no thoughts that the *potín* would not say.

Only then did Canning notice Ford's right arm in a sling.

"Have you been into the *potín* again, Colm?" Ford's voice was deep and the tone friendly, fatherly even, as he looked down on Canning with his hoary beard and white mane. He was a gigantic man, easily two of Canning. "Is that what happened to the wife and children? Were you drinking *potín*?"

Canning had begun to shake again, and he couldn't answer.

Now that he no longer had to deal with the boat, the soul
sickness—as he thought of it—had also come on. A world-
darkening gloom that made him think, if he had the strength
or the means, he'd kill himself there and then. It was the same
self-loathing that seemed to feed upon itself, making him say
and do things that caused him to hate himself all the more.
Like blabbing to O'Grady. Christ—he might just as well have
rung up the cop.

"Do you think you have a drink problem?"

Canning might have laughed, did he not feel like he was
wearing every nerve in his body on the outside of his skin.
Even the top of his head was burning. But the worst thing
was the feeling in the pit of his stomach, the hollowness,
knowing he was lost. His life was over at thirty-one. "Of
course I have a drink problem," he managed to say. "I don't
have any." It was supposed to be a joke.

Ford did not laugh. Instead he moved aft to his kit bag and
produced a large bottle. And it was not just any bottle but a
bottle of fourteen-year-old Jameson Red Breast. Like a
feckin' miracle, thought Canning.

"I.R.A. anesthetic," Ford explained. "The 'doctor' who
tended my arm said it was the only prescription he could write
that I could get filled." Ford also produced a cup from the
top of a thermos. "I could never drink whiskey straight, what
about you?"

Canning could not reply. He was seeing something like
birds or bats or bears moving through the periphery of his
vision now that his eyes were fixed on the bottle.

"What's the humorous line about Red Breast?" Ford
asked, nearly filling the cup. "Drink too much, it'll give you
an inflammation of the chest."

No, it'll give you feckin' brucellosis, Canning's brain was
screaming. Brucellosis was the punch line, you British prick.
Fifty years here and he couldn't even get that right.

"Water?"

Canning wrenched the red plastic cup out of the man's one
good hand, slopping most of it onto the berth. The whiskey
stung the gash in his mouth where Packy had hit him and
scorched down into his empty stomach. But—and here was
the sad part, Canning thought—in mere seconds it also

soothed him more completely than Mother's milk.

"Well—that's for now." Ford topped it up again. "Just to get you settled. You should sleep, if you can. After this thing is over, please God, I'll help you get your wife and children back." Placing the bottle on the floorboards between his feet, he tamped down the cork with his good hand. "I say this not because I just lost Breege, but because I'd like you to go on as you were—how Breege and I knew you when you first came back to the island full of hope and promise. And not how you now are. Maybe you could even get back to the writing?"

"How?"

"Well—first we'll get you well. Then we'll get you over to—where is it again, California? There you'll have to deal with the decision of what's best for the lot of you, remaining there or coming back here. But you'll be able to decide that all the better without this." He pointed to the bottle.

It sounded wonderful to Canning, in fact, too wonderful. He knew himself and knew it would never happen. Following his wife out to California would be just another admission of failure made all the worse by having to do it sober, repentant, and admitting he had "the failing." The *disease* of alcoholism—Canning had read the pamphlets. And alcohol was so cheap in America; he had summered there once with some American cousins, disastrously as it had turned out.

With the bottle in his hand Ford shuffled toward the companionway, having to stoop nearly in two before mounting the ladder. "I'll keep this up by the wheel. You did us the favor of coming to pick us up. We'll do that back for you. But sleep, now that you have the chance."

"Stuff California up your gansey!" Canning bawled, the malt now surging through him. "Money! I need *money,* like you promised. And whiskey! I know you have more than one!"

Packy's puffy, windburned face appeared in the companionway. "One more squeak out of you, and I'll toss your sorry arse over the rail. And that's a promise."

He knew Packy was serious, but Canning felt almost joyful that he was suddenly drunk. And out came "Ah, feck off, yeh big cheesy bollocks. See this?" From under his rain slicker, he pulled out a large-caliber automatic, just like the two others that he had brought along with the Armalite assault rifles. "Yeh come down here again, I'll put a bullet through yehr big pink puss." And he would too; it was all he could do to keep himself from pulling the trigger right then.

But the gun drooped from Canning's hand and fell onto his stomach, as his eyes closed.

PART IV

Plunder

CHAPTER 21

NOT MANY YEARS ago, a large new ferry had been brought to Clare Island by the owner of the Bayview Hotel. She was a spacious craft of about fifty feet and able to ride out the sudden, intense storms of Clew Bay. Painted red and white, she had a flat deck that could carry several vehicles or, say, a flock of sheep.

But in a blow one morning shortly after she was commissioned, her engines failed. The new boat had just left the shelter of the Clare Island breakwater, and she drifted onto a rocky beach, breaking up into two large pieces that could be seen there to this day. The owner escaped uninjured.

Now, ferrying to and from Clare Island was performed by a variety of boats large and able enough to make the sixteen-mile round trip profitably and safely. During the three-day "O'Malley Rally," every sort of craft was pressed into service, most for profit, some others for the convenience of celebrating relatives.

One such boat was curious. She was about forty feet long with a planing, sportfisher-type hull, a small enclosed fore-deck, and only a doghouse with a canvas top shielding the control console. Today with warm and sunny weather, the canvas was rolled forward, and a tall broad young woman with white-blond hair and a deep tan was at the wheel.

Deftly, she cut the largely open boat past the massive bul-
wark of the Roonagh Point breakwater that carved a small
sheltered harbor from Clew Bay. Wearing only a mango orange spandex bikini, she immediately collected the eyes of
the young male O'Malleys waiting at the harbor. They were
already deeply involved in "spotting form"—as the phrase
had it—of their felicitously distant relations of the opposite
sex.

As she spun the wheel and played one engine off against
the other, the stern of the boat swung round and the name on
the transom could be read plainly—*Grainne Uaile*. She then
cut the engines and drifted toward the wall.

Hands on the pleasant curves of her hips, she cocked her
head up at the throng that had gathered on the edge to look
down at her. "Any O'Malley *women* care for a free lift over
to *Cliara*?" It was the Irish word for Clare and meant Island
of the Clergy.

Several of the girls swapped glances, scarcely able to believe their luck. "But what do we do with our tickets? They
cost sixteen quid return."

"Flog them to some of the others. I'll wait. I can take
twenty of yiz tops," she said in the pancake accent of a Dubliner. "And 'specially any women with a yen to do some
divin'." She swept a hand at the suits, flippers, tanks of air,
and diving buoys that lay in the stern of the boat.

Some one of the men muttered, "At which she's a champ,
I'd hazzard." The male laughter was quick, deep, but diffi-
dent. And not one of them challenged her until an older man
stepped out of the crowd with a towel draped over his head,
like a shawl. He was visibly drunk, and had something bulky
stuffed under his jumper to simulate breasts.

"Hold on, luveen," he said in a high falsetto voice. "Don't
shove off without me. I'm just the diver for you." Scuttling
down the concrete stairs, he threw his kit on board, but the
woman threw it back.

He then attempted to climb on board, but she easily pushed
him away with a smile, saying, "Funny—I don't quite believe you're for real." She even squeezed his "breasts,"
which brought shouts from the men.

Finally, he attempted to jump on board, but she caught

most of him, which she deposited gently over the rail and back onto the stairs. "I'd ask if you've had enough, but it's plain from the smell of you you have."

"Fair play to her," said one of the other O'Malley lads. "She could have dropped him in the drink."

"I've had me tumble with Grainne. Now I can die happy."

"And should have too, yah sot," said another woman. "Great girl yah are!" And she gave the young woman a thumbs-up.

"I'll buy ye' a pint on the island," the man went on, picking himself up and pulling the towel from his head. "McCabe's Bar. It's right there in the harbor."

"You will not." The young woman was helping her passengers aboard the lurching boat. "You'll buy me a gallon or nothing," which got laughs.

"Only if you promise to be gentle." Which got more.

Crossing from Roonagh Point to Clare Island harbor in a converted fishing boat takes about twenty-five minutes under the best of conditions. And at least another ten when burdened with as many passengers as can safely be carried.

Noreen McGarr with Maddie by her side watched the faster *Grainne Uaile* power past the corner of the breakwater and plane off across the bright turquoise water toward Clare Island. She only hoped that Ruth Bresnahan and Hugh Ward, who had arrived on a Garda launch during the night, were there to greet the boatload of young women when they arrived.

Noreen's responsibility was the several "ferries" that were plying the bay on this, the first day of the O'Malley Rally. Her husband had so arranged the scheduling of the boats that there would be only one going and coming each hour. It would mean that a number of the O'Malleys might have to wait a while on the mainland, but at least some of the boat traffic over to the island would be monitored.

McGarr had taken himself up to the south slope of Croaghmore, where he could keep an eye on two of the other possible launching sites. They were in and near Portnakilly. The fourth site near the northeastern corner of the island was being watched by Paul O'Malley from his "quad's quad" on the

top of Capnagower. And finally, Bernie McKeon had a clear
view the Gottschalk buildings, the Ford cottage, and the cliffs
as far as Croaghmore. McGarr was in contact with all via
handheld VHF radios that he'd had Bresnahan and Ward
bring from Dublin the night before. Noreen kept hers in the
camera bag that was strapped over her shoulder.

"Excuse me," she now said to the person closest to her.
The ferry had left the dock at Roonagh Point for Clare Island
and she would have to work fast. "I'm from the O'Malley
Rally Committee"—she pointed to the name tag that was
pinned to her jumper—"Are you an O'Malley?"

The older man nodded and allowed his eyes to run down
Noreen's figure. Her trim and angular body was wrapped today in a red tartan body suit and a short black suede A-line
skirt. Her stockings were black, her flats were brilliant red.
With her bright copper-colored hair and turquoise eyes, she
knew she looked perfect for the part.

"Where are you from?"

"Biloxi, Mississippi, babe." And sounded it. "And you,
where you all from?" The man winked at Maddie.

"Down home." Noreen jerked a thumb at the island.
"We're attempting to put out a yearbook with the names and
photographs of every O'Malley who attends this year's rally.
We're hoping to make it free of charge because of donations
and adverts. Would you care to be in it?"

"For you, darlin'. Anything."

"What did he call you, Mammy?" Maddie asked.

Noreen ignored her. "Then let me snap your picture. You
have the rare good fortune of being number one."

"Wouldn't be satisfied any other way. What kind of camera is that?"

"It's electronic, a digital camera—no developing, no pro-
cessing, it works like a video recorder, but the images are still
and can be stored on the disk. And, of course, you can get
prints, if you have a color printer."

"My, my"—the man shook his head—"and all I ever
heard was how backward this place was."

Noreen swallowed an acid reply and wrote the man's name
and address on her clipboard, before moving to the next passenger. All the names and addresses would be sent immedi-

ately to Garda headquarters to make certain Irish persons of
those names existed and to Customs & Immigration authorities to check them against the computerized list of foreign
nationals in the country. McGarr would show the portraits to
the barman and the two patrons at McCabe's Bar who had
seen and spoken to the crewman of the *Mah Jong* the night
of the murder.

And so it went throughout the day. There were O'Malleys
from Sweden, Argentina, Uruguay, Brittany, South Africa,
Canada, Malaysia, Anguilla, Chile, Djbouti even, with a small
army from the States. But the only actual "Irish" O'Malleys
seemed to be young people who had "come to party with the
blood," said one gawky young fellow with pimples. "Incest
Is Best" was the hopeful pronouncement on the front of his
voluminous T-shirt. He was dressed in "grunge," so he told
Noreen.

"Names and faces, faces and names," said Maddie, tiring
of the duty during only their second "crossing" of the morning. "When can we go swimming?" Every time they passed
the fine sandy beach that ringed the north side of Clare Island
harbor the six-year-old peered wistfully at the other children
splashing in the sunny water. Unlike the frigid Irish Sea south
of Dublin where they usually tried to bathe, the water here—
heated by the Gulf Stream—was warm, as they knew from
their earlier visit to Clare Island.

"After lunch, kid," Noreen replied, repeating one of the
many endearments she had been called by the various and
high-spirited O'Malleys.

The best was yet to come, "Hai, chick—aye-n't yah gonna
tike my pict-yah?" asked a young man with a shaven head
and a brace of gold rings pierced through the lobe of one ear.
Wearing a muscle shirt, he had tattoos on both immense biceps, made more obvious because of the whiteness of the skin
on his upper arms—a death's head with "K2" beneath it on
the right and a Celtic cross on the left. There was a blue bat
in flight on his deeply tanned neck.

"A thousand pardons. I wanted to make sure I'd snapped
everybody else before attempting yours," Noreen replied, off
put by the appellation.

Sitting on the cap rail of the transom of the boat, he craned back his head and laughed. "Red hair. It's fire for sure. Chick is a compliment where I come from."

"And where is that?"

"Aus-tryl-ia, a' course. Where else?" He was wearing leather climbing shoes with a thick wrap of hard rubber around the leather uppers. In front of him was a rucksack with a long-handled climbing ax protruding from the flap.

"He called my mother a chicken," Maddie said to the only other person whose picture they had not taken: an elderly man with wire-rimmed spectacles who seemed uncomfortable in the presence of the—was he?—skinhead.

"What's that maike you then?" The Australian ruffled Maddie's brilliant, red curls.

"An egg?"

"Nai, you're way beyond the egg staige, luv. You're a pull-it." He gently tweaked her nose. "That's what you are— a pull-it." He reached for her again, but she scurried behind Noreen.

"I didn't get your name," Noreen said, raising the camera.

"That's because I didn't give it." Placing his hands beneath his biceps, he flexed his muscles like bodybuilders of old and tried to look stern. The neck of the muscle shirt had opened more completely to reveal a large wheel of purple bruising with a bright red center. "It's Brando O'Malley," he growled through his teeth.

Noreen lowered the camera slightly. "Brendan."

"Brando."

"You're having me on."

"With any luck at all. Me parents were big fans. They bought a projector and showed *On the Waterfront* to everybody on the ranch, the aborigines included, until there wasn't a man jack within fifty miles who couldn't recite the script from heart. It's said I got my start during the love scene." He pulsed his eyebrows. "I only hope I can avoid Brando's curse."

Noreen snapped the picture and waited.

Brando O'Malley puffed out his cheeks and extended his arms at his sides, as though pretending to be fat. "Boffo-lo-itis."

Noreen couldn't help herself he looked so comical; she started to laugh.

"Hubby around?" he added. "I'll buy you a beer."

Noreen gave him a look, as though to say now he really was overstepping himself.

"Don't let me looks fool you. I've got more degrees than a summer afternoon and a tux in me tuck." He pointed to the sack.

Noreen turned to the final man with the wire-rimmed glasses, who said, "Don't bother. I'm not an O'Malley."

"Really? And you're coming out to the island? I hope you have lodgings booked."

He nodded. "I haf' a place to stay." He was an older man who was wearing a tan windbreaker and cap to match. Gloved hands were folded on the leg of twill trousers, and the stout walking shoes on his feet were mahogany in color. Like the young Australian, there was a sack in front of him, contents bulging.

"German, are you?"

"Swiss. Schweibert's the name, Doctor Ernst Schweibert."

"And you've been to Clare before?"

"Several times. I spent the summer of 1990 here."

"As part of the study?" Noreen meant the follow-up to the study that had been conducted by the Royal Irish Academy in 1909–1911. Employing teams of scholars and naturalists, the Dublin group had examined every aspect of island life from flora to fauna to the underlying causes of emigration, which was then also a problem.

The sixty-seven reports were bound under one cover and detailed everything from small species of fungi and algae that had never before been examined in Ireland, through "the razorbills that breed up to a thousand feet on the great cliff of Clare Island" in colonies too numerous to count, to the history, archaeology, place-names, family names, Gaelic plant and animal names, and agriculture.

One of Noreen's great buys was a well-preserved copy of the massive tome for a fiver which she found at a bookstall on the Dublin quays. "I priced that yoke by the pound, and there's no hagglin', missus. I've spent half me life humpin' it in and out o' the van."

Because of the comprehensiveness of the effort, there were continual calls throughout the rest of the century for follow-up studies. By the 1980s not only had scientific knowledge advanced but also investigative methods had improved so markedly that there was some suspicion that Praeger and his cohorts might have missed something. Which proved to be the case.

"What's your field?" Noreen asked the man.

"Palynology. Actually, I'm a paleobotanist."

Now Noreen's interest was piqued. Having closely followed the reports of the symposia that were given in 1989, 1990, and 1991, she knew how successful the recent study had been. In both archaeology and paleobotany, it had been something akin to hitting a mother lode or winning the World Cup. And dramatic, since the earlier study had claimed that, whereas Achill Island to the immediate north abounded with identifiable Mesolithic structures, there was none on Clare Island.

But taking a walk one morning, an Irish archaeologist, who had decided to explore as much of the island as possible, happened upon what he thought was a Bronze Age monument, a *fulachta fiadh*. When he returned with his colleagues, the group immediately found four more.

The same archaeologist was then told by islanders of another site that "might be something." Hiking to it, their guides brought them past two more *fulachta fiadh* before pointing to a large collection of stones. The archaeologist rushed forward, unable to credit what he was seeing—a Stone Age court tomb or burial vault. It meant that people had inhabited Clare Island for at least fifty-five hundred years. Or perhaps seventy-five hundred. It was difficult to date the site precisely.

Another spectacular find occurred in paleobotany. "Were you present when that core sample was brought up?"

The elderly man nodded. "Not only was I present, but it was at my suggestion that Coxon took the sample where he did. Of course, he's never acknowledged that." The man raised his head and surveyed the island that they were fast approaching.

Coxon was Peter Coxon of Trinity College who, in taking

a core sample from a *fulachta fiadh,* came up with a complete, unopened, and glistening hazel nut. It was as fresh as the day it fell from the tree, seven thousand years ago.

Which was the kind of touch with the past that Noreen thought of as mystical. Bending to Maddie, she now said, "You know the ice I told you about?"

"The glacier that was once here?"

"That's right. After it melted, the first plants to appear in the glacial debris were grasses, docks, and meadowsweet. Then trees appeared, one of which was hazel."

"Like the nuts?" They were a favorite of Maddie, especially when wrapped in Cadbury milk chocolate.

"Within only two hundred years of its first arriving here, hazel trees covered this island, some of them growing to forty feet. Two hundred years is no time at all in the history of the earth."

Maddie gazed up at the bald eminence of Croaghmore and its green and treeless flanks. "I don't see any trees. Aren't there any left?"

Noreen turned her head to Professor Schweibert and waited; it was her test.

"After hazel, other varieties of trees appeared, until around seven thousand years ago when man began using wood for heat and shelter and perhaps even clearing some land for cultivation. The climate then was a degree or two Celsius warmer and drier than it is now, and it remained so for about two thousand years."

Curiously, the man's accent had disappeared; he sounded like an anchor on the evening news.

"But when it changed and became cooler and wetter, the soil could not replace the trees that were taken, as farming techniques improved and the population increased. Blanket bogs and iron pan appeared. Even so, in the sixteenth century, Grace O'Malley describes Clare Island as being partially wooded. In the next century, however, the British cleared Ireland of its trees for various reasons but mainly military, a wood being a place of refuge.

"Now, to answer *your* question, little one." Schweibert looked down at Maddie. "There are still some hazel trees, an oak or two, some birch willow and holly—all confined to a small area in the lee of a hill up there in Lassau.'' He pointed almost due north, as the boat now entered the harbor. ''But they're mainly dwarfed. There's too much wind and rain and too few nutrients in the soil.''

Schweibert glanced up at Noreen, his smile thin, his eyes clear and hard.

CHAPTER 22

"DID YOU MANAGE to meet that boatload of young women?" Noreen asked Ruth Bresnahan. She and Maddie had just joined McGarr and his staff at the Bayview Hotel for a working lunch.

From the windows they could survey the harbor. There Garda Superintendent Tom Rice was presently stationed to photograph and interview any celebrants arriving by private boat. McGarr had also asked the "ferry" captains to suspend operations for the noon hour.

"You mean the Amazon in the mango bikini? Moira O'Malley from Howth?"

"Yes, I don't see her boat anywhere." Not only was the harbor crowded with private boats, the picturesque lane that traced the shoreline was thronged with strolling O'Malleys in various stages of undress. The balmy weather was holding.

"She mentioned something about diving."

Said Ward from the sideboard where he was making a plate from the platters of sandwiches and salads that had just been delivered, "After she asked you—well—*out,* I guess you'd call it. What were her words again? 'Do you swim? Of course you do—you're *made* for swimming. We must plunge together. I could teach you how to *dive*.'" Bresnahan's jersey didn't help.

White, skintight, and sheer, it said "Oh!-Mmm!-Alley-Cat" across the protrusive front; on the back was "If you tickle me fancy, I'll purr in your ear." Beneath the garment could be seen a black strapless bikini. Her shorts also were sheer, exposing her well-tanned, shapely legs and much of her lower-middle anatomy. Unlike Noreen, who freckled, Ruth Bresnahan was a redhead who, with carefully measured exposures, could acquire a nonred color.

"Ah, you're just jealous she didn't ask you."

"She could tell from my lack of diving equipment"—Ward waved a hand at his chest—"I wasn't her tank of oxygen."

"Speaking of good air—how's Bernie doing up at the lighthouse?"

Noreen assumed the question was addressed to her, since her husband was in the next room showing the electronic portraits to the barman and two patrons from McCabe's. "Great, as far as I know."

"Not grousing yet?"

At the sideboard, Noreen began fixing Maddie a plate. "Peter said he was surprised there've been no complaints."

Bresnahan eyed Ward. "But wouldn't he be better placed here at the hotel?"

"Why?"

"Oh, I don't know—considering how he fancies chat and all. I'm sure he'd be on a first-name basis with half the O'Malleys in one short session."

It occurred to Noreen what was afoot, having glanced at a brochure in the Roonagh Ferry of the new guest accommodation at the lighthouse. "The Last Temptation" was surely *the* temptation to succumb to, when on Clare Island: a big bed in a turret on a four-hundred-foot cliff overlooking the wild Atlantic; Continental cuisine prepared by a master chef; long restorative walks in the brisk air with all those marvelous views of Clew Bay, Achill Island, and Grand Turk to the south. All on the Garda Siochana and so far from Dublin that no police snoop would cop on, as it were. "You could ring him up, see how he's faring."

"Splendid idea. I'm glad you thought of it. After all, four eyes are better than two." Bresnahan reached for the phone.

Unless, of course, they were locked into each other.

"Bernie! Bucko! How's every little thing up in your ivory tower?" There was a pause, and then, "What do you mean, who's calling? It's your colleague and sometime acolyte in matters of the spirit—whoever did you think it was?"

As Bresnahan paced the carpet by the phone, Noreen decided not for the first time that Ruthie was without a doubt the most beautiful, big woman that she knew. She had at once voluptuous size, shapeliness, and color. Add to that definite spirit, not just a little bit of Dublin wit, and a goodly measure of Kerry country craft, and you had a rather spectacular human being. Little wonder that she had corralled, so to say, the wandering Ward.

"Speaking of higher callings," Ruth continued, "where do you think I'm phoning from? I won't make you guess, which is cruel. Why, the bar of the Bayview Hotel." Ruth winked at Noreen. "It's a brilliant place. Great *craic* with O'Malley-this and O'Malley-that splashing out gobs of money. This round is from the cousins in New York, that one from Sydney. It's like a bidding war in an auction room with everybody on a first-name basis."

She listened for a moment. "So—the bar at the Bayview doesn't have a phone. Call it . . . poetic licensed premises. You seem a bit glum, chum. Tell me, now—has solitary assignment made you a little gah-gah? Or goo-goo? You know, the one white wall that surrounds you. Or, could one be the loneliest number that you'll ever know?"

There was no response, and Bresnahan could only assume that McKeon—Dubliner that he was—had never been forced to listen to country and western music, as everybody who switched on a radio in the West did. "Hang on, Bernie, the chief is passing the cabinet. Excuse me, Chief—as long as you're up, I'll have that other glass."

Again she listened. "What do you mean, what do I want? Do I have to want something? I was just checkin' in—one gumshoe to another—to find out if you've grown feathers yet and can fly without flappin' your wings. Know what Hughie and I have been given?"

Bresnahan waited, but there was only silence on the other end of the line. Usually McKeon would have a rapier-like comeback. "The bleedin' hotel is what, and I hate to say—since we're working and all—but it's *party time*."

Still she waited. Finally she decided to come out with it. "Want to make a swap?"

The others in the room watched as Bresnahan's eyes widened. "Of course Peter is here. He's in the bar." There was a pause. "I *am* in the bar. Like I said, it's packed, and—" Bresnahan lowered the receiver and stared down at it.

McKeon had rung off. After all, his specialty was interrogations.

Behind the door to the other room, the barman from McCabe's could be heard saying, "I dunno. It's hard to say. Wasn't the bar dark and him in the orange deck suit and all. Looked like a navvy off one of them Spanish factory ships. Beard. I don't think he'd shaved in a week."

Said one of the patrons from that night, "He kept a billed cap on, like the kids wear these days."

McGarr clicked the screen back four faces. "Like that?"

He nodded.

"Baseball."

All three men stared at him, none probably knowing a baseball from a softball. The transom of the *Mah Jong* said she was from New Orleans, Louisiana. No such boat was documented or licensed in Louisiana; of the seventeen boats named *Mah Jong* worldwide, none was a schooner. McGarr had pulled out every stop he could think of, but he was worried that time was running out. In a matter of hours the island would be teeming with more people than could be monitored or tracked, and he would have to take steps to protect Mirna Gottschalk and her son, Karl, who was still staying with her.

If only he knew more about the raiders, then perhaps they might narrow the focus. Hating the thought of diminishing his numbers on Clare Island even by one, McGarr decided nevertheless to send Ward back to Dublin. He was young enough to know computers, E-mail, and so forth that were necessary to extract information from other sources worldwide, and yet he was veteran enough to have more usual connections.

"And another thing," said the barman. "He kept his hand up to his face, like leaning on an elbow."

"The bigger problem is the pictures, if I can say so, Superintendent—"

"You can say anything you want."

"—them photos there, they're in color. But bars, now, bars is different. Bars is in black and white, like. In bars yeh don't think this color, that color—hat, coat, shoes. In bars, everything is . . . gray, since ye've got yehr pint and chat to take care of."

McGarr could credit the notion, especially round closing time which it had been.

"And there's only so much starin' you want to do at a stranger, never knowin' where they're from or what they might do," put in the barman.

"There's nary a word of lie in that."

Amen, thought McGarr. He began clicking through the women on the off chance they might have seen any of them before. There was the evidence of the small man or large woman's footprint in the soft ground around the Ford cottage. To say nothing of Paul O'Malley's sighting through his Swarovski scope.

Out in the other room, the phone rang. Bresnahan snatched it up, hoping that McKeon had changed his mind. But a decidedly feminine voice said, "May I speak to Garda Superintendent Hugh Ward of the Serious Crimes Unit, please."

It took Bresnahan only a heartbeat—literally—to know who it was. The admiring tone was unmistakable, along with the distinctive Dublin brogue. "One moment. Please hold." She cupped the phone to a hip, saying to Ward, "It's for you. I think it might be personal."

Ward frowned; he'd had no personal life since becoming involved with herself. "Who is it?"

Bresnahan arched an auburn eyebrow and shook her head. "I have an idea it's an admirer."

Noreen was all ears, wondering if she was about to be party to some revelation of Ward's infidelity. It was rather expected, given his past and storied romantic history.

"Ward here."

"Hughie—it's Leah Sigal from Sigal and Sons."

"Yes, Leah."

Bresnahan nodded, having been right; but she did not move away from the phone. As it was, they were practically shoulder to shoulder, she being the taller party. Ward—dressed in a blue buttoned-down, Oxford-cloth shirt, blue jeans, and penny loafers—looked like one of the younger American O'Malley revelers, and certainly nowhere near his thirty-six years.

"I phoned your office, and yehr mahn, Swords, put me through." It was said in the best Dublin voice. "I have a confirmation on the ring."

Ward's head went back.

"It is—as I thought—part of a parure. In fact, it's part of a famous set of diamonds and sapphires that had been given by the enormously wealthy Count Cyril Kraczkiewicz to his betrothed—I'm reading from the report I requested—on the occasion of their marriage in Gdańsk in 1934. Kraczkiewicz, a noted collector of gemstones and jewelry, disappeared in East Prussia with his wife in late 1944, and were never seen or heard from again, victims—it is supposed—of either the Nazis or the advancing Russians.

"The value of the ring? I should think my estimate was low both as a single piece or as part of the parure. My fax hasn't had a moment's rest since I sent out the request. I'm being besieged with offers to buy. The service must have a leak."

Free enterprise being even freer on an anonymous fax line, thought Ward.

"Hughie"—there was a huffy pause, as though the woman was summoning the courage to continue—"it was good to see you again, and I hope what I found out has helped. My son, Lou? He's going through his grandfather's records of any Clare Island or Clement Ford dealings.

"But, well—what I want to say to explain why I acted so odd when you called at the shop is . . ." She paused to gather breath. "It was because . . . well, because I was dismayed that you didn't recognize me. Have I changed that much? Hughie, are you there?"

Ward grunted and tried to turn himself and the phone away

from Bresnahan, sensing that more was coming.

"Hughie—I'm Lee Stone, your history reader the year you were at University College."

In a stunning flashback that, he knew, was revealed on his face, it all came back to Ward.

"What's wrong?" Bresnahan asked.

During that spring—how many? Fourteen years ago—Lee Stone and he had had a torrid affair. Only a few years older than he at the time, she had been a research student who assisted the professor who lectured the course. Although she had been married at the time, it had been like love at first sight. Her office, her car, his flat, Phoenix Park—they had been unable to keep themselves apart. Ward had even grown anxious that he was not devoting enough time to his studies and might fail his exams.

But then his father had died, and he had gone home to Waterford to bury him. After that, she had come down once to visit him and tell him that she was going to divorce her husband, whose name was Stone. Ward had either never asked her maiden name or, if he had, he had forgotten it. As he had her until now.

And then it occurred to him that her son was just about fourteen. . . . Ward drew in an anxious breath of his own. "What about your son?" His dark brow knitted. "Lou."

"He doesn't know, I didn't tell him. As far as he's concerned, my ex-husband is his father, though he's never seen the man. He emigrated to Israel before Lou was born. I've encouraged him to know something about you without letting on, though there was oft and many a time I thought I should. But divil the bit of courage could I muster to pick up the phone and disturb your life because of a decision I had made so many years ago."

But now the boy should be told, Ward decided without having to debate the issue, at the same time wondering if there were any possibility that the child was not his. No—he shook his head—he had met the boy, seen the similarity in their dark looks. There was no possibility that he wasn't.

"I know it's a great weight to drop on you after all this time, and I haven't had a moment's rest since you came into the shop, hammerin' my head off the wall whether I should tell you. But I decided God had put you in the way of us again, just at the age when a boy needs some male guidance.

"But I'll leave it up to you if you want to see him or let him know. As I said, I never wished to intrude on your life, which is the reason I didn't tell you earlier, and we can continue on like that, if you wish. He's got his uncles and cousins, whom he sees. Also, please don't think this is the beginning of any attempt to bind you to us or to secure monetary help. His grandfather took care of that for Lou, and fortunately the business is good. Too good. I scarcely have time to care for myself, as perhaps you noticed."

There was nothing to say to that either.

"Hughie—are you there?"

At the continued silence she rushed back into speech. "Sure, it must be a devastating lot to take in all at one go. But I'll leave it up to you. Do you have our number?"

"Yes."

"Good-bye, Hughie."

"Good-bye, Lee."

She rang off, and Ward lowered the receiver into its yoke. Looking up, he found three pairs of eyes on him; from the other room he could hear McGarr's voice saying, "What about this bloke? He's about the right age, and he looks stocky, like you said."

"I've got a son," Ward announced.

"The kid from the jewelry shop? Sigal and Son?" Bresnahan asked.

"You're not in earnest surely!" Noreen said. Dubliner to the core, being privy to a breaking story of such import concerning two people who were not only known to her, but who were also particular friends and prominent in their specialties was meat and drink to her. No, *three* people, since Ruth was unquestionably involved. "Leah Sigal's son? You have a child by my Leah Sigal?"

Ward only looked at her; it was as though she were speaking Swahili. He could hear the words, but he still could not comprehend the meaning. He did not know how or in what way his life had been changed, but it had.

"I think it's absolute *magic*! Leah is one of the best people I know. I often wondered how the boy ended up with such a downright Celtic name. It's spelled ell, you, gee, haitch, you know. Lugh." Noreen enthused before remembering Ruth. "I mean, when and where did you know her?"

"In the *biblical* sense," Bresnahan put in acidly. "There's no *other* knowledge for some patriarchs."

Said Maddie, "But Hughie isn't married, Ma. How can he have a son?"

"You certainly spread yourself thin." Bresnahan eased herself into a chair.

"More than a decade before I knew you," Ward managed, moving woodenly toward the sideboard. But he had lost his appetite, as well as his idea of himself as being essentially a free spirit. What was that statement by one of the German writers? When your child is born, it is you who is the dead one. Or, at least, it is your freedom that dies. Ward could not piece it out completely; it was too early.

Also, a child was such a responsibility; there were so many pitfalls and traps out there, as Ward knew from his own experience. But he also felt a profound pity and sorrow for the boy—*his* boy—who had not known his own father for fourteen years.

As surely, Lee—or Leah—had taken a chance. He wondered if the boy would ever forgive her for keeping them apart for so long.

"Hughie—please don't keep us waiting. Give us the details." Noreen was beside herself to learn when and where. In her own cosmogony, the two were worlds apart—a Ph.D. historian with a refined taste in jewelry and objets d'art, and Ward, who was without a doubt the second toughest man (in the best sense) that she knew. Her own being the first. "You had an affair—when?"

But Ward said nothing.

"He can't remember, there's been so many. Also, he's your archetypal 'gentleman.' You know, the one that kisses but never tells. Can you imagine he once said that to me?"

"But have you ever seen the lad? Now that I think of it, he's the—" Noreen caught herself.

"If you say spit and image I'll never speak to you again, so help me," said Bresnahan.

"Well"—Noreen looked away, not wishing to wrangle—

"the resemblance is certainly remarkable. But then Leah is dark too."

There was a long pause, during which they listened to McGarr's continuing questions in the next room, mingled with shouts, laughter, and revelry both in the hotel proper and down in the lane below the windows. The O'Malleys were in party form.

Finally Bresnahan said, "Cripes—how do I compete with the woman?" She held up three fingers. "She's wealthy, I assume?"

Noreen shook her head. "I have no idea, but I assume—"

Bresnahan did as well. "Bags of money. Two, she's produced a veritable clone of the man and weathered fourteen years as a lone parent without a complaint that he ever heard. And three—she still worships the very ground he trods. You should have heard her there in the shop, falling all over herself with flattering questions—the boxing, the cops. If himself and I had a child, we'd toss up a mutt, half dark, half red."

Noreen raised a hand to stop her. Some things said, even half in jest, could never be taken back. And it wasn't as if Ruth and she were having a private chat, woman to woman. There he sat, the impregnator himself, right across from them.

"And have you ever seen her?"

Weekly at least, thought Noreen. Not only did they own complementary businesses, they were friends. They checked in on the phone, went places together, even met for a drink and gossip at least once a fortnight. Suddenly Noreen realized why Leah had always seemed so interested in the Squad with clever questions tactfully put to elicit information about Ward. But their friendship had not been based on that alone. No. Noreen could remember scads of other occasions—at auctions, sales, and estate closings—when they spoke only about the matters at hand and had lunch and a laugh afterward. Ward could do worse than either woman. What a delicious dilemma.

"I asked you, have you ever *seen* her?"

Uh-oh, somebody big and dangerous was waxing wroth. Noreen nodded. Now, if she were to retain Ruth's friendship, she knew she could utter only the truth; anything less would be transparent. "I'd say there was a time that she was nicely put together."

"Yah—like *now*. I can only imagine what she was like before."

Well, one thing for Hughie, Noreen thought—he always had great good taste in women. But fortunately, all that came out of Noreen's mouth was "I've seen her at charity affairs and so forth looking ravishing. But always alone. During the week, it's as if she doesn't try."

"And talk about *one love.*"

Noreen was happy Ruth had said it, because the thought had occurred to her too.

Ruth stood and moved to the sideboard and Ward's brimming plate. She carried it over to him. "Looks like you've got your plate filled, me mahn." Ward only set it aside.

The door opened, and McGarr entered the room. "What's this—a séance? There's a boat anchoring in the harbor." He pointed out the window. "Rice might be there, but we need somebody with a camera." He glanced at his watch. "And the ferry's due any minute."

"Oh, Daddy—do we have to?" Maddie complained. "I want to go swimming with the other kids."

McGarr reached for his daughter, who was his love and life, and hoisted her into the air. "And swimming you will. Humpty and Dumpty over here will pick up our slack, being paid for it," as Noreen and Maddie were not. It was then that he noticed Ward. "What's with you?"

"He's just been told he's a daddy," said Bresnahan.

"No—" It was out of McGarr's mouth before he could take it back, but, he supposed, it was inevitable.

"Congratulations" was his second thought. "When can we expect the addition?"

"Ah, yehr late," Bresnahan replied disgustedly. "Fourteen years, in fact."

McGarr looked to Noreen for an explanation, but she averted her eyes.

"I'm sure he'll fill you in, man to man."

"Later then. Right now, Hughie, I want you to get back to Dublin and see what you can do with the Clare Island Trust, the possibility of some Republican connection, and the lists

we put together of the people who came to the island today.
Once you get in place, we'll send you tomorrow's additions,
and so forth. Can you leave immediately?''

Ward stood. ''If I can get off the island.''

''Rice will arrange that.''

McGarr turned to Bresnahan. ''Something wrong, Rut'ie?''

''Ah no, not a thing. I was just thinking how convenient it
is, lashing back to Dublin and the ready-made family. Is it a
setup? Did you two choreograph the entire blessed revelation?''

McGarr was at a loss, but when no explanation was offered,
he simply walked back into the other room and closed the
door.

Thought Noreen: given the country's approach to contraception and abortion, Irish women with unwanted pregnancies
had typically gone to England to give birth and had then given
their babies up for adoption. Years later, those same children—wishing to know their birth mothers—had successfully
met the other and then carried on with their lives.

Here the shoe was on the other hoof. Albeit cloven.

CHAPTER 23

BERNIE McKEON'S BRIEF touch with serenity was over, he could tell. With a resentment bordering on anger he watched the bikers, hikers, trekkers, and even joggers heave into view from the south of the island, singly and in clutches—in one case of nineteen. They were on the roads, in the treeless meadows and bogs, even now climbing the steep gray-green flanks of Croaghmore. The O'Malleys had obviously arrived.

From the east and west boats had also appeared, one of which had gathered McKeon's attention rather more grippingly than the others. It also corrupted the feeling of "fleshless beatitude" (he had dubbed it) that he had been nurturing since his reclusion in the lighthouse turret.

For at the wheel was nothing less than a great blond and bronzed goddess, who, in squatting to drop anchor and a second time to deploy a rubber dive raft, presented for McKeon's optically enhanced delectation the most shapely and ample pair of orange cheeks that he had viewed in many a moon. McKeon liked his women big.

Running up a blue-and-white international code flag, she also showed him the rest of her generous and nearly bare anatomy, before ducking down into the small cabin in the foredeck. But nobody else seemed to be aboard, which was a no-no for divers who were warned time and again never to dive alone. McKeon's sixth son was a diving enthusiast.

She soon reappeared, dressed in a wet suit with a mask, tanks, flippers, and the complete regalia including a curious-looking belly pack. McKeon had not seen the likes of it before and wondered what she had in there. From a deck locker, she pulled out a speargun, and without further ado got into the rubber raft and paddled in toward the cliffs, out of McKeon's field of vision.

And, sure, weren't there several other boats farther along the cliffs, fishing with rods in the turquoise shallows and one now pulling in a lovely big mackerel. Suddenly McKeon was hungry. *And* thirsty. He was just a fleshly sinner after all, he concluded.

The final boat was so far along the cliffs by Croaghmore that McKeon could barely make out the two figures on deck, but they appeared to be loading a net into a skiff. One man then took the oars, and they soon too were out of sight, rounding the cliff beyond the Ford cottage where McKeon had lost the woman and nearly drowned two nights before.

Also, there was some new action on the southeastern flank of the mountain, a single figure trudging up a goat path. He was heading toward a ridge that was cast in deep shadow, now that the sun had begun to decline. McKeon recognized the man's gait, his build, the khaki hat and jacket; the figure then turned his face to him and waved. It was McGarr. Unclipping the VHF radio from his belt, he held it up and shook his head.

McKeon understood what he meant. They could chance using the radio only in an emergency, so as not to scare off the raiders. Even if they used the police channel with DSC (Digital Selective Calling) that transmitted digital messages to only specific receiving stations, or if they employed a complex scrambling code, they could not be sure they would not be heard.

While costly, the electronics needed to interdict such systems could be purchased on the open market. The best were portable, some even handheld, and every major drug dealer in Dublin had them.

McKeon glanced down at his own handset to make sure it

was still functioning. Every once in a while throughout the day, a voice had come on chatting almost exclusively about fishing or the weather or asking a boat to pick up something on the mainland.

The most often heard voice was that of "Paulie-O'," who McKeon assumed was Paul O'Malley. He always had something to tell the various captains about catches, conditions, and the presence of water bailiffs, sometimes citing what he called "other sources."

By that McKeon guessed he meant the Weather Fax and Fish Fax services that he subscribed to and read off to a inquisitive captain when asked. He invariably added what he had picked up on his other radios that could be heard in the background whenever he came on.

McKeon watched now as McGarr chose a perch on the side of the mountain. Removing his own binoculars from a case, he settled himself under a low ledge that virtually obscured him from sight. Had McKeon not seen him take the position, he would not have been able to tell he was there.

Which cut McKeon's area of sweep in half. Beginning at the far perimeter, he began raking the binoculars back and forth in horizontal bands, ever closer to his own post there in the lighthouse. Once the sweeps were completed, he then checked all figures that he had seen or anything else that seemed different or suspicious, particularly in the immediate vicinity of the Gottschalk residence, including the glimpse he could catch of the cliffs and the ocean below. He then swept the entire grid vertically, from the fields near the lighthouse to the edge of his perimeter, which was roughly half the distance to Croaghmore. McGarr, he knew, was doing the same with his half.

But apart from the dive boat with the goddess, none of the O'Malleys—pushing out from the harbor after finding all rooms taken—had gone anywhere near the Gottschalk place which lay as far north as it was possible to walk. Tents were now being pitched wherever the landscape offered shelter from the wind. In fact, Timmermans had said he'd heard that some of the O'Malleys actually preferred camping out. "You know, to make contact with the earth where most of the generations of their clan were conceived, passed their days, and were buried. It's said some of them go away fulfilled.'' There had been a twinkle in the Belgian's eye.

Shades of a pagan rite, thought McKeon. No, some *excellent* pagan rite, Christianity—or, at least, *his* Christianity—being no more than a light gloss on the surface of his personality. Whenever it was scratched, up came the battle helmet with horns, the cudgel, the flagon, horses, hounds, and women—all glimpsed in his mind's eye under a full summer moon. McKeon howled lightly, then scanned the area below the cliffs. The mermaid had yet to return.

Already McKeon could count eleven tents up with several others on the rise. It was only a matter of time before they discovered the sheltered boreen running from the main road to the Gottschalk compound of buildings. And night was only a few hours off.

Now a solitary figure had appeared at what was marked on the map as a standing stone in Ballytoohy, due south of the lighthouse. He was a short, square, older man in a cap and spectacles who had a large rucksack strapped over his shoulders and some sort of device in his hands. It was long and thin with handle spokes for . . . turning?

After examining the standing stone on all sides, he laid the device on the ground, pulled off the rucksack, and removed a notebook. Carrying it over to the plinth, he squatted down on the far side where he was no longer visible to McKeon, and certainly not to McGarr both because of the distance and an intervening ridge.

Anyhow, it was then that the radio bleated, as a scrambled voice came on, perhaps from one of the "factory" fishing ships that earlier had been working the waters to the west of the island. Spaniards, they had been catching tuna, Paulie O' had told some of the local fishermen. There was a reply, and yet another from a third source with a deeper voice. And then nothing.

As with all other transmissions—especially now that Chief Superintendent McGarr had given him the duty—Paulie O' had taped the exchange, which he ran through his computerized code descrambler that copied the unscrambled voices on a disc. He then listened to the transmission a third time and immediately activated the voice-recognition telephone that was attached to his robotic wheelchair. He spoke the number that Chief Superintendent McGarr had given him.

The language was not Spanish, and Paulie had heard the language only once before. It was Afrikaans.

When the Dublin number answered, Paulie played the un-scrambled voices a fourth time to the man on the other end, who was a translator. "Is that all of it?"

"The lot."

"Do I tell you what they said?"

"If you would." Paulie was trying to sound calm and cool, as though all of this was just S.O.P. to him, when it was without a doubt the most exciting challenge he had faced since the accident that had crippled him. His mother had wanted to help, and they'd had a dreadful row with Paulie making a run at her in the automated chair. When she fled down the stairs, he locked the door.

"Are you ready?"

"Ready." Paulie switched on the recording function of the telephone answering machine which gave off a bleep.

"The first voice says, 'Helmet here, in place. Can you read me, Heather?'

"The second voice—the woman's voice, I take it—replies, 'Yes, Helmet, Heather here. In place.'

"Then the first again, 'Good. And you, Ducal?' or Dugald, I couldn't make out which.

"Ducal answers in a playful voice, 'Yes, Father. Don't do anything foolish. I have you in my sights.' And that's it."

Paulie thanked the man and rang off, only to be faced with an enormous decision—to alert McGarr that the raiders were back and on the island, "in place" by their own assessment.

McGarr had told Paulie, "I'm going to leave it up to you. Be judicious. Contacting us could tip our hand, but anything vital we should know."

Paulie now thought—their taking the chance of checking in like that, telling each other they were in place, could only mean that not all of them were visible to each other (only Ducal or whatever his name was could see Helmet) and that they were in the places from which they would strike. And confident! Paulie did not speak Afrikaans, but the playful tone was unmistakable.

Problem was—Paulie could see just about everything everywhere that McGarr and his man up in the lighthouse could (and better because of the power and quality of his Swarovski spotting scope), but there seemed to be nothing unusual. Just like the "Rally" before and the one before that and before that, the O'Ms were raising tents and starting campfires.

Musical instruments had been brought out, and he could see people singing. A donkey pulling a cart with a big barrel of Guinness on the back, which had collected a crowd in one place. Others of Paulie's clans people were moving from one fire to the next; the "partying" had obviously begun and would continue at many campsites right through to the dawn.

It was a perfect blind for the raiders, and at the very least McGarr should know that they had established themselves somewhere among the crowd. With his chin, Paulie activated the VHF, but he decided to forgo the police band and leave off the DSC signal and scrambler which is what the electronically adept would expect of the police. And then, had they been monitoring Channel 16 for any length of time, which he was sure they had, they would have heard him signing on and off, speaking with the local fishermen.

"Paulie O' to Fish One." It was the call name they had agreed upon for McGarr.

"Fish One here."

"Fish One, how's the luck?"

"Miserable."

"You mean, you don't have your limit?"

"There's not a squid between here and Nova Scotia."

"Have ye' checked that limp thing in yehr britches lately?"

"Paulie O', if I was there, I'd catch yehr neck, and then what?"

O'Malley laughed. "I'll try to forget you said that, yeh shagger. Me callin' with where the fish are."

"In the market or a seal's belly. Or is this where I begin the penitential prayers?"

"Well, now—that's better. For a wee afternoon of velvet scoops, I'll tell you this; there's mackerel, tuna, and hake."

"Where?"

"Whoa, buck—are we agreed?"

"Jaze—how many scoops fill a wee afternoon?"

"As many as I can keep down."

"No problem, then—ye're on. Two it is." McGarr tucked the speaker into his chest and laughed, as though to suggest that there were others listening in the cabin of a boat. "As for the mackerel, tuna, and hake?"

"Ye' bastard, yeh—I shouldn't tell yeh this, but on 'Turk." He meant Inishturk, which was another island to the southwest of Clare Island.

"Where off Turk?"

"Haven't I got three reports?"

"Of mackerel running? The bloody Spics have probably hoovered up the rest."

"Strong and clear. All on the surface."

"You mean, walkin' round, just waiting for the net?"

"Depends on who's handling the net. The boats I spoke with say they got their quotas, and the schools keep narrowin', like they'll link up soon. But it should take *you* the rest of the night. I'll give me love to your missus."

"I can't thank you enough."

"Not to worry, she will. She always does."

When McKeon looked up from his own VHF that he'd been staring at, concentrating on every little word, there she was— McGarr's missus. With her daughter, Maddie, Noreen was at the south edge of McKeon's sector. And what were they doing?

He raised the binoculars to his eyes.

They were staring down at what looked like a mound of stony rubble. As she spoke, Noreen was scrabbling the toe of a shoe through the debris.

And something else had changed in McKeon's sector. But what?

Pulling down the binoculars, he surveyed the mile-square sector with his eyes alone, looking for the anomaly. What was it? The tents were all still in place, one more of them fully up; the large family had secured an enviable spot in the lee of a flat mound of land where they had a strong turf fire burning and their other gear was being pulled from tuck bags; the three mountain bikers had joined up with a fourth and were trying to negotiate a bog.

There it was—the man at the standing stone had been joined by another person. McKeon raised the binoculars to his eyes again.

She was a rather large but pleasantly made woman dressed in boots and khakis with something like a bushman's hat over her blond hair. Her well-tanned face was framed by tortoise-shell sunglasses. Reaching down for the device that the old man had been carrying, she followed him away from the stone.

McKeon began working the grid again, with renewed dedication, now that they knew that the raiders had arrived. Still, there was nobody even remotely close to the Gottschalks' compound. The big new Land Rover was still parked near the house. Smoke was coming out of what McKeon supposed was the kitchen chimney. He glanced at the door, hoping that Timmermans would not forget his tea, now that the lighthouse was overrun with O'Malleys. McKeon would not dare leave his post.

"Another name for *fulachta fiadh* is burnt-stone mound. Do you see the burnt stones here among the rubble?" Noreen asked.

Maddie nodded. The mound they were looking at had been cut by the hoe of a tractor, so that a cross section was exposed to view. The bottom layer was composed of the rubble of a glacial moraine. Above it was a clear sign of what had been turf—a thick layer of sod that had grown there perhaps as many as three thousand years earlier.

"The people then dug a horseshoe-shaped trough here on the banks of this stream so they could divert some of the water into it. Once it was filled, they closed it at both ends. At the same time, they had built a fire to heat rocks that they pushed into the trough until the water was boiling and hissing and steam was pouring out. That was when they put in the meat, and the cooking began. It was from heating the rocks over and over and over again that they cracked into pieces, like this." With the toe of her shoe, Noreen pushed a few of the shards around. But today they provide us a record of what went on in *fulachta fiadh*.''

Maddie looked dubious; her brow was furrowed. ''It seems like a great lot of bother to cook some meat.''

''Actually, I think it's rather ingenious myself. They've discovered over thirty of these on Clare Island so far, and no major watercourse was without one.''

''Why didn't they just use a pot?''

''Because metal that could withstand such heat hadn't been found.''

''Then why didn't they just hold the meat over the fire like a barbecue or put it on some of the hot rocks, like a grill?''

''Good question. I've often wondered about that myself. Perhaps they preferred boiled meat. Another explanation is that these horseshoe-shaped trenches are actually hot baths. That after they got the water to a good warm temperature, they jumped in. But because there're so many of them on so many of the islands off Ireland and Scotland, the people who study these things tend to think they were ancient kitchens. Not baths.''

''I like the baths better.''

Preferring grilled meat like your father, thought Noreen. ''Oh look—there's Professor Schweibert. Let's ask him what he thinks they were used for.''

Maddie ran ahead toward the two people who were engaged in setting up a tent on a raised bit of land along the boreen leading to the Gottschalk place.

''What are you doing?'' Maddie asked, obviously startling the man whose bare hand jumped toward his rucksack. The other was still encased in a glove.

But the woman with him intervened. ''Now, what does it look like we're doing? What's your name?'' She kept spreading out the tent.

''Putting that up?''

''I knew you were a smart one the moment I looked at you.''

''Her name is Mattie,'' said Schweibert.

''Maddie,'' Maddie corrected.

''She's the little girl I just told you about that I met this morning.''

"The one with the mother?" But catching sight of Noreen, she added quickly with a smile, "Everybody has to have a mother at one time or another, don't they? And here she is, I assume."

"That's right. I'm Noreen. Did I meet you on the boat too?" Noreen displayed a brilliant smile and offered her hand.

"Helene, is mine. I'm afraid not. I'm certain I would have remembered you. And Maddie."

"Then you came by private boat?"

Before she could answer, Schweibert said, "Of course she did. Helene is my assistant, and she brought over the project boat. What with these 'ferries,' as they call them, and 'water taxis,' and all this blasted dither with this clan of fools—we'll get nothing done."

Noreen glanced round, hoping he had not been overheard; it was an opinion best kept to oneself.

"We require secure, dependable transportation, so I rang up Helene."

"Project? Really? I wasn't aware that you're engaged in a project."

"The *study*!" he barked.

"Did you put in at the harbor?"

"Yes—she put the boat in at the harbor. It's there now."

"Are both of you going to sleep in that wee tent?" Maddie asked.

"Really, young miss—that question is impertinent, and I think both you and your mother are far too inquisitive for my liking."

Bidding them a good evening, since it was fast approaching, Noreen took Maddie by the hand and beat a quick retreat. "I bet you're hungry. Ruthie is waiting dinner on us at the hotel, so we'd best hurry."

Maddie kept turning her head to look back at the tent raising.

Night came on with two warnings for Peter McGarr. The first was from the wind that ceased with an abruptness so sudden that the silence seemed loud. Then it got dark.

Positioned on the east side of Croaghmore, McGarr could not see the western horizon, but he could tell from the way some of the campers now gathered on the cliff edge to point out to sea, that something ominous was gathering there. One of the men moved quickly back to his tent and put all his gear inside, zipping the flap, then checking the fly sheet and tent straps and pegs. And yet the sky to the east was a limpid blue just the color of a robin's egg.

The second warning was quite different and made McGarr question his strategy. Was he taking too many chances—with the Gottschalks, his staff, the congregated O'Malleys? He even had his wife and child out there, like it was a holiday. And finally with his own life.

Feeling a few grains of sand drop onto his neck and trickle down his collar, he glanced up at the ledge that was in back of his head.

Standing there looking down at McGarr with—was it?— an ax in his hands, was a wild-looking man with a great shock of white hair but whose face was in shadow. "Whatever are you doing there?" he asked.

McGarr had heard that voice before. "And you? I could ask the same of you."

"Me? I suspect I'm doing your bloody job for you, since it's plain you can't."

Turning on his heel, Fergal O'Grady moved into the darkness, as though he would climb Croaghmore, the blade of his slane an even brighter patch than his unruly hair. In the renewed breeze, it was standing on end.

CHAPTER 24

WHEN HUGH WARD got back to the office in Dublin at dusk, he did not go straight to the chief's office. Instead he only waved to Sinclaire and two undercover operatives who were meeting in there. For more than a year they had been trying to bust "the Penguin," an oily, squat, adder of a man who controlled the flow of heroin into Dublin north of the Liffey.

Ward labored under no illusions about the effect of any one arrest, but he imagined that a great deed would be done the city, could they put the Penguin away for one of the many murders that had been committed in his name. At least until some other piece of work stepped into his spats.

Also, at quarter to ten of a fair summer evening, he could not have it seem that he was hard at work. Diligence of the forever-panting sort was frowned on, even for the police, and, when ringing up his "sources," he would have to make it seem as though a wee question had occurred to him over a pint or at dinner or on the links.

Thus he repaired to his own tiny cubicle and closed the door. Since he was an officer assigned to the Clare Island investigation, copies of all replies to queries and other memoranda had been placed on his desk. After ringing a clerk for coffee, he removed his jacket and sat.

The first report was from Scotland Yard replying to the query about any possible public school or Ox-bridge graduates by the name of Clement or Clem Ford or Angus or Helmut Rehm or Angus Helmut Rehm. The only perfect match was for Angus Helmut Rehm, a Scot, who had attended Aberdeen Grammar until 1932 and graduated from Cambridge in 1935 with a first in modern languages.

The Yard information officer had launched subsequent searches; British Immigration & Customs reported the following: Angus Helmut Rehm had left England 11 October 1935, departing from Dover and bound for Bremen, but there was no record of his ever having returned.

Also, Inland Revenue said that there was no current, taxpaying British citizen by that name or one who owned real property in the British Isles.

Finally, Yard criminal records were examined: Angus H. Rehm had been arrested and charged with the crime of inciting to riot 1 May, 1934, when he and a "band of hooligans" attacked a Communist party gathering in Hyde Park. He gave his permanent address as Crovie, Grampian, Scotland. At his court appearance, in which charges were reduced to a disorderly persons offense when his victim failed to identify him, he gave his present address as Magdalene College, Cambridge.

Which made him the same Angus Helmut Rehm.

The Yard information officer added that Rehm was involved in another altercation in the fall of 1935, after having graduated from Cambridge. It seems that, to settle an old score, he along with four others attacked a fifth man, and all but Rehm ended up in hospital. When the victim—one Klimt Dorfmann—refused to press charges, the Cambridge constabulary did, because of the severity of the beating. But the victim, appearing in court, would not identify the four charged men as his attackers, and the case was dismissed.

"I noticed that the address given for Klimt Dorfmann was also Magdalene College, Cambridge," the Yard information officer had written. "The only other information about him was that his permanent residence was listed as Harwich."

The phone rang, and Ward's hand plucked up the handset in a reflex action. "Ward."

"Superintendent Hugh Ward?" a barely adolescent voice asked.

"That's right."

"This is Lugh Stone. My mother thought it would be all right if I phoned you directly."

Ward leaned back in the chair and smiled. To think that it was his *son* who was speaking to him was nearly too much to take in. "Yes, Lugh," he managed. "How are you?"

"Well, sir. Thank you. I'm phoning about my grandfather's records. I'm after having gone through them."

"Good lad."

"I think I've found something. Or I've found the only Clare Island reference in the entire nearly seventy-five years that Lou did business here. He died in his nineties."

Ward liked what he was hearing; the kid sounded intelligent, focused, and competent. Of course, his mother was brilliant, from everything that Ward had known about her fourteen years ago, and he had confidence in his own intellect. "Go on."

"From what I can put together, it seems that a man came into the shop in March of 1947. He said he wanted to sell some gold in the form of bullion, which means ingots or bars. He had ingots—two of them to begin with in pure form. Lou was a careful man, and he asked for identification. The man produced a British passport that Lou corroborated was genuine, and from that point until Lou's death in 1982, the two of them traded regularly—gold, silver, gemstones of every sort, and some jewelry. The man's name was Klimt Dorfmann from Harwich, Suffolk; that's what the passport said. His address in this country was care of Peig O'Malley, Clare Island, Westport, Mayo."

Ward's head went back. "Lugh—I can't tell you how important what you just told me might be or how much I appreciate your effort on this. I owe you a night out and a slap-up dinner. I'll ring up when this is over."

"I'd like that. My mother says to tell you hello."

"My best to her." Ward hung up and immediately turned to his computer. Not only was there the run-in that Klimt Dorfmann had with Rehm in 1935, there was the statement by Paul O'Malley's mother (contained in one of McGarr's reports) that she believed Ford was from Harwich. In fact, she said he had told her he had inherited property there. And finally—it occurred to Ward, as he accessed his E-mail service and typed in the Klimt Dorfmann name—that it was a partial, "poetic," and adumbrated anagram of Clement (Klimt) Ford (Dorf) with the "-mann" elided.

He checked the time of the Yard report, which had come in only three hours earlier, which meant that same information officer could still be on the job. He would E-mail the officer directly, which would save the time of going through channels which with delays might result in some other person dealing with the follow-up. He wrote:

> *"Klimt Dorfmann = Clem Ford. Please check all Harwich, Suffolk, Cambridge University, and any other references at hand for Dorfmann. It is rumored that Dorfmann inherited property in Harwich from his mother, name unknown. Am making a formal request in case you're off work. I owe you a pint."*

Signing off, he added his formal title—Detective Superintendent, Serious Crimes Unit,—so the researcher would understand that it was a felony investigation.

After completing the formal request, Ward turned back to the desk, wondering why Rehm had not returned to Britain after the war. Perhaps he'd been killed, or, as a Nazi sympathizer, he had been unable to return. Who else would have attacked a CP gathering in Hyde Park but some right-wing organization that resorted to violence? Certainly there had been many in Britain during the depths of the Depression who believed that fascism with its state control of commercial enterprise was the answer to the boom-and-bust cycle of capitalism.

From his studying history, Ward also knew that by 1935 Hitler had seized complete control of Germany, having abolished the Reichstag in 1934, repudiated the Treaty of Versailles, and begun a program of massive rearmament. Could Rehm with his German-sounding last name and first-honors degree in modern languages have removed himself to Germany to aid in the cause?

Another possibility was that he had been recruited by MI-6 as a spy, and all the Nazi sympathizing and brawling that had brought him before the courts had been nothing more than cover.

Of course, Dorfmann's name was German as well and meant . . . villager, Ward seemed to remember from his study of that language.

History. Ward thought of Lee Stone again, his history teacher, and *their* Lugh, which was history on the most personal level. He glanced across the cubicle to the stack of books from which he culled names when in need of an obscure "source." Among the telephone directories and membership lists of various clubs and organizations was the UCD annual from the year that he had been at university.

Forcing his mind back to the matter at hand, he picked up the second memorandum that reported on the identity check on all persons who had arrived on Clare Island that day. The lists of their purported names and addresses had been faxed to Serious Crimes Unit Headquarters in Harcourt Street where a team of information-processing clerks was keying the information into the computer that was tied to both Garda Siochana and Customs & Immigration mainframes. But with 1,178 names and addresses, the supervising officer had no hopes of fulfilling the request before midnight, which could be too late.

Ward picked up the phone. "May I speak to Sergeant Johnston, please? Hugh Ward here."

He waited, and when another voice came on, he said, "Sheila—how's the list coming." He listened to her tale of woe—she had one clerk on maternity leave, another on holiday, the third could barely key in her own name.

"Sheila—may I ask you something?"

"Yes, of course. Anything."

"Do *you* type?"

"I do, sure. How do you think—"

"Then I'd appreciate you rattling the keys for me on this tonight. I type. Do I come over there and pitch in?"

"Oh no—Jesus! Don't you dare." Since she'd never hear the end of it.

Ringing off, Ward now had nothing more to do than wait.

His coffee had arrived, and he carried it over to the stack of books. When he picked up the UCD annual, it opened immediately to the group portrait of the faculty of history. Had he looked at that page often in the past, or was it just coincidence?

And there she was in all her dark beauty—*his* dark lady. He wondered if she could have been pregnant at the time the photo was snapped, since she looked luminescent compared to the others. She glowed. And like a scent jar of past experience knocked from the shelf, everything they had shared together—their youth, their hope, their expectations, sex, love, Proust even—came flooding back to engulf Ward in a vivid, heady moment that left him with a pounding heart and feeling slightly dizzy. It was as though he could feel her again and feel how it was then.

How could he not have known? How could he have been so blind and self-centered?

"You can't imagine what it's taken to defend this table from the O'Malley hordes," Ruth Bresnahan said when Noreen and Maddie finally reached the crowded and noisy dining room of the Bayview Hotel, looking wet and frazzled. "Especially now with the weather closing in and the tenters in rout. Is the storm as bad as they say?"

Not knowing what had been said, Noreen could only nod. The blast had struck when Maddie and she were only halfway back. First the sky had darkened almost as if night had fallen, except for a sparkling band of rich golden light at the very edge of the horizon. There had been many gawkers who had never seen so dramatic an ocean vista.

"Isn't it beautiful?" one O'Malley had asked, as Noreen and Maddie had hurried past. Having summered on Clare Island, Noreen understood what well might follow. "I'd find some shelter fast, were I you." But her advice was disregarded, since the air was still, the evening warm from the heat of the day, and . . . well, the O'Malleys were among themselves and a power in their own right. What possibly could go wrong?

But when the wind came on again, it had changed direction, swinging around nearly one hundred and eighty degrees.

And it came on with a faraway roaring that sounded like the howl of some oceanic turbine. "We're in for it now," Noreen just managed to say, before it struck them full in the face and knocked Maddie's feet out from under her.

Noreen, swinging the child around into her lee as she turned her back, could barely move forward. And when a frigid rain began, it raked them in a horizontal torrent that pounded their skin right through their rain gear.

"I can only pity those poor campers," Noreen now said in the dining room of the hotel. She settled Maddie in a chair and looked round for a waitress who could get them tea and cocoa. "If that wind caught them the way it struck us, they're now tenting on Achill."

"But could you not see it coming?" Ruth was always amazed at city people who seemed oblivious to the elements until it was too late, since she had grown up on a farm in the South Kerry Mountains, hard by the wild Atlantic, and to this day she kept one eye on the clouds.

"I think I did, but we were all the way out by the standing stone in Ballytoohy. I can remember feeling that we should get back. But then, a question arose about the purpose of *fulachta fiadh*, and who should we bump into but Ernst Schweibert—the professor from the boat this morning."

"You mean, the one non-O'Malley tourist of the day?"

"There weren't any others?"

"Not that I know of, apart from resident Clare Islanders and two journalists whom I recognized. Tom Rice thinks the 'Rally' and the report of the murder are keeping other tourists away."

So much the better, thought Noreen, both for them and for the investigation. "What about his assistant?"

"*She* was nice," Maddie pronounced in a most grown-up voice, only to add, "Mammy—*when* are we going to eat? I'm famished."

"Soon, luveen—if I have to get it for you myself."

"Which assistant?" Ruth looked into the teapot on the table that she had long since drained, hoping that there might be some wet in the bottom.

"Didn't you interview the woman? She said she came on a boat that's presently in the harbor—at Schweibert's request.

She's a tall, strong-looking girl in her early twenties, well capable of turning down a core drill. He had one with him.''

"She told us her name was Helene,'' said Maddie, ''and they were going to sleep in the same tent.''

Noreen's eyes flashed at Ruth, who said, ''Well—perhaps her middle name was Helen, but I reviewed the lists for duplications and any Louisiana or South African addresses, and there was not a single Helene among them. Quite a few Helens, given their family tradition of tossing up strong women. But no Helene.''

Noreen thought for a moment; certainly Schweibert had appeared to be the real thing. It could be checked with a single phone call to Peter Coxon at Trinity College, who had unearthed the seven-thousand-year-old hazel nut. ''So we have to conclude that his assistant, Helene, either has a different first name and her last is O'Malley, or that she somehow managed to slip on to the island without our taking her name or snapping her picture.''

Ruth shook her head. ''Not if her boat is in the harbor, and you met her all the way out in Ballytoohy. She must have put into the harbor, what—''

''At least an hour before that.''

''—to have hoofed it all the way out there. And I can tell you I personally went over every boat stem to stern until seven o'clock, when one of Rice's men took over.''

''Maybe she was already here?'' Finally Noreen caught the eye of a waitress close by, who raised a finger to say she would be with them in a minute.

''Not possible. The chief personally visited every house on the island, and now it's like we've got a team of one hundred and forty confederates. There isn't a Clare Islander who's not on the qui vive.'' Bresnahan stood. ''So tell me—did Schweibert give you an opinion about *fulachta fiadh*? Hot baths or boiling pits?''

''To give the divil his due, it was no time for idle chatter.''

''Well, let Professor Ruthie set your minds to rest—they were both.''

Noreen and Maddie stared up at the tall, auburn-haired woman.

''Sure, nobody wants to tell the truth about the matter,

since it'd be an admission of ancestral guilt. But remember, I'm from Kerry where there're so many *fulachta fiadh* that people claim they were invented there.

"Now then, follow me closely. First, consider the size of your average Bronze Age maritime intruder." She held a hand out from her shoulder. "Now think of the dimensions of the *fulachta fiadh* you saw today. It would hold him neatly, no? And last, imagine the state of his bodily cleanliness— how many years ago?"

"Five thousand. Conservatively."

"Certainly before Sunshine soap appeared on the scene."

Noreen and the waitress nodded; Maddie was wide-eyed.

"Having said all that—would you want to eat your enemy without washing him first?"

Noreen laughed; Maddie smiled but plainly had not understood; Bresnahan rose to leave.

Said the waitress, "The specials is roast leg of lamb with mint sauce, entrecote of beef grilled to order, and Dover sole."

"Where're you going? Aren't you going to stay for dinner?"

"I just want to peek at the harbor. I'll have the steak, rare. The 'Intruder' cut." It was while passing through the lobby that the VHF radio in her purse beeped, then issued the garbled squawk of an electronically scrambled voice. Of an actual intruder.

Bresnahan stopped, even though she knew she would not be able to understand what was said. But no more was.

After unscrambling the transmission, Paul O'Malley heard:

"Dugald?"

"*Hier.*"

"*Ons 'n poging waag.*"

"*Alle voorspoed!*"

O'Malley activated the telephone and spoke the number of the translator in Dublin.

Bernie McKeon in the turret of the lighthouse had heard the brief bark of the scrambled transmission, and he was waiting for more, when he thought he saw a figure moving up the boreen toward the Gottschalk house.

Ever since the beginning of the storm, his surveillance sector had been thrown into such chaos that he did not know which figure among the dozens to follow. They were rushing this way and that, trying to get themselves and their gear out of the blast. Also, day was giving over to night, and the strange low clouds that had enveloped the turret that morning, seemed to be returning. Wisps kept bolting past the window, obscuring his view for whole seconds at a time.

The question was, should he switch on the infrared enhancement in the night-seeing binoculars? Or should he assume that the raiders, if they were out there, would possess the capability of knowing they were being observed?

With the figure now in the yard between the Gottschalks' buildings, he had no choice, but it took his eyes a few moments to adjust to the pale green and yellow shapes that now appeared, and by then she was at the door of the house. A tall, square, young woman dressed in something like a field uniform.

As she was knocking, McKeon remembered where he had seen her before: with the man whom Noreen and Maddie had spoken to earlier in the evening; *and* in the dive boat below the cliffs during the afternoon. There was no mistaking the sculptured shape of the backside that she now turned to him, as she waited for the door to open.

What about the boat? McKeon swung the glasses but had to wait until another patch of cloud whisked by. There it was, anchored off the cliff but now hobby-horsing on its rode in the stiff storm chop. How had she gotten up here without climbing through the cut near the Ford cottage where both McGarr and he would surely have seen her?

It was then that another voice came on the VHF. "Chief, Bernie—it's me," said Bresnahan. "I'm breaking in because I thought you should know: I just got off the phone with Hughie, who says Clem Ford is or was actually a person named Klimt Dorfmann, son of a Borkum island merchant sailor and a Harwich woman. He was at Magdalene College, Cambridge, with Angus Helmut Rehm, a Scot whose father was a German national, like Ford's or Dorfmann's.

"Rehm, however, was an avowed Nazi sympathizer, and there seemed to be some antipathy between the two. After graduating from Cambridge in 1935, Rehm returned there with three other men and attacked Dorfmann. The court transcript says Dorfmann was a huge man, who put three of them in hospital but ended up there himself. He then returned to Harwich to recuperate.

"At the trial, however, he refused to identify his attackers, even at the insistence of the magistrate, saying it was dark and he couldn't remember who they were, and the charges were dropped. Rehm then left the country shortly afterward, never to return according to British records.

"*But*—and here is the big one—Rehm was named at Nuremberg as a war criminal, and is still on the active list of the Wiesenthal organization." That pursued Nazi war criminals, McKeon knew.

Now the door was open, and Mirna Gottschalk—after saying something into the house, evidently to her son—pulled on an anorak and accompanied the young woman out into the drive. They moved off down the boreen toward the tent that she had put up earlier with the old man and had been one of the few that had survived the onslaught of wind. Another cloud bolted by.

"Rehm is described by Wiesenthal as five feet nine inches tall with a stocky build, blond hair, and blue eyes."

A genetic Nazi, thought McKeon.

"As a Waffen SS colonel during the war, he was captured by the Russians and interrogated by the NKVD. He was tortured and lost all the fingers on his right hand, before he is said to have killed his captors and escaped."

Turnabout being only fair play, butcher to butcher. McKeon kept his eyes on the house.

"He would now be in his early eighties, so all that might have changed."

Not a great deal, thought McKeon, who had watched him erect the tent and pound down the stakes, in spite of the missing fingers.

"The capper is the fact that Customs and Immigration have no Ernst Schweibert legally in the country. Hughie, through a contact at Trinity, got Schweibert's home phone number in

Switzerland. It seems that the Dr. Ernst Schweibert who participated in the recent Clare Island study disappeared three months ago while on a dig in Umbria. He just never returned to his hotel one night. The Italian police say he was last seen in the company of a much younger woman, but with no corpse and no report of violence, they're treating it as a missing-person case.''

Very missing, McKeon concluded—like for eternity.

"Also, we can find no entry documentation for Brendan or 'Brando' O'Malley, who purported to be an Australian national. He's about thirty-five, close to six feet, powerfully built, shaved head, and had what appeared to Noreen to be hiking or camping gear in a kit. He also had tattoos on both biceps and his neck and a large bruise on his upper chest, as though he'd recently been in a mix-up or an accident.''

Now at the tent, the younger woman pulled down the zipper and held the flap open. Mirna Gottschalk bent and stepped in. The girl followed her.

"And finally, there is no known person by the name of Moira O'Malley at the address she gave in Howth, and we don't have a record of having interviewed any Helenes, which is the name 'Schweibert's' assistant gave Noreen when she spoke to her this afternoon.''

They then heard an electronic ringing in the background. "Wait, it's my phone.''

"Peter,'' McKeon interrupted, while keeping his eyes on the tent. "The assistant is the girl from the boat, it's still below the cliffs here, and Schweibert is Rehm, I'm sure of it. Build, age, the one gloved hand, the works.''

Now the tent flap opened again. "Worse still, they're both now with Mirna Gottschalk. She's got his arm on one side, the girl on the other, like they're helping him walk, and they're moving toward the house.''

"Can you get down there?''

"Before they get back inside? Not a chance.'' It would take McKeon all of twenty-five on-the-trot minutes to even approach the house.

"I can't see a thing here,'' said McGarr. "The blow has pushed the clouds right down over me.''

"That was Paul O'Malley,'' Bresnahan interrupted. "He

says the last transmission was the older male voice telling the younger male to begin the operation. Also, it could be that they know they're being watched by infrared.''

Sitting with his back wedged into a crevice of stone that shielded him from most of the wind and rain, McGarr had a decision to make—to rush the house, now that they knew who Rehm and the woman were. Or to wait until they were out in the open again.

The problem with either scenario was the safety of the Gottschalks, which would damn him either way if they came to harm. But, of course, Rehm wanted something from them, which might buy time. The even greater problem was the probability that their voices were now being monitored. Which could not be helped.

"Bernie, you stay put and report anything and everything. Ruth—you get Rice and the others to close off the compound. Make sure everybody . . . extraneous is out of the area.'' McGarr pushed himself out from the protective nook into the stiff breeze that was thick with wet, gauzy cloud. "Understood?''

"Understood,'' McKeon and Bresnahan said together.

CHAPTER 25

AS HAD ANGUS Rehm. He was clutching the VHF scanner/decoder to his chest like a heart monitor, which Heather had told the Gottschalk woman it was. "My father, please—he's having problems with his heart. I'm afraid he'll die if I don't get him out of that tent." The wire, however, led to a plug in Rehm's right ear.

And what had he understood? That he had underestimated the police. Now there was little time to get what they came for and leave. As the two women helped him through the front door, he punched down the transmitter and said one word in Afrikaans, "*Nou!*"

Earlier in the day before the storm had struck, Dugald had climbed down the cliffs about fifty feet, where he could be seen only from the sea. He then traversed the cliff face about a half mile horizontally, until he was even with the Gottschalk house and came upon the rappelling ropes that Heather had strung to facilitate the evacuation from the island. Using those, he had quickly gained the top of the cliff, which coincided, neatly, with the onset of the storm. For the last nearly two hours, he had waited in a shed near the back door of the cottage.

Now at the door itself, Dugald raised a climbing shoe and dashed its hard-rubber sole into the wrought-iron latch. It

227

broke cleanly, as he knew it would. The thin cubby door
sailed off, smacking into a tier of shelving boards and dump-
ing whole rows of potted plants onto the concrete floor with
good dramatic effect.

There was no way anybody in the house could have missed
that sound, Dugald thought, as he stepped across the cubby,
pivoted, and raised his foot again. Just as in Lesotho in the
early 1980s when he was a young recruit with the South African Defense Force and was rousting ANC criminals from
the shantytowns around Maseru, he kept the barrel of his
Steyr AUG assault rifle pointed at the door, so he could kick
it open, fire and fall away. The police might soon arrive; time
was critical.

But all he heard was his father's voice somewhere deep in
the house, saying, "Is that your son? He's about to meet
mine."

Moving quickly into the well-appointed kitchen, Dugald
squeezed himself between a fridge and a freezer, again pointing the barrel at the only possible place that a threat might
appear. And did.

A tall, dark young man with a square bony frame walked
quickly into the kitchen toward the broken frame of the now
open door. When he stepped by the fridge, Dugald reached
out, grabbed a wrist, and pulled the man down and toward
him, while his left knee snapped up into the groin. As the
head descended, Dugald popped the neck once with the thick
butt of the AUG's bullpup stock that had been designed just
for that purpose. The man dropped limp, out before he even
hit the deck. And hard. His forehead bounced on the terrazzo
tiles.

Quickly, professionally, Dugald patted him down. No
weapon. Without war to keep people hard and vigilant, they
grew soft. The man—Karl Gottschalk, Dugald believed his
name was—had to have known they'd be coming, his mother
or the police having told him. And yet there he lay, helpless,
probably not even having seen who or what hit him. Dugald
had half a mind to whack the back of his useless head. But
they might need him for the mother.

Still, Dugald pressed a climbing shoe against the small of
the back where the hands could not reach. This time there

would be no screwups. Unlike his brother Malcolm, Dugald would not die for his father's ego or his sister's vanity.

Rehm called to him now. "Would yeh bring the boy in now, please, Dugald? There's little time."

Standartenführer Rehm, thought Dugald, giving orders. He'd had enough of that in his life. Snatching up the limp form by the belt and rushing him into the long hall, he skidded the son, like a curling stone, across the slick tiles toward the three people who were still standing just inside the front door. Heather hopped out of the way and the body, tumbling and turning, slammed into the door.

The mother dropped to her knees and raised the bloodied face. Like a peach, the skin of the forehead had popped, and blood was tracking into his eyes and across the pale discs of his sclerae. "My God, you've killed him."

"Not yet."

"I'll not ask ye' again," said Rehm. "Give us whatever Clem Ford brought ye'. It was not his and never was."

"Nor yours either, as I understand it." She rose from the floor and began moving down the hall, as though she would walk away.

Heather stepped in front of her. "Where do you think you're going?"

"To get a plaster for my son's forehead. To stop the bleeding."

"Better bring the box, he might soon be bleeding elsewhere." There was color in Heather's cheeks, her eyes were bright; she was enjoying herself, Dugald could tell.

"Please get out of my way."

"So," said Rehm, "Clem did bring it here?"

"*Fuck!*" Dugald roared. "We're getting fucking *nowhere*! We're wasting fucking *time*!" His hand shot out, grabbed the woman by the face, and pulled her toward him. "Is it under the fucking *hearth*?" he bawled into her face.

Mirna could not speak; she was frozen with fear. Enormously strong, his fingers felt like steel springs pressing into her flesh, bruising her bones. In a wild arc, her eyes took in the shaved head, the rings in the ear, the look in his eyes that proclaimed to Mirna louder than he could shout that he had killed and would willingly again. "Yes," she managed.

Releasing her, Dugald turned to Heather. "Get it."

"What? You bastard, you get it your—"

The backhand slap, sweeping up from Dugald's belt, snapped his sister's head back and sent her on a stagger into the sitting room. "And bring it all here."

Rehm moved forward to help, but Dugald shoved him back against the door. "I hear a peep out of ye', ye' won't have the chance to savor yehr muckle sweet revenge," Dugald taunted in a broad Scots burr. "Malcolm would want ye' at least to *glam* the *geld.*"

Dugald's hatred of him and the sister, who had kissed the old man's arse from the time she could talk, was not recent. While he was alive Malcolm, who had been loved by all, had acted as mediator among them, but now that he was gone . . .
"Give it here"—Dugald swung the barrel of the AUG at Heather, as she rose from a choke of ash dust with the metal box. He'd pop her without thinking twice.

And he could tell she wanted to say something, to assert her new primacy with their father, who shook his head. Warning her against any such foolishness, warning her against her own brother, his son. The middle child, Dugald had really never felt a part of them, and he knew what they thought— it should have been him and not Malcolm.

So be it. Snatching the metal box out of her hands, he stepped to the table in the hall and dumped the contents under a light. They had created the division, they had wanted it. How much could there be to share?

He scanned the page with the two names and addresses and also his father's name at the bottom of the page, all written like the correspondence they had found in the cottage. He then surveyed the map with "Cave" marked plainly on it at what appeared to be a three-hundred-foot level.

Clipped to the map were some Polaroid snapshots showing what looked like ammunition cases brimming with jewelry and gemstones, and not one or two but at least six that Dugald could count. "Come here," Dugald said to the woman.

She took a timid step forward, turning her head back to her son on the floor who was beginning to come to.

"What's this?"

"Clem's map of the cave."

"Where is it?"

"On the Great Cliff of Croaghmore. It can't be seen, you have to climb there."

"How big is it?"

"Big. Several large galleries and maybe a chimney."

"You mean, there might be a second entrance?"

"I don't know. I couldn't tell. My light wasn't strong enough."

"And these? Is this what's in there?"

"Yes."

"Did you take these pictures?"

Mirna nodded.

"When?"

"Two nights ago."

"Why?"

"To show to my son."

Rehm now dared to approach Dugald. "Ach—would ye' look a' tha'. Diamonds, rubies and *gold*. Did I na' tell ye', son? Was I na' right? All the kiaugh we've gone to has paid off."

Dugald ignored him. "What's this?" He picked up the thick sheaf of yellowing composition paper with the red wax seal that was broken. Opening it up he discovered more of Ford's eccentric script. It was dated 1947.

"It's Clem's memoir about how he came by all of that."

"*He* came by it? Woman—*I* personally put it all together with no help from him. He *stole* it from me in the last days of the war."

"That's in there too."

Flicking through the pages, Dugald saw that she was not lying. He handed it to his father, saying, "You should burn that."

"What—are ye' crazy, mahn?" Rehm fanned the pages. "It's confirmation of all that I ever told ye' about what happened there in Bergen. It's his bloody confession."

But also the link between you, a war criminal, and my fortune, you old fool. And it cannot continue to exist. Snatching it back, he tossed it to Heather. "Burn it."

He could see she wanted to challenge him, to say, Burn it yourself. But she knew what would happen, and they needed

232   Bartholomew Gill

him more than he did them. She moved toward the hearth.

"What's this name mean?" Dugald pointed to the names Monck & Neary. "I'll ask you but once."

Mirna did not hesitate. She was terrified of the man; she could still feel where his fingers had dug into her face. "They're solicitors in Dublin, the firm Clem told me I should see."

"About the investments he made?"

She nodded.

"And this?"

"Jewelers. The one he dealt with in Dublin."

"For what's left in the cave?"

"Yes."

"See?" Rehm said. "I told you he was telling the truth. He knew he had to."

To murder Malcolm, as you said yourself. Dugald shook his head; it was still hard to believe that Malcolm was dead.

"Heather—please don't, I beg of ye'."

But she took a match from the box on the mantel and struck the flame. With a burst the old paper ignited and was quickly consumed. She dropped the blazing mass into the hearth.

"Ach, Dugald—ye' shouldna' ha' done tha'." His father's pain was real, making Dugald wish there was more to destroy.

He turned to the woman. "This is the most important question of your life. You answer it true, you live. And your son there, he lives. You lie—I'll kill him first but slowly until you tell.

"When we get to Monck and Neary, what do we say? How do we identify ourselves to secure control." Ford would have left a key—some word or phrase or series of phrases—that would identify his successor.

As though steeling herself, the woman clenched her fingers at her waist and looked him in the eye. "Now, I tell it you, and you let us live—my son and me?"

Dugald smiled; she was as naïve as her diction was quaint. "You tell it to me."

"I have your word?"

He nodded; for what it was worth, she had his word. Neither of them could live, not with what was at stake and what had already transpired. People—soft people—were ignorant of the world as it was. They refused to *see*. At least this one had courage.

"Yes? Say, yes."

"Yes, yes, yes. We'll need you, though, to come to Dublin, just to be sure."

"What about Karl? My son."

Dugald glanced at the young man who had managed to push himself up against the wall; he was now trying to wipe the blood from his eyes. "I see he's got climbing shoes on, and is that climbing gear in that backpack by the door? Was he going to climb to the cave tonight?"

He could read in her eyes that he was.

"Then, I'll tag along. You should never climb alone." Dugald noted the eye contact between father and daughter; they were thinking, Right—you go for the tangible assets, Dugald, the ones Ford thought too readily identifiable to convert and too difficult to carry away from the cave and transport off the island. While we take care of the anonymous, easily transferable, financial instruments and probably the lion's share of the hoard with Ford having had nearly fifty years to build up the principal.

But there was nowhere in the small world that war criminal Angus Helmut Rehm could occupy that Dugald would not find him. Or them. And their betrayal of him, as they had betrayed Malcolm, would make it all that much easier.

Said the woman, "You're to say, 'Dorfmann sent me.' When she says back, 'But I don't know a Mr. Dorfmann,' you're to say, 'Klimt says you do.' Now, if my son takes you to the cave, then what?"

"Mother," Karl said groggily from the floor, "I can take care of myself."

Dugald shook his head; it was a pleasant prospect. But what would she believe? "The problem with Clem was Clem was greedy—in his own way. He couldn't have partners of any sort, he did not want to share. But we're different. We're prepared to let bygones be bygones. We even told him that before he pulled out a gun. And there's obviously enough to go round for you, your son, for us. If we work together, if we cooperate."

She opened her mouth to speak.

"I know. There's the other man who also came at us with a gun."

"Kevin O'Grady."

"I'm sure we can help his family, some way."

The woman only looked off, suspecting he was lying but wanting to believe, since she had no choice.

"You agree? Time is flying. You keep our confidence, we keep yours, and your son comes back no worse off than he is now. How are your legs?" Reaching down, Dugald snatched Gottschalk off the floor and set him on his feet. "Can I carry your kit?"

"No, I can manage."

And to the mother, "You pull the van round in front of the door. Make sure you switch off the interior lights so they don't come on when a door opens. You know how?"

She nodded.

"Then the three of you"—he turned to his father and sister—"out the back. I wouldn't tarry in Dublin too long. Make contact, establish control, and leave. I'll be in touch."

"How?" Rehm asked.

Dugald smiled. "Leave that to me. I'll find you."

"Do I see lights moving in the drive," asked McGarr, speaking into his radio. Having to pick his way through the boggy headland in the dark, he had gained only a half mile. But he could now hear the cataract above the Ford cottage, somewhere off to his left. And he could still see the Gottschalk place about a mile away, whenever the clouds or fog or mist lifted.

"It's the woman, Mirna. She's pulled the van round to the front door, I think. I can't see her because of the house."

"Is she alone?"

"I couldn't tell. Uh, there it goes again." The car now moved away from the house but at a creep. McKeon switched off the infrared, but it was no better. He switched it back on, as the car topped a short rise.

And then he thought he saw some other movement near the house. Swinging the glasses back, he surveyed the entire cliff edge as far as the Ford cottage, only to decide it had probably been more vapor scudding by. Both boats were still in place, although only the fishing boat off by Croaghmore was showing a light.

When he brought the glasses to bear on the drive again, he watched the van proceeding at the same snail's pace until it moved down into a small ravine that had been cut through ledge rock. "Do you see it, Peter?"

"Only the glow from its lights. The soup here is thick."

"Why is it moving so slowly? Could she be hurt? Or could it be a feint?"

Or a trap, thought McGarr. "How long did they have it there by the house out of our sight?"

"Two minutes, three tops."

Plenty of time for an experienced bomber to rig a previously prepared device to a door. "How far until it reaches Ruthie's position?"

"I can see it now, Chief," Bresnahan replied, "coming straight at me about a quarter mile off. It looks like she's stopped or is driving slowly. The road is poor here, and with the fog—"

"Mind yourself. If she's alone, make her stop and tell you what gives."

Standing in the middle of the boreen, Bresnahan scissored both hands in front of her, as she had been taught in traffic control when she had first joined the Guards ten years ago. If Mirna Gottschalk were not alone, she would ask her for a lift to the harbor.

But the van, still proceeding at a crawl, did not stop. Jumping from its path, she tried to peer past the glare of the lights through the windshield. As the driver's side window approached her, Bresnahan's right hand moved to her hip, closer to the 9 mm Glock that was concealed under her jacket in a holster at the small of her back.

But there was nobody in the car that she could see. Pulling out a pocket torch, she shined the beam directly down at the wheel that had been lashed in place by a web of shock cord. As the van jounced along the rutted road, the steering wheel could move, but the elasticity of the cord kept the car tracking along the ruts in the road.

"It's a feint. There's nobody in it, and the wheel's tied

down,'' Bresnahan said into her radio, as she watched the van roll away.

"Bernie, I'm going in," said McGarr.

"I'll join you."

"No, you stay there. I'll need eyes."

There was a pause, and then, "Maybe you won't. I think they're already gone."

"Gone where?"

"Gone on the dive boat. I don't know how it happened, but one moment it was there, and now it's gone. I think. There's clouds." A paused ensued, and then, "Yes, it's gone. They didn't even bother to take the rubber raft aboard. I can see it floating off toward Achill."

"Can you see lights?"

"No, they must be running blind. The only light I can see is on the fishing boat, the one that's anchored off the Great Cliff."

"Bernie, ring up the Naval Service and see if they can track it. I'll make sure the house is empty."

It was the harsh squawk of the VHF radio, carried on the wind across the bog to the very edge of the cliff, that alerted Dugald Rehm to McGarr's presence.

Squatting down and pulling Karl Gottschalk with him, Dugald waited until he heard the noise again and located the probable position. "You follow me and do what I do. And remember your mother."

CHAPTER 26

CLEM FORD WAS at a loss what to do. Anchored in Colm Canning's fishing boat a good two hundred yards off the Great Cliff of Croaghmore, he could make out two figures climbing the cliff face toward the cave, now as day broke.

His first thought was that Mirna and Karl had decided to view the cave together. But as the day wore on, he could see that the climbers were both men, who were knowledgeable and quick, wasting little effort as they scaled the sheer face of the headland. Could they have come off the boat that he heard start up and leave without showing any lights about an hour earlier? Could they be the Rehms? Not unless they had added to their number, since Ford was certain Angus Rehm could not negotiate the cliff at such speed.

Keeping himself in the cabin where he would not be seen, Ford pulled the binoculars from the clip by the wheel. With only one good arm, he had to struggle to focus in the pitching boat. As well, his old eyes were hard put to the task. But in the few glimpses he got of the two, he suspected the second climber was Karl, with his square shoulders and long thin legs. In fact, having taught more than a few generations of young Clare Islanders how to climb, Ford recognized some of the lower man's moves as his own.

They were free-climbing with the exception of a single

chock or camming device that the lead climber had inserted
in the last difficult rock passage just below the cave. That
proved he had never climbed before with Karl, who could
negotiate the hazard easily. But who could he be, with Karl
climbing willingly behind him? Could he be the surviving
Rehm son, tricking Karl into showing him the cave through
some subterfuge? What was his name again? Dugald, he had
heard Angus call him.

Ford kept trying to get a clear look at the man, whom he
believed he would know anywhere now after the debacle at
the cottage. But whereas the blocky, powerful shape resembled Dugald Rehm's, the man was wearing a blue or purple
climbing helmet and, of course, he kept his face to the cliff.

In any case, there was nothing Ford could do. The one hope
was that Packy, who was now up in the cave, could keep rein
on Colm Canning. Because of Packy's bad hand, it had taken
them most of the night to reach the entrance, and Canning
had agreed to go along, only after being promised a bottle on
top.

Ford despaired. How could two old men and one a drunk
manage to confront the Rehms, who had obviously planned
their attack to a fare-thee-well. He glanced at the Armalite
rifle by his feet. But how could he aim and fire a weapon
with any degree of accuracy when he could barely heft binoculars? All in a bobbing boat.

"*Breege!*" Ford moaned, his eyes again sweeping the dark
cliffs, the flitting clouds, and the two figures who were nearing the entrance to the cave. "*Ah, Breege!*" That their life
together was over and he had made such a cock-up of things
was too much to bear.

Dugald Rehm smelled the stench of whiskey just as he was
about to squeeze himself into the cave. On the still air, the
reek was heavy, sweet and close.

Wondering who it might be—some errant O'Malleys who
had blundered across the entrance to the cave and were now
toasting their luck? Or perhaps Clem Ford and some friends—
Dugald glanced down at Karl Gottschalk. He was some
twenty feet below and still climbing the cliff. Dugald's eyes

then swung to the boat that was anchored a few hundred yards offshore.

He had seen it there the evening before with two men in a dory working nets or pots close in to the cliffs. Now the dory was back on the boat, meaning that they had returned there. But Dugald could see nobody on deck or in the cabin, the windscreen of which had swung away now as the tide was turning.

Perhaps they had gone away with some other fisherman on some other boat. Or they could be below sleeping, waiting for the tide to carry the fish back in. In any case, whatever threat they posed was distant by several hundred yards of sea and sea cliff.

Not so Karl Gottschalk, now that Dugald suspected there was somebody in the cave. The young man was only fifteen or so feet below him, and, anyway, he had served his purpose, bringing him here. And climbing accidents were conveniently inexplicable for those who free-climbed alone.

Having secured the end of the rope to a rock horn, Dugald waited for Gottschalk to attach a carabiner and load his weight onto the tether. It was then Dugald jerked the rope up with all his strength and freed the camming device from the crack. Gottschalk plunged—not silently as Dugald would have wished—but, rather, screaming all the way down until his cries were drowned in the roiling sea three hundred feet below.

Dugald quickly climbed up onto the face of the large rock that shielded the cave entrance; that way anybody stepping out to look down would not see him. The sound had been unmistakably human and was bound to bring whoever was in there.

Now a head appeared in the cleft below Dugald. The man looked out. He was large and strongly built by the size of his shoulders, with curly hair streaked blond and a full beard that beat in the breeze. It was from him that the smell was coming. There was a bottle in his right hand.

Swinging his twenty-two-ounce ice ax on its thirty-two-inch aluminum shaft, Dugald plunged the sharp, wedged claw into the center of the man's forehead. Holding him there erect, Dugald snatched the bottle away before it could fall and break. With a tug he freed the ax and let the corpse slide away from him, over the edge of the cliff.

He did not hesitate. Dropping down onto the ledge where the man had been, he called out in his best Irish brogue, "That takes the biscuit, altogether. Oi've had enuff o' this." Moving quickly into the cave, he tossed the bottle in front of him, knowing that his body would be silhouetted in the bright daylight and his face virtually invisible to whoever was waiting in the darkness there.

The bottle landed at the feet of Packy O'Malley, who had been dozing under the painted warning of Peig O'Malley, his second cousin twice removed. Coming to with a start and wrath in his heart, he pushed himself away from the wall saying, "Colm Canning—yeh lout and yeh sot. *Yeh*'ve had enough? I'm sick to death of yehr antics."

Exactly, thought Dugald, stepping quickly over to the old man before he could gain his feet.

"I told Clem it was not on—bringin' this bottle up here, and now no more for you no matter how ye' beg." He reached for it, but Dugald kicked it out of the way.

Packy looked up; Colm had changed. He had shaved, and everything about him looked fresher, bigger, brawnier. It was not Colm. "Where's Colm?"

The man smiled. Deeply tanned, he was wearing a blue and purple climber's hat and a strange class of eye goggles. There were tattoos on either arm. Packy began pushing himself up, but a powerful kick, delivered to his shoulder, sent him sprawling into the fine sand on the cave floor. Like a dart through his spine, another foot was then punched down into the small of his back. "Feck ye', ye' pooling hoor's melt!" Packy bawled. "Ye' squid's inky get! Clem Ford'll do ye', sooner or later. Don't think he won't!"

It was only then Dugald noticed that the man had lost all the fingers on his right hand, just like his own father, and he silenced him with a short, sharp kick to the back of the neck. Grabbing the body by the belt and the hood of the fishing jacket, he scuttled the heavy corpse to the entrance of the cave, and tumbled it over the cliff.

Would the three bodies be viewed as a multiple climbing

accident, he wondered? Only if they were not carried away by the tide, which was more likely.

In any case, he doubted an official would bother climbing up to investigate why they had fallen or to question the strange shape of the wound in the forehead of the drunk. After all, it was Ireland where details were ignored. Witness how easily they had got what they came for, this second time with him in charge.

From his pack, Dugald pulled out a halogen lamp and turned back into the cave to advance upon his fortune.

McGarr was tired. He had not slept the night long, and when in Mirna Gottschalk's house he discovered the doors broken open and blood on the kitchen tiles, he felt beaten. More so when he found the keystone pulled out of the hearth and a metal box empty.

He had known the raiders were coming back, yet he had allowed them to waltz right in and take away what they were after, perhaps along with two more lives.

More out of force of habit than any real confidence that he could come up with a lead, McGarr began searching the house, then the shop, and finally the studio. There in a wastepaper bin beneath the photocopy machine, he noticed a sheet with Clem Ford's handwriting.

Sure enough, it was a copy of a sheet of lined paper. It had not been centered high enough on the scanning bed and had lost the last few lines. It said it had been written by Ford here on Clare Island in 1947 and appeared to be the first page of a reminiscence of his war years.

Obviously McGarr had not searched as thoroughly as he should, and he began anew. But he found nothing. Anyhow, how could a half-century-old document help him locate the Fords, Packy O'Malley, and the Gottschalks, who had probably come to grief by now, given how the raiders had dealt with Kevin O'Grady.

Out in the yard, McGarr radioed McKeon and told him to pack in the surveillance effort. "Get some sleep."

"What about yourself?"

"I'm going to wander over to the Ford cottage and look round."

"Again? There's not a thing in that place you haven't looked at twice."

"And, worse, I'll be making you feel guilty."

"Don't count on it. I'm only a short stagger from the bed." He signed off.

The wind had eased, the sky was bright, the day would be fair. Already, fearless O'Malleys were returning from whatever shelters they had found for the night to pitch tents again on the rolling, treeless greensward. To the south beyond the harbor, he could see more boats advancing upon the island from Roonagh Point.

On the north side of the island—directly below the cliffs—there was none, not even the fishing boat that McKeon had reported as working the waters on the day before. McGarr asked himself why he had not put a watch on the few that had gathered there? Because of the height and the steepness of the cliffs. And in his own defense, he actually had. McKeon, who was his best.

Granted, the weather, the darkness, and the sheer number of O'Malleys near Mirna Gottschalk's house had conspired against him. But the long and short of it was—he had simply been outwitted. Stopping by the cataract near the Ford cottage, he dug out a cigarette.

One thing, he should have been better informed about the practices of the "Rallyers"; the whole scene had taken him by surprise. And two, he should have recruited some of the locals to act as spotters with binos and VHF radios. Like Paulie O'. But thinking of Fergal O'Grady, he wondered how possible that would have been, McGarr being a *seoinin* and all.

McGarr took a puff or two. The roar of the tannin-rich bog water, surging into the dingle, was soothing to him, and he squatted down to rest, his eyes following the second trail leading away from the Ford cottage. It weaved back and forth, climbing the mountain, as though it had been used, say, by a donkey bearing a burden rather than a person who could save steps by climbing straight up.

What possibly could Ford have been carrying down from the top of the mountain? Turf? It was a possibility, since peat existed in virtually every setting in the West of Ireland. Also,

Fergal O'Grady—who had climbed that way—had been carrying a slane on his shoulder when he surprised McGarr on the night before. On his way, said he, to do McGarr's job of work for him. McGarr bristled to think of how completely the man had got the drop on him. And lucky he didn't get a bullet in return.

McGarr now wondered if the old man could have stayed up there. If so, he might have seen the direction that the dive boat was headed when it left the island from its anchorage below the cliffs. Jumping across the sluice, McGarr began climbing the mountain straight up. The sun was warm on his back, the air crisp and storm-scoured clean; at the very least he'd get some exercise.

Dugald Rehm could not believe his luck. First, there had been the easy way that he had dispensed with the opposition. True, they had been a yuppie, a drunk, and an old man, but there might not even be an inquiry, if and when the bodies were found.

Second was the plunder, and it certainly was. Rings, brooches, diamonds, emeralds; there was a tourmaline that scarcely fit in his palm, and great round slices of solid gold with six-inch-diameter holes in the middle, looking like glittering cangues. Ford had either tired of melting them down or had decided that he already had enough in Dublin. Why bother.

Bottom line: His father had not lied. It was a magnificent treasure in every way, and he only wished Malcolm were there to share it with him. Dugald would carry it away, backpack load by precious backpack load, which, of course, would take some time. He'd buy a house somewhere on the mainland where he could hide the booty. He'd tell the islanders he was studying gannets or puffins or choughs, so none of them would question his frequent visits to Croaghmore. They were used to their island being studied.

Dugald found his third piece of luck in the chimney that the woman had mentioned; he knew then that he had been destined to take control of the fortune. Not only were there bolts and pitons fixed into the wide barrel of the stack, there were also runners, carabiners, and sturdy Enduro climbing ropes that were in excellent condition, here where the elements were not a problem. The line rose at least as high as Dugald's excellent light could shine. When he struck a match, the flame flickered slightly. There was a draft, which meant there was a hole at the top—the second entrance.

After loading up his pack with a few of the choicest pieces that included an actual crown, Dugald began his ascent of the chimney. He would return to the harbor and mingle with the O'Malleys until he could catch a boat back to Roonagh Point. If he moved fast, he might even meet up with his father and sister in Dublin and relieve them of their obligation to join him in partnership.

Strapping his light onto his backpack so he would have some illumination climbing the dark aven, Dugald started up the chute slowly, carefully, methodically. Now was not the time for derring-do; now was the time for careful steps that would remove the treasure from the cave and provide him the life that his father had wanted for himself. And for which Malcolm had paid the ultimate price. Now Dugald would have to live it for both of them.

The chimney narrowed but then opened into another gallery where—Dugald suspected—the ancient stream that had worn away the limestone fissure in the mountain and had created the cave had once collected and pooled. There he rested where, it was obvious, Ford had taken a breather in the past. In a corner was a large bottle of what looked like water; also there were burned matches and small piles of tobacco ashes, where the man had knocked out his pipe.

But Dugald could now smell fresh air laced with the tang of brine from the sea, and he began climbing again. Five minutes later he could hear wind wailing past whatever opening the aven led to, which had to be near the very top of Croaghmore, given the length of the climb. Dugald rejoiced; he'd been right. The entire setup was perfect, which was why it had taken his father so long to discover Ford.

Now seeing light, he switched off the torch on his backpack and pulled himself up toward the dim glow.

From perhaps a quarter of a mile away, McGarr saw the figure near the apex of Croaghmore, hunkered down with his *brat* wrapped around him and his white mane flying, looking himself like another rock or a white-capped dolmen. The slane was on his shoulder, and he was so still that McGarr wondered if something might be wrong with him.

But then suddenly Fergal O'Grady got to his feet, and with his head still lowered toward the rocks in front of him, he took a cautious step backward. Slowly the slane rose off his shoulder, gripped tightly in both hands.

McGarr himself stopped, wanting to see what the man would do if uninterrupted. But O'Grady just stood there for another long time, until McGarr decided he should use his binoculars to see what he was looking at.

As McGarr glanced down to find the tab of his jacket zipper, however, he saw something flash. Like a thunderbolt, the bright silver head of the slane had swung around, and an object shaped like a rock—no, *two* rocks—rolled away from O'Grady's feet.

Looking round, he now saw McGarr, and, quick for his age, he scuttled over and picked up one of the rocks. Then, with his back to McGarr, he moved to the edge of the cliff and tossed it over, down into the waves below.

The breeze caught the second object, which appeared to be blue and purple, and it skidded away from the cliff, only to bounce and tumble and sail down the flank of the mountain where it found its own place in the sea.

Picking up the hem of his *brat,* O'Grady appeared to wipe the blade of his slane on an interior fold, before turning and walking triumphantly, defiantly even, directly at McGarr. The tool was back on his shoulder.

"What did you just toss off the cliff?"

"Garbage. It's how we disposed of it, before the likes of you."

CHAPTER 27

WHEN THE THREE people walked into the office of Monck & Neary on Merrion Square in Dublin the next morning, they found a man dressed in a swallowtail coat, morning trousers and spats. He scarcely looked up from the newspaper he was reading.

Beside him on the desk, a television was monitoring price quotations from the Dublin and several international financial exchanges. To his other side, a computer was also scrolling through lists of figures. It was torrid there with an array of caged birds raising a din. Otherwise the Georgian room was light and airy.

"May I help you?" the man asked. He was young and handsome with black hair, a good tan, and dark eyes.

"We're here to see Monck or Neary."

"In what regard?"

"In regard to a trust."

The man smiled and turned from the paper. "Trusts is us. But you want to speak to Neary, who's in charge of such matters. Top of the stairs, second door on the right. Knock first, please. I'm Monck. I handle the markets"—he swung a hand at the monitors—"and the birds." His smile became more complete, as he unabashedly surveyed the feminine particulars of the two women, each in her turn. "Perhaps you require a guide."

"No, I think we'll find the way," said the larger of the women. She was tall, broad, and fetching. A blonde, she was dressed in a smart but conservative summer suit of brushed linen with a broad-brimmed sun hat to match. Like her shoes, her large purse was brown patent leather and gleamed.

The other woman, however, was smaller, older, and dark with white braided hair; she was wearing some out-of-doors costume. Her shoes were wrapped with wide bands of rubber for climbing rocks.

The man, who left the room last, was a match for the younger woman. Although elderly, he looked fit. His pale blue eyes were clear, his skin deeply tanned, and he possessed a full shock of silver hair that he wore swept back. Looking jaunty in a blue seersucker suit, he kept his right hand in his trouser pocket.

"Yes?" Neary asked, when they knocked.

"May we come in? We were told we could speak to you about a trust."

"Please do."

They entered the room to find a large but shapely auburn-haired woman sitting at a desk surrounded by papers and computer printouts, and what looked like a stack of fax transmissions was in her lap. "Pardon me if I don't get up? I'm rather . . . involved. How can I help you?"

Heather Rehm rather liked what she saw—the shape and cut of the black-bordered, chrome yellow suit, to say nothing of the strong face and smoky gray eyes of Neary. She immediately checked her hands—no rings, which was encouraging. Yes, she could do business with this woman. At the same time, there was something disturbingly familiar about her. "What's your first name?" Heather asked.

"Astrid—and yours?"

"Heather." There was no point in using an alias, if they were going to take control of the Trust. They would move the money directly to South Africa at the earliest possible opportunity.

"And you are?"

"Louise," said Mirna, having been instructed not to give her own name.

Bresnahan turned to Rehm.

"Call me Gus. My friends do." He smiled.

"Good, so, what can I do for you this morning?"

"We're here about the matter of a trust," said Rehm. It was without a doubt the most exalting moment of his life, the apotheosis of having persevered and bent every effort to right the wrong of what was now the distant past. He had found Klimt Dorfmann and supervened. And yet, somehow, he felt cheated that it was not Dorfmann who had brought him here to witness the transference. "Dorfmann sent me."

There was a knock on the door. It opened. The head of Monck appeared. "Excuse me. A thousand pardons, Astrid. Is there a Missus or Miss or Ms. Gottschalk here? I hardly know what to say these days. She has a phone call."

"Me?" Mirna asked. "How does anybody—"

"I think it's your son. He said to tell you it's Karl."

"Of course, *he* would know," said Mirna, glancing at both of the Rehms as she stood.

"I'll go with you. Father, you can handle the—"

"He says it's personal," Ward put in. "And urgent."

"Can't she take it here?" asked Rehm.

"He rang on the public line. I handle public calls in order to free Ms. Neary for—" Ward pointed to the impedimenta on the desk.

Mirna Gottschalk broke for the door. "I'll be right back."

"See that you do," Heather barked. "Remember me to Dugald."

Ward swung the door a bit wider, and she squeezed out, only to stop in the shadowed hallway, shocked by what she saw in Ward's right hand.

It was a gun. He closed the door and pointed to the stairs, whispering. "There's a Garda car outside. It will take you to him. He's had a nasty fall, and he's in hospital. But don't worry, they say he's out of danger."

Inside the room, as Heather sat back down, it occurred to her where she had seen the woman at the desk before.

"Dorfmann sent me," Rehm said again to Bresnahan.

Snapping open the top of her patent leather purse, Heather plunged her hand in.

"Mr. Monck!" Bresnahan barked at the door, pushing the stack of faxes to the floor and snatching up the Glock in her lap.

The door burst open, and Heather swung some sort of machine pistol at Ward, who fell away as the weapon spat a burst of silenced fire at him that was punctuated by four loud blasts from the Glock. The first punched Heather back in the chair, the second spun her round. As she began to slide to the floor, the third and fourth removed her linen sun hat, bursting as wide plugs from the back of her head.

Ward picked himself up.

With the gloved right hand gripping the arm of the cushioned chair like an old black claw, Rehm stared down at his daughter dead at his feet, then slipped his other hand into the jacket of his seersucker suit.

"Don't!" Ward warned.

"Take your hand away!" Bresnahan stood up from the desk, the Glock locked in both hands and pointing down at him.

When the hand—tanned and rumpled with veins, like an old claw—came out from under the lapel with something shiny, a stunning fusillade riddled the man, knocking over the armchair so that he lay there, feet raised, the thin bones of his old legs exposed.

Ward straightened up from his firing crouch. "You okay?"

Bresnahan lowered the gun. "I think so." It was the first time she had ever shot anybody, to say nothing of having killed two people.

The air in the room was filled with the sweet stink of gun smoke that was sifting slowly through the morning sunlight.

They heard footsteps on the stairs, as other guards rushed up to the room.

"It's all right," Ward called out. "We're in here. No problems."

Bresnahan was not so sure. On quaking legs she lowered herself back down into the seat and tried not to look at the face of Heather Rehm with the two large cratered holes in her forehead. It was a sight that—Ruth knew, even then—

she would never scrub from her memory. Something had changed for her, but she did not know what.

Dressed in flak jackets, helmets, boots, and carrying automatic carbines, the other guards stepped cautiously into the room. Their eyes fell to the bodies. Said Ward, "Yehr woman there pulled that gun and sprayed the place. We had no choice. Then yehr man followed suit. We warned him, but it was like he was committing hara-kiri."

Ward had been in this position before, and he knew it mattered very much what story was bruited about in police circles. Sooner or later it would become public, indiscretion being gauged by the pint. The truth without any imaginative flourishes was always best.

He jacked the clip from his Beretta. "I'm out, Ruthie. What about you?"

Bresnahan nodded. She did not have to check. At some point in the execution of the old man, her Glock just would not fire anymore. "Has anybody got a cigarette?"

Ward glanced over at her, concerned; she did not smoke.

But one uniformed guard smiled at another and produced a cigarette. "Certainly, Inspector. D'ye' need a light?"

Smiling up at him, she accepted both cigarette and light, then crossed her long, well-formed legs—clad as they were in black lace. Exhaling the smoke, she looked out the window there by the desk, into Merrion Square.

It would be the better part of the "inside" story, Ward knew. "Didn't she whack the both of them right where they sat, then took a vacant chair and had a quiet smoke with the stiffs dead at her feet." Her stock would soar in cop circles, more decidedly with the Rehms having been cop killers.

PART V

Dispossession

CHAPTER 28

TWO DAYS LATER, while lying on the beach at the harbor on Clare Island, watching Maddie gambol in the surf with some other children, McGarr opened a photocopy of Clem Ford's (or Klimt Dorfmann's) memoir.

It had been found in a pocket of Karl Gottschalk's belly pack that was still wrapped around his waist when, injured, he had been plucked out of the sea by a fishing boat and taken to Westport Quay. From there he had been flown by medevac helicopter to a hospital in Dublin.

The tall old man with the great snowy beard who had radioed Westport and arranged for the helicopter did not give his name. The moment the chopper was airborne, he shoved off in his boat.

Having taken the boat's numbers, however, Gardai in Westport determined that it was owned by one Colm Canning, also of Clare Island. Canning did not answer his telephone, nor was he home when McGarr tried to call there.

McGarr now looked down at Ford's backward-slanting script.

11 November 1947
Clare Island, Mayo
Eire

I write this while the details are still fresh in mind and so you who succeed us will know the source of the cargo that I brought to this island. I write also for posterity and my God, who shall judge me; it was war, but it was also a struggle between forces. I knew that back in the mid-1930s. The pity is, not well enough.

First, a word about who I am, since beginning in 1945 I had to abandon my true identity, again because of the cargo. I arrived here under circumstances that were, at the very least, covert and perhaps even criminal, when viewed in the light of history.

I was born in the middle of the First World War in 1916, the son of a German maritime trader and an English woman with whose family he had dealings. With his captain's license, my father was soon conscripted into the German Navy, serving with distinction during the fateful Battle of Jutland. I grew up in Harwich in Suffolk. English was my first language, although I began speaking German at an early age.

After the war, my father removed us to his own family's base on Borkum Island where he operated a legitimate import/export business by day, while he smuggled at night. Petrol, liquor, tobacco—any contraband that was profitable to bring into the Weimar Republic via the shallow water along the Friesland coast and the Ems. The fall of Weimar and the beginning of rearmament brought other opportunities, however, and he began trading with South America for raw materials then in short supply—mostly tin, nickel, bauxite, and manganese.

Since the tradition on both sides of my family was nautical, I learned to sail as a child. During my summer holidays from mainly English schools, I gradually gained mastery over a variety of vessels of ever greater tonnage, until in my seventeenth year in 1933 I became a fully licensed captain. It was something that my father had wanted me to attain.

My mother's traditions were different, however, and a place was found for me at Cambridge, where my maternal grandfather had studied. There I read history, and one of the regrets of my life is that I did not finish. Because of a misadventure in my third year at the hands of some thugs whose political beliefs I did not share, I was injured in a brawl. I had to return to Borkum to mend, and the fate that befell my father at the beginning of the First World War nearly became my own.

But rather than be conscripted into the German Navy, I decided to join the Submarine Service where lay Germany's only hope for naval supremacy, as it was apparent even then. Because of my father's honorable record and my having captain's papers, the height restriction for submarines was overlooked. I joined the DVC (Doenitz Volunteer Corps, as it was called informally) in January 1936.

You, who will read this, might know the story. During the early years of the war up until February 1943, German submarine technology was equal to any defenses that Allied convoys could mount against us. In that month our submarines sank 44 boats and 21 ships, a total of 142,465 gross registered tons of Allied shipping. But only three months later, we lost 35 U-boats, 1,026 submariners, and we sank a mere 96,000 gross registered tons.

As early as 1937, naval planners had known that the superiority of the Type VII subs that became the backbone of the fleet would be short-lived. Even then other larger, faster, quieter boats were on the drawing boards. But instead the High Command, which was dominated by Nazis or Nazi toadies, chose to squander Navy funds on a surface fleet that was doomed from the start and proved to be little more than a fatal grand gesture.

Suddenly in the midst of fog and darkness, when a submarine commander thought it safe to run on the surface, Allied aircraft began to attack with such accuracy that there was barely enough time to dive. Also, convoys seemed to know of our approach, zigging and zagging away while their escort ships attacked us with steadily increasing success. It was as though the sea were made of glass, and they could see our every wallowing move.

And yet with its usual Nazi bombast the High Command kept sending us out in the old Type VII iron coffins to die. Over 30,000 of us did, which was a casualty rate of 85 percent. Some 5,000 others were lucky to be captured. By 1944 we had been driven out of Europe proper to Bergen, Norway, with only a handful of active boats, little fuel and spare parts, and a dearth of experienced crew. At twenty-eight I was the oldest living active sub captain, while the flotilla commander was an ancient thirty.

On 8 May 1945 (the day of Formal Surrender) I returned to Bergen after a run of six weeks, during which I had spent most of the time hiding in the coves and holes of the continental shelf off Ireland and Scotland. I ventured out to attack only twice and was nearly sunk both times. I remember the day of return in every particular, since it is a day that has shaped the rest of my life. It is about this day that I write.

It began when we passed through the sub nets and surfaced in the fjord to a leaden spring sky. The bridge of my Type VII-C submarine was so beaten that it was a length of twisted, torn steel that was scarcely afloat. From there I saw a strange sight drifting through the icy water of the fjord a few hundred meters off our bow.

It was a Walter boat, the most advanced of the new submarines that had been promised years earlier but had never been delivered. "Miracles of German technology," they had been called, that "would win the Battle of the Atlantic." As I stated earlier, they had known this eight years earlier.

Maybe at that time boats like the Walter might have mattered, had we been given the ninety we had been promised. Scanning my crew, I doubted how effective any number of new boats could now be.

The ragtag assembly of children (I can only call them) were swimming in the long gray leather jackets that had been made for submariners, for men, *not the boys before me. They had thin chests, bony arms, and even after six weeks at sea few had beards. For the first time, a boat under my command had gone out without sinking a single enemy ship. The truth was, I had been lucky to get them back alive.*

I can remember feeling hot and bitter anger. My mate had only just handed me the morning radio communiqué from Berlin to all forces in the Atlantic Command. "Be strong," it said. "Do not falter! The foe, too, is weary." It was more Nazi bombast and smacked of a passage cribbed from the Edda and "heroic" death. Not only did they not care if we died, they actually wanted us to die to fulfill the necrophilic dimensions of their horrid myth.

Here was the apparition of a new submarine with its anti-sonar rubber skin and complex radars protruding from its conning tower, arriving among all the shattered hulks of our once proud submarine fleet now at the end of The End, like a macabre joke. See? (Berlin was saying.) We delivered our miracle of German technology, what could have made you invincible. To do what with, now? Well understanding their humor, I had an idea.

Let me write here for the record, I hated Nazis; in fact, I had fought them since my days at Cambridge. There I had been singled out by the handful of Nazi sympathizers because I was German, I am large, and I did not agree with them on any issue, including (now in 1945) the destruction of Germany.

"If you hate them so much," my then wife, Ilsa, once asked, "why do you fight for them?"

"It's rather simple," I had replied. "I am a German man, I am also a German sailor, and my country is at war. My father served in the German Navy and his father before him."

By 1945, however, Ilsa too was dead, killed in a bombing raid on Kiel where she had been living with her parents while I was in the subs.

At any rate, before my battered boat reached the sub pens that day in Bergen, Conrad Geis, who was my chief engineer and the only other experienced man in my crew, appeared beside me with a second message. It was from the flotilla commander, congratulating me since, as the most senior submarine captain, I would now be given the Walter boat. Some hours later, Geis and I went to inspect the new boat.

She was a fair-sized craft of about 200 feet and, I guessed, 1,200 tons. What I liked about her immediately were her fair, whale-soft lines and her two batteries of 30 mm antiaircraft guns that were fitted sleekly, fore and aft, into the top of the conning tower to reduce drag. I loathed some of the other new designs that lacked a deck gun, for once forced to the surface for any reason, you were defenseless.

Instead of a submariner to greet us, however, a man in a soft hat and civilian clothes met us on the foredeck, "Commodore Dorfmann," he called out. "But of course, who else could you be? I was told to find the biggest man in Bergen with a half-pint sidekick."

Geis only appeared so in contrast; actually he was of average height for submariners—a dark wiry man whom I considered a technical genius worth two men twice his size. There was nothing he could not fix or fabricate.

"Who the hell is he?" I asked.

"Probably some stuffed shirt from the Todt Organization."

It was the contractor that had built most of the subs for the Third Reich since 1933.

"You take care of him, I'll look round at what they brought us."

"And you are?" I stepped up on the rounded, rubber-sheathed foredeck. With the other arm I swept Geis past the man.

"Axel Schmelling, Todt service director. I'd like to give you a tour of your new vessel, Commodore."

It was the second time that the man had overstated my rank, which was merely Kapitän and a giant step from Commodorezursee. But he quickly launched into his speech, calling the Walter boat a true *submarine— and not just another submarine-type boat—that could remain submerged for an entire tour of duty, yet maintain speeds of most surface vessels.*

As he spoke I turned my back to him and climbed the

*ladder of the conning tower. Apart from brief furloughs,
I had lived on submarines and survived the experience
for nine years, and I could see at a glance what the
boat contained. Also I was in no mood to suffer a fool
who had spent the war constructing a weapon, no matter how superior, that had arrived too late. Not when
so many of my comrades had gone to the bottom.*

*The interior of the tower stank of fresh welding scars,
new paint, and all the artificial rubber of gaskets and
seals. When my eyes had accustomed themselves to the
shadows, I discovered that the Walter had been built in
two tiers, the lower given over to a massive battery.*

*"On one charging she can produce a submerged
speed of five knots for four days or sixteen knots for an
hour,"* Schmelling said over my shoulder. *"With snorkeling she will cruise at twenty-four knots submerged,
which is faster than most Allied antisubmarine craft."*

*He who had only ever to outrun a sub-chaser on a
drawing board.*

*"In that mode, the boat need never surface. As well,
the engines are whisper-quiet turbines that run on per-
oxide, which eliminates the problem the Fatherland has
of obtaining petrol-based fuels."*

*The Fatherland? I decided Schmelling must be a Nazi,
which was how he, and people like him, had kept themselves out of the war. Nazis fought best with their
mouths. He proved it. As I climbed to the second tier,
he went on about the boat's radars and its capability
of sensing when it was being tracked by enemy radar.*

*"And finally there is the new 'Lut' torpedo that's
impossible to defeat."*

Or, at least, there should have been Luts.

*Geis appeared in an open forward bulkhead and sig-
naled me to follow him. The torpedo storage bay was
empty. Cranking the wheel of the air lock of a torpedo
tube, he bade me look in. Nothing. And another. Still
nothing.*

"No eels."

*When I turned back to Schmelling, there was another
man, who was dressed like a soldier, behind him.*

"Where are the Luts?"

"They'll be here shortly."

"You mean—you ran from Bremen to Bergen defenseless?"

"Without incident. There's nothing out there that can track or catch this boat. And we figured we'd better get it out now."

While we can, was implied.

Geis and I looked at each other; things must be worse at home even than was reported.

"That's fine if you're in a race," I said. "But this is war. How do you expect me even to defend myself, much less hunt and defeat the enemy?"

"That'll be all, Schmelling. I'll take over now."

Without another word, Schmelling left, and the other man stood there, as though waiting for us to recognize him and make the first move. His uniform, however, was a distraction; also it had been ten years since I'd last seen him. I felt older than time.

He was wearing a long gray raincoat that was open, and the flying blouse and baggy jump trousers of a paratrooper. The color, however, was not the dark blue of the Luftwaffe, but rather the gun-metal gray of the army. With a difference—on the officer's cap was the skull and crossbones of the SS along with his rank badge, which was Standartenführer, the German equivalent of colonel. His jump boots were polished to a mirror sheen.

"Don't you recognize me, Klimt?"

Only then, when he said my name, did I; it was Angus Helmut Rehm, a Scottish national but also a Nazi zealot who shared with me a German patrimony and who had been in my college at Cambridge. Enraged that I had rejected everything about National Socialism and Nazism, and had once cruelly branded him "Der Scots' Rump Führer" during a public debate (a name that was quickly adumbrated to a derisive "Dour Rump" and became Rehm's unshakable monicker), he and three others equipped with cudgels had attacked me on a

Cambridge street. It was those injuries that kept me from finishing my degree.

"Don't tell me I've changed that much."

In fact, he had not; it was as though he had not aged a day.

"You haven't."

It was a lie. My knees were shot; I now had a permanent stoop. Little sleep, poor food, bad water, and foul air had taken a toll.

"You only look more . . . mature. I know I certainly am. Much has happened to mellow us. I hope you're willing to let bygones be bygones, I know I am. And I'm here to apologize."

Out came his hand, which—after a moment or two of reflection—I took. We had both been rash and callow youths whose beliefs were yet to be tempered by experience. War, of course, is the great forge; at that moment in Bergen I think I believed in nothing but survival.

And there was something wrong with his hand. I looked down.

"A thousand pardons." Rehm raised it. All the fingers of his right hand had been cut off down to the second knuckle. The grafted skin on the stumps was a bright pink color.

"Stalingrad. Or, at least, retreating from Stalingrad. My battalion got overrun and captured. For a time."

He waited, the clear blue eyes and handsome face assessing if we understood that he was a fighting Nazi soldier, an officer of the Waffen SS, and not just another Nazi. Also he wanted to make sure that we had noticed the medals that were visible on his chest, now that the raincoat had opened more completely.

I glanced at Geis who looked away. Among us submariners it was bad form to speak of our victories, especially when we were losing the war.

"I see you have Lieutenant Geis with you."

Rehm was a short, strongly built man; the blond hair showing below his cap was clipped short.

"I've heard a great deal of good about you too, Lieu-

tenant. I'm sure both of you are wondering what
brought me. Let me put your minds at ease—I'm here
to deliver you these.''

From his pocket he pulled out an envelope and
handed it to me.

"Along with the new 'Lut' torpedoes. Most are already here in Bergen. The last four are being flown in
perhaps sometime today. We've had some problem with
. . . logistics, let us say. Things are rather problematical
these days.''

Again Geis and I traded glances. As far as either of
us knew, nothing had been flown in or out of Bergen
for months now, because of the lack of air transport
planes and the constant presence of Allied fighters. Also
conventional torpedoes weighed three thousand pounds
apiece, and the "Lut" was reported to be heavier still.
And finally, since when was the SS in charge of arming
submarines?

"Everything will be in order by tomorrow, you'll see.
In the meantime, I was hoping to have a word with you,
Commodore. And the lieutenant too, of course. Could
there be some place close by we might get a good meal
and a few drinks? My treat of course. You might open
up that envelope, Klimt. I know you'll like what's inside.''

In it were the badges of a Commodorezursee, along
with a letter promoting me to that rank.

McGarr glanced up from the pages to check on Maddie
and the other children who were now playing in the gentle
waves. It was a peaceful scene to be sure, compared to what
he was reading.

Certainly Ireland had experienced her troubles, to say nothing of the War of Independence and eight hundred years of
British domination. But because of the isolationist and anti-
British policies of Eamon De Valera, the regnant politician
of the time, twenty-six counties of the country had the good
fortune to avoid the cataclysm that had so decimated most of
the rest of the continent.

She did not go unscathed, however. Attempting to punish

Ireland, Britain kept her in economic thrall after the war until she joined the Common Market in 1973 and was able to trade directly and freely with the Continent. And accept twenty billion in "backhanders," according to Fergal O'Grady. McGarr glanced up at Croaghmore, before returning to Clem Ford's—was it?—confession.

Bergen during the war was not much more than a large Nordic fishing village of wharves, canneries, and smokehouses grouped round the harbor with ranks of timber-built houses stacked up on the surrounding hills. Even in May of the year there was snow on the mountains and bits of ice in the fjord.

I remember noting how many SS were about the area that fateful day. As few as six weeks earlier, an SS officer had been a rarity; now Rehm's maimed hand kept flapping up and down as we passed one after another group of storm troopers who seemed to be gathered at key streets and intersections.

I took Rehm to one of the grog shops that had sprung up round the harbor in Bergen with the arrival of the Atlantic Command. In Norway, making a profit by serving liquor to the enemy was rather less dishonorable than in other occupied countries. Most Norwegians considered drinking bad for everything, including the health; thus plying us with alcohol was in a small way a subversive act.

But no sooner were we through the doorway than I was surrounded by other submariners who rose from their tables to welcome me, since it was seldom now that a boat actually came back.

"Wolf!"

It was my nickname.

"You're back! How many did you get?"

"None—but I fired three eels. After that I spent most of the time with my belly in the mud. But, you know"—I looked round at them, loving each and every one and also seeing in my mind's eye the many who were no longer present—"I like the mud, and, what's more important, the mud likes me!"

The others laughed volubly, eager to share in my humor, if nothing else. I had told them in the only language that we knew, which was boats, that I—their veteran, in many ways their fighting chief—had failed, that we were beaten, that the end had come.

Yet they laughed with me, they smiled, they gathered round to feel what nine years and nearly a half-million gross registered tons sunk felt like. But they too, like me, were glad it was over, even if we now had to acknowledge defeat. Too many of us had died. And now it was time to make an end.

"How about the new boat, the Walter? It's just arrived, and we hear it's yours."

I shrugged; everybody wanted the boat, but far be it from me to list its advantages.

"How does it look, Connie?" an engineering officer asked Geis.

"Like something that should have been delivered years ago. Fast, quiet, well-armed from all I hear." Geis's eyes met mine; it wasn't well armed yet.

"What about us? When do we get to see it?"

"After I've had my beer," I said. "And incidentally—from now on it's Commodorezursee Sea Wolf to you snorkel rats. I expect a lot of bowing and scraping, to say nothing of a lifetime of free drinks."

Opening the envelope Rehm had brought me, I propped the silver-and-gold rank boards on each shoulder; snapping a finger, I flicked them off into the crowd, who roared their delight.

It was only then that some of the others noticed Rehm. I watched their smiles fade, as their eyes moved over the death's head emblem on his cap. It did not seem to matter that he was also wearing a gold wound badge and an Iron Cross first-class on his chest, or that the ultimate medal—the Knight's Cross with oak leaves and swords—swung from a chain around his neck. Perhaps he had fought often and well, but he was police. Worse, he was Himmler's secret police from the political party responsible for our defeat.

We took a table, and a tray of drinks was delivered.

I picked up a glass. "What shall we drink to, Colonel? To 'Final Victory'?"

"No, Commodore. There's not a chance for Final Victory anymore, or even a negotiated truce, I'm afraid. It would be better for us to forget this shit." Rehm touched his SS collar insignia. "It's over. Germany is broken. Final defeat is only days away."

"I'll drink to that," I said. "To Final Defeat!"

"And to your health and well-being after the war." Carefully lifting his glass with the stubs of his maimed hand, Rehm clinked it against ours but only touched the liquor to his lips.

Geis and I, who had not tasted anything but tepid water in weeks, drank ours off. "And this is why you're bringing me torpedoes—to discuss after the war?"

"To tell you the truth, Klimt—that's exactly what I wish to discuss. After the war. What are your plans? Will you be going back to Kiel or Borkum?"

I only regarded the man.

"Kiel has been bombed into nothingness, but you know that."

Since my wife had been killed there.

"But your mother and sister are still alive on Borkum. Isn't it the third house on the right, just past the bank?"

Still I waited. It was a small table, and the liquor had made me regret having accepted the man's apology. In Cambridge they had come at me with lead-weighted bats. I had never killed a man with my bare hands, but there was a first time for everything.

"I understand your people were lucky and got through the war quite well. Not like some."

Now my gall was high. We had lost our father, my wife, and on more occasions than I kept track of I had been lucky to have escaped with my life. But Geis nudged me under the table, then narrowed his eyes and looked away, as much as to say, Hear the bastard out. He wants something from us. Let's find out what it is. After that, we can deal with him.

Rehm got right to it. "So, what is it for you after the

war—'importing,' like your father, for want of a more accurate term?''

Which was smuggling, although my father had done little of that in later years and had a small fleet of ships at the beginning of the Second World War.

"Have you ever sailed to South America?"

He knew that too. I can remember glancing at the clock behind the bar and figuring Herr Knight's Cross had two minutes left.

"Did you see this?" Rehm pulled some folded sheets of paper from under his tunic. "It's the telex of surrender that came in only an hour or so ago, while you were docking. Would you care to see it?"

Geis and I were dumbfounded; more, when he added, "Or, rather, I should say it's the extract from your Admiral Doenitz. Did I tell you that in addition to being chief of staff of the navy, he has now been named der Führer?"

"What happened to Hitler?"

Rehm shrugged. "He wasn't the leader we thought he was."

Which was an understatement I would have found macabrely humorous, had I not begun to read the message with its lugubrious hyperbole that had proved so deadly to so many of my cohorts. My eyes caught on the passage:

> The dead command us to give our unconditional constancy, obedience, and discipline to our Fatherland, which is bleeding from countless wounds.

The word "surrender" was nowhere mentioned, and it was signed, as Rehm had said, by Karl Doenitz, Führer.

I showed it to Geis, who was never one to mince words. "Does that son of a bitch think we should go on dying for the dead? Is that what he wants? Sitting there in Berlin and surrendering his desk."

"Well, he won't get it from me," Rehm was quick to

say. "I've done my bit for the Fatherland, like you two
have done yours. How many years did they send you
out in that iron coffin I saw you in this morning? To
do what? To die. That's what they intended. Now it's
time for us to live and think of ourselves."

That was fast, I thought. Now we were together.
"What do you think will happen to your Walter boat,
now that we've packed in the war?"

Given how advanced it was, the Walter would be
taken to a British or American shipyard, dismantled and
copied.

"Wouldn't it be a shame not to take it for one final
cruise?"

I waited. It was why the man had worked something
of a miracle to get himself to Norway at the bitter end
of the war to seek me out with all the rest that he had
brought, in spite of our sorry history together.

"Say, to South America. You, me, Conrad here, your
pick of crew from anybody you like." He nodded to the
bar. "It's a big boat. I myself will have a dozen com-
panions. Maybe fourteen. With me that's fifteen. The
rest will be yours. How many can a boat, like that,
carry?"

Thirty-five in a pinch, I thought, counting half as
crew.

"I need only give them word that you have agreed,
since they want you as captain. Even better is what
we'll share when we get there." Rehm smiled and
reached for his glass; this time he actually drank.

"Gold and diamonds. Your share will be equivalent
to five hundred thousand U.S. dollars, half when we
sail, half when we dispose of the boat. To show our
good faith, I have this for you." From a uniform pocket
Rehm pulled out a small sack and tossed it on the table.
"Go ahead, open it."

I did not move.

"Its value is equivalent to at least fifty thousand dollars. Yours to keep, whether you choose to be our captain or not. I figure I owe you at least that much. You
lost a year, as I understand it." And did not com-

plete my degree, went unsaid; and surely would not
now, at least not at Cambridge.

"Certainly somebody else here will jump at the offer," Rehm scanned the crowd. But we wanted you because of your knowledge of South American waters, to
say nothing of your reputation as a captain. And then
I know for fact that you're a man who can keep his
mouth shut." Rehm attempted a smile.

The sack that he had handed me had a Polish phrase,
I thought, stitched through its supple leather with gold
thread. The draw strings were also of woven gold.

I can remember thinking how five hundred thousand
dollars was quite a sum and would go far toward setting me up with a vessel. After all, I had my mother
and sister to consider. All of my father's vessels were
sunk, his wharves and warehouses bombed into obliv-
ion, including himself. And yet I was hesitant, suspecting that Rehm, in spite of our rapproachment, could not
be trusted.

In the shadows of the table where only Geis and I
could see, I opened the sack and poured the contents
into my palm. It was a handful of cut and polished gems
of differing shapes, but all of obvious clarity and size.
With the edge of one, I cut a line down the side of my
beer glass.

"You'll find they're virtually flawless and expertly
cut. If anything they're worth far more than I said, say,
in Buenos Aires. That one you're holding, Lieutenant?
It's an estancia in Paraguay. Add another—all the peo-
nes you would need to create your own new world.
Europe is destroyed. Dead. There's no hope of building
anything of real value here."

Not after you and your kind, was my immediate
thought.

Rehm stood. "You think about it. But I'll need your
answer by morning." He left.

Geis and I sat there in silence for the few minutes it
took our cohorts to realize that Colonel Death's Head
had departed and to join us.

We tarried another hour or so before heading back
to the pens.

CHAPTER 29

━━━━━━━

McGARR GLANCED UP at Maddie. She and some new-found friends were building sand castles—their own little world—at the edge of the beach. He turned the page.

When we got back to the harbor an hour or so later, we discovered that Rehm had taken control of the area around the new Walter boat. Fire teams of SS storm troopers armed with Schmeisser machine guns were positioned at both sides of the pier, with another clutch at the gate to keep out the crowd of submariners who had gathered to tour the boat.

Seeing that, my anger surged. I had just enough alcohol in me and just enough sorrow over our defeat and all those who had died needlessly to make me fearless. Without thinking, my hand leapt over the shoulders of the submariners in front of me and seized the throat of the SS officer who had been facing them down. I slapped my Walther against his temple and forced him to his knees.

"Shoot me!" I roared at the SS guards. "And I shoot him! They shoot you!" My cohorts had now also drawn their sidearms. "You want to die?" I asked the officer, who was gagging and trying desperately to pry my hand

*from his throat. But he was soft, a desk warrior who
had no strength, and I began dragging him toward the
Walter boat, where Rehm now appeared on the conning
tower.*

*"What's this all about, Klimt?" he asked in a mild
voice.*

*"It's about your Gestapo! These men only want to
inspect the new boat, which is their right. Since when
has the SS declared a German Navy vessel off limits to
German sailors? And what's this here?" Sweeping my
hand that held the gagging officer, I sent him tumbling
down a gangplank toward another group of SS who
were trying to hoist a torpedo in the yoke of a crane.*

*"This boat is my command," I went on. "Up until
the moment that I'm issued a direct order by a superior
naval officer to stand down. Nothing occurs aboard her,
nobody comes on board without my expressed permis-
sion." Now I had the gun pointing directly at Rehm
and the four men who had appeared behind him. "Is
that understood?"*

*Rehm smiled. "Then you've decided to accept my
offer? Something else has just come in. I think you
should see it." He raised a sheet of paper.*

*I stepped up onto the boat, then helped the smaller
Geis aboard. He said to me, "Maybe it's time we covered our own asses. It's a long way to Germany." He
meant either in a U-boat running on the surface with
a white flag flying from the mast, if there was fuel
enough even for that. Or by road and ferry, with more
than a few angry partisans along the way.*

*Up in the conning tower, Rehm handed me another
transmission from Berlin to the flotilla commander, or-
dering him to keep all boats in port and all personnel
in place until "an Allied naval presence" arrived to
take charge of "all men and materiel." Since they were
just offshore—I knew from my own recent experience
there—they would be here within a day.*

*"Do you want to be around for that, Klimt? I most
certainly don't."*

I straightened up and surveyed the men standing be-

hind Rehm; one of them looked vaguely familiar. While dressed similarly and nautically—blue caps, pea jackets, dark trousers—they were not in uniform, and looked more like merchant seamen (and British at that) than military officers.

I certainly did not wish to witness our defeat, much less give myself up if I did not have to. As a dual citizen who had voluntarily fought for the other side, I would without a doubt be singled out for some special attention. My concern was not so much for me, since I had made the choice and now would have to live with the outcome, but for my mother's relatives in Harwich, a city that had been bombed during the Blitz.

"What about Geis?"

"What about him?"

"He gets the same as you offered me."

Rehm shook his head. "Half."

"The same, or you get somebody else. There's not a man out there who's so much as made landfall in South America." I waved a hand at the other submariners, who had still not dispersed.

"Three hundred thousand U.S. dollars or its equivalent."

"No, the same."

"Then, we'll find somebody else."

"Good. You men down there!" I bellowed at the boaters below me on the dock. "Stop what you're doing and come up here. Take these bastards off this boat."

"Wait," said one of the men behind Rehm. "Commodore Dorfmann should not be expected to sail without his chief engineer. And Lieutenant Geis should be compensated for his extraordinary service and talents."

Rehm said nothing. Obviously the man—the same one whom I thought I recognized—was in command.

"What will my other crewmen be paid?"

Said Rehm, "One hundred thousand U.S. dollars or the equivalent in the currency of the country of our destination."

"Which is?"

The other man pointed to the ladder. "We'll decide

that when and if we can get out of here, and already
we've wasted too much time. Now that Commodore
Dorfmann is aboard, gentlemen, we should leave him
to the loading of the torpedoes. It will go more
quickly."

"Do you think that's wise, sir?" Rehm asked.

"Wisdom is a commodity we can no longer afford,
Helmut. It takes too long to acquire."

The other men laughed, and they left the conning
tower, retiring into a forward area of the boat.

I waved to the submariners, bidding them to come
aboard; one by one I planned to take the crew we would
need aside and make them the offer. I would show them
the order of surrender, tell them what Berlin had said
about their wanting us to die for them.

But Geis was not at work five minutes before he decided that there was something strange and wrong
about the ten Luts that Rehm had flown in. Unlike the
old acoustic torpedoes that could be fired at an angle
of no more than ninety degrees, the new torpedoes
could set their own course, zigging and zagging toward
a target. Also as many as six Luts could be fired in one
salvo from as deep as 160 feet to swarm up and anni-
hilate an enemy ship.

But the torpedoes that Rehm had brought seemed too
heavy, inordinately so, and balanced wrong with all the
weight forward of the midline. Fourteen years of sub-
marine-engineering experience told Geis that once
those eels were shot out of the tubes by compressed air,
they would promptly sink to the bottom of the ocean.

"I don't care what they've used for a propulsion sys-
tem," he confided to me, as we surveyed where the
strap of the winch had to be placed to balance the thing.
"Not even a rocket could keep that nose up." Even
after he added a four-thousand-pound addition to the
counterweight, the crane only just managed to raise it.

A thought occurred to me. I could not imagine Rehm
and the four others with him leaving Europe empty-
handed, not with the opportunities they must have had
for plunder. It was, surely, the difference between a

soldier and sailor at war. The sailor had only the company of his mates and his boat with the pitiless sea beneath him and sometimes months of patient hunting before quarry was even sighted. A soldier, on the other hand, had land under him, and women and wine. Preferred soldiers—political soldiers—had the best of that, on principle.

"Let's get them aboard," I told Geis quietly in the cabin of the crane, "then we'll see what they are."

In the early years of the war, a crew of dockworkers called "torpedo boys" was responsible for the loading of eels aboard submarines. By 1945 those crews had either been killed or had become submariners themselves. Therefore, we armed our own boats, and now, as I added men to the crew, they gathered round to help Geis.

The process was difficult, time-consuming, and dangerous under the best of circumstances. A conventional three-thousand-pound torpedo had to be greased, fitted with a protective harness, and then hoisted by crane over the submarine. Slowly it was then lowered onto a loading trough and slid through the torpedo hatch into the sub.

There the harness was removed and by means of a system of pulleys, the torpedo was maneuvered into the bow or stern torpedo stowage bays. The torpedo mechanic then armed it with a warhead and recorded its number in his munitions log.

Looped with other bands of steel and chain, it was again hoisted aloft by six men and dragged into its tube or stowage cradle. Fourteen acoustic torpedoes—a total of some forty-two thousand pounds—was the usual complement aboard a Type VII sub. This boat had ten twenty-one-inch-diameter eels that were fourteen feet long; there were six in the bow and four more broadside forward, two to port, two to starboard. It was 3:00 in the morning by the time we got them all aboard, and I sent all the submariners but Geis to retrieve their belongings from their berths or billets and to report on deck no later than sunup.

Geis and I immediately repaired forward, second tier, where the torpedo bay was situated, and we were surprised to find an SS storm trooper positioned there. "Who are you?" he demanded.

My first impulse was to disarm and perhaps even kill him; I had told Rehm the conditions under which I would join them, and here, only hours later, one had been violated. But we had other literal fish to fry. And I realized he was just another young boy dressed in a man's costume, like my own aboard my last several commands.

Pushing the barrel of his Schmeisser aside, I said, "Why, son, I'm the captain of this scow. This is my engineer, and we've come to arm the torpedoes. Surely you wouldn't want us to sail out of here unarmed. Are you coming with us?"

His eyes said, I hope not. "I was ordered not to let anybody in here."

"I just told you"—I raised my arm, forcing him back so Geis could duck in—"we're not anybody, I command this boat. Standartenführer Rehm wants this to happen." I had to perform my special contortion to get myself through the hatch of the bulkhead, and when I straightened up as much as I was able, I saw the young man's eyes widen; he had not expected a submariner to be so large. "You sit yourself down and watch. You might learn something. What's your name?"

"Hans." Who was not a day over fifteen. In his hands the Schmeisser looked like an abomination.

"My name is Klimt, that's Connie. Has anybody told you the war is over? We surrendered today." Obviously nobody had; his eyes were wide as saucers. We advanced on the eels.

At the first sling, Geis removed the firing pin/plunger cap and bent his head to peer into the detonator cavity. He turned to me and smiled. With the blade of his long-shaft screwdriver he tapped the back of the cavity. "Just like I thought, it's solid. These aren't torpedoes, they're—" He shook his head; he didn't know what they were. "Shine the light in there." I complied.

The black paint was easily scratched off, exposing a bright, soft metal below. Geis smiled more completely and kept working the screwdriver until it had produced a small pile of shavings. Scooping them out, he handed them to me, saying, "Why don't you see if there's any ersatz coffee in the mess, Commodore. I can take it from here." And to the boy, "I like the war being over—now I can give that big bag of wind orders."

But the boy scarcely smiled. It was past his bedtime, and his eyes were closing. By the time I returned with three cups, our storm trooper was sprawled against the bulkhead, fast asleep, and Geis turned to me triumphantly. "It's gold, isn't it?"

I nodded.

"Well, take a look at this." Glancing down at the boy to make sure he was asleep, Geis led me over to one of the torpedoes and quickly and expertly removed the propeller and tail section housing. But instead of finding a propeller shaft and the aft end of some propulsion device, I saw a long, brown tube that was rumpled and soft.

"It's like a big waterproof bag. I think it extends the length of the eel. Feel it."

There was something in it or—rather—many things, some bigger than others.

"Let me show you." Stepping around the thing, Geis squeezed open a slit that he had made on the hull side of the "bag" and shone the beam of the torch in. "All that glitters is not gold," he said. "It's gold and silver and diamonds and rubies and anything else that they could get their hands on."

It was obvious it was just that—pillage, plunder, booty; most of it was spectacular jewelry.

"All ten are the same, I've checked. They must have mocked up a Lut torpedo, leaving it an inch shy of the twenty-one-inch diameter. Then they made a mold and cast these things in gold, leaving the interior ten inches of the twenty-inch-diameter hollow. These inserts came next, stuffed with diamonds and jewelry, the whole thing then being encased in the shell of a Lut with a cast-

iron warhead, cowlings, propeller, and all. Real enough to fool anybody on first sight.

"The one thing they hadn't counted on is the weight. But with the war over"—Geis shrugged—"there's no need for them, right? And all they have to do when we get to wherever we're going is to pop them out of the tubes with compressed air into some shallows near a beach, then put themselves off in a raft, and scuttle the boat.

With us in it, I thought.

As had Geis. "With all this"—his hand swept the torpedo bay—"they can't let us live. How did they get this stuff? Who'd they steal it from? And who are they— the others with Rehm? There must be a reason they're bailing out of Europe."

I shook my head. I did not know. I'd been at sea for most of nine years and knew only what I'd been told in communiqués. I don't think I had read even so much as a single newspaper in the last six months.

"And even if the boat is found with us shot or poisoned or suffocated, so what? It'll be passed off as just another wartime accident or mutiny. Something that happened to some Krauts off the coast of South America."

In retrospect, I know it was selfish, but I can remember feeling the outrage welling up inside of me. Helmut Rehm, who had tried to murder me once before, had traveled all this way with his Nazi masters at the end of the war and for what? To get me to transport their doubtlessly criminal plunder to some sanctuary where he would complete the crime he had botched in Cambridge and do me in.

"I have a plan," I said to Geis. "Here's what we're going to do."

Noreen sat down on the blanket beside McGarr. "What are you reading?"

He showed her the handwriting.

"Clem Ford's memoir? Is there a chance I can see it next?

What about these pages that you've already read?'' She picked them up.

McGarr's eyes slid over to Maddie and her playmates, then refocused on the page he had been reading.

CHAPTER 30

REHM AND THE others with him awoke around dawn and found us in the control room with the turbine engine purring, charging the batteries. Geis and I and my crew were busied reading gauges and making notes on clipboards. It was all a charade.

"Well, Commodore, are we ready to cast off?"

I knew he was not, if he intended to depart with fifteen in his company. So far he had only five.

"I'd say in an hour's time. We'd like to run some tests. Did you arrive here on this boat?"

Rehm shook his head. "We flew in."

"Then, who—" Geis asked.

"Schmelling and a crew from the Todt Organization."

"Well—they're here by sheer luck. The inertial guidance system that controls underwater navigation is off by at least three degrees. We'll have to submerge to correct it."

Rehm's eye narrowed in suspicion.

"Here at dockside, of course."

"Also, there's the tanks," said Geis. "Metal fragments—flashing bits from the welding process, dropped rivets, metal shavings. It's typical of a new boat, but *can be fatal, if a dive can't be accomplished under fire or we can't dive fast enough to avoid being seen and marked.''*

Rehm's brow revealed that he did not want that.

"All minor problems." I smiled down at him, *for your experienced crew. "And I have some advice—you should have yourself a good shore breakfast with real food and stretch your legs one last time for the next month.''*

"A month? I thought it would take only twenty days.''

"How did you figure that—running at twenty knots?''

Rehm glanced at Geis. "I thought this boat could do twenty-four knots.''

"Snorkeling," he said. *"But snorkeling can be seen from the air. If you're not concerned about that—"* Geis hunched his shoulders.

"Three points," I put in. *"One, we don't know that this boat can make that speed for any sustained period of time. It was probably built round the clock by at least some inexperienced boat builders who were probably being bombed and forced to scrimp on materials. I hope she can make twenty-four knots, but we'll have to see. Gradually. Increasing speed a little at a time. We don't want a breakdown.*

"Two, there are ocean currents that we will have to buck. And, finally, there's the unknown. In my experience, the unknown always occurs. It's inescapable." I smiled more completely; it was the point I hoped he would understand best. *"You tell us how it's to be— breakfast here, breakfast there. You stay here, you stay there.''*

It was breakfast there, with the ten missing complements of Rehm's group, who now arrived, remaining on the boat while we completed our "tests." Even at first glance it was easy to see what the new additions were— Rehm's killers.

Although they all wore some item of Waffen SS gray, not one had on the entire uniform. Nor did they carry similar weapons, but rather whatever they had fancied and removed from fallen foes—Kalashnikovs, M1s, Colts, Enfields, Webleys.

Most noticeable, however, was the way they peered round the control room as they descended the ladder—like the pipes, tubes, and gauges were an alien, hostile world, and all their boots, knives, guns, and bullets would not avail them much here. In a word, I could smell their fear, which had probably kept them alive on the ground wherever they had been, but could now be exploited. And would.

"Commodore Dorfmann—I'd like you to meet Sturmbannfürer Beust. He has served me well and will now be my eyes and ears while I'm having breakfast. He's told me he's enamored of submarines and should have been with you and not me. Now he has his chance. Please inform him what you are doing, step by step. And don't let his looks fool you. Beust is a quick study. Who knows, he might change careers in the Argentines and become an admiral."

I smiled down at the man who was not much smaller than I and much more fit, I could see. His muscles strained at the cloth of a Russian Army general's uniform shirt, if I was not mistaken. His face was as square as those shoulders, and he had been told about me, I could tell. His dark eyes had that dead look that said it was only a matter of time. I was his target.

Rehm left the boat with his four similarly blue-clad friends, and I turned to Beust, explaining to him what we were seeing on the dials and meters. "The deck lines have been loosed, and we shall dive in place, operate the inertial guidance system, then surface and check its accuracy against the bridge navigation instruments." It was all a charade, of course.

Beust, however, tried to understand none of it. It was clear he was nearly out on his feet. His eyes were glassy and kept closing in the heat of the control room. Yet he remained on my heels, like the guard dog he was.

Perhaps forty minutes later after repeated dives, Geis handed me his clipboard. "Here's the present varia-

tion. Can we live with that? The note on the board said, "9 billeted in forward bay, sleeping. Hatch closed, locked. Descend, flood?"

I nodded. "We can live with that, but I don't think Standartenführer Rehm would like it, arriving in Tierra del Fuego and not the mouth of Rio de la Plata."

Beust remained wooden.

We dived again and remained submerged for only a minute or two, before I ordered the boat to the surface again. Immediately thereafter, I climbed the ladder and moved out on the dripping, frigid bridge to take the wheel and maneuver the boat in closer to the dock.

The torpedo hatch suddenly popped open, Geis appeared, and the storm troopers scrambled out, soaking wet. Most were dressed only in their underwear, and there was not a weapon in sight.

Geis jumped onto the dock and skidded a boarding plank down onto the deck. The storm troopers scrambled off.

"Halt! Stop!" Beust shouted. "Where are you going?" When he turned round to me, as for help, he found the barrel of my pistol pointing at his head.

"You're next. Climb down the ladder and get off."

Now he smiled, then shook his head. "You'll have to shoot me. I bet you've never killed anybody up close. It's all been—what?—two hundred yards, five hundred, a mile. It's easy, like that, isn't it. Impersonal. Push a button, wait. Poof—up goes the ship." He gestured with his hands, and I nearly shot him then.

"Down goes the periscope, and it's all forgotten. Well, this is different, isn't it? If you want me off this boat, you'll have to shoot me. Go on." He took a step toward me. And another. Now we were very close. When his hands jumped for the gun, I put a bullet through his brain, then shoved his body down the ladder onto the deck.

Rehm now arrived, having run down the dock. His partners were not far behind.

Hitting the sticks and spinning the bridge wheel, I edged the sub away and the boarding plank fell into the water. Geis now joined me on the bridge and swung the aft pair of 30 mm antiaircraft guns around on Rehm and his mates.

"You won't get far. I ordered the sub nets closed last night. They can be opened only at my orders. Rehm meant the steel-cable nets that were strung across the narrowest part of the Bjørnafjord. Also positioned there was a battery of powerful guns.

" 'Dour Rump Führer' that you are," I said, nudging the props up a peg so that the boat would slip out into the harbor.

"We should kill them," Geis said from the gun he had trained on them. "If he's not bluffing, we'll never get through submerged."

But Rehm would also have to convince or coerce the gun crews to fire on a German boat. Even if he did, I doubted they could hit us at the Walter boat's top surface speed, which was nearly thirty knots. Also, Beust had been right—I had never killed like that before, and my judgment was still clouded by the experience. But Geis was right too, and my decision not to take them out there and then ultimately cost him his life.

For even though I punched up the turbines to full power from the moment we left the sub pens in Bergen, they were waiting at the batteries and firing when we first rounded the bend leading to the net. Was the net drawn? I suspect I'll never know, and in retrospect I believe that we should have submerged and probed it; the water there is deep and, if we had found it closed, we could always have gone back up round the bend to surface and gain momentum before making our run on top.

But tide was running out and the current, which was strong there, was pushing our speed in excess of thirty-five knots. Added to that, I could tell from the initial shelling, which fell far short and then far long, that Rehm and his storm troopers must be manning the batteries, not the trained crew.

"We're flying!" Geis roared at me from the 30 mm guns that he was still manning, and in a trice we were over the position of the net, passed the batteries, and surging out into the Atlantic. But I no sooner ordered a white flag hoisted in case any Allied warships were in the vicinity before we could submerge, when a volley from the batteries—late and long—tore down from the sky and smashed into the conning tower, killing Geis instantly and the two other submariners who were with us on the bridge. It riddled my back and legs with shrapnel.

I went down and out, and the boat, still coursing with nobody at the helm, skidded over one of the many rocks that dot the mouth of the Bjørnafjord before others of the crew could take the wheel. Gone was the lower stabilizing fin of our rudder, and the shaft was damaged in a way that made the prop spin eccentrically. Like that, it was only a matter of time before the vibration tore the boat apart. Gone as well were our snorkel, our radars, and our main radios.

Using a sextant and traveling on the surface only at night, we managed to limp the roughly thousand miles to Clew Bay, where often, during the war, I had lain in the rocky depths or charged my batteries in a narrow inlet at night. I knew the bottom and the currents. And in the teeth of a wild spring storm I sent my final radio message using the auxiliary radio that I and the three remaining members of my crew hauled out on deck. I sent only the coordinates of our position, in case any of the others whom I had told as insurance about our mission might be listening. If we did not live, I wanted them to have the fortune.

We maneuvered the boat as close to the Great Cliff of Clare Island as we dared go, before expelling the cargo into a hole I knew of. The torpedoes would be virtually invisible but still relatively easy to retrieve. By then the boat had rattled itself so loose the pumps were barely able to keep the leaking water from submerging the turbine, which occurred just after we had released the final "torpedo."

But mercifully the turbine (truly a miracle of German technology) carried us away from the rocks so that at least one of us (I, the lucky one) managed to survive. I tried to get us to a trench that I knew of where we could scuttle the boat. I was still on deck at what was left of the bridge, not wanting any of the others to risk being washed from the twisted wreckage by a wave. It was what saved me, being washed overboard and not sinking in the confines of the Walter boat. I was beat and tumbled and smashed into the cliffs. Yet I lived.

I was saved by a woman, who I learned was Peig O'Malley. Her solitary cottage sat in a cleft of the cliffs. Having heard us maneuvering there during the night, she had come down to the beach with her blind niece at low tide to discover what we had been about. At first she thought me "a Brit," as she told me when I recovered, dressed as I was in the blue togs of a British merchant mariner and carrying a Webley automatic.

I had discovered the clothes in the lockers of Rehm and his "friends," after we had gotten clear of the Norwegian coast. They had evidently intended to pass themselves off as English, wherever it was that they had intended to land. I thought it an expedient ruse, given my own command of the language. But the first words out of my mouth were "Wie heissen Sie?" as I looked up into the star-burst blue eyes of her niece. And from that moment I was safe. Peig O'Malley was an ardent Irish Republican who despised the British.

It took me over a year to winch the torpedoes, one by one at night, up into the cave that Peig showed me, and almost another to establish the Clare Island Trust and find a quiet way to fund it. Now it belongs to you who are reading this. I write only so that you know the probable source of the wealth. I hold you to nothing that I have begun or is being done with the funds while I live. Its disposition is up to you.

                              Clement Ford
                 (Former Commodorezursee Klimt Dorfmann)

McGarr closed the sheaf of photocopied pages and handed it to Noreen, who read it much more quickly than had McGarr.

After handing it back, she thought for a while before saying, "I think it's truly wonderful what he and Breege and obviously Peig chose to do with that wealth. Given Peig's sympathies, they might have funded the I.R.A. instead. Or squandered it on themselves and—what's the phrase?—creature comforts.

"Still, none of it fell from the sky. Somebody—some-*bodies,* most likely—owned all that stuff." She turned to McGarr. "Now what?"

He did not know. He was faced with the dilemma of making public all that he now knew and thereby destroying the Clare Island Trust that had done so much good for the area. Or of colluding in the cover-up of without a doubt more than a few egregious crimes.

"So, where is this cave?"

McGarr had an idea, but he said nothing. And would not, until he decided.

"And do we know what happened to Ford and his wife?"

McGarr thought he did and he told her: that after Clem Ford—or somebody who looked remarkably like him—had ferried the injured Karl Gottschalk into Westport harbor, the boat he was in was seen motoring past Clare Island due west. In addition to the Fords, Packy O'Malley was still missing, as now was Canning. It was his boat.

McGarr had contacted the Naval Service to learn if they had received any reports about it. But they had not, save for a sighting by one of the Spanish tuna fleet vessels of a small, probably Irish fishing boat some two hundred miles off the coast, still headed due west in heavy seas.

"In other words, he decided not to carry on."

So McGarr assumed. Ford had lost his wife, a good friend in Packy O'Malley, and also Kevin O'Grady and Colm Canning. And there would be too many questions.

McGarr stood.

"Where are you off to?"

"A little unfinished business."

At the hotel he changed into his walking gear, then loaded and checked the action of his PPK. It would not do to confront unarmed a man who had proved himself capable of killing so easily and so well.

CHAPTER 31

HE DID NOT knock. With the barrel of his automatic pointed at the door, McGarr kicked it open and found Fergal O'Grady standing on the other side with a slane in his hands. "Put that down."

O'Grady's eyes were wide with fright. "Are ye' going to shoot me now, ye' *seoinin* devil?"

"Only if I have to. Come with me." McGarr turned and walked round the house, heading off across the fields toward the mountain. O'Grady followed slowly at a respectful distance, knowing full well where they were headed.

It took them the balance of the afternoon to scale the bald rocky bluffs of Croaghmore. The O'Malleys not resident on Clare Island had gone home, and the two men were the only figures on the mountain. As they climbed up through the summer heat the cool breeze off the Atlantic increased in strength until on top it became a gale that they had to turn their backs into. O'Grady's woolen *brat* flapped wildly, exposing his gnarled old legs.

Yet the wind wasn't strong enough to keep seagulls and crows from gathering round a thistly depression at the very top. Squealing and cawing, they dived at and fought with each other, trying to get close to what appeared to be a cleft in the rock there. Every so often, one of the lucky would disappear within.

Nor was the wind strong enough to keep off the smell, once the birds had departed. It rose from the hole in foul puffs.

McGarr pointed at the hole. "I'm showing you this, so you know I know. Who's down there?"

"Sure, if you know so much, you know that too."

"It was his head that you carried over and threw off the cliff."

"Is *that* what it was?" The old eyes widened in mock wonder.

"I'll ask you again and only once more—who was it?"

O'Grady thought for a moment, as though deciding if he should answer. But then he nodded once, his white mane bobbing in the breeze. "You'd not be asking, if you were taking me in."

McGarr did not reply.

"The answer is, damned if I know. I never saw him before in my life. But I'll tell you one thing, and that thing I *do* know—he's the man who killed my son."

"How do you know that?"

It was O'Grady's turn to stare at McGarr, but pityingly.

"He was climbing out of the cave."

O'Grady's expression did not change.

"How long have you known about this cave."

"If I said, you'd not believe me."

"What's down there?"

"I think you know."

"And you know."

"Amn't I after saying I do?"

"And what do you think of what's there?"

"The gold, the jewels, the lucre? That it's deadly. That it could and would and did kill. Pity it was my Kevin. But— I've seen to that, haven't I."

"And knowing about it—how long?—you never let on?"

"Why? It's death. I said that from the beginning."

"Or were tempted to take some for yourself."

"Never. But don't think Clem Ford never offered. Don't think he didn't try to buy me off. Wake up, man—*this* is the evil in the world!" O'Grady jabbed a finger at the hole.

"With this comes the power to make other people conform to *your* plan, to make the world into your image. Which is what Clement Ford tried to do. Buy me, buy you, buy everybody with his Clare Island Trust, as long as you did what he wanted. Go here, go there, go to university like Colm Canning who came back here emasculated and lost everything, including now his life.

"And trust! Trust *what*? Trust him, trust modernity, trust *seoinini* when we know, like our ancestors knew for ages before us, that we can only trust in the earth, in our legends, and in our gods. The rest of it kills!"

"How did you know your son's killer would come out here?"

"Don't snakes always come out of their holes? I knew it as surely as I know what you're after here."

McGarr felt his nostrils flare; he was rapidly losing patience with the didactic old man.

"Five good people died that we know about, and at least three are on your head. And you—you're trying to clear your conscience, which you'll never do. You failed, you scut, and but for me the man would have got away with my son's murder."

"So—what happens now?"

"To what's down there?" O'Grady blinked and shook his head, as though astounded by McGarr's ignorance. "Mirna Gottschalk, another *seoinin,* will carry on, of course—dispensing the corrupting largess to the ignorant, the damned, and the greedy who will take it at their peril."

"Instead of living the good life according to Fergal O'Grady."

O'Grady turned on heel and left McGarr to the wind.

In Mirna Gottschalk's sitting room three hours later, McGarr asked her, "What are your plans for the Clare Island Trust?"

She did not seem surprised that he knew. She shook her head. "I have none."

"By that, you mean it will continue?"

"Of course it will continue—as a memorial to Breege and Clem. They sacrificed their lives to help others, and I plan to carry on in that vein."

McGarr listened to the wind roaring past the house. "And you're not unhappy about the probable source of the wealth?"

"I am, surely. I've thought of little else since Clem brought me the packet. But how would one go about naming the original owners and finding and compensating their heirs, lo these fifty years later? Making it public isn't the answer. The courts and the government—" She shook her head. It was plain she shared the distrust of so many others here in the West.

"I've been in touch with Leah Sigal," she went on. "She says there's a possibility of tracing the more spectacular pieces back to their rightful owners, but discreetly. Also, Astrid Neary tells me she knows of organizations that have been set up to compensate persons who had their assets looted during the war. And now that Eastern Europe is opening up, the Trust might contribute to those groups.

"But if there can be good news, it's that Clem was careful, Monck and Neary dutiful, and there's enough in the Trust to do all that and more. *If* we're allowed to continue."

McGarr checked his watch. It was getting on toward dinner, which he did not want to miss, having moved from the hotel to the lighthouse for the duration of their holiday. "I'll leave this with you." He placed the photocopy of Ford's memoir on an arm of the chair. "I didn't make a copy. Do you have another?"

She shook her head.

"Do you *know* of another?"

"Not unless somebody copied it when Karl was in hospital."

McGarr shook his head. The copy had been found on Karl when he was rushed by helicopter to hospital in Dublin. Along with his other personal effects, it had been stuffed in a plastic bag that was then sealed. Ward had been the first to open it.

"Then it's up to you. If anybody asks, I'll say I never saw it. If anybody asks you if I ever saw it, you say no. Are we agreed?"

She nodded.

McGarr said good night.

EPILOGUE

SEVERAL MONTHS LATER, after having taken Lugh Sigal to gyms, weight rooms, boxing matches, films, the theater, to dinner with and without his mother, out for a weekend with the Frenches (Noreen McGarr's parents) in Dunlavin, and even down with Ruthie and him to Sneem in County Kerry for another, Ward summoned his courage and sat the boy down.

They were in Mulligans in Poolbeg Street, a pub not far from Ward's own digs that he frequented largely to read the papers over a quiet pint.

"What are you having?"

"Whatever you are."

"Two pints, please."

Lugh was shocked, overwhelmed, entranced. He was actually going to have a pint of stout with his favorite person in the entire world. And there he had just turned fifteen. But in Ward's company laws did not seem to matter. He did what he thought was right.

Ward carried the brimming glasses over to a banquette by the windows, other men turning their heads to Ward in greeting or saying a few words, as always happened when they were out together.

"Is this your first pint?"

Lugh nodded.

"So—I have a bit of advice about anything like this. Drink slow, make it last, see how it feels. Today you'll not get another." Ward turned and faced him, making sure their eyes met before they clinked glasses.

Lugh sipped and tried to mask his disappointment. There wasn't much chance of the pint—a full twenty ounces— not lasting. The bitter brew tasted like an oily yeast soup; he wondered how some men could drink gallons at one sitting.

"So." Ward was nervous and repeating himself. "It's a day to remember. And I hope you will." Was there any chance he wouldn't? "Because—" No, that was the wrong approach.

Ward took a healthy tug from the glass and grimaced; he didn't fancy stout either, and had only ordered it—and not lager—so his son could say, in Irish fashion, that he had his first pint with his father.

Ward breathed out; he was at sixes and sevens. This was harder than anything he had ever done in his life. "Okay— you know how people have babies?"

Lugh tensed, wondering if Ward was going to try to explain about the birds and the bees; he'd had all of that at school. And elsewhere.

"You do?" The dark eyes flashed his way, and Lugh nodded. "Good. Because—are you ready for this? No, you couldn't ever be ready for this—I'm your father."

There was a pause in which the brakes of a bus, arriving at the terminus at the bottom of the street, thumped, then squealed. A patron at the bar said, "Excuse me, are you ready? Good. I'll have—" and he proceeded to order for a group. Pint in hand, Ward stared down at his coaster.

Lugh said, "I don't get it. Is this a joke?"

Ward shook his head and swung his eyes back to the boy. Ward was not a coward, not even an emotional coward, which he had long thought he was. "I'm happy it's not. You are my son, I am your father. Can I tell you how I met your mother?" And he did.

When he was through, Lugh did not know what to think,

or even to think at all. After a while, he blurted out, "Jesus—this is great. But why didn't my mother tell you sooner?"

"Because she didn't think I was ready for marriage and all the responsibilities of being a father. And she was right."

"But why did she let me think my father was . . . Sol?"

"Because she was married to Sol when she became pregnant, and she couldn't tell you about me without my knowing too."

"Then why didn't she tell you—" But he knew the answer to that; he looked down into his pint. "She didn't love Sol, she told me that. That's why they got divorced. Didn't she love you?"

"I think she did."

It occurred to Lugh that she still did; once she started speaking of Hugh Ward, it went on and on. And then, whenever the three of them were together, she looked different, dressed different, even sounded different—younger. "Did you love her?"

"I did."

"But you don't now."

"It's fifteen years later."

"And you love Ruthie."

Ward tugged on his pint, then again turned to the boy. "The point is, I'm glad Leah told me. I know this is hard, and it's something you're going to have to think about. But I've gotten to know you, and you're a good man. We still have the rest of our lives together, which should be a long time, please God. But what's past is past. Are we agreed?" Ward raised his glass; they clinked.

After a while Lugh asked, "What are the chances of you and my mother . . . ?"

Ward did not know that either. Every time he saw her she looked better and better, and he was reminded more and more of how they had been together. And one night when they were alone together while waiting for Lugh to return home from school, Ward had been tempted. Sorely. He had to make an excuse and leave, he had wanted her that much.

"What happens now?"

"That you know?" Ward hunched his shoulders and

wrapped his arm around the boy. "I have a son, and you have a father. It's new, it's different, I like it. More to the point, we've got to know each other, and I like you. Let's enjoy it." And try not to think of your mother.